With the explosive ac____ ___ __
the steely authenticity of *Black Hawk Down* . . .
Owen West uncovers the reality of front-line combat
in *SHARKMAN SIX*

"*SHARKMAN SIX* is truly a war novel for the New World
Order. . . . Owen West takes a minor military operation and
makes it an important morality tale as well as a metaphor
for the way things really are."
—Nelson DeMille, author of *The Lion's Game*

"A superb war book—absorbing and deeply expressed.
Owen West really puts you inside the minds of the Marines
on the front lines."
—Mark Burnett, creator and executive producer of *Survivor*

"*SHARKMAN SIX* crackles with intensity."
—Andrew Huebner, author of *American by Blood*

"Excitingly assured prose. West recounts with tragic wit
the war in Somalia. . . . The rounds are singing off Clancy's
helmet."
—*Kirkus Reviews*

"West shows staggering insight . . . in this powerful debut."
—*Publishers Weekly* (starred review)

"A riveting tale of modern warfare."
—*Abilene Reporter-News* (TX)

"A new military classic."
—*Flint Journal* (MI)

SHARKMAN SIX
A NOVEL

OWEN WEST

POCKET **STAR** BOOKS

New York London Toronto Sydney Singapore

This book is a work of fiction. Names, characters, places and incidents are products of the author's imagination or are used fictitiously. Any resemblance to actual events or locales or persons, living or dead, is entirely coincidental.

 A Pocket Star Book published by
POCKET BOOKS, a division of Simon & Schuster, Inc.
1230 Avenue of the Americas, New York, NY 10020

Copyright © 2001 by Owen West

Originally published in hardcover in 2001 by Simon & Schuster, Inc.

ISBN: 0-7434-4816-2

First Pocket Books printing May 2003

10 9 8 7 6 5 4 3 2 1

POCKET STAR BOOKS and colophon are registered trademarks of Simon & Schuster, Inc.

For information regarding special discounts for bulk purchases, please contact Simon & Schuster Special Sales at 1-800-456-6798 or business@simonandschuster.com

Cover design by John Vairo, Jr.; photo credits: Paul Edmondson/Getty Images, George Kavanagh/Getty Images

Printed in the U.S.A.

To my father and all the others
who fought so well for the Republic

PROLOGUE

I was born in Vietnam's sunset. Twenty-five years later a slice of that fireball lingers and I live in the long shadow it paints, especially dark for a third-generation Marine trying to follow two divergent combat boot tracks. I was given my own fight two years ago in Desert Storm. Gift wrapped. Tonight, I await the opening bell of my second.

Mine was supposed to be the generation that never had to fight. Somehow it would all be done by remote control—turn on the monitor, align the crosshairs, flip the switch, and poof! Scratch one bridge from a world in which none are "too far" for our NASDAQ war chest. In Desert Storm, you could count the number of American infantry commanders who lost people to direct Iraqi fire with your digits, a short list of the few and the damned. Guess what? I'm on it, and sometimes I think I'm the only one.

Am I viewed as a disgrace because of a quick decision and an Iraqi rocket-propelled grenade that ended its horrible path in one of my men's helmets? No way it's going to happen a second time. Not in this body bag of a country. We all come in, we all come out, heads high.

Heads whole.

PART I

Two men stepped out of the woods, one of them trailing a shotgun by the barrel.

—JAMES DICKEY, *Deliverance*

– 1 –

9 DECEMBER 1992

> *Butch:* Then you jump first.
>
> *Sundance:* No, I said.
>
> *Butch:* What's the matter with you?
>
> *Sundance:* I can't swim.
>
> *Butch:* Why you crazy . . . the fall will
> probably kill ya.

I am floating in a black rubber Zodiac on a black ocean at night, waiting to enter a country that is darker still. I strain to hear the clack of an AK-47 coming off Safe, or the abrupt, metallic snick of a machine-gun bolt, but the rapid breathing in my boat makes it impossible to pinpoint the faint noises coming from the beach. It is just past midnight and we can't wait to crash this party.

My left arm is dangling over the side of the boat but I'm leery of dipping it into the Indian after the intelligence brief on the dangers below. I take a quick, quiet swipe to test the ocean's temperature and it is so thick with phosphorescence that five bright green streaks follow my fingers through the length of their swim, glowing for a few seconds after my hand has retreated. My right hand remains gently draped over my M-16, my only girlfriend at this moment, a sleek beauty with whom I have snuggled for two years.

I have to fight the urge to stand and scream. I'm excited not so much because we may be able to shoot at some folks tonight—that's just a bonus, really—but because this landing might very well make us famous. For a generation raised by celebrities and those who report on them, fame—however fleeting—is the grunt's modern medal. In The Good War, the press were the cheerleaders, and medals—real feats—distinguished soldiers. In Vietnam, the press were the critics and medals were ignored. We learned from that. The press need us—and we can freeze them out if we so desire, just like we did in Desert Storm.

We grunts will never make the "Star Tracks" section of *People,* or be featured on *Entertainment Tonight* walking our Christophe-coiffed dogs, but CNN has guaranteed an Oscar celebration for us tonight. And maybe this time the world will learn the names of grunts instead of generals and fancy weapons. We don't really care which of us, just as long as it's *one of us*—a brother SEAL or a Ranger would be all right, but a Marine grunt would be better. Just not a general or an admiral or a pilot. If you go home to a full meal and a bed, you're not one of us.

Welcome to the world's greatest karaoke party. Just don't forget to bring your rifle!

"Sharkman, this is Photograph, over," says the tiny plastic speaker shoved into my ear. A thin, rubber-coated wire connects it to the black Motorola radio taped to my shoulder harness. It is the SEAL platoon. They entered the water twenty minutes ago and swam in to the beach, and now they must be feet-dry. Why they didn't wangle a better call sign for this operation I don't know. I mean, come *on*. Our platoon workout T-shirt has a drawing of a huge, bare-chested man—with a grinning shark head for a face—emerging from the sea, firing an M-16; underneath him the slogan reads, "Kill 'Em All, Let God Sort 'Em Out."

What do the SEALs wear? A picture of a camera? A Def Leppard *Pyromania* tour shirt?

"Photograph, this is Sharkman, over," I say, hand cupped over my mouth so the throat microphone catches most of the sound.

"Let me speak to your six, over." The number means he wants to speak with the unit commander. Don't ask me why the military doesn't use "one" instead. So our platoon's second-in-command, Gunnery Sergeant Jarius Ricketts—who, like every Marine who holds the rank, is known simply as Gunny—is "Sharkman Five," and the numerical references end there or everyone gets confused; by rank the platoon has several "fours," lots of "threes," and one troublesome Marine who was just reduced to a "two" for flattening the nose of a British MP in Hong Kong three months ago.

"This is Sharkman Six, over," I say.

By virtue of a college education and the completion of officer candidate school, I was deemed fit for USMC consumption, had my lieutenant's bars pinned on my dress blues by my chuckling, inebriated grandfather—who slammed the pins deep into my shoulder muscles and shouted, "Them are your first blood stripes, butterbar! Now see if you can avoid screwing up the lives of your men like the rest of these zeros!" even as the other newly commissioned ROTC lieutenants were huddled in quiet conversations with their parents—and was placed in charge of an infantry platoon, forty-five Marines recruited from across the socioeconomic spectrum, bound by a manic thirst for adventure and, ultimately, war.

Following a full two-year infantry tour complete with a 100-hour war, I applied to become a reconnaissance platoon leader. I endured a grueling day-long physical fitness test, passed the interview, and was selected. On the day I departed my infantry battalion for recon, my battalion commander said, "Most lieutenants would kill to get to recon, but don't be tempted to mistake a good physical fitness score for tactical superiority. It's not a reward. I didn't overrule your selection, because I think it can do you some good. If you don't learn sound decision making with those seasoned NCOs, well, then I'd say you never will."

Most officers never engaged the enemy in Desert Storm and most of them were decorated for their service. My platoon attacked a trench in a fierce firefight and conducted a forced coronation ceremony for thirty-two Iraqis, making them instant kings in the eyes of their god, like it or not, do not pass Go, do not collect $200. Of course, I also lost a good guy. When I faced my battalion commander hours later under a billowing black sky, his words were rapid-fire, all kill shots. "I thought my orders were to bypass all occupied trenches, Lieutenant. What was it about that you didn't understand?"

"I didn't have a choice, sir."

"You always have a goddamned *choice*, Lieutenant. You're an officer and an officer always has choices. You just *chose wrong* and a Marine's dead because of it. Dead!"

He turned suddenly and stormed off toward the burning well spit, twenty feet of fire lighting the rally point like some terrible death pyre, nowhere to hide from the circle of flickering faces staring at me, a ghostly jury just returned with the verdict. The dead Marine's name was Tommy "T-Bone" Bonneger.

The dead Marine's name *is* Tommy "T-Bone" Bonneger, and he may be Desert Storm's only grunt casualty.

When I arrived in recon nine months ago, I was determined to prove to my new platoon that I was a good officer who would listen to his men (as my grandfather had so often lectured), look out for them, and lead them—though with just two years of experience it is a fair question to ask how a youngster like me could possibly lead men like them.

Recon Marines are in a little better shape and are a touch more maniacal than regular grunts, if that is possible, and most of them are older and far more seasoned than I. Enlisted men swarm the rigorous tryouts for reconnaissance platoons because of the promise of independence; recon Marines patrol in small teams devoid of officers and their concomitant micromanagement. So here I sit, the leader of a platoon of men who do not want to be led at all.

I am twenty-five years old.

"We are Disneyland. Repeat, we are *Disneyland*," the radio tells me. SEALs have the annoying radio habit of repeating phrases they consider to be important or particularly dramatic. As if simple code words require extraordinary digestion. Actually, for SEALs they might. "There's press people on the beach north of us. No signs of enemy. Repeat, beach is green. *Beach is green*, over."

"Roger. Did anyone see you land? Over," I ask. The military radio jargon sounds dorky and superfluous but it keeps things clear once we begin shooting.

"Negative. But there's lots of reporters . . . right on your Mickey Mouse site. Reporters! I mean *right* on it. Can you see 'em? Over."

"Wait one, over." I point at Sergeant Armstrong in the bow and give two hand signals. We communicate with hand and arm signals when the enemy is near and enforce a strict code of noise discipline. Draw your own conclusion as to the label we've applied to our beachgoers.

Armstrong picks up the laser illuminator and slips on his night-vision goggles. I point in the general direction of the beach and bring my hand, two fingers extended in a horizontal peace sign, back to my face as if I am going to poke out my eyes. The other five Marines in the boat put their NVGs on, too, having seen the hand signals. A powerful laser beam shoots across the water from Armstrong's hand and lights up the dark continent, in a fifty-meter diameter, like a spotlight. The infrared laser is invisible to the naked eye; unless they have NVGs, the forty-odd bodies on the beach have no way of knowing they're being watched. I adjust the focus of the magnifier on my goggles and can make out cameras and cords. Between fifty and a hundred people. *No rifles.*

The Pentagon must have given them an eight-digit grid coordinate; they are *right on* my landing site. Armstrong sees the same thing and signals "seventy-seven people," which I believe to be within ten; he's a terrific observer but cocksure. He then signs "No enemy in sight" somewhat dejectedly. Of my twenty Marines, I'll have to watch him most closely once we're ashore. Like most bullies, his self-esteem is linked to domination.

He's also the Marine I want most on my side if we exchange metal.

I give him the hand signal for "Prepare your team to swim." Armstrong nudges the Marine next to him, and when he has the boat's full attention he hand-signs "I love you, sir." He gives me an exaggerated wink, the white of his eyeball disappearing momentarily, replaced by a shit-eating grin that breaks through the dark, more teeth flashing in the night now that the others have seen this. Armstrong's trying to show just how cool he is under fire . . . or, potential fire.

I'm tempted to zing him right back, something like "Love you too, One Nut." Sergeant Jake "Stretch" Armstrong is happy to tell you all about how his extraordinary high school football career ("twice an *All-State* tight end, sir . . . and that's *Texas* football, not some pussy New England prep stuff") was ended when the family tractor rolled and crushed his pelvis. What he won't tell you, though, is that he lost a testicle in the accident. I know this because as his platoon commander I have access to his medical records, which is also the reason I can't engage in tit-for-tat grasps at attention. I smirk and turn back to the radio.

The whole action takes less than fifteen seconds.

"Roger, Photograph, we make out about seventy-five news bubbas on the beach. We'll see you at Goofy, then. Over." I'm happy they weren't made because I want my platoon to be the first ones to take advantage of the photo op. Talk about fifteen minutes of fame! I'm surprised the SEALs didn't take advantage and throw out a few bombastic quotes. It's not like them.

Don't get me wrong, Marines understand the lust for glory as well as anyone—a jealous World War II Army officer likened our propaganda machine to Joe Stalin's— but ours is a much more stealthy approach. Put it this way: The professional wrestler Jesse "The Body" Ventura was a SEAL: "I ain't got time to bleed!" John Glenn, on the other hand, "is" a Marine. "I think we would be remiss in our duty if we didn't make fullest use of our talents in volunteering for something as important as this is to our country and the world in general right now." Enough said.

"Roger. We're heading to Goofy now. Out," whispers Photograph. The Disney code words are probably unnecessary given our encryption technology, but it's good practice and it sounds cool. It helps get the Marines into character. The SEAL mission is to "di-di" (a Vietnam slang holdover for "go fast") to the airport just a few hundred meters inland, link up with the Pakistanis on deck, and ensure that the runway is clear for the heli-borne force. My Zodiac is flanked on either side by the two other boats carrying six Marines each; our job is to secure the beach landing site for the tracked amphibious vehicles that will be carrying a few hundred infantry jarheads. We'll be the first Marines to land in Somalia as part of "Operation Restore Hope."

My recon platoon is going in first tonight because it's our job—scouting ahead and putting eyes on the enemy before the big forces arrive; a toe in the water. Roughly the same theory applied when you handed your kid sister a glass of Coke and some Pop Rocks. The platoon is made up of three six-man teams of hard-core, patriotic whack-balls, each of them led by a seasoned NCO like Sergeant Armstrong and used to operating on its own. Gunny—my impressive platoon sergeant—and I are riding in with the teams because the entire platoon has been tasked. And because, frankly, we didn't want to be watching this landing on the ship's televisions.

I call headquarters back on the *Tripoli*. "Vader, this is Sharkman. Seventy-five press personnel are right on the proposed Mickey Mouse site. Should we still keep it primary? Over."

A ten-second pause. "Sharkman, this is Vader. Affirmative, over."

The Pentagon wants to show us off.

Ted Koppel is waiting for us on the beach as we speak. I know this because we watched him on television yesterday announcing our forthcoming arrival. "The operation is expected to begin tomorrow at midnight with the arrival of elite Navy and Marine reconnaissance units that will pave the way for a larger follow-on force."

We're not exactly following Sun-tzu's advice on surprise here.

You won't hear any arguments out of us, however; we relish the opportunity. My generation hasn't seen a big war, but we've been assuaged with some quickies. When the other 1,500 Marines arrive at dawn, we'll teach some punk warlords what true domination is all about, open up the clogged food supply lines, and save a starving nation.

Armstrong's six-man recon team slips quietly over the side. I'm clumsy and the added caution I use in order to avoid a loud *Splash!*—and the ensuing snickers of my Marines—allows Armstrong a small head start. He's a decorated Marine who gnashed his teeth when he heard that his team wasn't going in alone, angry that his gunny and lieutenant decided to accompany him to meet and greet. Rank is a bitch.

The ocean is too warm and feels as thick as a milk shake. As I slip the heavy rubber fins over my desert combat boots, I think of the sharks circling below and my first instinct is to catch the other Marines to reduce the odds that Bruce will pick me out as the lame calf.

A defunct slaughterhouse sits just at the eastern tip of the entrance to Mogadishu Harbor, about two klicks (slang for "kilometers" for all you civilian types who don't watch movies) up the beach from our objective. Built on stilts and attached to a small jetty, blood and guts were ripped from cows, camels, and Lord knows what else and dumped directly into the ocean for all to see. It was an efficient

Third World solution to waste that gave rise to another evil.

While children at Coney Island might dodge bandages in the surf, Somali children were snatched by sharks and devoured in the waist-deep waters. It became a minor epidemic for which there was no reasonable cure. The crumbling, prickly dirt found just inland made soccer too painful for the barefoot Somalis. Soccer is life in the Third World and sand is soft.

Though fishing nets were erected, an occasional ball sailed over the nets and into the water. The *only* ball. The sharks, creatures that can smell a thimble of blood in an Olympic swimming pool, were driven mad by the constant flow—*gallons* of blood!—in the water. With their senses on full alert and their appetites raging, the small splashes were investigated immediately and violently.

The blood stopped flowing from the slaughterhouse a few months ago; crops went untended and animals starved, so the slaughterhouse shut its doors. The clans began hoarding food and fighting over it. Which caused a famine. Which drew CNN's attention. Which is why I'm here.

By the time I link up with my swim buddy, Gunny, who is also my right-hand man, Armstrong is already forty meters closer to the beach. I can just make out heads and contrails in the strip of moonlight. No matter, both Gunny and I are strong swimmers and will reel them in quickly, much to Armstrong's chagrin. Armstrong is from rural Texas and though he's got the build of a big swimmer at six foot five, he's better in a barroom than he is in the water.

I swim up to Gunny and he winks at me. He has camouflaged his eyelid like an eyeball: all white except for a black dot, centered, perfectly proportioned, a trick that has freaked out many a foxhole buddy at night.

His black face is streaked with tiger stripes of light tan

and green paint, which is ironic because my white face is covered in black and green. We were ordered to cammie up, unusual because it's never an explicit order, it's standard. But camouflage makeup makes for better TV.

And you thought supermodels were bad.

I'm not swimming so much as finning, my long legs propelling my torso forward with steady, rhythmic kicks of my swim fins below the surface. Legs straight and locked, hips swaying for most efficient power. Both of my arms are streamlined against my sides, like a squid, my left hand pressed flat against the seam of my utility trousers and my right hand wrapped around the barrel of my rifle. The sling of the weapon across my chest keeps it snug, and when I inhale I feel it tighten and pull the rifle slightly into my spine, the front sight post digging into my lower back sharply, very nearly drawing blood. It is a comfortable feeling.

My wake in the black ocean is green and sparkling. The Indian lips around my head and expands in a rippling V as I slice toward the beach. It takes ten minutes before Gunny and I catch the six Marines of team one and it will take another ten to touch the dark continent. I hear the men breathing because they are excited, the low, mechanical hiss skipping across the surface like a distant steam engine, but there is no other noise, no telltale splashes.

I look at Gunny's square head, framing the eyeball, two meters away. His warpaint scheme is totally sinister, especially given what lurks underneath the water. I want to giggle because this is just not going to be a fair fight. And because I'm a little nervous—I'm not exactly the bravest guy in The Few and The Proud.

I swim headlong into the Marine swimming in front of me, who has stopped for some reason. He shudders, absolutely terrified, and spins around, reeling and snorting. He thinks I am a fish come to kill him. Then his eyes and brain connect and his mouth closes again, his face a mix of relief and embarrassment, and he points to an area in front of Armstrong, who has stopped as well. I swim forward and Gunny grabs my elbow.

"What's that?" he asks. "SEAL submarine?"

A mass of glowing green is moving rapidly toward the team like an underwater comet, moving just below the surface. Fear tingling in my stomach, shooting down my arms now the way it did just before I crashed my father's truck. I try to get my rifle out in front of me but the fish is too fast. It closes to within two meters and turns abruptly, gliding past me, streaking a bright contrail of phosphorescence behind it. A wave of pressure lifts me backward gently, right into Gunny's arms.

"*Holy Shit,*" I say. It is hard to tell exactly with the tailing glow, but the bulk of it is easily ten feet long. It circles around behind the team, then turns again, carving out a dimming figure eight.

Armstrong is suddenly moving past me, whispering orders to the team. "Break up and get to the beach as fast as you can. That thing—"

"Hey," I hiss. "Listen up. Everyone get in here tight and face outboard. *Now.*"

"Sir! This is *my* team. We need to get to that beach . . . it's, what, maybe two hundred meters away? We keep fucking around out here and—"

The fish closes in again, this time from behind, and streaks below us. I watch as the glowing particles from its wake flutter up past my fins, now tucked tightly against my hamstrings, my body in a cannonball as I watch it pass, my nose bubbling as I try to put my eyes as close to the slick as possible. The Marines are already moving by instinct, huddling together for protection like a school of bait fish, spinning with the shark.

"I am in charge of this platoon," I whisper, almost believing it.

"Sir! My team . . . *we* need to get to shore—"

"This is now *my* unit, Sergeant, so you'll do exactly what I tell you." Sergeant Armstrong has six years, five inches, and forty pounds on me, but I have rank and that is all that matters right now. I turn to the team.

"Form a tight circle, shoulder to shoulder, and face outboard. When he makes his run again, jab your rifles underwater and keep your feet up. It's okay to break your waterproofing and noise discipline. If you have to fire . . . *fire.*"

The comet turns and moves in again, steadily and slowly, deeper this time. The shark is directly under the circle of Marines, perhaps seven meters below—a faint ball of green that my eyes strain to discern—when it turns and streaks for the surface, the glow growing exponentially, my legs fleeing from the fish as if they are in competition with my torso, trying to push me up and out, my rifle moving forward. The shark shoots up and out of my view, behind me, and I cannot turn in time.

Then the deep pop an M-16 makes—nearly muted—when it discharges underwater, Gunny lifted halfway out of the water, his rifle jammed into his ribs, the slap of the tail on the surface, Gunny up higher now like a pole vaulter, me rolling back from the force of the water wave, the Marines turning in all directions like a herd straining to see the predator that has come to take a meal.

"Gunny!" I whisper, not expecting an answer.

His big head breaks the surface and he spins in a tight circle, treading water like a water-polo player, frantically looking down at the water, froth all around us. "Oh my *fuck!* He . . . see that, sir?" he pants. "Big . . . He came at me. Got my rifle in front of him and he drove it into my ribs . . . on the . . . on the way up. Up to take me. Put the barrel right on his head and shot him. Shot that motherfucker! Pushed me out of the water and onto his back."

"You're lucky. Let's—"

Armstrong swims out from behind one of the Marines and hisses, "*Fuckin' A, he's lucky.* Never should have been sitting here in the first place. We got to get the fuck out of here. That thing took off . . . get out while he's gone. This is stupid, sitting—"

I turn to him and put my finger in his face. "*You* listen. If—"

Gunny is between us, pushing Armstrong back.

"How about this? How about this, sir? We stay together, like you said, which probably saved one of our lives"—he glares at Armstrong and then turns to me again—"but we swim now. As a group. *Together.*"

I look at Armstrong but he just stares back. "Make it happen, Gunny," I say. "You and I will take the tail-end Charlie positions and look backward the whole way."

"Gotcha, sir." He leans in to Armstrong's ear, whispering furiously, the Texan's equipment harness wrapped around his fist as he lectures, and seconds later we are on our way to the beach like a tight pod of dolphins, Gunny and I watching the six, hanging on to the harnesses of the Marines in front of us.

After five minutes I hear Gunny whisper, "Hey, sir. Why d'you think that shark picked me?"

"Just bad luck I guess," I whisper back.

"Nawww, sir. Once you taste black, you don't go back."

"I heard that, Gunny," whispers Lance Corporal Terrel Johnson, Armstrong's assistant team leader and most loyal henchman, a black Marine from the Los Angeles suburbs who was recently busted down a rank for that Hong Kong brawl. "And I don't like bein' on the clock. Can you two swim faster? You're slowing us down."

"Uh, hey, sir, you seeing what I'm seeing back here? Coming from five o'clock? I think it's another fish," Gunny whispers.

"Don't fuck with me, Gunny," whispers Johnson. "Seriously. My shit's freaked out right now and I don't wanna look like a puss in front of the cameras."

———

Fifty meters later the team has stopped again. I look over the bobbing row of heads, toward the beach, and can make out people and vehicles. They are talking quietly and occasionally I hear the group laugh. There are women present. Hubba-hubba. Hey, it's been three months.

I see Armstrong give a few hand signals and four Marines break off from the huddled group, two swimming right and two left. They fin away from us, parallel to the beach, to provide flank security. I wish them Godspeed because I really don't want to get eaten while I tread water. Armstrong remains in the center with Johnson and is doing his best to ignore us, but his excitement boils over and he swims up to me and smiles. The prodigal son. He signs that, if the shit hits the fan, Gunny and I are supposed to hit the water first while he provides covering fire from center beach. Right. Imagine Gunny and me returning to the *Tripoli* to explain why the two senior members ran from their platoon. But I placate Armstrong with a smile and a thumbs-up.

The wind picks up slightly and it's an offshore breeze because I can now make out a conversation. There is no smell to Somalia yet. I expect the entire country will reek of disease and death and corpses and blood and sand.

"Where the hell are they?" says a man on the beach. "I'm fucking bored."

"Maybe they're already here, Don," says a woman.

"Yeah, check your jeep, Donny. Maybe they're hiding in it," says another.

"Pshhh. These macho idiots don't sneak around. They bumble. You'll see," he says.

I want to swim around their flank and sneak up on Don, just me, perhaps grab his throat and cut off the airway with my left and put my Ka-Bar knife up next to his eyeball with my other hand, wearing a scary war face, fangs extended, then apologize and say that I wasn't sure if he was a friendly—postal workers don't have the market cornered on screwy fantasies. But I also want to hear their excited gasps as we emerge from Loch Ness in full regalia.

Armstrong checks his watch—it's 0030—and signals the Marines on the flanks. All six of them begin to fin slowly, in a line, toward the beach. Their rifles are no longer slung across their backs; mine is in my hands as well. I see Armstrong's shoulders pop up and know that he's in shallow enough to stand. Like all of my Marines, I am scanning the darkness behind the reporters for bad guys, moving my eyes quickly back and forth and looking out of the corners the way I was taught: The rods and cones in the eyeball work more efficiently at night this way. I'm looking for vehicles that look out of place, people moving a little too quickly, and torsos dug in. All Marine rifles come off Safe.

Tension.

Our inherent paranoia—that the media will somehow screw us over—does not explain away all the jumpiness. Somalia is a dangerous place and Gangbanger bullets will kill you just as dead as Soviet ones will. Whoops, sorry, *Russian* ones.

Thirty meters from the beach the Marines are all moving forward in various crouches in waist-deep water, rifles being furiously unwrapped from their plastic shields like Christmas morning, Armstrong now on his belly, low-crawling on elbows and knees to keep his M-16 dry, when a woman spots him and shrieks, "Ohmygod! THEY'RE HERE!"

Once more unto the breach, dear friends, once more.

– 2 –

Captain Willard: Who's the commanding
officer here?

Soldier: Ain't you?

There is a surge of vocal orders near the vehicles and people begin running, sprinting, down the beach. It is a total goat rodeo—the first derivative of the clusterfuck. Some people are clapping and cheering. There are metallic *clangs* and *thumps* and *riiippps* as car doors are opened and slammed shut and cameras are dragged out of flatbeds. There are "Let's gos," "C'mon, Todd, hurrys," and "I'm comin', I'm comin's."

Armstrong is quickly surrounded by the screaming throng and, on one knee with his rifle in his shoulder, I am convinced he will plug somebody, possibly in front of the 40 million Americans watching back home. I quickly yell into my radio—"Mickey Mouse! Mickey Mouse!"—the code word for "feet-dry," no contact. Then I focus on Sergeant Armstrong, the platoon's Lone Star. The only hope is that the NVGs he is wearing, which make precision shooting difficult because you cannot use the sights, will hamper him just enough to prevent a kill shot on a national anchorman. Given the choice, I know he will kill someone of distinction. *Better to burn out, sir . . .*

The Gunny and I might have assigned one of the other two teams as the scout swimmer team—and left Armstrong to arrive by Zodiac with the other twelve Marines once the beach was secured—but you don't keep your best Marines in reserve. You put them on point. Jake Armstrong walks a fine line, but he does it because he believes in his job and his men. The fact is, if a firefight erupts, I'll be looking to him for clues, not vice versa.

I look right and left and see that flank securities are feet-dry, undetected. But our noisy landing has, I'm sure, penetrated all of Mogadishu proper. I imagine clan leaders four miles away standing outside their huts, listening to the celebration on the beach. Laughing. No need to watch it live on CNN when you can stand outside and watch. I imagine that hundreds of evil red eyeballs are watching our fete. The throng encircles Armstrong and begins to press in tightly as if he is a famous defendant. Armstrong stands, weapon at the ready, shoves a photographer and yells, "Get the fuck away from me!"

Cameras poke through the crowd and I see little red lights in the darkness. They are filming, probably with civilian night-vision scopes. I'm happy they're smart enough not to use lights. Armstrong seems to take notice and yells for all the world to hear, "I am a United States Marine here to do a job, so please get out of the way and let me do it! We're here to feed starving children and all you can do is think of your ratings!"

I am standing in knee-deep water. Three things pop into my mind. First, he has obviously rehearsed this line, perhaps daily for the last two weeks. There is just no way in hell. Second, the colonel must be going ballistic right now and I'll have some serious explaining to do. Third, I'm jealous and hope the cameras still roll for me.

The soliloquy triggers a reflex in all of the camera people and instantly we are bathed in light. Flashbulbs erupt, floodlights lock in, and the night is gone. I lose my night vision in an instant. I see only blinding white light, and imagine Gangbangers sneaking in between the reporters to plug us. I know Armstrong has ripped off his NVGs by now. He is cursing loudly and tries to push through. This is not good.

Gunny and I sprint forward, onto the beach, trying to draw attention away from Armstrong and succeed. I hear a *beep!* from my Motorola—HQ calling—and ignore it. Gunny moves forward with his right hand on the trigger housing of his weapon, his left hand extended like the Grim Reaper.

"We'll address all of your questions, ladies and gentlemen. *So you better get those fucking lights off my Marines,*" he says.

The lights swing onto us and two anchormen move into the attack, holding microphones. It dawns on me that they are broadcasting live. This really *is* a karaoke party. I feel a strong grip on my arm—it is Gunny—and he pulls me down on a knee so I don't look like a deer in the headlights, literally, to all the folks back home. We go into a stealthy, conspiratorial whisper mode for the cameras, and though it is only acting we have done it enough to make it look good: two painted warriors leaning in cheek to cheek, a portrait of diversity, eyes and weapons outboard, looking for danger, whispering hasty plans of destruction and death as if the cameras did not even exist.

I send Armstrong forward to recon the road while we keep the press occupied, then shield my eyes from the lights with my hand in a mock salute. The CNN logo is suddenly in my face and that good-looking Gulf War woman with the supercilious accent, Christiane Onomatopoeia or something, is on my left. Some fatty photographer in jungle safari dress—come to think of it, all these bozos are dressed for a designer assault on the outback—nearly backs into her and she deftly smacks him in his head and pushes him back. She's still talking but I cannot see the camera now so I scoot forward to give her a better backdrop, which blocks the Gunny. He whispers, "Hey, sir, you're blocking me out here. Rotate back so we can both get in." He winks.

I recognize Ted Koppel from ABC and wonder why Jennings didn't make it. Dan Rather has the cool designer safari jacket on that he's worn since he arrived last weekend, and I am nearly overcome by the urge to rush over, grab him, throw him down and scream, "What's the frequency, Kenneth?" which will certainly get me launched from the Corps, folk-hero status notwithstanding. Brokaw is here but no Scud Stud.

A photographer says to another correspondent, who I can't make out, "Can you do that again with the Marines in the background? I missed the picture."

"How's it feel?" says some guy stupidly.

C'est magnifique mais ce n'est pas la guerre. "Good," I say. "We're excited to get in here to help."

My radio beeps again. I turn to answer and a camera lens jabs me hard in the mouth; I feel a trickle run down my lip and taste the blood when it curls under my lip. I'm the first casualty in Somalia.

"Are you expecting trouble tonight?" asks a woman. Woman. Female. Procreates with males. Three—*long*—months. Thank you, Easter Bunny.

"We're always expecting trouble, that's why I have a

problem with all the lights." I am stale and feel like a tired athlete slurring banal answers to banal questions, just like Nuke Laloosh.

Gunny rescues me. "Aidid said he's glad we're here and looks forward to working with the Marines. I have something to say to him, from me personally: Be careful what you ask for, you just might get it. I don't like people starving young kids."

"What's your name? Who are you?" they all ask, excited.

A boom mike comes swinging through the crowd and settles, hovering over Gunny's head like a mechanical bumblebee.

"Hey!" I shout at the crowd. "You are compromising the safety of this mission and the safety of my Marines with those lights. *Turn off your lights or we will turn them off for you.*"

Tell me Middle America won't eat *that* one up. I nod at Gunny. He winks, tosses the rifle from his large right hand to his left, takes two menacing steps forward and hisses, "You heard the man. Do it."

Cell phones begin to ring in the crowd and everyone is shouting that New York is telling them to douse the lights, douse the lights, DOUSE THE LIGHTS. All the lights go off and suddenly it is dark again. No doubt the Pentagon brass on their case, having realized their error.

One photographer can't resist the image, however, and keeps snapping away at the large man in camouflage, the flashes lighting the Gunny like lightning. The wet utilities are outlining his body, especially the upper mass, and I think it will make for a great picture in *Time.*

He says, "Hey, motherfucker, I've had about enough of you," and the man stops immediately. To the seasoned brawlers within the paparazzi ranks, Gunny must make Sean Penn look like a little schoolboy. They back off nearly twenty-five meters, which gives us some room to think.

"Sir," Gunny says, "don't you think you should call the colonel?"

Oh, shit. *Well, to tell you the truth, I kind of forgot myself in all this excitement.* The colonel will be highly pissed. DEFCON 3, I'm sure. He gave me explicit orders to keep in constant communication with him. Constant, not just code-word calls. This is a bad, bad mistake. In the Marines a direct superior can destroy a career with a simple performance report. This nationally televised operation will make or break him, an operation that, for a man who missed Vietnam and was left home during Desert Storm, means *everything*.

"Yes, Guns. I'm just letting him sweat a little." I wink, trying to be casual, but I am worried. *Really* worried. Lieutenant Colonel Vin Capiletti is fully aware of my actions in the Gulf War, lectured me on following orders when I reported to the battalion—"No room for reckless actions in *my* unit, Lieutenant. I'll make sure you'll never have to struggle interpreting commander's intent; I make my orders clear and I don't pull punches. Your job is to carry them out well"—and has a thermonuclear temper that can be combatted only by employment of an equal show of force, interpersonal MAD. Which is to say, if you are a subordinate, not at all. Oh, and I don't want to forget this fact: The colonel also controls my career and, by extension, my life.

"Besides," I whisper, "there's nothing much to report."

Gunny likes this. He chuckles and shakes his head as if to say "You officer types are crazy." Gunny hates Lieutenant Colonel Capiletti.

"Vader, this is Sharkman. Mickey Mouse, over." It's been, what, five mikes (if you were visiting Canada when this became colloquial, it's short for minutes) since we hit the beach? What's five mikes? About five weeks of ass chewings and five months of sweating over my next fitness report. "Vader" used to be the colonel's sarcastic nickname until some sycophant told the old man, and he liked it so much he kept it as his call sign. Now the lieutenants have given him two new, secret nicknames: Bison Breath and B-Squared, for obvious reasons.

"Sharkman, this is Vader Six! Get your six on the radio, over!"

"This is Sharkman Six, go, Vader." This is not a cheer.

"What are you *doing?* Over. I want those lights turned off, ASAP! What was that Marine doing speaking on TV? And you! What's the situation? Over. Are you in control of the situation? *What's going on? Over.*"

His voice is squeaky, though it could be the encrypted radio. The Gunny pretends to check his weapon, but he's not even moving his head, he's straining so hard to overhear. The next transmission will be reported back to the troops if I don't screw it up—officer conversations hold particular interest for the men because they glean insight into their own commanders. I'm tempted to request, "Say again all after 'doing,'" but that would really be pushing it.

"Situation resolved. Press misled by HQ. Marines did well. Mickey Mouse, over."

"Sharkman, I say again, *where is the press now?* The commander of the Joint Task Force is going *ballistic!* What is the situation? Are your Marines doing reconnaissance or giving quotes? GIVE ME AN UPDATE, OVER. OVER!" *So great is his pain that he does not scream but roars.* Lieutenant Colonel Capiletti has blown a gasket. He's lost it. I actually have to turn down the volume on the radio.

"Vader, this is Sharkman. Press have retreated. No casualties, no choices. Preparing to Minnie Mouse. No sign of Gangbangers. Over."

"Hey, let them through," says someone behind the press circle. A reporter shouts, "Excuse us! We need to get through. Excuuuse us, please!" Someone important is trying to get to us, and the herd is following. The radio beeps and I hear Armstrong's voice, but I have to address the oncoming throng first.

It's two Italian officers, part of the UN force already in country, and getting their pee pees slapped by the Somalis. We shake hands and the Italian colonel holds on for too long and actually smiles for the camera. You'd think it was Yalta.

Some photographers snap a few pictures, but they are hesitant now. No flashes go off. No floodlights. The colonel is somewhat puzzled, but eventually releases my hand and says, "I am Colonel Calizzi. Can I give you a ride to the airport? That is where you will set up the operation. We have met the SEALs already!"

I want to ask him if he plans to reveal the *entire* plan to the press now, or only the landing. Add some elephants and a few tents and we've got a three-star circus going. *Step right up!*

"No, sir," I say. "And I'm going to have to ask you to follow my gunnery sergeant here back to the news trucks. We've got this under control." It's dismissive and arrogant considering that an Italian general has been placed in charge of the United Nations operation here, but certain militaries have screwy ways of doing business and they are best avoided.

I turn to the reporters and say, "That goes for everyone. Fun's over. Let us do our jobs. No more questions will be answered."

The prospect of facing my own colonel has my full

attention, and I am overcome by regret for not dismissing the cameras earlier. The colonel must have watched our big interview! With the Desert Storm focus on smart bombs and generals I guess I just got greedy. Dumb.

Gunny takes his cue and shouts, "You heard the man! All you people follow me back to the jeeps."

The Italians stare at the Gunny for a second—thankful that he's a good guy—before they nod and walk away, the media mass following. No more live shots for the evening news.

The radio beeps and I hear Armstrong again. I take a knee and am about to respond when I hear a noise behind me. It's a woman in a CNN cap, cameraman in tow. "Excuse me. Hi. Are you in charge here?" Her J. Crew blouse is still damp from the squall and her safari vest is open, so I notice the outline of her bra, light green in my night-vision goggles. It's clear she's been in Somalia for a while; she's darker than the rest of the pasty group fresh in country for the landing.

"Sorry. No more questions, ma'am."

She ignores my remarks and walks right over, kneels next to me, hand extended. She has dark eyebrows that plunge sharply toward her nose and she's really quite good looking. Though, truth be told, even the Gunny has started to look handsome, as long as it's been. "I'm Mary Thayer-Ash. Are you Lieutenant Kelly?"

It's too dark for her to read the name tapes stitched onto my uniform and I search for an answer. Finding none, I ask, "How'd you know that?"

When she flips her head back toward her cameraman, her black hair swings around and exposes her neck. Her hair bunches at the end of its ride and moves back gracefully to its natural position fanned across those wide shoulders of hers.

She ignores the question.

"I'd like you to answer a few questions—for the good of the mission."

I like that. Blackmail posing as patriotism. If I don't respond, I'm letting down the team; if I do respond, she can damn well ask me anything and edit it later.

"Do you expect any trouble from the warlords who have been terrorizing the population?"

It's my turn to ignore her.

The radio beeps again and I whisper, "Excuse me, call waiting," and stick the earpiece in deep. I put my hand across my mouth so Ms. Ash won't hear me—our throat microphones transmit noise directly from the vocal cords—and whisper, "Sharkman Six, over."

I hear Gunny clearly in a shouted whisper. "Six, this is Five! Roll to platoon frequency!"

The last time I heard inflection like this I was in Kuwait and someone was screaming that my radioman was dead. My throat closes and I turn from Ms. Ash and her cameraman. I roll to the private freq and hear, "Six, I'm with Armstrong. We've got one dead Somali Gangbanger over here. Another beaten up but still breathing and tied up. Both were armed. I'm fifty meters north of the road. We need to unfuck this *ASAP.*" *Oh, shit.*

I turn to Thayer-Ash. "No more questions. Please. Just go back to the vehicles and stop interfering." I am trying to remain calm but my head is now swirling with anxious images: dead Somalis, the colonel screaming disobedience and recklessness, the brig, dishonoring an already scarred family . . .

I am a third-generation Marine. My family's military history, though rich, is binary. My grandfather, Red Kelly, is a warrior forged in World War II and the Korean War, a hero of hyperbolic status for me, the embodiment of manliness and the benchmark by which I judge myself. A man who spent his formative years robbing young Japanese, Chinese, and Korean men of theirs. When I look into the mirror and shave off pieces of my inheritance, I see tangible bonds to him that have grown stronger now that I, too, am a Marine—a *man*—my breeding flushing proud, manifest in my wars. For I have craved, hunted, and bagged *my* adventures, *my* tests, *my* stories—elusive and skittish prey in a world where most baby boomers point to their portfolios when asked to name the biggest risk they've ever taken.

My father joined the Marines to fight in Vietnam, but disgraced us, my grandfather and me. Discharged from the Corps under "other than honorable" circumstances and sent home halfway through his first tour, my father has never discussed his war or his failure, and it remains an awful secret, a spur in my grandfather's shoe that he cannot dislodge and a consistent reminder of the cowardice that defined my early years. "The boy sure as hell didn't inherit the penchant to play pussy from me," I heard Red Kelly tell my father once when I came home crying after yet another schoolyard rout.

My father wears a wicked skull tattoo on his forearm, teeth rigored shut around a dagger with five long blood slashes forming a base for the tattoo. He refuses to discuss its origin except to say, "Vietnam," a mystery that maddened Red Kelly, made worse by the fact that his son had a cooler tattoo than any of the five faded units Red advertised on his own body. When I was five I told my grandfather as much and he was so bothered that he went out and got a new tattoo stitched into his chest—a massive man with a shark's head, carrying a machine gun. Underneath the Sharkman it reads: "Undefeated."

Twenty years later I requested Red's old call sign and was given, along with it, the chance to prove that I, too, am a fighter. But now my platoon has killed a Somali and modern wars come with modern rules. I am a third-generation Marine. Will there be a fourth?

Miss Thayer-Ash is taken aback by my tone—I haven't covered the significance of the radio message as well as I'd hoped—but she nods and stands up. "Okay, Gavin Kelly, take it easy. Maybe we can talk later?" She turns and walks away.

I start to answer her but realize that I don't have any saliva left. It is all I can do to nod and focus on the sand under my combat boots. My earpiece beeps again and I hear Gunny hiss, "Sir! Give the Zodiacs the signal to land and get over here. I need you *right now.*"

And suddenly I know why Mary Thayer-Ash knows my name.

– 3 –

10 OCTOBER 1988

When we last met, you were the master and I
was the pupil. Now I am the master . . .

I am a college senior. My best friend, Darren Phillips, and I
are in a preppy biker bar called the Bow and Arrow. Such
things are not contradictions in Cambridge, Massachusetts,
where old money Harvard students dress down so they
might bond with the working class between visits to the
Upper East Side and the Hamptons. Darren is over by the
bar buying a round while I scan the crowd of women and
pick out a few I'll watch intently all night but never speak
to. I see Darren glare at two Massholes who are wearing
their baseball caps backward as he makes his way over to
me with the drinks; Darren's gritted teeth and foamy
mouth are not unusual given his general intolerance for
things that rub his worldview raw—"What's the purpose of
wearing it like that if the lid's on the other side?" he once
asked me, spinning my hat around. "Marines don't pull this
showy shit." Problem is, the men he's locked his radar on

are laughing with the bouncer. As a general rule, you don't irritate the bouncer when you're underage.

Darren bulls his way through the crowd and hands me a Guinness. He is scowling but it is impossible to tell if the Massholes are the salient cause; Darren Phillips is cheap as hell, doesn't drink, and deeply resents his turn to buy the round—he feels he's overpaying given the fact that a Sprite costs a third as much as a Guinness.

"What's your problem?" I shout over Axl Rose, a wildly overreaching question that might elicit a wide slew of answers from "this vile music" to "the fact that Michael Dukakis was allowed in an M-1 in the first place."

"Heard an ignorant comment I shouldn't have. I may need you in a second, Kelly."

He turns back to squint across the bar at the men, sipping his Sprite through a straw, and my stomach roils. Darren keeps his head shaved and I see the skin around his ear stretching toward his jaw, then relaxing, then stretching again the way it does when he grinds his teeth.

"Welcome to the jungle, baby!" Axl screams. "We got fun and games!"

He hands me his Sprite and pushes his way back through toward the entrance, his head glistening as he passes under the flashing lights of the arcade basketball game. Black guys look good bald, I look like Frank Perdue. I keep my hair in a flattop as long as ROTC regulations permit so the Harvard women can at least leave one box unchecked as to why they won't date me.

My eyes move past him and find the bait; one of them has extended an arm so a woman can't move past and the other is leaning in from her six o'clock, pinning her next to the wall. The bouncer is just sitting there, watching the men laugh. Now I know we will fight; Darren Phillips often ignores insults leveled at him—he views them as manifestations of either jealousy or ignorance, both beneath him—but he never passes up a chance to play the hero. He moves up, weaving stealthily through the crowd, grabs the Masshole's arm and snaps it down. I cringe; just like Phillips to act before he thinks it through! There is an animated argument and much finger-pointing. A chair falls down, a bottle breaks, and necks extend, heads craning. Though I am safe in a DMZ fifty feet away, I find it hard to breathe.

"Welcome to the jungle! Watch it bring you to your knees, knees! I wanna watch you bleed!" Axl squeals.

Darren turns abruptly and storms over to my safe haven, his lips pursed and his features folded up like a bulldog. "I need you outside, Kelly. Fight's on!"

"Jesus! Do you even know that chick? Maybe she's friends with those guys."

"I need you outside with me *right now*, Kelly."

"Shouldn't we just call the cops?" I call after him, but it's just a finger drag mark on a cliff. Darren is already heading toward the three men, squaring his shoulders and swiveling his head on his neck—a wrestling warm-up, I figure—following them out the door.

The old panic rises and freezes me in place, a gift from my father, a virus that I will not manage to root out until the Gulf War. My mind races and I am both awed by and ashamed of the excuses that prevent me from leaving this bar: Sorry, I got into a scrape inside with two other friends of theirs. I slipped and hit my head. Bouncer stopped me. There was a fire. Chick was choking on a peanut. I didn't hear you. A fight? I thought you were just going home early, like usual you lightweight. Why didn't you say so? You know I got your back covered. *Semper Fi.*

I am comfortable with self-contempt when it comes to violence, and the feeling isn't a sharp guilt, just a dull throb with which I have lived since my grandfather first discovered that I was a coward.

In 1975, when I was seven, he took my father and me to Fenway Park. Red Kelly is an ardent Sox fan so I, too, became another fanatical and tragic victim. We sat in the bleachers behind two shirtless drunk men—in retrospect I suppose they were in their twenties—who were drinking prodigiously. Occasionally they would burp and swear at a player, and I would look at my grandfather with wide eyes and an open mouth. It seemed unconscionable that those fat, hairy drunks could have anything bad to say at all about Yaz and Fisk!

"Did you hear what they said, Red?" I asked.

My grandfather has insisted I call him by his Marine nickname from the time I could first speak. In fact, my first word was "Red," a bitter subject for my parents, both of whom blame my grandfather for a force-fed, two-day carpet bombardment of his name during a visit when I was thirteen months.

Eventually Red could take it no more. "You two shut your sucks or I'll shut them for you." My grandfather is a big man, and though he was over fifty years of age he seemed incredibly imposing and brave.

"Cool down, Pop," my father practically begged.

The drunks glanced back, laughed dismissively, and continued the onslaught.

My grandfather's face began to flush red, a sign I recognized as a natural warning, the way a snake rattles or a shark arches its back. He handed me his beer and stood up. "You fancy yourself tough?" Red hissed at the two men.

He was much bigger than they were, and a step higher he seemed to be a giant, red stubble bristling out across the width of his face, darkening his hue and framing a nose that zigzags as wildly as a lightning bolt. My father rubbed my head and winked. Still, I wept openly.

"Easy, Pop," my dad said.

One of the men looked at my grandfather. "Don't push me, man. I'll embarrass you right here."

"Do—you—fancy—yourself—tough?"

"Go fuck yourself."

Then one of the men pushed my grandfather in the chest.

Red yanked him clear out of his row and slammed his face into the back of a seat. He jerked the man's head back by his hair and smashed it down into the metal again, grinding his teeth into the backrest, taking his time. The man let out a loud wail and his face was bright red and wet. Red lifted him to his feet and wrapped his left arm around his neck in a choke hold and looked at the man's friend, who was just standing there stunned, as frozen as I was.

"You gonna help your buddy out of here? Huh?" Red asked. "Because it's your turn next, you hippie bitch."

The man said, "Jesus Christ! Yeah! Just let him go. Security! SECURITY!" He grabbed his friend and started to help him up the aisle.

Red looked at us and smiled. He seemed totally at ease. Actually, he seemed genuinely happy. He said, "I'm going to escort these fairies outta here. You can stay with the boy, Tom, since you're not going to join in. I'll be right back, *kids*. Are you all right, Gavin?"

I was still sobbing, and lacking the lung capacity to blurt out a coherent sentence between breaths I stuttered, "Red . . . I thought . . . Red . . ."

"He's got a lot of his father in him, doesn't he? Jesus, calm down, Gavin. Man's never got nothing to cry about. Certainly not for a fight. Look at this one. He's even more nervous than you two." He pointed at the man as he walked past us up the aisle with his wounded friend and I saw that his cutoff jean shorts were dark with urine, the hair on his thighs slick against his flesh. "That's what happens when you don't take beaver and root it out of a man early in his life."

Bryan Jenkins filed assault charges and brought a civil suit against my grandfather for a broken cheekbone and seven broken teeth. My grandfather was terrified; he wasn't afraid of any man, he told me, but lawyers were not human.

When Red went to the Boston police precinct to answer questions, an old desk sergeant said he'd already ripped up the charge sheet. Red nodded his thanks and started out the door.

"Hey, Red Kelly," the cop yelled after him. He pointed a thumb at himself. "Marine Corps. Nineteen fifty to fifty-six. First of the First. Warred in the forgotten war with you. I read about you in the *Globe*. Several times."

As do I whenever I visit my grandfather's house. The articles about Red Kelly's exploits in the western Pacific and Chosin line the walls of his South Boston home, neatly encased in custom-made cedar frames, perfectly aligned so that when you enter the house and move down the narrow hallway you feel you are running a gauntlet of sorts, the glass faces twinkling, beckoning you to read the words of intrepidity that bulge beneath. A test of your manhood. A dare to compare.

When I was young Red would read the articles to me, adding editorial comments, sound effects—"Then that little Jap, right? I fire at him again but this time he gets it in the head. *POP!* And he still keeps runnin' for the line, crazy little Tojo! So I pop him again. *Thwack!*"—and charades. Eventually we would reach the living room, as pristine and rich as a museum, trophies neatly arranged and ready for viewing. Japanese pistols, a North Korean flag, a samurai sword, and, of course, the medal case. He would take the cedar case down, unlock it, and step away, watching me proudly as I devoured the contents. I liked to rub my fingers across the colorful ribbons, and by the time I was six I could recite the story behind each of them. Most are adorned with tiny brass *V*s for valor in combat. Bravery in the face of the enemy.

So it does not shock me that, at the age of twenty, my feet are glued to the bar's sticky floor when my best friend needs me outside. No, it's no surprise, but the disappointment is as palpable and tasty as bile.

I gulp down my Guinness and grab the pay phone.

"911. What is your emergency?"

"There's a fight right outside the Bow and Arrow in Cambridge!" I shout. "There may be knives!"

"Okay, take it easy. We've got a patrol car right near there. Now, what is your name and how—"

Welcome to the jungle! It gets worse here every day! Ya learn to live like an animal! In the jungle where we play!

I drop the phone, walk toward the door, stop, peer out the window, breathe, fight the fear, steel myself, and step into the street. The cold air scratches my lungs and it is hard to draw air. A dry leaf crunches under my sneaker. One of the men is already unconscious on the brick sidewalk, his baseball cap—"BU Hockey"—lying next to his head. Blood from his shattered nose is brighter than the red of the brick, gurgling and popping out of the hole in the bridge, thin round bubbles filling with air then bursting and trickling past his eye.

He's breathing. Why can't I?

The second man is also on his back, but still struggling. Darren straddles him like a grizzly over a fresh kill, blood and saliva drooling from his mouth, painting the man's face. His fist is up in the air, then rocketing down again, the sharp *craack!* of that big black paw striking the face, the other hand choking him. This one's cap is off, too.

"Take it easy, Darren," I try to say, but it's just a whisper.

He tilts his head up toward me and he nods, drooling, teeth clenched but enjoying it. "You got him," he hisses, jerking his head at a man who is rushing by me.

I tackle him and can't even encircle his legs, they're so thick. We're grappling on the pavement. The bouncer. He frees one of his legs, foot slithering out of my grasp, then returning with the force of a mule kick right in my chest, exploding my lungs. I fly back and slam into a parked car. The bouncer rolls to his feet and thunders forward but he's not fast enough. Darren shoves him hard into a light post and I see him tumble sideways and hear a *kah-pop!* The bouncer crumbles backward as if he's a crashed car and screams something about his shoulder.

Darren sticks out his hand and I grasp it. He yanks me up.

"I thought for a second you were going to let me take all the glory again, Kelly."

"I . . . tried . . . to get out here quick . . . I figured that if . . ."

He claps me on the shoulder. "Easy, brother. Catch that breath first. If they counterattack, you'll need it." His black eyes dart across his victims the way they do when he's revved up, predatorlike, surveying the situation, feeding him information. "Not that they're gonna come back for seconds. They lack the good old Marine Corps spirit! You know, Kelly, you just need to learn to act on instinct like they taught us at OCS. Don't think things through if you're just going to waste time. Marines don't twiddle their thumbs, hemming and hawing, they adapt to a situation and *act!* When we get out to the fleet, there's no officer handbook that will make decisions for us."

It was one of many lessons Darren Phillips delivered to

me, perhaps his most loyal henchman. Darren was a prodigious lecturer, far more eloquent than my Harvard professors and much more striking because his subjects were grounded in the deep realities of the world he had made and then conquered, intricate power plays doggedly implemented to slingshot him—and those who would dare to follow—up and over mountain after mountain until there were none left to climb. His creed was grounded on simple principles: Follow the rules and separate yourself from the pack, not with pomp and flourish but with the sheer determination to beat them. "There may be people who are smarter than I am," Darren told me once, "but I'll be damned if I've ever seen one who's willing to outwork me." Darren took me under his big wing in college, and while he still brags that his mentoring enabled me to get through ROTC and Marine Corps officer training unscathed (true), it is also true that I was his only real friend; most of our peers kept a friendly and awestruck, but leery, distance from the tiger.

The last lesson I learned from Darren came in October 1991. Eight months earlier, a stray Iraqi bullet shattered his kneecap and ended his Marine Corps career. More than that, it cracked the cemented plans of a man who writes down weekly, monthly, and yearly goals in a notebook I once discovered called "Life Tactics and Strategies." Darren's dream was to become a Marine Corps general officer, make a name for himself, and run for office. On the flight to Saudi Arabia, he said, "Let's say I do some good in the desert. Kill a few Iraqis, earn the unbreakable respect of my men. I think I have a legitimate shot at becoming the first black president seventeen years from now. That's assuming General Powell won't run first, of course. Because if he does, he'll avalanche it."

His doctors acted out the cliché and gave him fourteen

months of convalescence following his bitterly disputed medical discharge from the Corps. Six months after a plastic kneecap replaced bone, Darren and I were racing for the Clydesdale trophy in the Marine Corps marathon—the Corps has a special place in its heart for big guys and the winning Clydesdale would collect a trophy as large as the first place bulimic's, assuming he or she tipped the scales over 190 pounds. We talked of finishing together but with two miles to go, Darren accelerated and said, "Gotta go for it, Kelly, sorry, man, keep up if you can but I gotta do this thing." I plodded next to him for a mile before my legs burned and my lungs seized just enough to spur him into his sprint, sensing it. He finished in just under three hours, and my time is not important since I finished behind someone; as Darren says, "Better dead than second."

Still, the Marines refused Darren's request for reinstatement and he found work, of all places, at CNN as a "combat technical adviser." CNN! This job for a man who once threatened to shoot a reporter who escaped from the Gulf press pool to follow his platoon.

Mary Thayer-Ash knows my name because Darren is on this Somali beach somewhere. I should have expected him—this is CNN's exercise, and with Marines making up the landing force for Restore Hope, I am sure there weren't many other articulate, decorated, by-the-book and follow-the-rules former Marines hanging around Atlanta begging for the assignment. His presence was inevitable. He's smart enough to stay hidden; the last thing he wants is to be associated with the gaggle fuck on the beach. But he's here, watching over my shoulder. Watching the man who switched places with him.

I entered the Corps to right a family tradition and initially intended to serve the four-year minimum required of the ROTC scholarship. After Desert Storm I warmed to the idea of a career, and after seeing Red Kelly's face at the Gulf War parade, after hearing him talk with my men about what a good job I had done in the war—the first time I really did well at anything—I'm suddenly vying for lifer status and the same run at general that Darren was making before he was clipped. He's probably staring at me through a civilian night scope right now, muttering a string of fantasized commands, putting himself in the place of his pupil.

- 4 -

Rules?! In a knife fight? No rules!

"That one there's the dead one, Lieutenant Kelly. This one's still among the living, just a little bruised. He's playing possum, is all." Gunny points at two small figures lying face down in the dirt, their hands flexi-cuffed tightly behind their backs.

The plastic handcuffs—roughly the same design as plastic straps that bind stacks of newspapers—are drawn so tight that their hands have swollen like that awful Howie Mandel balloon prop, in itself as troubling a cultural misfire as Vanilla Ice. The prisoners are lying side by side and head to toe. Their mouths are duct-taped shut. No whispering allowed, not that the dead one is going to start singing "The Body Electric."

"How can you tell this one's alive with your boot on his head?" I hiss.

Gunny looks up at me and his eyes are *wide,* glowing light green in the crystalline haze of my night-vision goggles, otherworldly; he looks like an excited but nervous father whose son has just tagged one 300 feet over the Little League fence and into the windshield of a Ferrari.

"Checked his pulse as you were walkin' up, sir. He's alive, all right. Watch." He lifts his boot and drives it down onto the prisoner's hand. The man squeals and thrashes forward, moving like a deranged inchworm. "See?" Gunny returns his combat boot to its original bar rest and the man lets out a muffled grunt but stops struggling.

I have been on the beach fewer than fifteen minutes and one of my men has already erased someone. Considering the presence of the press herd fifty meters behind us, this is not exactly the kind of development about which a young officer fantasizes when he plots his military career. "Guns . . . how did this *happen?*"

"It was a righteous kill. I got Armstrong set up on the road there in case any more show up."

"I didn't hear any firing."

"No, that's the best part, sir. Armstrong used a *bayonet.* Didn't want to endanger any of the reporters behind you. Is that old school, or what?"

I look up the road with my goggles and see Sergeant Armstrong moving back toward our position, using a bush to sweep away the footprints and drag marks the bodies have made on the road. I hear the live prisoner breathing heavily now, more rapidly than I am . . . and I started hyperventilating when I heard the radio transmission five minutes ago. Little dust clouds are forming with each exhalation and drifting across his face. It smells like human excrement. "This one just shit his trou," whispers Gunny. "Nasty beast."

Join the Marines. Make your journey into manhood an adventure, travel to beautiful, faraway lands, meet people from myriad exotic cultures.

And kill them.

"Don't crush him with your boot, Gunny," I whisper. "Last thing we need is an accusation of excessive force."

He steps over the dead Somali, who's splayed across a shrub, frozen in a violent sprawl, and slides his combat boot down from the living Somali's head, stopping on his upper back. "Well, sir, I think we got that box checked already. We already killed one." Gunny smiles widely, pearls against his black skin, but when he reads my frown he closes his mouth and affects a grave air.

I see a large shadow gliding soundlessly across the dirt and recognize Sergeant "Stretch" Armstrong before I see his face; no one else in this country is that big and scary. He crawls over, nods at Gunny, then stares at me proudly. His face is painted like the Grim Reaper that he is. "I was reconning this road out in front of you-all and I seen these two walkin' down the road with AK-47s. I tried calling you a bunch of times, sir—"

"We were keeping the press off our backs then, sir. When he probably called, I mean. That was all the beeping on your radio," Gunny interrupts. They've discussed this story, but Gunny will keep it honest. At least to me.

"Anyway, so I remembered the rules of engagement and all, and I fixed my bayonet on my rifle. I didn't want to exchange shots with the press and you-all behind me. When they got close, I jumped 'em and told 'em to give up. Then that one fucker just raised his rifle at me. Him, sir. Raised the rifle up! So I had to stick him. It happened real fast. The other Skinny fuck tried to attack me, too—tried to unsling his AK—but I butt-stroked his ass. Clubbed him real good. Didn't kill him or nothing."

I kneel by the dead man and roll him over. He's very light and his head snaps back abnormally, exposing a long, dark gash that runs from his Adam's apple clear through his neck to his spine. The rank smell of human feces in combination with the sight nauseates me and I raise my head and shut my eyes for a moment, breathing through my mouth. The feeling passes and in the green haze of the night-vision goggles I see there is blood all over him. All over . . . everywhere. There is a big hole in his chest. Huge. As in fist size. As in I can drop a grenade through his body. Oh, he's been "stuck" all right. For a second I find myself admiring the sheer physical strength required to make a man's neck disappear and then put a hole clear through a man's rib cage. *This was no boat accident.*

I feel for the pulse out of some television habit and notice that my hand can almost fully encircle his neck. The NVGs don't provide depth perception up close and my thumb sinks into the neck wound about an inch before I yank it away. He's still warm, a cherry pie. His eyes are open but this is just a corpse now. I try to pull the head back toward the shoulders but my hand keeps slipping. I am weak. My forearms are so tight that I couldn't open a jar of spaghetti sauce right now. Can't grip with warm blood all over my hands. I think of lots of things at once: *Do I have cuts on my hands and is there HIV in this blood? Was this a righteous killing? Gee whiz, isn't he warm.*

This is the first corpse I've touched; in Kuwait the dead we created were policed up by REMFs—Rear Echelon Mother Frickers, supply weenies like my father was— though I did step in a man's rib cage once. Gunny reaches over and grabs my forearm. "He's already dead, sir."

"Yeah," I whisper a little too shakily considering Marines, like wolves, can sense fear. Gunny and Armstrong cock their heads and share a brief glance.

I use some silence to reclaim my voice—it is a macho game and I know The Rules—then, "Thanks, Sherlock." Smooth. *Smith, Wesson, and me.* "So they both had weapons. Armstrong, they have any extra ammo on them? We're going to have to get everything in place under the rules of engagement."

"Negative extra ammo, sir, we searched them. But this is a good kill, that's obvious. Their magazines have about twenty rounds each and the little fuckers aren't starving, that's for sure. They were fucking *shaking*, they were so scared. That one shit his pants."

His dismissiveness pisses me off. The rules of engagement are strict for Restore Hope and have dominated our preparations for this landing, taking up more scenario rehearsal time than combat preparations. We have landed in the middle of a chaotic civil war that is claiming five thousand lives a day, a hurricane of violence and blood, but Somalis are allowed to carry personal weapons; deadly force is authorized only if an American life is directly threatened, and each incident is sure to be assiduously investigated. I can feel my heart thumping steadily now, boom, boom, *boom*. Many Marine officers pray for moments like these—tangled leadership problems that they can cut through with swagger—but I am *terrified*. "No, it's *not* obvious. He pointed the rifle at you before you stabbed him. Correct?"

"What the *fuck* is this, sir? *Yes*, I said," Armstrong hisses. "He raised his fucking rifle. Sir, I tried calling when they were coming at me and *you didn't answer*. I had to *act*." In a moment our relationship has changed and I don't like the cliché upon which it is forming.

The Gunny steps between us, tapping my arm reassuringly. "The lieutenant ain't accusing you, Stretch. Smarten up. He's trying to *protect* your white Texas ass in case there are questions."

Armstrong nods at me and whispers, "My bad, sir. I'm still keyed up."

"Okay, we'll take 'em off your hands now. Get out on

the perimeter with your team. You did the right thing and you sure as hell saved our asses. I'm just asking the questions they'll ask me." I grab his shoulder and look him square in the eyes. No sense flustering him now; there may be more bad guys en route. "Keep your eyes on the road. Expect a whole caravan of news folks to come back down the road at about 0400, when the colonel arrives, so let the rest of your team know not to go shooting any good guys."

"What about the press, sir?" asks Gunny lightly, as if the matter is closed.

I turn to Gunny and smirk. "That's who I'm talking about, wiseass." He smiles back. Then Armstrong smiles widely, huge teeth in an ice field of angles. Even in my goggles I can see the terrible British genes Armstrong has inherited and I giggle, too. Hey, so we just murdered some Gangbanger. That was then and this is now. Doesn't mean we can't make a joke at the expense of Sam Donaldson now, does it? Ho, ho, ho.

Armstrong crawls forward to brief his team. I jerk my head toward the beach. "Let's drag these two back about twenty meters, where we can figure out who they are."

Gunny says, "I got it, sir," hands me his weapon, reaches down, and, grabbing a Somali's armpit in each hand, drags them both back, the live one kicking briefly until the edge of the Gunny's flat hand chops into the back of his neck. I glance back to see the dead Somali's head bouncing along in the dirt and . . . the neck tears a little more. I twist my head away quickly and concentrate on breathing. We kneel down and Gunny rubs the blood off his hands, in the dirt. He raises them and they are muddy, another human being on him. "Nasty thing. What do you think, sir?"

My pulse has accelerated and it's still climbing. The

words come out in bursts, full auto. The smell of blood's not helping, either. I try to whisper on the inhalation like I was taught, but I am too panicked to concentrate on hunter-killer skills. "I think we fucked up and as a result Armstrong was forced to kill someone, that's what I think! I mean . . . they were coming down the road armed, so it was legitimate, but we should have been there. A *bayonet* takedown? Jesus! Why didn't he do it like we drilled? Challenge these two verbally—from a covered position—then plug 'em if they didn't comply? And while we were talking to the press! First few minutes of the fucking operation! I mean, the colonel is going to fucking *kill* me. He told me to keep him appraised the entire time and to keep *all* the Marines in sight. This Gangbanger's throat is slashed, it looks like he caught a mortar round in the chest, and the other one's been beaten to within an inch of his life."

Gunny takes my forearm and whispers, "Whoa, sir. Slow down. Just cool out." I am shaking badly and his voice is soothing; I've relied on my platoon sergeant for many things over the last year, but I have never needed his help more than now. At thirty-five, Gunny is the oldest man in the platoon, a career reconnaissance Marine who has rapidly ascended the ranks: assaulted Grenada as a lance corporal, bitterly watched the Panama action on television as a sergeant on recruiting duty, led a recon team through Desert Storm as a staff sergeant, and now oversees three teams as a gunnery sergeant. He has so many decorations that when he squeezes into his dress blues, his left breast covered with a pound of bright, multicolored ribbons, he could pass for a Red Army general. I lean on him for advice and to keep the platoon's house. Of course, he *is* a house.

"We can handle this, sir," Gunny whispers. "We done

him right by keeping the press occupied. Otherwise it would have been a total goat fuck. I think this mother-fucker and his buddy here, right, were looking to fight. No other way for Armstrong to do it. Otherwise you risk a firefight and a dead Dan Rather. Hell of a thing, really. Saved our asses from some real Gangbangers, the AK-47s and all."

I shake my head. "NFW. These here were armed, but they aren't the droids we're looking for." Gunny just stares—he only remembers quotes from war movies. "Only twenty rounds each, walking *alone* down the *middle of the road*? Doesn't make sense that they'd be coming to ding some Marines like this. *Not with twenty rounds.* Let's find out."

Gunny rolls over the live prisoner, gives him the "You best stay quiet or I'll kill you" sign and rips the duct tape from his mouth. The Somali grunts and squeals, "Noose! Priss! Noose!"

Gunny takes his right hand and squeezes the prisoner's cheeks together so that they touch inside his mouth. "*I told you to shut the fuck up,*" he hisses and shoves the man's head back against the dirt with a solid *thunk.*

"Priss . . . America priss," the Somali whispers, tears in his eyes.

Press. Oh, shit.

"He's saying he's with the press," I whisper. I pull out the laminated country guide that each Marine is carrying in his left breast pocket by order of the Bison—the guide itself an elucidation of just how tangle-fucked this mission may get—but my NVGs can't quite focus on the text. I remove the goggles and stick the card and my red-lens flashlight up past my belt on the inside of my blouse, next to my bare chest. Then I put my chin on my chest and pull the collar up over my head, buttoning the top button to seal off any light so I can read it without giving away our pos. I read the card for what must be the fiftieth time.

Key Somali Customs

1. Somali men greet each other with a hug and a cheek kiss. This is a sign of friendship and is not to be ridiculed by Marines.

2. Avoid showing the soles of your shoes to Somalis. This is considered an insult.

3. Demonstrate your verbal skill when you can. Verbal facility is highly valued in Somalia; if you can recite a tongue twister or poem, you will win esteem for your skill.

4. It is customary for Somalis to stand "close" during conversation. Do not move away.

5. If you see a dead Somali, try to cover the body with a "shroud." This is custom.

Key Phrases

1. We are Marines here to help you. *Wa Inaan Indin Marines Cawwino Ayaan.*

2. Do you speak English? *Ma Ku Hadli Kartaa Ingissii?*

3. What do you need? *Maxaad Doonya?*

4. We have a doctor and food. *Wa Dakhtar Ha Cunto.*

5. What is your name? *Maga-a?*

6. **Stop! Lie down! You are a prisoner!** *Joogso! Jiifso! Maxxbus Baad Tahay!*

7. **Do what we say or we will kill you!** *Hubkaa Ohig Toogan Jarta!*

"*Maga-a?*" I whisper, the instrument of choice for a bad case of modern white man's burden. Nothing happens.

"Answer the man, you little fuck," Gunny says and wraps his hand around the prisoner's throat. Talk about a bad cop. Of course, it's hard to be friendly with a man who was stalking the platoon, little bastard. I know the Somali is just not getting my pronunciation so I try again in both Somali and English.

"Mahmeloti. Mahmeloti," he whispers.

"He ain't no reporter," Gunny whispers and starts to put the duct tape back across the Somali's mouth. "I don't see no press pass on him." Everyone associated with the press—including Somali bodyguards and interpreters—is supposed to be wearing a big plastic identification card, fluorescent yellow and glowing in the dark, to mark them as a friendly and to prevent situations just like this one.

"Wait, Gunny. You. Why did you have weapon? Kill us?" I exaggerate a bunch of movements and pick up his AK-47; I was always pretty good with charades.

"No! No! I sleep. Wit priss! Wit enbecee!" He speaks English.

"Keep your fucking voice down!" Gunny hisses. He squeezes Mahmeloti's throat shut and covers his mouth at the same time. Then he starts to grind the Somali's head into the deck. "You got me, motherfucker? You best—"

I grab Gunny's arm. "Ease up. Gunny, let him go. He speaks English. Let him go."

Gunny releases him and Mahmeloti gasps and begins to

weep. "Priss. Am wit America priss. Enbecee. Enbecee!" The tears glisten and reflect in the green light of my goggles.

"Embassy? Are you with American *embassy?*" I ask dreadfully.

"Yes! Enbecee!" The Somali nods emphatically and forces a smile. His eyes are already welled up. Mine are dry, but I'm deeply shaken. Have we killed . . . *an embassy guard?* No, there *is* no embassy anymore.

I grab the AK. "Why you have this? You shoot America? You shoot Marines?"

He shakes his head violently. "No! No, I sleep. I wit enbecee. Tom Brokaw. Tom Brokaw!"

Gunny looks up at me and says, "What the *fuck?* This little crying bitch's spinning you some lies, sir. He's saying he's embassy and we don't even have one here no more. Then he's saying he's *Tom fucking Brokaw.* Did you just hear that? This motherfucker's a Banger, no doubt."

Gunny grabs the Somali's head and begins to grind it into the dirt again, twisting it back and forth and digging a hole with the friction. "How you like that, Mr. Brokaw? HUH? You like to lie to me some more? Huh? Huh, bitch? You think we're fucking *stupid?*"

"Let him go and put the tape back on his mouth," I say in a whisper, understanding now, clarity invading my body in lockstep with the nausea. I bow my head and try to think of an exit strategy. *I. Am. FUCKED.*

Gunny tries to gag him but the tape is too dusty, so he unwraps some duct tape from where we keep it on the stocks of our M-16s and encircles the Somali's head several times. I am extremely nervous and I want to go back a half hour and start this all over again; I am adrift and dreading everything that will follow this moment.

"No, he's not a reporter, Gunny. He's a bodyguard. He's a bodyguard for NBC, not the embassy. We're fucked!"

Gunny puts his head down and freezes for a good twenty seconds, then nods suddenly. "Sir, this is going to get clusterfucked, we don't play it right. If the press gets hold of this, we're dead. They live to screw over the military. Their bodyguard! And this motherfucker here wasn't sleeping, sir. After *that* landing? He's a liar, sir. He's a *fucking liar*, sir."

Gunny always throws in lots of "sirs" when he debates with officers so he can argue passionately without being accused of being insubordinate, though it's hard for civilians to understand how this huge man can even *be* subordinate to *anyone*. And at this moment, even though I have the rank and it's my call, I'm hoping to follow his lead.

"What do you suggest?"

"We need to do what's right, sir. First—*inbound!*"

I see his rifle come up, pointing over my shoulder, and he yanks me to the ground, both of us shouldering rifles now, me scanning the shrubs beyond the dead Somali's body. I see a woman's torso rise over the bushes as she approaches. It's Mary Thayer-Ash.

"Relax. It's just a reporter."

"Relax? That's the enemy, sir," Gunny whispers.

The moon has set, so she is having difficulty maneuvering across the brush and rock. She has a nice figure, and lying behind this shrub, watching her through night-vision goggles, I feel the guilty pleasure of a Peeping Tom. She's noisy and uncoordinated.

Gunny whispers, "She moves like you, sir. Look at them long legs. Is there a Kelly sister on deck?" He's trying to mend my frayed nerves but I can hear the tension behind it.

"She can't see us in the dark. Let's be quiet and she'll pass."

The Marines all around us are absolutely silent, no doubt hoping this will encourage some more Gangbangers to come play. In the silence I hear Somalia for the first time. There are some typical Third World noises—babies coughing and hacking in the distance, generators humming—but others are missing: There are no dogs barking, there are no chickens squawking, and there are no humans talking. In their place there is a singularly disturbing sound, audible only during stronger gusts, eerie in the dark: A woman is crying. Fingernails on a chalkboard.

Ms. Thayer-Ash hears the sobs and is spooked. She looks back twice at the jeeps from where she came, then back my way. We are invisible. She turns around and takes a step to the road, stops, and pivots around again. "Hello?" she says softly. Pause. "I know you're out here." Louder this time. No doubt the other Marines are peering at her through NVGs now. "Come out, come out, wherever you are. I have to talk to you guys. C'mon, don't be like this. I'm going to stand here all night if I have to . . .

"Hey!" Shouting now. "Where are you?"

I pick up a small rock and throw it five meters to her left, startling her. "Hey! Very funny, guys. I'm not leaving until you come out."

"This is getting fucking ridiculous," I whisper. I pick up my rifle and creep over to her. She waves at me as if I am going to miss her in the dark and I take her arm and pull her to a knee. "Hey! This isn't a joke. Please go back to the vehicles and stay put. You're being dangerous."

She yanks her elbow away. "I can go anywhere I damn well please. This isn't the Gulf War, Lieutenant. I've been in Mogadishu for three months and I know a lot more about it than you do." I absorb the rebuke and am starting to speak when she says, "Sorry. Look, I'm a little stressed. I'm looking for two bodyguards. Friends of mine."

"Who?"

"Somali bodyguards. NBC's, actually, but they were my

personal protectors for two months until they were hired away. Deeper pockets, you know? Anyway, when NBC left for their hotel, I told them I'd find them. Two men. They've been helping the whole press crew out and they apparently went somewhere behind the jeeps before you guys arrived."

"What are their names?" I ask, and realize immediately that this is a suspicious and stupid question. She doesn't seem to catch it, though.

"Said and Muhammad Lahti," Thayer-Ash says. No doubt our Mahmeloti. "They're brothers. And they speak English. They were bodyguards for the Red Cross for many years before I hired them. Did you kill them or something?"

"No, Ms. Thayer-Ash." I say it slowly and with a smirk, like I'm talking to a six-year-old. I sigh like she's wasting my time. "We didn't *kill* them. Are they armed?"

She nods her head slowly. "Unfortunately. I objected, but they had their AK-47s."

"We were briefed that they should have some form of press pass, correct?"

"Yes," she says quickly and matter-of-factly. "They always wear theirs. *Always.*" She holds up the big plastic card dangling around her neck, about six by six inches— believe me, I know that measurement. The card has a bright yellow fluorescent border, glowing brightly in my goggles. "This keeps them alive in Somalia," she says.

"You saw them tonight?"

"Actually, no. I didn't. But they'll have the passes, believe me."

Restore Hope is fewer than thirty minutes old and I feel like I've already lost control of the situation; my arms begin to tingle when the dread rolls my stomach, just as it did when the shark arrived, except this time he's coming for me.

It becomes hard to think in the chaos. I believe Armstrong has lied to me about the press passes. I *know* Muhammad Lahti is lying about being asleep when we arrived. Does one cancel out the other? "I'll put the word out, ma'am. If they come in the perimeter, I'll bring them directly to you. I bet they went home when we arrived, though. Now please go back to the jeeps. We're your bodyguards now."

"Spare me. Hey, let me try those night goggles." If I humor her she'll leave. I hand my NVGs to her and she puts them on. "They're all fuzzy." I reach up and twist the lens on the monocle and she puts her hand on mine briefly. It's warm.

"Okay, it's working now. Cool. Hey, your pants are still all wet." I look down and my trousers are splashed with one of the brothers' blood.

"Hear the crying?"

"Yes, it's . . . it's just awful. Some of the Somalis cry all day, but at night you can hear them better for some reason. It makes me so sad." She looks past me at the faint glow of Mogadishu. Her nose is long and thin, the focal point of her face, aiming point for two very sad eyes. "I'm glad we got the story out and finally got Bush's attention, though. And look, here you are because of me." It is a wildly over-reaching statement, but it is also partly true. CNN started this intervention. In fact, there is a rumor that Ted Turner claims he will send cameras to Bosnia next to stop the atrocities there. Foreign policy by cable news. "Aren't you young to be in charge of these guys?"

"Yes," I say, "but between you and me, don't tell the Corps I have a belly ring. It's against regulations."

She reaches out fast and rubs my stomach. "I can't feel it. Hey—eeww, what is that?" Her hand is covered with Lahti's blood and she looks down at it, palm up. It is so dark I have a chance.

I grab her wrist and wipe her hand clean with my camouflage blouse, chuckling. "Sorry about the motor oil. You should ask before touching—that's harassment, isn't it?"

"Something Marines know tons about, I'm sure." But she lets me continue rubbing her palm clean. "You never asked me how I knew your name."

"Oh. Yes, I've been——"

She stands abruptly and says, "You'll see. It'll be a surprise. See you around."

———

I am alone on a knee, facing the ocean. I need just a few minutes to think. We have a dead Somali who is a good guy. Not just any friendly, actually, but a personal friend of Tom Brokaw, Ms. Thayer-Ash, and some other reporters who are, by now, suspicious. His brother claims they were asleep—with press passes—when Armstrong approached. And we have put a tennis-can hole through the corpse's chest cavity, hacked an ax slice from his neck, and watched him bleed to death.

My mind is flooded with courses of action, none of them good . . . a spectrum from Dudley Do-Right to the GoodFellas option: Kill the other brother, bury them both, and fuhgeddaboudit. I have four hours to decide on a coherent story before the colonel arrives, and all decisions point to an investigation. As the commanding officer, I am responsible for the actions of the platoon and Armstrong's decision will fall on my shoulders, as it should. But what conclusion will the investigating officer reach? Will he conclude that Armstrong had to react quickly to protect his platoon and the press, that Lahti is lying, that the rules of engagement didn't fit this situation, that it was ultimately a case of a Marine acting as he was trained—defending himself—while his leadership was forced to deal with a screaming throng of reporters led to the landing site by the Pentagon itself? Or will he conclude that Armstrong murdered an innocent—who may have been sleeping—while his lieutenant ignored orders, lost control of his platoon, and toyed happily with the press? If it's the latter, I'm going to make my father's discharge seem honorable; the Corps does not tolerate incompetence in its officer ranks and they'll hang me on the Tree of Woe.

Though the night is clear, there are few stars and the moon is gone, so the darkness is pure, untainted by light. The air smells sanguine and salty—of course, my upper lip is beaded and I may be sniffing my own sweat. I cannot see the amphibious ready group that is going to pounce in a few hours—three ships and a thousand-man infantry battalion of Marines—only black on the horizon where they must be. I think about what Ms. Thayer-Ash said. Apart from some State Department weenies on deck, I am The Man here for four more hours. Certainly the senior military man, anyway, and the only kind that will count if we get down to business. I don't even consider the Italians.

At twenty-five I am the tip of the spear: American foreign policy personified come to make the world right, come to restore hope to an entire country. Come to assuage our guilt.

– 5 –

Nigel: The sustain! Listen to it.

Marty: I don't hear anything.

Nigel: Well you would, though, if it
were playing.

I slip my NVGs on again and notice that my hands are
shaking. I crawl back toward Gunny and hear, "Halt.
Advance and be recognized." It's the platoon's Navy corpsman who must have been placed in a rear security position
by the Gunny. Doc has the bad habit of pointing his rifle
where he shouldn't, so I go flat on my stomach.

"It's me, Doc," I whisper from a small depression that
may save me if Doc's brain-housing group malfunctions
again. "You saw me coming. White. White. White."

"Snow," he hisses.

"*White,* goddamnit. I already said 'white.'" I'm pissy, but
he's just doing his job, as thick-headed as he is.

Doc has an IQ under a hundred and once told me he
wanted to be a vegetarian when he retired because he liked
the idea of helping people's pets. Last year he kept a pet rabbit in his squad-bay hooch against regulations because he
was lonely, a modern-day Lenny for whom trolling through

San Diego bars for women was an impossibility. One Sunday morning Doc returned from sunrise service and the bunny was missing. Gunny said he screamed and ran around the recon area calling its name between sobs for six hours before he eventually broke down on the basketball court and had to be carried home by Johnson and Armstrong. "That sweet ol' rabbit probably went up to the hills where he's runnin' free," Armstrong told him soothingly. Gunny also said that Johnson and Armstrong had come in from a wild drunk the night before, kidnapped and eaten the rabbit after a stint in the platoon microwave— Armstrong taking the eyeballs first because they're apparently full of protein and would contribute to his ripped physique—but couldn't bear to tell the corpsman after the Asian display of grief.

I'm constantly tempted to lay into Doc, but he's also a born-again Christian, so my conscience usually overrides my need to scream at him or choke him.

"Come on into the perimeter, sir."

I sneak over in a crouch and say, "What's up, Doc? You were watching me the whole time, weren't you? You knew it was me."

"Yessir, but I had to make sure it was you up close. You never know, what with it being Somalia and all." As I crawl past him he says, "And I got the 'what's up' joke. Bugs Bunny, right? Am I right? I get that a lot 'cause I'm a corpsman." His statement is frightening because he reminds me that he is, in fact, supposed to be the medical expert in the platoon and he is dumber than the shark that attacked us.

"Doc, you are depriving a village somewhere of an idiot."

He shrugs and says, "I'm here to help this platoon now, though, sir."

I crawl up to Gunny Ricketts and he nervously whispers, "Sir, I got bad news. The colonel's on his way. I had to tell him about the dead Gangbanger."

"*What?*" I expected to have four hours to think this through.

"He radioed, sir, and I didn't have no choice. Whole landing force is on its way. What'd the reporter want?"

"Here's the deal. These are NBC's bodyguards, and she's looking for them. She says they were wearing big fluorescent press passes like the ones we saw on—"

"They don't have press passes, sir."

"Let me *finish*, goddamnit, Guns. We gotta get our shit *square*, here. Here's what I know. These two are bodyguards. They speak English. We need to find out if they had their passes on. I think they did. Next, they had weapons and under our rules of engagement Armstrong had the authority to use deadly force *if* they looked like they were going to fire. They shouldn't have had weapons . . . but under the rules they're allowed to have small arms. So the question is—that we need to know, that I *have* to know—were they walking down the street and did they have the press passes? Or were they asleep like he says? Because if they were asleep, we have a murderer on our hands."

"Armstrong's no murderer, sir. No way they were sleeping."

"You know it and I know it. Problem is, this prick is going to stick to his story and which side do you think the press is going to take? Let's go get Armstrong and have a talk. We need to unscrew this now. In about fifteen minutes there's going to be some investigating officer asking all the same questions."

He grabs my arm. Hard. "No, sir. Let me do this. You

don't want to be near this conversation. Please . . . *please*, sir. I know him."

I stay put and Gunny crawls off into the black. He and Armstrong have a history, and though I know Gunny will not lie to me, I suspect the bond between them is deeper and more powerful than Gunny lets on. History is important in the Corps and the loyalties that develop have a way of building like a flood and overwhelming the rule book. Sergeant Armstrong served in Gunny's recon team in Desert Storm, saved Gunny's life, and now holds Gunny's former job.

About two years ago, on a night just before Desert Storm's ground war was launched—when I was shivering in a damp hole in the Saudi Arabian dirt, not fifteen klicks away—Gunny was briefing his six-man reconnaissance team, Armstrong among them. The sun had disappeared days earlier and though he was bent over a map in one of the world's hottest climes, Gunny blew into his cupped hands before he pointed to the team's objective.

Satellites had detected Iraqi armored columns moving south, toward the coalition forces in Saudi Arabia, and Gunny's team was tasked with getting eyeballs on the approaching enemy. They were inserted at night into a Saudi border town and discovered that the Saudi army had abandoned their post. Gunny moved his team through the center of the deserted town and established a forward outpost on the roof of the tallest building overlooking the main highway.

"What's all this?" asked then Corporal Armstrong, holding up a helmet and some binoculars he had found in the corner of the roof. "I think it's the Arabs'. Think they got captured?"

Gunny shook his head. "First of all, Stretch, it's the *Saudis* that were supposed to be here—everybody's an Arab—and second of all, no, they ran, they didn't get captured."

Later that night four Iraqi armored vehicles rumbled into town and set up a defensive perimeter. Looks like an advanced guard, Gunny thought, which is very bad news for a team outfitted only with rifles, grenades, and radios. *Semper Gumby.*

The team had scrambled some aircraft to deal with the personnel carriers when Armstrong, who was looking through the thermal telescope, whispered, "Staff Sergeant, there's seven T-55s headin' this way! And a *fuckload* of other vehicles!"

The team soon found itself in the middle of a town filled with an entire Iraqi armored company. The six Marines had no chance against all the armor, so they simply locked the door to the roof, booby-trapped it, and reported on the situation. A platoon of American Light Armored Vehicles was dispatched to join the fight, but before they arrived, some Iraqis made the mistake of investigating the Gunny's building. When the Marines heard Iraqi chatter in the stairwell, Gunny decided that he could wait no longer for the precision strikes of the aircraft. The only way out was to start pounding them immediately with artillery, hoping the inaccurate fires would scare them enough to effect a breakout.

It took about five minutes but eventually, over the mechanical rumbles of the vehicles revving around him, Gunny heard a thunderous ripping sound, as if mile-wide sheets of paper were being torn in the sky above. The 155-millimeter shells seemed to peel back folds of the air itself. The earth groaned, and for the first time in his life Gunny felt small. Insignificant. Vulnerable. He had his head sticking over the roof's small wall like a dog leaning out a car window. He saw a bright flash where a tank was parked and a second later he felt the shock wave washing past him, forcing his mouth open and squeezing out his breath, reverberating violently in his gut. The rush of air from the blast swept over the team, knocking over radios and causing some men to squint, others to cover their heads and curl into the fetal position. Arty shells won't kill the tanks without direct hits but they'll sure as hell get their attention, thought Gunny. *Run, you motherfuckers.*

Some Iraqis began to fire, loosing long tracer bursts into the sky as if fighting the will of the night itself. Others ignited their engines and raced out of town, zigzagging away from a premature rendezvous with Allah. Looks like they're not as eager to die as they claim, thought Gunny. He kept the artillery coming, shifting the fires with precise radio instructions that bracketed the stubborn vehicles and eventually broke their will to remain in the town. Far better to face Saddam than a Marine and his radio.

Suddenly the fleeing vehicles began to erupt in showers of sparks and, overhead, he heard a nearly continuous roar of jet engines, increasing in volume, shaking the entire building. This was the first battle of the war and every pilot in the theater wanted in. Invisible smart bombs glided down through the black and the *cahruuunch* and *cah-hhraaack* and *sssssssssiing* as the shrapnel whizzed past, peppering the building, bouncing across the sound barrier like deadly rubber balls. The roof shook and the deep vibration of the shock waves bounced the radios across its cement floor. The night was soon day, so illuminating were the burning vehicles.

Gunny heard an explosion over by the door to the roof and knew the Iraqis had tripped the Claymore mine, welcoming over three hundred steel ball bearings with their bodies when they opened the door. But they kept coming. A communist grenade—probably tossed by some lucky survivor in the stairwell—bounced once on the roof and skidded right between Gunny and the other five Marines in his team. This is it, Gunny thought. It's been a good run. He screamed, "Grenade!" and tucked his head between his legs.

He heard the explosion a moment later but felt none of the blast. When he looked up, Armstrong, who was grinning, panted, "Got that sucker just in time. Exploded right after it left my hand! I threw it off the roof!"

The Iraqis soon realized that the only way to survive was not to run, but to stay hidden in the town, hugging the buildings. Gunny directed two strikes on these vehicles before the rest found haven right next to his building—the tallest in the city. He brought a Harrier in tight, but the shrapnel from the strikes began to tear into the roof, slightly wounding one of the Marines. If the team was going to escape, the vehicles would have to be destroyed with close air attacks, and in destroying them, some of the ordnance was certain to pepper the roof.

"Stretch!" Gunny shouted. "Take the team and storm down to the next floor! I'm gonna finish off four vehicles and I'll be right down! We'll break out to the west if we get separated . . . Meet at the primary rally point!"

Armstrong apparently hopped up, screamed, "Fuck yes! Let's fuck these motherfuckers *up!*" and led the other four Marines in a sprint to the rooftop door. They blasted their way down the stairwell with a wave of bullets and grenades, killing six Iraqis, and tossed three grenades onto the next floor at different angles. When they burst in seven more Iraqis were dead and three were stunned and wounded, on their knees moaning and babbling. Their ears and noses were bleeding.

One of them looked up at the Marines and screamed, "*Allah Akbar!*" He began to crawl over to his rifle and Armstrong shot him in the ear. The left side of the Iraqi's head remained intact, but the right side disappeared in a red powder that covered the wall and dripped slowly before it coagulated to a stop.

Armstrong sent two Marines to secure the door leading downstairs and booby-trap it, then did something bizarre, something that sealed his reputation. He peered out the window and saw that one of the vehicles remained untouched, parked right next to the building. "Let's show these motherfuckers what they're dealing with!" he yelled. He grabbed one of the bodies and hefted it through a window.

All of the glass had been shattered and Armstrong said later that the only sound he heard next—even though artillery was crashing on the streets around the building— was the loud thump that the body made when it landed on the Iraqi vehicle. He howled and told another Marine to help him; together they tossed out six more bodies. Sure enough, the vehicle revved its engine and made a desperate break from the village.

The Gunny spotted it and sent in a Cobra gunship to end it.

Armstrong and the other Marines below were cheering when one of the Iraqis staggered to his feet and made a drunken, shell-shocked rush at the guarded door. One of the Marines raised his rifle and the Iraqi stopped, turned, fell down, stood, and began to run back to the center of the room in a daze. He was met by the butt of Armstrong's M-16. The blow was so harsh that he spun 360 degrees in the air, like a diver, and came to rest on his stomach. His face had been collapsed such that when Armstrong rolled him over, he said he looked like E.T.

It got a good laugh.

All in, Gunny's six-Marine team had destroyed over twenty vehicles, captured seventeen Iraqis, and killed over a hundred.

Gunny recommended Armstrong for the Bronze Star. And when he talks about it, his reverence for Armstrong is clear. "Although I must admit," he said once, laughing, "that young Devildog should be kept in a glass case labeled: 'Break only in the event of an emergency.'"

———

Gunny crawls back in five minutes. We have fifteen more before the cavalry arrives and I feel the pressure and inevitability of the rising sun. "All square, sir. They was walking down the road, just like he said. I saw the blood on the road. Wet clumps of dirt, sure as shit."

"For Chrissakes, Guns, it just rained. What about the press passes?" Gunny will not lie to me.

"He told you none, right?"

"I'm asking you."

Pause. "Sir. I can't let you . . . just. . . . Armstrong told you no passes, so let's leave it at that. I'll handle it. He w—"

"Gunny!" I whisper. "Yes or no. I'm the fucking *platoon commander.*"

"Which is *exactly* why I want you to leave this alone."

"Cut the bullshit, Gunny. Yes or no."

He shows me two bright yellow, fluorescent press cards, each of them containing the Lahti brothers' photographs and press affiliation. They are glowing in the dark. Scratch one bodyguard from NBC's payroll. *Requiescat in pace.*

Gunny puts them back in his pocket and sighs. "He *did*

not see the cards when they were walkin' down to us. I can't say I would have seen 'em either, what with the AK-47s. I think the rifle demands your attention first, don't it, sir?"

"Doesn't matter what I think."

Gunny gets in my face and whispers, "Yes it *does*, sir. When he saw he had killed press personnel, Armstrong hid the passes and lied—to protect himself, but you and me too, sir. From this shit we're hashing out right here. I believe him about the road. Stake my *career* on it."

"We may have to." They teach you the Marine Corps book at basic officer's course—six months of leadership training and decision making under pressure—but I feel wildly unprepared for this. The ideal officer might snatch an obvious solution, but if it's out there I can't find it in the murk. Perhaps that says something about me. Strike two.

"Like I said, sir, you never saw the pass. Look, we both know it was a righteous kill. This pass just fucks things up, and the *press* is gonna believe this little Skinny was sleeping!"

"This sucks."

"Yessir. But this is why you get paid the big bucks."

"Exactly. So I'll do the right thing." How did we get into this? My best combat Marine kills an armed bad guy and now I have to struggle for a story? I glance down and see that Muhammad Lahti is scooting away like an earthworm, so I stomp on his back.

"Sir," Gunny whispers. "That's all I'm asking. Do the right thing. *That's all I'm asking.*" He leans in close and grabs my forearm. "Sir. I know Jake Armstrong. If he had killed this one for no reason, just murdered him because he could, then I would have his big ass in the brig in a heartbeat. But it didn't go down like that. They were walking down the road with rifles and Armstrong was trying to raise us, but we were occupied with those cameras, so he *acted* and killed a Gangbanger armed with an AK. He couldn't see the pass . . . and even if he *did*, these two were posing a *deadly threat* and it was a legal kill."

Gunny's neck is spackled with loam and tan camouflage paint but I can still see the big vein that crisscrosses up past his Adam's apple and disappears under his chin. He dips his face down so he can meet my eyes but I avoid his and stare down past his chest at his cartridge belt, focusing on the Ka-Bar blade he keeps sheathed there, just behind his two magazine pouches. In the movies you often see action guys with their knives taped upside down to their shoulder harnesses, as if they can access them best there, so when I reported to recon I wore mine that way, too—until the Gunny yanked it off my strap on my first night patrol and gave me a mild lecture about losing gear in thick brush.

"Hey! Sir! *Sir!* Forget the press passes, they're just fucked-up parts of these *fucked-up* rules of engagement. I mean, come *on*, sir. He can't be expected to just sit there while armed enemies walk toward us! What's he gonna do, out there alone, shout a challenge and endanger himself? Force protection's the priority in Somalia, right? Well, he was protecting us.

"Sir, in the Marine Corps there have always been published rules . . . then there are The Rules. We need to protect our Marine."

The Gunny is right about force protection—it's our first mission in Restore Hope. No American life is to be lost, which tells us that no Somali life is worth that of a Yank. Neither of us agrees with it, but why not use it as a safety net for a fall like this? The United States has developed a violent aversion to casualties and my overriding mission here is to keep my men safe. Please don't ask me how this meshes with the task of opening up food lines in the middle of a civil war; I don't have the answer. After all, if force protection was truly overriding, we would still be floating on the *Denver*. Hell, we might be kept inside plastic bubbles until World War III erupted.

We were sent to intimidate a warrior people who have been forged in violence. At the same time I am supposed to be keeping my unit safe, I am supposed to enforce rules that make Somalia a much more dangerous place, rules that allow Said and Muhammad Lahti to walk toward an amphibious landing site with loaded AK-47s. How to reconcile the two?

The tug on my moral code is palpable now, a war among my sense of loyalty to my men, a distaste for this operation's rules, fear of the press, and the overriding principles of Marine leadership: Do not lie, cheat, or steal.

"We'll have to lie for him. Those two fights he got in in San Diego . . . and that brawl in Hong Kong . . . he's got a pattern of violence that the press will—"

"*You* aren't involved. *I'm* the one who saw it go down when I was walking over."

"You . . . you'd *do* that?"

"Sir, this Skinny thing is going to continue to lie about sleeping. Sleeping through *that* clusterfuck on the beach? Come *on*, sir. NBC will side with this little Gangbanger, and Armstrong's record will be torn apart. They'll just see the fights. But they can't tear my record apart. Armstrong needs me, needs *us*. I'm asking you as a Marine to back me. I'm willing to stake my career on this."

Gunnery Sergeant Jarius Ricketts has five daughters and a wife to support, twelve years invested in the Corps, and an impeccable record that has jumped him up the ranks. He is a career Marine who has latched on to the Corps with a fanatical fervor and this is the first time I have seen him violate rules. What am I risking?

In the distance a child is squealing again. Then another joins in, waking once again to a hunger you and I have never known, a hunger that has sparked the most powerful nation in the history of the world into intervening. We have a higher calling in Somalia, and these two brothers got in our way. It was not supposed to be like this.

There is no school solution. I need to act on instinct . . . just like Armstrong did.

"I'll back you," I say. Gunny squeezes my forearm and closes his mouth, nodding his head. "First, get rid of those passes. Second, you get it totally square—I mean *totally* airtight—with Armstrong. The other Marines know shit, right? Third, I want to see the road myself."

In the distance a faint buzz swells until I hear the engines of the AAVs grinding out over the Indian, an onrushing swarm of hornets. "Let's go. The redcoats are coming." We jog over and get on our knees in the middle of the dirt road.

"Here, sir. This might be blood. Remember, all those cars drove over this. Plus, Armstrong swept away the tracks."

I look at the little wads of dirt. "Oh come on, Gunny. Who the fuck knows?" I crawl over to the small bush where Armstrong must have dragged him. I can't see anything on the leaves, but it is still very dark. I glance up at Armstrong's position and most of the team members are staring out into the hinterland, watching their respective sectors and ignoring me—officers are always doing screwy things. But not Armstrong. He is staring right at me with a frown, clearly a challenge. *What do you think you're doing, Lieutenant?* I see him, I mean really *see* him, for the first time.

I glare back but Gunny breaks my contemplation. "Sir!

Lord Vader's shuttle has arrived, as you like to say!" He's buoyant now, his mood moving inversely with mine now that the colonel has arrived.

"Go square it with Armstrong. Hurry."

The first amphibious vehicle rolls out of the darkened sea like Godzilla in one of those Japanese movies and skids to a halt just to my front, dripping itself dry, drooling all over the sand it now owns, marking its territory, twenty feet high and forty feet long, tan color scheme just a day old. The press is snapping away and shouting, but I notice that the big anchors aren't up yet to cover the landing. Poor Colonel Capiletti. Dan Rather's snoring through the colonel's big moment.

Several other tracks land and motor over the beach, heading straight down the road toward Mogadishu, .50 machine guns and automatic grenade launchers locked and loaded in the event Aidid should get some balls. *Be afraid. Be very afraid.*

The rear hatch opens in the track to my front with an ominous *whirrrrrr* and Colonel Vin Capiletti comes rushing up to me, a surge of Marines moving past us with rifles ready, flopping down in the sand, up again and moving, down again. Bison Breath leans in close to my face and hisses, "Lieutenant Kelly! Where are they?"

The nickname has an obvious origin, dual in nature: The colonel is a close talker who moves within intimate striking distance during all conversations—in itself a horrifying event—and his mouth smells like a mouse crawled under his tongue two years ago and died. While eating tuna fish.

The colonel is a big man with hefty, short arms that poke out of his uniform disproportionally, like a T-Rex's. Even with the Barney reach, however, he managed to win the naval academy boxing championship in 1973. He has sculpted the perfect build given our working uniform: Like cops, it is protocol to beef up the biceps to fill out the rolled camouflage sleeves. When our Marines start pulling this crap—working on beach muscles for aesthetic purposes—Gunny and I run the extra meat off until they view the weight as a burden, but there's not much you can say to a senior officer.

"Got them secured over there, across the road, sir."

"Show me."

He glances up and seems to be startled by the group of reporters who have surrounded us. They're shouting questions and suddenly old Bison Breath seems to positively glow. "Ladies and gentlemen," he says. "I have a brief statement, then I'm afraid I have an operation to run. My name's Capiletti and I command the battalion landing team of Marines you see landing from the air and sea around you. We've got a very important job to you—I mean, to do, and we aim to do it. And do it well." The colonel is losing his course, fast. I know he's lusted for this moment since he missed Desert Storm—perhaps for his entire career. He coughs and grins, gathering himself. Perhaps he should hire Armstrong as his personal spokesman.

"We have one goal," he continues. "To feed these people and put an end to the bullying brutality." Well, sir, that's two, actually. "Oh. And I really should thank you for that reception tonight. That was quite a welcome for the Marines!" Everyone laughs. Maybe he'd be better at comedy.

Reporters begin to shout questions at him. Soon he is answering them in bunches, each time mentioning that this is the last one.

I don't blame him. Ours has been a thankless occupation as of late, so it is hard to resist talking with people who are genuinely interested. I'm also hoping that he is fast understanding what a goat rodeo it became down here, reporters sent to a potentially dangerous landing beach by the NSA *before we even arrived.*

After five minutes we're on our way; I'm supposed to be leading the way but somehow the colonel is in front of me, processing subtle clues in my track and magically continuing in the proper direction. He hates to walk behind subordinates. When I glance back all of the reporters are questioning the newly arrived Marines except Ms. Thayer-Ash; she's staring after us, hands on her hips.

"Saw you on CNN, Lieutenant," a gravelly voice whispers.

"Press was all over the place, Sergeant Major," I say to the small man who has sneaked in behind me. Sergeant Major "Big Duke" Duncan is the senior enlisted Marine in the battalion, and as such he's supposed to be the colonel's closest adviser on matters like that which we are about to rip open. What Gunny means to me, Sergeant Major Duncan should mean to the colonel, though the truth is that the colonel doesn't get along all that well with human beings.

Big Duke is tacitly in charge of all the enlisted Marines in the battalion and absorbs their gripes when they are reluctant to bring them to the college boys. Or when they are *about* the college boys. Nicknames are frowned upon in the Corps, but the sergeant major insists on being called Big Duke, his Vietnam call sign. You can get away with things like this when you're a Silver Star winner and a veteran of two wars. Big Duke was recon in Vietnam and has taken a special liking to our platoon, largely because of Gunny. On paper I am senior to him because I am an officer, but the reality is that nobody orders Big Duke around except the colonel.

"That landing was the craziest thing I ever saw, but consider this a head's-up, sir: The colonel's pissed," Big Duke whispers. I turn to him and see that he has a wad of chewing tobacco stuffed under his upper lip, bulging it. He has a fire-hydrant build and a deeply wrinkled face, perpetually tan. Too many walks in the hot sun, too many frowns at the actions of lieutenants like me. His giant scar, running from his left eyebrow clear down the length of his nose, looks white in my goggles. No Viet Cong knife, though—his wife hit him with a frying pan by accident. That's what years of snooping and pooping get you, I guess, a stealthy advance toward the thick wafts of sizzling steaks on the stove that even your wife does not detect. And when you're five-foot-five, a sudden turn with a hot skillet can end you.

"How's Armstrong doin', sir? Gunny said on the radio he saw him stab that Somali in the heart."

He raises his eyebrows so I say, "Armstrong's gonna be fine, Big Duke."

"Oh, I know he is, sir."

The Gunny greets us just past the road by popping up out of a thicket and waving us over; when we creep across, Gunny walks right past Bison Breath to Big Duke—a slight that the colonel doesn't catch in the dark—and shakes his hand.

"Wild night, eh, Gunny?" says Big Duke.

"Nothing we couldn't handle, B.D.," Gunny says seriously. "They were careless."

"Last mistake they'll make. It's tough when the veterans show up at rookie camp."

"Yes, it is. Iraqis learned the same thing."

The colonel feels awkward in the midst of the conversation—an enlisted discussion of combat—and interrupts. "Well, what the heck happened?"

Gunny begins to walk toward the Lahti brothers and gets halfway through the story when Big Duke coughs and says, "Help you, ma'am?"

The colonel spins around in time to hear Ms. Thayer-Ash say, "Just wanted to ask the colonel a few more questions." I can tell by his face that he has finally met the enemy on a battlefield: She has a quick wit, carries a microphone, and can ruin your life with a sentence.

"I've got nothing more to add, I'm afraid," the colonel says. "You'll have to speak with the public affairs officer when he arrives." He smiles and adds, "Sorry."

Doc is suddenly standing next to the group, nervously shifting from one foot to the other. Everyone turns and regards him. I make the mistake of asking, "What do you need, Doc?"

Doc is a skinny young man who, like most corpsman, does not fill out his uniform and wears his hair a little long. He was the butt of platoon jokes for six months before the Marines realized that he was too stupid to understand and take offense at their personal attacks. Marines don't attack unless they have damage to show for it, so they moved on. Probably to richer target areas like my personality. "Oh, I don't need anything, sir. Just making sure."

"Making sure of *what* exactly, Corpsman?" asks Big Duke.

"That ... it's not a pretty sight, Sergeant Major Duncan. For her, I mean. I wanted to make sure you-all kept your distance from the corpse. It's pretty gross. His neck is, like, fully hacked open."

Over his shoulder I can see the two bodies, dark shapes against the sand. Damn you, Doc. "Go back over to your post, Doc. We'll be there directly," I say, too late.

"*What?* What's going on?" Ms. Thayer-Ash asks. The

five of us hesitate too long. She looks right at me and says sharply, "What happened? Did you kill the Lahtis?"

"Ms. Thayer-Ash, go back—"

"Did you? Did you *kill them? Did you kill my friends?*" Her voice is screeching and her dark eyes suddenly fill with tears. All of us are taken aback by this turn of events and she tries to push through to see. I am struck by the drastic shift in her emotions.

Gunny grabs her and she struggles, trying to peel his fingers from her biceps. "Sirs?" Gunny asks, frantic and desperate for an order. Mary Thayer-Ash twists herself around and throws her head back wildly, trying to crunch into his face, a bucking bronco. This is not the kind of hand-to-hand they prepare us for.

The colonel takes control immediately and I marvel at how sure of himself he is. We razz Bison Breath for a lot of things, but command presence isn't one of them. "Sergeant Major Duncan," he says calmly, "get an AAV up here and put the prisoners inside. Ma'am. Ma'am! Calm down! Please calm . . . stay calm and he'll release you."

Gunny's grabbing her has made it much, much worse. "You killed them!" Thayer-Ash sobs. She snakes an arm back and scratches at Gunny's face, catching an ear and raking it raw. "Let me go, you bastard! *Let me GO!* Help me! HELP ME!"

I see the reporters in the distance staring at us, waving to each other, the group growing and moving along the road toward her voice, running now and lights popping on again, a glowing phalanx.

"Shit," the colonel says calmly. It is the first time I have ever heard him swear. Bison Breath believes that there's no place for foul language in the new Corps, that we're "dumbing ourselves down," and he's been praised by his superiors for this attitude. It's a pretty fucking good point, really.

"Lieutenant Kelly. Get your men up and in front of the prisoners. Form a wall. Now. Don't do anything dumb."

I shout to the three teams. Armstrong's arrives first and I say, "Close ranks in a circle around these prisoners. Don't say a word. Don't do a thing. If a reporter forces his way through, let him be. No violence. Enlarge the circle when the others get here." I'm hoping that a show of force will rule out its necessity.

Armstrong nods and barks an order. One of his Marines looks down and says, "Oh my God. His head is cut off almost. What happened?"

I move over next to the colonel, who has his arms stretched out toward the closing throng like a man about to be hit by a train. "Stop! Ladies and gentlemen, please stop there! I'll answer all your questions."

Gunny moves forward and extends his arms, handing Ms. Thayer-Ash to the crowd as if to say, Here, you take her. She is sobbing and screaming that we have killed the Lahtis and that they're dead behind us. A cameraman sets down his tool, grabs her, and pins her to his body, where she squirms even more violently.

The other reporters look over my shoulder, bobbing their heads for a glimpse, and I push gently against the few up front, giving the colonel some room. Lights now and cameras pushed up and over my head, panning slowly in hopes of a shot of the bodies. I peel off my NVGs and squint. Someone tests my will and I push back, unable to see if it's a woman or a man.

"What happened?" asks a reporter. "What are you hiding? Colonel, what are you hiding?" asks another. They are so undisciplined that several are speaking at once, and yet something is preventing them from having a look-see themselves. Probably the guys with the rifles behind me. I glance back; the other two teams have joined the cordon and enlarged it, the Marines standing at port arms with their rifles, waiting. They look menacing enough. I suppose the reporters don't want to risk a Kent State repeat. *Four dead in So-mal-ya, how many more?*

I have to stifle a giggle but there is nothing funny about this. Not a single thing. At all. I've had this reaction to pressure—an automatic tendency to joke when I'm terrified—since I was in the fourth grade, when the Montgomery twins first began what became a long cycle of beating the hell out of me in school. I developed a penchant for wiseass comments because it was the only way to salvage any pride, and I'm still fighting a tendency to quip at inappropriate times. My mother says it's the devilish Celtic blood in me. My grandfather thinks it's an alien gene—like my timorous nature itself—that somehow penetrated the Kelly clan, probably through the mailman since he doubts my father's testicles ever descended.

"Ladies and gentlemen, quiet down!" shouts the colonel. "Quiet down and I will tell you!"

The posse has turned inward and they are pushing and shoving each other now, the reporters with the microphones extending them like rapiers, hands on shoulders, yanking the front-row seats back and down, hissing at one another. Civilians have such poor manners.

"This morning, as you know, we landed reconnaissance to ensure that the beach was safe." The reporters begin to hush. The colonel repeats the sentence and continues, "They were providing security when two armed Somalis, in violation of the orders we spread widely through our advance party, were sneaking toward the landing beach. I say again: They were armed with AK-47 *automatic weapons* and were a *direct threat* to everyone, including yourselves."

That's it, sir.

"But, Colonel they—"

"Let me finish! Please, folks. We have strict rules of engagement as established by the UN, and our Marines followed that to the letter . . . and risked their own lives to carry out those rules. The Marines moved to capture and question the two Somalis and the Somalis resisted to the point that they posed a deadly threat . . . and one of them was killed . . ."

There is a rumble behind the crowd and the AAV swings wide around the reporters and stops behind my Marines, its huge turbine engines roaring, drowning out the crowd. The tracks grab the earth and rip parallel lines of its skin free, branches and shrubs pulling up roots, pulling up dirt and sand, clouds of particles dancing like a glowing mist in my goggles. Most of the reporters cover their ears and grimace, backing away. I nod to Gunny and he rushes over to Armstrong, whispers something, and they disappear into the middle of the circle. I hear the tailgate whir open, then shut almost immediately, just behind the group of Marines. Gunny reappears and nods, and I lean over to the colonel and shout, "Prisoners're in the Amtrack, sir!"

"Ladies and gentlemen!" The colonel is forced to yell over the track's engine. "When I know more you'll know more! I promise you . . . the matter will be thoroughly investigated and I'll get you those answers! Now, if you'll excuse me."

There is a burst of questions that allows the colonel to whisper to me, "This better be right. I'm telling you, Lieutenant, *this had better be right.* You get in the vehicle with me now. We need to chat."

Before I climb up onto the track, I remove my NVGs

and look at the real Ms. Thayer-Ash, not the glowing-green video-game version. She is staring right at me, knowing. But knowledge is not, in this instance, power. Not without proof. I cannot tell which is her salient emotion—anger or sadness—because, though she is crying, her teeth are gritted and her eyes are narrowed. She is screaming at me but I cannot hear her for the track's engine. She holds up her hand, palm out, and thrusts it toward me several times.

The bright red lines of blood caked on her wrist and in the tracks of her palm are clear in the sparkle of floodlights that polish the act, illuminating this country for the first time, reheating the dirt, waking Somalia from its violent slumber, the promise of peace and food lodged in the rifle I hold.

PART II

"Do you want me to do anything about them Indians?" Call asked.

"Which Indians?" Augustus asked. . . .

"Those that shot the arrows into you," Call said.

"Oh no, Woodrow," Augustus said. "We won more than our share with the natives. They didn't invite us here, you know."

—LARRY MCMURTRY, *Lonesome Dove*

– 6 –

15 JUNE 1974

No bastard ever won a war by dying for his country. He won it by making the other poor, dumb bastard die for *his* country.

It is my seventh birthday and my grandfather has finally agreed to take me with him on his lobster boat. It is a brisk fall day and a heavy chop greets us when we pass Castle Hill on our way out of Newport's harbor, the southwester slicing into the tops of the swells and sending salt froth into the windshield like pellets from a shotgun. Red doesn't have a pair of bib overalls that will fit a small man, so he gives me the shirt off his back and tells me not to get it all gunky with the bluefish guts we're going to use to bait the traps. His shirt billows around my feet, so I tie it tightly around my waist with a knot that makes me look like a girl, Red says. "But hell, leave it, leave it. A little camel toe'll cure a hangover every time. Right?" I don't understand most of my grandfather's jokes but I laugh anyway.

Red wheels his boat around in a tight circle and with

the gaff I snag the pot on my first try. He barrels aft, snatches the funky line, and hefts it above the pulley. When he leans back to demonstrate the technique—I'm supposed to time him on this one so we can compare speeds when I pull my first up from the depths—his bare skin stretches as taut as the vibrating rope with the beads of saltwater popping clear of the seaweed. The bright pink scar where the Jap stuck him with the bayonet flattens smoothly, its shiny surface catching the sun. Below the scar the two faded tattoos on Red's back dance. I watch the bulldog bark for a while before I remember the Sharkman, so I sprint to the gunwale and watch the crackling muscles on his red chest move the creature. The bullet hole near his shoulder is the size of a quarter and I can see it peeking through his red chest hair.

"You payin' attention to the technique, sport?" he grunts.

"Wanted to see the Sharkman move."

He nods his approval. If you're ever in trouble with Red Kelly, just tell him you were working out, getting a haircut, or pondering The Good War and he's off your back in a heartbeat.

He slings the pot out of the water, the wooden cage flush with brown lobsters, tails snap-snap-snapping, and says, "Time!"

"Fifty seconds."

"Shit! That's slow 'cause I got six keepers inside here!"

He smiles and tosses the lobsters across the deck at my Docksides. I snatch them up by their backs and plunk them into the holding tank, then get a glob of bluefish remains and scamper over to Red, just barely baiting the trap before he slams the lid shut and sends it overboard with a *kerplash!*

"Look at that! You can see my damn ribs, almost!" he

says, flexing his pecs so the tattoo moves because he knows I like that, his bare chest smattered with goose bumps in the cold breeze. "Ain't seen them ribs since The Big Dance. I remember once, musta been about a week after the Navy left us in Guadalcanal, I was lying prone, behind green shrubs. Still, I felt exposed in that Guadalcanal jungle! Too long, not blending in, scanning the bush over my iron sights, leaning hard on my raw ribs. I lost the fat meat from my belly when my unit ran out of food and, *man*, was I skinny. Almost as skinny as you!

"I was alone again and I cursed that damn BAR. You remember why the other Marines ran from me, right? Why I was always fightin' alone?"

I grab the gaff and stick it back into the rod holder. "Yes, Red. The Japs try to kill the BAR man first."

"Goddamn right, they do! Goddamn right, Gavin. But the other Marines needed my firepower! That slow, steady, pounding roar, *boom-boom-boom-boom!* so loud it drowned out the cracks from the M-1s. And the M-1 is a powerful rifle! So when a firefight was raging, my team leader would scream my name and wave me closer. But if I flopped down too close during a rush, he'd roll away and scream, 'Get away from me! Keep your dispersion, goddamn you, Kelly! You tryin' to get me killed?' Man, it was a confusing place for a seventeen-year-old. But I didn't have no choice; no one else in the squad was strong enough to carry the BAR and a full load of ammunition without an assistant."

"They were all weak?" I asked.

"Oh, hell no, boy. A weak man don't end up a Marine at the Canal. We were volunteers! They were just weaker than me."

I pull a lobster out of the tank and step on the crusher claw. I grab the mallet and one of the wooden claw pegs, center the peg in the lower-outside corner of the lobster's pincer claw, and start to tap it, more as an investigation than anything else, waiting for Red to provide instruction. But he's into a story and you never interrupt Red Kelly during story time, even if they get weird.

"So anyhow, Gavin, I'm alone and there's thick vines all around me. I stand and try to bull my way through, BAR first, when I see three animals coming at me from the left. Now, I didn't have schools like you got now so I think that maybe Clark—you remember, my buddy that got shot in the face later? Clark?—wasn't screwing with me about the tigers after all. He told me there were tigers, right! I was afraid of no man but a tiger, well, that's a different story, sports fan.

"I try to run but I tangle myself badly. There's no escape, right? So I turn to see what's come to eat me and they are *human beings*, tiny, tan, naked Japs. No clothes or weapons! I rip loose, grab my BAR, and spin it around just enough to slam a long burst into the bastards! Two of the Japs disintegrate. I mean it. Gone!

"The recoil rips the BAR from the vines like a jackhammer and puts me on my back. I stand and run around a tree to reload, where I run smack-dab right into the third Jap!"

Red eases the throttle into neutral and waves his hand to signal that the good part of the story is coming up; I stop tapping and tilt my head back so I can see him looming above me, the boat yawing violently in the swell but my grandfather shifting his weight so he can act out the finale.

"*Baaammm!* I smack into him like a linebacker. The little Jap sprawls backward and curls up into the fetal position, right where you are to me now. So I put my big combat boot on the Jap's head and what do you think happens?"

He's standing above me with a fishing boot held high in the air above my head but I'm not worried; Red lives by a strict code where beating up women or children is punishable by firing squad. "You take him prisoner?"

"Nooo, Gav, how many times I gotta tell you? I didn't fight in the European theater of operations—that's where Patton was, remember? No, the Japs took no prisoners, and because of that neither did the Marines. We killed every Jap we seen because they would do the same to us. Hell, our corpsmen scratched the red cross from their helmets because those crazy Japs would shoot the wounded and the doctors. Bastards!

"Anyway. So I reload, put the barrel of the BAR against the Jap's back, and squeeze the trigger. My weapon malfunctions! Doesn't fire. I mean, can you believe it? I slam the BAR against the tree to free the jam but it just gets more fouled up. My buddy Clark runs up. 'Any more around?' he yells, panting, like this, 'Ahahahah.' Then he points at the quivering Jap and says, 'He's naked! Probably used his uniform for the shits, like us, huh?' Most Marines cut the bottoms out of our trousers in case we had a bout of the jungle crappers while we were on the move. And my utilities were dotted with holes where I cut out pieces of hasty toilet paper 'cause we were out and the leaf gave me helluva rash on my ass."

"Did you kill him, Red?" I ask. "The little Jap?"

"That's just it. Clark wants to take him in! He says, 'I ain't killing him! We got to take him back with us.' Now, Clark is in charge of me, but I know an unlawful order when I hear one. I say, 'No way. We got the dope on that. No prisoners. What're we gonna feed him, anyways?'

"A few minutes later we walk into the company area with the prisoner. Some of the other Marines gather around the CP to watch. 'I ain't goin' in to see the cap'n with him, Clark,' I says. 'This was your foul-up.' But Clark tells me, 'I'm the squad leader now and that's exactly what you'll do.'"

I forget the lobster for a moment, totally taken by Red's story. I vaguely feel the lobster struggling to spring up on its spider legs, trying to gain some purchase with its fanned tail. "Well, what happened?" I ask.

Red knows he's set the hook, so he smiles. "We walk into the company tent, and my captain looks at the prisoner, then at us, then back at the prisoner. 'Well, this is *dumb*. You know what policy is on prisoners, Kelly. We don't have any food to share. Wait outside.'

"I am *barely* out of the tent when there is the deep pop of a forty-five. The captain shot him! The Jap runs screaming out of the tent, holding the part of his chest that's missing. He sprints like a crazed chicken in a wide circle around the company area, trailing a thin jet of blood, then dies right near me like this—'*Awwk awwk awwk!*'" Red dances wildly and then collapses on the deck of the boat. He raises his square head, a big smile on his face, and winks. "Most of the Marines were laughing like you are, but not me!"

I stop giggling in an instant when I see how serious his face is. "Were you sad?" I offer.

He smiles again and says, "Gotcha! Oh, *hell* no, I wasn't *sad!* I was pissed! I wanted to take a nap after patrol, and now Clark was gonna make me dig a grave hole for the mashed thing at my feet!"

My eighth birthday isn't nearly as fun. I'm playing catcher for my Little League team except there's one problem: It's tee ball and you don't *need* a catcher, so it's the position for the worst player.

Fat-ass Joey Montgomery knows this and when he

comes up to bat he says, "They put you at catcher because you suck, Gavin." His cheeks are so engorged that he looks like he's storing two extra baseballs in them. He and his brother both have been cursed with male breasts that jiggle even more than the rest of their body parts when they run.

Joey and his evil twin, Jay, have been harassing me for a year—thumbtacks on my chairs at school, lunch money donations, water balloons at recess—and I've been working up the courage to do what Red tells me I *have* to do to forever remove the big twins from my back: fight. I wear a catcher's mask and it makes me feel brave, maybe for the first time in my life.

"I suck at what?" I ask.

"Tee ball, stupid," laughs Joey.

"Oh. Well, that's better than sucking my brother's fat banana tits."

Joey steps out of the batter's box and nearly trips. "*What?*"

"Sorry, Joey," I say, holding up my hands. "I didn't mean that."

"You and I are gonna fight soon, Gavin. You better not mean it."

"I didn't. What I *meant* to say was, sucking at tee ball's better than being a cocksucker like your dad."

Joey drops the bat and steps away from me, as confused as I am as to what the word means—it's something Red called Mr. Callahan last month when we discovered that some of our traps had been cut. Of course, none of the traps have been touched since Red separated Mr. Callahan's shoulder in that fight right in front of Aquidnick Lobster.

Joey finally realizes it's an insult. "Say that again, Kelly, and I'll hurt you."

"You already are. Hurting my eyes, I mean."

"Stupid!"

"I know you are, but what am I?"

Joey charges and knocks me to the ground, straddling me. He bats at the sides of my head with his doughy fists but I am more relieved than hurt; I'm finally fighting and it isn't so bad. His breath is ragged and labored. I claw at his arms for a while and manage to roll him over by arching my back and turning my body. I can hear the other kids yelling. I grab one of the three folds in his neck and cock a fist behind my head, Joey below me now and scared for the first time—I think somewhere below the din of my screaming teammates I even hear him say, "I give," but I'm going to hit him anyway.

Someone snatches my arm in midair and jerks me free of Joey, lifting me into the air. I dig my fingernails into Jay's fat forearm but it's as solid as oak, and when I look down I see the tattoo—the white skull grinning up at me, dagger clenched in its teeth, the entire thing framed by a blue diamond, five blood stripes dripping down below where the forearm grows truly massive. It's my father. "Stop it, Gavin!" he yells.

"Let me go!"

"That's enough, young man," he says. He pins my arms to my sides and pulls me behind him.

There are grown-ups in the melee now, telling the team to take their positions again and calm down, and I see Joey's dad rush up to the circle panting. "What the hell're they fighting for?"

"He called you a cocksucker!" yells Joey, pointing at me.

"*Excuse me?*" says Mr. Montgomery, three hundred pounds of him still heaving from his fifty-yard dash, wiping his brow with his Yankees baseball cap.

"Did you, Gavin?" my father asks sternly.

"I don't even know what it means, Dad! It's just—Joey's been picking on me all this year!"

My father faces Mr. Montgomery and says, "I apologize for it, Herb. I'll wash his mouth out with soap or something when we get home."

"Yeah, well, that ain't good enough, Tom." Mr. Montgomery points at me. "That kid's got a big mouth and if he don't learn to shut it now he's gonna learn a hard lesson one day. Damn, he's rude! Callin' me *that*? Maybe we should just let 'em fight it out."

My dad laughs. "Yeah, well, that's ridiculous, Herb. And let's not forget how this started. It was *Joey* and *Jay* who we've been talking about this past year. This never would have happened without their harassment." My father has visited the Montgomerys twice to appeal for peace, but the talks were as effective as the Tet cease-fire.

Mr. Montgomery levels a glare at my father that's unnerving. He steps toward us. His head is as large as the Great Pumpkin's (I file the observation away for future use).

"Don't go making excuses for your wiseass son, Tom. You just sound foolish."

"This is a *Little League game*, for Chrissakes, Herb. Now who's the one playing the fool? Let's just calm down here," my father says.

Mr. Montgomery sneers and starts to breathe hard again. "Fool? You calm down! You calm down, Tom! I'm not the one who called somebody a '*cocksucker*,' am I, Tom?"

My father lifts me up and starts to carry me, over his shoulder, toward the parking lot. "This is absurd. You're losing control over nothing, Herb."

"Yeah, yeah, yeah, Tom," Mr. Montgomery calls after us. "Run away. That's right! Big, tough Marine runnin' away. 'Cause I'm right here if you need me, Tom, calling *me* absurd? Calling *me* a fool? Huh? Want to say it to my face or are you gonna talk behind my back like that punk son of yours?"

I watch Mr. Montgomery all the way to the parking lot—he is rubbing Joey's head, nodding, even sharing a laugh with my coach. "Why didn't you get him, Dad?"

"Fighting doesn't solve what you think it will unless both parties agree to the rules ahead of time and stick to them. No unexpected repercussions."

"What's that mean?"

He sighs and sets me down next to our Volkswagen Beetle. He glances back at the baseball diamond and Mr. Montgomery, who is still standing at home plate watching us, and who raises his arms as if to say, Well, here I am. My father shakes his head and rubs my head. He looks almost sad and I take it as fear, his eyebrows slanted up toward the center of his forehead and the corners of his mouth drooping slightly. "It means that if I went over there and punched Mr. Montgomery, he'd probably have me arrested. So in solving one problem I'd have a much bigger one. Understand? He only wants to fight if he wins. But if I win, he'll sue me or throw me in jail. So there's no way I can win. And you don't fight to lose. That's what I mean when I tell you fighting doesn't solve your problems, not unless you're allowed to win. Understand?"

I nod and stare at that sinister tattoo. What a faker, Red had said during the Tall Ships Festival when we were out on the boat, a supply guy getting a tattoo like that. So now I understand, and what I understand is this—my father is afraid of Mr. Montgomery and everyone knows it. My father is a wimp.

"Well, let me fight Joey, then. He won't tell on me."

He smiles and opens the car door. "Joey's a big kid," he says. "Just remember that there's always someone tougher than you are. If Joey or Jay bothers you on Monday, I want you to tell your teacher or come straight home. I'll handle it through proper channels. Okay?"

"Okay, Dad."

He drives me to the marina and we step onto his boat so we can do our chores. My cleaning outfit is stored below the cabin and I clamber down the ladder well into the gear hold so I can change. When I emerge a few minutes later in my miniature set of rubber-coated coveralls, I climb up to the bridge and notice Dad outside at the end of the harpoon pulpit. He's gripping the handrail with all of his might, pulling and struggling against some unseen force. I consider popping open the windshield and shouting, "What's wrong?", but I'm embarrassed for spying on him so I just watch him pull and pull, his big arms vibrating and the back of his neck flushed bright red. Eventually he stops and I run back down into the cabin as he walks toward the cockpit.

On Monday morning Joey ambushes me at the bus stop in front of a small crowd that includes his brother, Jay, who is providing insurance. I know that if I start getting the best of Joey, Jay—who's much meaner—will come over and kick my head in or something, so the fight isn't in me. But it's a mistake. Joey seems to gain an immediate confidence by sucking it straight out of me, his fists coming faster and finding targets now, my lights being slowly punched dim, a pattern that will continue for over five years. I don't tell on them, though, because I'm not a rat. Red says that nobody likes a rat.

After the fight the Montgomerys are still laughing when the bus pulls up and I hear Joey say, "My dad says the only cocksucker in this town is your dad, that's why the Marines kicked him out!"

– 7 –

9 DECEMBER 1992

> Never get out of the boat. Absolutely god-
> damn right.

I am standing knee-deep in the foxhole that Doc and I
will share tonight, staring nervously at the white armored
personnel carrier that carries a big, black "UN" brand on
its flank like a cursed cow that's been selected for slaughter.
U.S. forces here fall under the "operational control" of the
United Nations Task Force commander who's been in
country for a few months, an Italian general named
Allessandro Bellissimo. Operational control is a vague
term that means we are supposed to follow "strategic
guidelines" handed down by Bellissimo while still retain-
ing the flexibility to follow our own chain of command
and reject "morally or tactically" objectionable orders.
Simply put, some policy wonks have come up with a confusing, fence-riding policy full of blameless bomb shelters
and escape routes should something go awry in Somalia.

The UN APC parked in our compound means that

General Bellissimo is paying a visit to Colonel Capiletti; the investigation into Said Lahti's death is no doubt complete, the only remaining question whether I will die by bullet or shark attack.

Sixteen hours have passed since the landing, an eternity in a 911 war.

We've dug in just outside the Mogadishu airport terminal, the temporary headquarters and staging area—the hub of Restore Hope—we're using as a jumping-off point for going to feed the needy. The configuration of the airport defenses: an oval ring of foxholes surrounding the two huge airport hangars, two men per hole. Our platoon was lucky enough to have been given rock-star parking and we're staring right at the wall that separates the northern edge of the terminal from Mogadishu, three miles away. Why have we dug in just behind a wall, you might ask, severely curtailing the maximum range of our weapons, especially given the fact that the wall—about eight feet tall—is low enough to climb over *and* dotted with huge, dishwasher-size holes? I'm asking myself the same thing but I'm in no position to question the colonel's orders, risky under benign circumstances and suicidal considering my current conundrum.

I give the three team leaders a quick order on tonight's defensive scheme and they are professional enough to keep their mouths shut; Armstrong would normally pipe up here, but he's in my boat—*Titanic, Bismarck, Andrea Doria, Pequod,* or *Orca,* take your pick. Our Team Two leader, Sergeant Jesus Montoya, softly tests the waters and I answer him firmly. Yes, we have to sleep here tonight, on 50 percent security, watching out for infiltrators. No, we can't booby-trap the holes in the walls because of the kids who are popping in and out of them. Yes, the same goes for barbed wire. No, we can't go on a night hunt tonight, we have to stay in our holes. No, you can't shoot grown men who walk up to your hole at night, even if they have rifles. They have to point them first.

I have the gnawing feeling that I'm letting my platoon down by not fighting this emplacement—that I'm endangering them by keeping silent—but the truth is that the colonel probably fought the rules of engagement, too. Once a Marine gets an order, he can argue it with its issuer, but he never, *ever*, gripes about it in front of his subordinates. He passes it along as if it is his own. General Bellissimo probably handed the colonel his orders, the colonel handed them to me, I talked them over with Gunny and am handing them to the team leaders, and they'll go hand them to their teams. No tears.

Still, it's hard to take ownership of these orders. And it's impossible to ignore all those times Red Kelly pounded this into my head: An officer has one duty, and that's to look out for his men. To keep them alive. "I can't tell you the number of zero pricks I seen who were more concerned with their careers than their own Marines. Gutless bastards!" my grandfather told me at my commissioning ceremony, the one my father avoided. Then he put a playful fist into one of the brass buttons on my coat and said, "If you're going to be the first officer in the family, you'd best do it right. So *listen to your noncoms* and you better goddamn well *do right by your men.*"

At the Gulf War parade, I told Red about my dead radioman, Tommy Bonneger, and asked whether or not I did right by him, one of only a handful who died in the war. "First of all," Red said, "yours wasn't no *war*. Hundred hours? Hell, that's not even a firefight. Second, this kid T-Bone shoulda been named Bone Head, from what you tell me! That's what war does: brings out the best in the country and rids it of both its very best and bravest men *and* the dregs—the stupid and such. This kid Boner didn't act smart and he died. And hell, that's just one man. *My entire company was wiped out in a few seconds at Tarawa.* No tears for one man."

"Tommy Bonneger was not a dreg, Red. He was a hero. He died because he was the bravest one," I whispered, turning away from him to smother my burning eyes.

"Hey. *Hey.* Whooaa now, sport. Okay, okay. Like I said, the bravest get shot, too. The worst part of war is that most of the cowards make it. Okay, so Bone Head was no coward. But don't go feeling sorry for yourself because one man done got himself killed. You want to feel bad? Go to the Iwo memorial and you'll understand that Boner was lost thousands of times over in *seconds* during The Big One."

Red winked, but Tommy Bonneger dug a trench across my heart that will never fill in. He was not dumb and he was not a dreg, and he was *much* better than me. Red said that cowards often make it through unscathed and I wonder about that . . .

I often think about T-Bone, playing out the death scene in that bloodstained trench whenever I meet someone from New Jersey, or shake hands with a Tom—my father included—or watch a pickup basketball game (the men used to say that T-Bone had "hops" for a white guy), or look at an upscale menu, or reread the letter of absolution from his wife that still closes my throat, or . . .

I've just returned from leading the platoon on a seven-mile run around the compound. And around. And around. We are not allowed to venture into Mog proper, so the run was like running on the flight deck of the *Denver,* where it takes fourteen laps to reach a mile, watching the same antenna or cleat whip past every twenty-five seconds.

The Marines typically hate the boredom of lap runs. Not

today. We're famous within the battalion because of the kill—*dude, with a bayonet!*—and most of the grunts cheered for us when we passed. Well, cheered for Armstrong.

Four Italian officers strut out of the hangar, General Bellissimo the tallest among them and by far the most animated, gesturing wildly as he hops into the UN vehicle, the brushed polish on his glistening uniform catching the sun and sending it into my eyes. He's wearing the infantry beret that, strictly in terms of fashion, makes Marines shudder; we still don't understand why our own infantry Army units get off on donning those goofy pancakes. Worse, we're now hearing that the *entire* Army is lobbying to wear them, a friendly fire fashion disaster that will rival crushed-velvet jumpsuits and feathered hairstyles.

The general's nifty cap is baby blue, United Nations issue—an alarm bell that there are goats and lassos lurking close by. He probably has no idea what I look like, but I crouch down in my hole anyway and watch the vehicle motor across the tarmac to the UN hangar—a larger hangar two hundred meters away that's rumored to have air-conditioning and cold sodas—from between Armstrong's long legs.

I was introduced to the general three days ago, when the *Denver* first cracked Somalia's territorial waters. The platoon was gathered on the flight deck, pointing excitedly at a brown-and-green coastline that had appeared on the horizon after three days of only midnight blue water and robin egg sky as we steamed across the Indian, a colorful present under a once bereft tree, a Christmas Eve expectation fulfilled.

"That the shithole country we fixin' to unfuck, sir?" Armstrong asked me.

"Fixing?"

"Yessir. Fixing."

"As in, 'preparing'?"

"No. Fixin', I said. Oh, damn it, almost forgot. You got to go get briefed by the Italian general, sir. Don't come back tellin' me we got to wear one of them blue helmets, neither." He handed me a folded memo and shrugged. Armstrong has ink black hair but his eyes are light blue and when his pupils contract and he squints, like he was then, his entire face seems to glow, master of all domains. "Hope you ain't late. I guess I got caught up in the excitement. Looks like we got to do more of that scenario training on the ROE."

I nodded, and as I walked away I said, "Well, I'll be fixin' to meet y'all after the brief then, Sergeant," as I studied the memo.

From: Vader
To: Commanders
Subj: Rules of Engagement Brief

1. All officers are to assemble at 1400 in the wardroom for a country brief by General Allessandro Bellissimo, commander, UNITAF.

2. Uniform: Pressed utilities and polished boots. This is a first impression, gents.

3. The media will be there to cover the brief and the subsequent rehearsals of the ROE on the flight deck. Keep a sharp eye on your Marines and bear in mind that these images will be beamed back to the States. I expect the Marines to be totally professional as they go through the scenario train-

ing. Conduct inspections on knowledge, gear, actions, and proper uniforms before you begin the rehearsals. First impressions are one shot, one kill, gentlemen.

Vader Out

I arrived at the wardroom early so I could get a seat as far from Bison Breath as possible, tucking myself in the corner by the bug juice dispenser; my boots are months away from reflecting even a glint of light and my ironing skills have never reached satisfactory Marine Corps standards. The rest of the officers soon filled the room, most of them complaining about serving under the UN command and wondering—as they would with any new commander—what General Bellissimo was like. Rumor had it that he was some sort of aristocrat, perhaps falling into whatever junior varsity royalty status the title "count" carried. The excited murmur died a head-shot death when someone shouted, "Attention on deck!" and in a second I was standing straight and narrow, every fiber of my body rigid except for my eyes, which locked on the two men and followed them as they paraded toward the podium, an American Marine colonel and his Italian boss, snapshot of the new world order.

B-Squared left us at attention while he strutted between the ranks to give the general a quick taste of Marine discipline, the starch layered so thickly on his camouflage utilities that they shone, but Bellissimo said, "My God, relax, gentlemen, relax! We cannot have this type of formal greeting every day we meet in Mogadishu, can we? Standing for me. A simple 'hello' will do, Marines!"

Bellissimo laughed and the room joined him. He was a tall, thin man with olive skin and the build of a tennis player—he was clearly fit but his smooth gestures and gait seemed upper class and soft in such close juxtaposition to Colonel Capiletti, who was rubbing a hairy forearm awkwardly and trying to fake a laugh, tension and explosiveness obvious behind the grin. Bellissimo patted Bison Breath on the shoulder and said, "They're big. What have you been feeding them, Vincent? Grenades and bullets?"

"Uh, no. No, sir. Just good old-fashioned Navy chow."

"Well! I'll have to have my chefs meet with your chefs! My men who have been in Somalia for four months would love to eat this 'Navy chow,' I'm sure. Perhaps you can give me a recipe?"

Colonel Capiletti understood that the request was facetious but he didn't know what to do with it. "Yes, sir, we do have cookbooks. I can give you one, I'm sure, sir."

Bellissimo shook his head grandly and smiled again, patting Colonel Capiletti on the back. He turned and looked at the room but addressed my colonel. "I was only joking, Vincent! It was just a joke. Did your family leave its sense of humor in Italy when it left for the United States?"

It was a condescending act that I initially dismissed as a cultural misunderstanding, but listening to the general call Bison Breath "Vincent"—and watching them standing side by side—I had the strong impression that the colonel was a heavy laborer to Bellissimo's architect, and that a few generations ago the Capilettis were tending the Bellissimos' crops, something that was not lost on either of them. My distaste for the command relationship blossomed and I, too, was standing there wondering how in the hell United States forces had ended up falling under a foreign commander in the first place. We might poke fun at the colonel, but he was *our* colonel.

"Gentlemen!" Bellissimo boomed. "I am *delighted* to have you join my ranks as our new foot soldiers. Please, sit down. You make me nervous, big Marines standing around me!" He laughed again, but this time the echo was softer.

"My force has been here for four months. This mission requires sophistication. It is . . . complex, to say so. Sophistication! And you Marines have never been known for your . . . delicate handling, eh?" He laughed again, and I think it was mostly the reporters who joined him. Marines get knocked all the time within the military for our thick heads—"jarheads," "bullet-traps," "steak-for-brains"—and I don't have a problem with it; when you spend your existence begging to be the first force to hit the beach, well, there has to be a widget missing somewhere. But we also believe there's not a finer force in existence when it comes to nasty, tangled missions, so criticism in that area doesn't sit well.

Bellissimo smoothed his wavy brown hair and nodded to the cameras in the back as if they were sharing an exclusive secret that we Marines might never fully digest. "You have called the Somali clans 'warlords.' I have read where you compare them to your own Mafia. Your relatives, right, Vincent? I'm joking again, of course, but here is my point: In Italy we have always had your 'Mafia' and we have always known how to deal with them. America struggled and knocked heads—that's the correct sentence? Yes. But in Italy we crafted 'strategy' and 'relationships.'

"Under my command, I want you to view the Somalia situation as you would view difficult corporate or political situations. My men have been here four months and we have been able to work with the Somalis and avoid bloodshed. I do *not* want shoot-them-ups, yes? I want thinking, not bullets, yes? Think."

I watched Bellissimo tap his finger against his skull and

I followed his instructions. My thinking: If he's been able to *work* with the warlords, why the hell did someone dial 911 and call us? The fact is, the UN has been getting its ass handed to it.

"The sector I have assigned you is mostly calm since we've been dealing there. It is the northern edge of Mogadishu and it is run by a young man named Hassan Farah, one of Aidid's lieutenants. Farah is no older than most of the people in this room, maybe thirty, but he's been fighting for his entire life. He's what you would call the 'mayor' of your sector. You should treat him like he is your old Chicago mayor Daley; he has his hand in every food ration and knows what everyone is doing. He is popular among his people because he protects his Hibr Gidr clan—Aidid's group, yes?—from the other warring clans.

"Farah works with another man called Ali and a group of young enforcers. Your 'warlords.' They have AK-47s and pistols, but they know the rules about big weapons and you won't see any. I have talked myself with Farah and he's concerned that the Marines will come in and . . . 'upset' things. I told him he has nothing to worry about and that you Marines, in turn, have nothing to worry about from him. That things will remain calm unless he violates the rules. He understood. There won't be a problem, yes? Not if you use your heads. Just keep the rules of engagement always in your minds and always be thinking."

Our intelligence officer followed the general with another lengthy brief on the ROE, a repetition of the scenarios we'd been practicing for a week but a good show for the general and the cameras. When the meeting was adjourned, Big Duke pulled me aside in the passageway and introduced an older, wiry man whose face was just as leathery and wrinkled as his chaperone's.

"Sir, this is John Smith. He and I served together in

Vietnam," said Big Duke. "He's quite familiar with Somalia and I'm bringing him around to visit with all the commanders."

I turned to face Smith and he nodded. He was wearing blue jeans without a belt, a Redskins T-shirt, and Docksides without socks—three separate violations of the colonel's strict code for liberty attire that was put in place to protect Marines from the spectre of sexually transmitted diseases; a Marine in Hong Kong for two days faces steep odds to begin with when he rushes down the gangplank and sprints toward Lang Quai Phong's bar strip, but they are crushed entirely when he's dressed as unfashionably as his haircut.

I liked the man already and I shook his hand. "Nice to meet you, Mr. . . . Smith. Agency?"

"That's right."

"Why didn't you just brief everyone after the general? Anyway, we already got our CIA country brief by message traffic."

Big Duke and the spook exchanged a look and Big Duke said, "His is not exactly the popular opinion right now, Lieutenant. And with the cameras running around, well, it wouldn't have worked out. His information isn't the kind of thing you'd find on a message. I just think it's important all the commanders hear it informally, is all."

I raised my eyebrows and Smith said, "This is just an opinion, and it's off the record. The Italians have been coddling these thugs and you can expect some problems when you go into that sector. Farah isn't a mayor—he's Al Capone. He'll prod and taunt you to show his people who controls his neighborhood. Difference between you and the UN is, Marines won't back down, and that's a problem. The *other* problem is that Farah has a goddamn copy of the

ROE. No shit. The UN thinks it will help both sides 'understand each other.' So he will use it to bind your hands. You'll probably never catch Farah red-handed, but he'll be incredibly active behind the scenes."

"Doing what?" I asked. "Stealing food?"

"Yeah. Yeah, there's that. And murder, rape, and pillaging. Oh yeah, Lieutenant, he's a real prince. Watch your back."

I nodded my thanks and walked off to my stateroom, thinking about the rules of engagement and my responsibilities as a platoon commander. I pulled the laminated card out of my left breast pocket and read it again, wondering how adjectives like "minimum" and "graduated" would mesh with nouns like "Devildogs" and "Leathernecks."

Rules of Engagement: Restore Hope

1. **Every Marine has the right to take all necessary action—including the use of deadly force—if he is in immediate mortal danger and must defend himself. This is overriding.**

2. **Always use the *minimum* amount of force required by the situation. Marine actions are to be both reasonable and proportional.**

3. **Use a *graduated response* depending on the situation.**

    A. **Warning (verbal, visual)**

    B. **Minimum force (maneuver, physical restraint)**

    C. **Warning shots**

    D. **Deadly force (last resort)**

I met my platoon on the flight deck three hours later during our scheduled rehearsal time, Gunny announcing the unit by screaming, "Combat!" before charging out of the hatch in full combat gear like some overgrown gladiator yanked out of his own time, the Marines running in formation behind him, howling, rifles held chest high, body armor thumping with each stride, sweat squeezing out immediately from beneath the Kevlar helmets, cartridge belts full of blanks, dummy grenades, canteens, first aid kits, and knives clinking and clanking.

"My God," said a cameraman standing behind me. "Who's that?"

"That's Gunnery Sergeant Jarius Ricketts and his recon platoon," I said, hoping that he might decide to film us a little. Bison Breath scheduled our platoon at the end of the day, *after* the reporters had gathered the necessary footage and had grown bored with the dress rehearsals.

"Hate to meet him in a dark alley," he said, camera case still idle on the tarmac.

Gunny sprinted up to me and skidded to a halt, breathing hard and wearing a huge grin. He inhaled deeply and I heard the Velcro chest zipper on his flak jacket rip slightly—XXL and still not large enough. "Platoon's ready to run through the scenarios, sir," he panted.

I turned to the cameraman and said, "Dark alley? It's high noon in a public place, I'm his platoon commander, and I'm scared shitless."

We moved over to the CH-46 helicopter that was playing one of the food trucks and practiced setting up a food distribution line, waiting for the bad guys to show up, all of us mimicking a soup kitchen as if it was a bad game of charades with the relatives. The first scenario was designed to run the platoon through the first block of the "three block war" that we're supposed to encounter often now that the Soviet Union has withered—an especially dangerous mission because it mutates from a humanitarian operation with scattered malcontents, to policing unruly crowds and armed rogue punks, to full-scale combat. We couldn't exactly fly the Somalis out to the ship to play themselves, so I tasked Team One with playing the aggressors, Armstrong cast as Farah and Johnson cast as his henchman, Muhammad Ali. We were briefed that Somali men could achieve great status by standing up to the Marines, so I told Armstrong to push the envelope a tad.

We heard their chants long before they emerged from the hangar bay; it was Armstrong's way of drawing the cameras to him and it worked. Those reporters who had long since packed away their microphones began giving snappy orders to the cameramen the moment *Clinton sucks! . . . Clinton sucks!* began to reverberate across the flight deck. Cameras were yanked out of aluminum cases and suddenly we had an audience, lenses whirring and reporters testing their sound levels, one two, test, test, hurry up, John, and get this footage!

Armstrong's team jogged toward us dressed in an assortment of T-shirts that ranged from "NWA Hell, Yeah" (Johnson) to "Don't Mess with Texas" (Armstrong). Armstrong himself was wearing some kind of white dreadlock wig that he had probably cut free from a mop.

"Somalis kick ass!" they screamed, all of them with raised fists, pumping them like the Black Panthers or something. "Clinton sucks! Clinton sucks!" They were supposed to act irreverent and chaotic—by God, I had cast them well.

"Team Two: Off the food line and on security, just like we drilled," I said evenly, coolest of the cats. "Don't let these punks provoke you. They're unarmed."

"Roger that, sir," said Sergeant Montoya, our level-headed team leader from San Antonio. He gave some crisp orders and his team rushed into a security position, quickly forming a protective cordon across our imaginary food point.

Across the flight deck I saw that the cameras had attracted Colonel Capiletti and he was jogging over to check on the training. Either that or Armstrong had recruited him as a bad guy and he was moving in for some crossfire. The Somalis were chanting louder now and Armstrong had moved his ragtag crew right up against Montoya's team, pressing forward against their blank-loaded M-16s, screaming wildly, "Clin-ton sucks! We want food! We kill Marines! Clin-ton *SUCKS! CLIN-TON SUU-UUUUCKS!*"

"Just ignore the yelling, Montoya," I said evenly, thinking I was in total control.

Bison Breath called out to me and I could see he was in a panic, for some reason, upper lip straining for his flaring nostrils like he was snarling. A camera crew trailed behind him and swooped in to join the other three that made up the edges of the arena. One of the reporters whispered, "Can they *say* that?"

"Just what the heck is going on, Lieutenant Kelly?" Bison Breath shouted above the swelling chants.

I assumed he was inserting himself into the scenario. "Just some warlords making trouble, sir. I'd advise you to stay back, though. They seem to be unarmed so I—"

"*You* tell them to cease this verbal puke *right-gosh-damned-fricking now!*" he hissed into my ear, unconsciously grabbing my elbow. He was in a rage and white puffs of spittle were spraying shotgun style, his eyes bloodshot and wild. This is not the position in which a lieutenant wants to find himself with a man who once snapped a lance corporal's surfboard in half over his knee for having the audacity to drive into the battalion parking lot with it strapped to his roof.

"Damn it, Kelly! Making statements about the president-elect of the United States is a violation of the Uniform Code of Military Justice! Jesus! The reporters are all over it! Look at them, for Chrissakes! I could bring your men up on charges!"

"Sir, they're *acting*."

He put a hefty finger deep into my pectoral muscle, flak vest notwithstanding, and practically screamed, "Does it *look* like they're *acting*? My God, Lieutenant! This will be shown on the evening news! Make them *STOP!*"

I was terrified. I spun around and practically sprinted up to my creation, Frankenstein preparing to kill his monster. "Sergeant Armstrong! Stop with the Clinton stuff!"

"Who you talkin' 'bout, my white brutha?" Armstrong replied in a bad Jamaican accent. He bounced up and down so his dreadlocks danced like Medusa's eels, clearly immersed in his role, a method actor who rivaled De Niro. "I don' know no Armstrong. When you talk to the supreme WARLORD FARAH, you show me some respect, Daddy-O. Or I break a cap in yo' white ass."

"That's 'bust a cap,'" Johnson corrected.

"*Both* of you shut your holes," I said. "And take off that fucking mop. Take your team back into the hangar and try this entrance again without acting up."

"But *you* told us to act up, sir," Armstrong protested.

"I know I did. Now I'm telling you different." I tried to roll my eyes back as a signal. "Understand?"

"No, sir. I don't think I'll ever understand officers." With that, he whistled and his team followed him into the hangar like a loyal pack of dogs, grumbling the entire way, the tar on the nonskid deck sucking in the sun and heating our feet right through the soles on our boots, so hot that just before Team One disappeared into the hangar the mirage broke them up and then swallowed them.

Our audience remained for take two, and it began well enough—Armstrong's team having a good time with their new slogan, "The U.S.A. is me-di-ocre! The U.S.A. is me-di-ocre!" B-Squared nodding his solemn approval after the reporters chuckle, Montoya's team keeping order by forming a human wall so the rest of the platoon can feed our imaginary friends. Then Muhammad Ali—aka Lance Corporal Terrel Johnson—grabbed Montoya's rifle and wrestled him to the ground. When Montoya's Marines swarmed in to peel Johnson away, Farah—aka Sergeant Jake Armstrong—grabbed one of them in a headlock, snatched the Marine's M-16, and put the barrel against the Marine's head.

By the time I had shouldered my rifle and pulled the trigger, at least a dozen other Marines had already fired: *Pop! Pop! Pop! Pop! Pop!* Warlords ran pell-mell, some faking wonderfully dramatic deaths, spinning and twisting, others crawling on hands and knees toward the cameras, screaming about a body part or two. The Marines cut loose from the food line and launched a full frontal assault on those of Armstrong's men who were still alive.

Lance Corporal Johnson crawled toward the CNN cameraman on his stomach, his upper lip curled as if he was in excruciating pain—it was really well acted, actually—screaming, "Oh, Lord! Oh, my Muslim Lord! I was unarmed! I just wanted food! *I was unarmed!*"

Then he snatched a Marine's leg and the Marine, who was out of ammunition, popped his magazine free on the deck, snatched another from his pouch, slapped it into his M-16, rode the bolt home, and fired at least twenty rounds into Ali's—er, Johnson's back: *Pop! Pop! Pop! Pop! Pop!*

Johnson shook violently, as if he was being electrocuted, while the Marine screamed, "I WOULDA CLUBBED THE FUCK OUTTA YOU, JOHNSON, IF YOU WAS A REAL SKINNY AND TRIED THAT!! I WAS JUST OUTTA ROUNDS, IS WHY I TOOK SO LONG, YOU SKINNY PUNK!!"

I looked back at Bison Breath and he was wearing a mask so fearful that he could have gone trick or treating with it, absolutely horrified and hateful at the same instant in time. His mouth opened and he screamed at me. A squad automatic weapon cut loose a string of blanks—BaaaRRUUUUPPPP!! BaaaRRUUUPPP!—that came in time to drown out his words, but I understood them.

Behind me I heard a reporter whisper, "You're getting this, right, Jerry? I mean, my God!"

"Cease fire! Cease fire!" I shouted in a full panic, Marines feigning death all around me, a massacre of steroidal ballerinas, spinning and spinning, screams of wilding echoing across the flight deck, me giving the "cease fire" hand-and-arm signal as well.

I waded through the Twister mat and closed in on Armstrong. "What the hell are you doing?!" I shouted above my echo.

"Whaddaya mean, sir?"

"This scenario was just supposed to be a feeding with light harassment. Exercises one and two. You took it to another level! You're going to get me fired!"

He shrugged and looked over my shoulder. "Sorry if I got you in some trouble, sir, but I think the platoon did real good. I took Stovell hostage and everyone shot me right away. See, the way I figure it, these Gangbangers we're gonna face ain't gonna tell us which scenario they'll pull before they do it. Since Farah is unpredictable—like you said—I told my team we should be unpredictable. Otherwise someone's liable to end up dead. And it ain't gonna be me or my men."

———

Three Hummers rev their engines and roar out of the airport compound. Watching the twelve infantry lieutenants brief their platoons, lock and load, and head off into the Somali hinterland to do some good . . . well, it's enough to give a guy a complex. Until the colonel's preliminary investigation into the death of Said Lahti is completed, however, my platoon has been placed in the penalty box. I expect the results any minute, though I've been telling myself the same thing for the past six hours.

The other two team leaders trot over to brief their men, but Armstrong lingers. "When are we gonna go get some, sir? We're missin' out. I got a reputation to uphold."

I ignore it. "Tell the other men that it's time for chow, Sergeant Armstrong."

The fact is, though, I'm as antsy as he is. A day ago, Restore Hope was going to cement my career, another chance to prove myself, perhaps enough to float me all the way to full bird colonel in fifteen years; it's hard enough to find one brushfire war in which to fight, but *two*? Combat is the crucible by which we are judged and I hit the jackpot when we were diverted to Somalia. If there was any doubt about my actions in the Gulf War, I was going to seal them permanently.

Marines are the first to fight. We kill bad guys. Enemies of the republic. And since the wall crumbled—along with our perfect enemy—we've regularly added folks to our most-wanted list, including old friends. Hey, any port in a storm.

To build the thirst for conflict, the Corps takes its troops away from their families and friends for six-month sea deployments every eighteen months and crams them into tiny holds below the waterlines of ancient troop carriers—nineteen Marines stuffed into a steel-walled space, bunks stacked four high from deck to overhead. The bunks are so cramped that the bigger Marines actually have to slide out of their racks to turn over, otherwise their shoulders hit the bunk above them.

The trip from San Diego to the hot spots always seems to coincide with brutal typhoons that violently pitch and yaw the flat-bottomed amphibs and throw the Marines from their bunks. Sometimes we have to strap ourselves in at night; each bunk comes with a canvas cargo strap for that singular purpose. Well, it also serves as a decent love rag if you're in a pinch. Then the Navy cranks up the boilers to make up for lost time, and the berthing spaces, located right next to the plant, begin to cook the sweat and flesh and vomit. Fistfights erupt over musical tastes and personal space and unwanted but unavoidable physical contact. Like tigers starving in a cage manned by two blond gay men in silver suits.

Okay, it's not *that* bad.

A month later the Dear Johns arrive—along with the occasional rumor of infidelity back home—and requests come in for emergency leave, Marines desperate to fly back and fix those things that have been permanently broken. We deny them, of course. Who would be left to dig holes into the Kuwaiti sand if we sent every broken heart home? As Gunny says, "If the Corps wanted us to have wives and girlfriends, it would have issued us some."

Finally, when the Marines begin to contemplate mutiny, the Pentagon sends a warning order like the one we received when we were cutting holes in the South China Sea: "Take a look at CNN tonight. You may get to take your frustrations out on someone."

Now we have done that, and I'm not sure if it was the right thing to do. As I walk over and join my men in the chow line, noticing the NBC and CNN trucks that must have slipped into the compound during our run, my entire life hangs on the colonel's willingness to fight for me and my platoon's version of Said Lahti's death, an awful turn of events.

– 8 –

I once thought I had mono for an entire
year. It turned out I was just really bored.

I am praying that there will be some USMC slop left
when the chow line finally dwindles its way down to me.
Marine officers eat last. The Gunny is standing in front of
me, the back of his green T-shirt caked white with salt and
stretched by his lats. Armstrong, next in line by rank if the
Gunny and I buy it, is in front of him, which means I have
to listen to one of the Marine Corps' endless debates as a
price for food. Armstrong is shoving some of his team
members around, arguing; the animals get restless just
before feeding.

"Stretch, you don't know the first thing about ant
strength." The Gunny uses Armstrong's nickname and I let
it slide. He and Armstrong are having classic Marine Corps
debate number six: relative strength. "I mean, it's just a stupid argument," he says. "A spider's much stronger."

"Bullshit, Guns. If I had the strength of an ant, I could
lift a fucking freighter and carry it from here into Kenya. A
freighter. Think about that. And since I'm the strongest in
the platoon, I could probably carry *two* freighters. Or

maybe one freighter and fifty chicks or something. Fifty fat chicks."

"But a spider's got *speed*, my man. I'd run around your ant ass and pounce on you. Plus, I'd have eight arms to beat the snot out of you."

"I don't know about them lazy New York ants, Gunny, but a Texas ant has speed."

"You callin' New Yorkers lazy, young stud?" Gunny growls, nearly human. "Let's talk about lazy. Let's talk about sittin' out all day watching cows eat. Now *that's* lazy."

"Compared to all them welfare motherfuckeds? Are you kidding me, Guns? Half of New York is taking a handout we're paying for. You and me both. Whole fucking city should be burned and rebuilt."

"Now that's just plain ignorant . . ."

A Lincoln-Douglas debate it isn't. I zone out and gaze around the hangar, searching for the reporters. I see two civilians—must be reporters—standing outside the colonel's office and I lose my appetite. I mean it, it's just *gone.* There's no way in *hell* they'll believe Muhammad Lahti had no press pass. And the lying son of a bitch will continue to insist he was asleep. My God, Gunny, what were we thinking? I grab one of the messmen and ask how long the reporters have been here.

"Aw, shit, sir. She's been here, what, over an hour now."

"What do you mean, '*she*'?"

The Marine narrows his eyes, surprised at the question, then turns and points at the chow tables, packed with Marines. "Well, that chick from CNN, sir. That's why we're so crowded in here. No one will leave until she comes out again. They want to see her. Problem is, she's got this big, black bodyguard with her who won't let any of the guys get autographs or nothing."

That's how she knew me, all right.

" . . . sir?"

"What?"

"Are you okay, sir?"

"He's no bodyguard," I manage. "He's a reporter, like her. But he's also a former Marine."

"Lieutenant Kelly, sir," a Marine says from behind. I'm getting it from all sides now. "Colonel Capiletti wants you. At the heavy bag."

Gunny glances at me—our fate is at hand—and I shake my head. I wipe the saltwater from my forehead and try to get my breathing pattern back to normal. Gunny pulls me aside and whispers, "Sir. Cool out. You're sweating. *Relax.* We did right."

"I don't know, Guns. *Shit.*"

"Sir, you're scaring me. Keep your chin up . . ."

Just as my face begins to flush red with both fear and embarrassment I turn it and avoid Gunny's eyes, hating the fact that I still have not managed to conquer my cowardice. I am supposed to be the leader and there isn't a more timorous Marine in the entire chow hall. It's petulant to resent one's father for inherited emotions but, my *God*, it's a difficult emotion to fight.

I jog over to the colonel's office, a transformed lounge that doubles as a private boxing area because he never travels without his precious equipment. I can hear the blows on the heavy bag before I turn the corner, my heart hammering away, and run right into Ms. Thayer-Ash. I try to catch her fall and my left hand lands squarely on a breast, as alien as, well, as an alien. She sprawls back and says, "Watch it! Jesus, what is it with this place!"

I reach down but she brushes away my hand and staggers to her feet.

"Oh! Excuse me, ma'am."

She doesn't recognize me without the camouflage paint

and she just pushes past me without a second glance. But I notice her, all right: coffee eyes, black hair encircling a strong, tanned face. My eyes follow her all the way out of the hangar, one pair of the thousand. I take a moment to gather myself and rap three times on the hatch. "Lieutenant Kelly reporting as ordered, sir!"

"Enter!" Bison Breath bellows like a foghorn. Marine Corps manners are slightly overdone.

I round the bend and enter his office; Bison Breath is pounding the heavy bag while Big Duke pushes forward against his punches, rocked back by each one more than I would have expected. *Thump! Thump!* The colonel is snorting with each punch, exhaling loudly, working himself into a lather, sweat flying off him like a sprinkler. The hooch smells like a locker room.

Darren Phillips is standing in the corner, leaning against the bulkhead with his big arms crossed. He's wearing khaki outback pants, iron-pressed with razor-sharp creases, desert combat boots that have been brushed free of dirt, and a white polo shirt with the eagle, globe, and anchor on it. The shirt is a size too small—one of his old tricks—and he looks like David Banner in mid-metamorphosis, pectoral muscles stretching flat the tiny cotton coils. He uncrosses his arms, smiles, and walks over with his arm extended. I shake his hand and he winks, still wearing the calm mask of confidence he has displayed for the eight years I have known him. My comfort level soars. I haven't seen him since the marathon.

"How you been, Kelly?" Darren has a deep voice that is both powerful and practiced; I used to hear him rehearse his speeches to his platoon in the bathroom when we lived together in San Clemente.

"Never better," I manage, trying to mimic him.

"Like I told Colonel Capiletti, here, I apologize for that

cluster on the beach. I tried to tell them, but . . . you know the press."

"Kelly," snorts Bison Breath heavily, in between punches, rocking his head and shoulders. "I understand"—*thump! thump!*—"you and"—pant, snort, pant—"Mr. Phillips here were roommates at that art school."

He wants me to correct him so he can say, Oh, that's right, Hahvahd, and everyone can laugh but I just nod. But Darren takes the bait. "Sir, I tried to take art at Harvard but Marine ROTC wouldn't allow me. Too many history requirements and not enough time for electives because of wrestling. Now I fear my softer side will never be discovered, sir."

Darren has no obligation to refer to the colonel as "sir," but he's after something and it is obviously working.

Bison Breath grins and throws a nasty combination into the bag, which nearly puts Big Duke on his back. "Yes, Phillips, but you're developing it now as part of the press corps."

"Don't remind me, sir," Darren says, laughing. The more things change, the more they stay the same. Darren Phillips is the most driven person I have ever met, but he is also a man who believes strongly in respecting authority, following rules, succeeding (and thriving) in bureaucracies simply by outperforming everyone else—and he developed a reputation as a kiss-ass as a result. Of course, he probably doesn't even know that some of our college and Marine Corps *companeros* called him "The Senator"; no one had the guts to tell him.

"I'd forgotten I'd become what I most despised. A reporter who's trying to hide his love for communism." He and Bison Breath laugh heartily.

It is a surreal scene, so much so that I think for a second about screaming and running around naked. But if you think military prison is bad, you should see their asylums. "You summoned me, sir?" I cut them off, impatient.

Bison Breath steps away from the bag and narrows his eyes at me. He grunts, "Ah, Darren, can you excuse us, please? The sergeant major and I have to chat with your former roommate."

Darren says yessir, and slaps me on the shoulder as he walks out as if he's supporting me in an argument that I have not yet had, some secret long since shared with B-Squared. "See you, brother," he whispers.

Bison Breath says, "One second, Kelly." He closes on the bag and attacks it again.

"No problem, sir. Gives me time to finish mine." I drop into the push-up position and begin to bang them out, Hap to his Willy. This is a caricature of Marines, something I would have laughed at five years ago, but I do not feel a stitch of awkwardness.

I watch Darren walk out of the office and all the old ROTC memories are here. ROTC required all midshipmen to don their uniforms twice a week for drills but because protesters burned the Harvard ROTC building in 1968—the administration hasn't welcomed ROTC back to campus since—we bussed down Massachusetts Avenue to drill at a ragged (and anonymous) shantytown on the MIT campus. Before my second drill I was waiting for Darren outside my dorm with my uniform slung over my shoulder, hidden in a garment bag. Military uniforms weren't the rage at Harvard. Darren came marching around the corner in his service dress blues, head and shoulders back, pristine white cover pulled down snug on his bald head, strutting. "Where's your uniform?"

"Didn't have time to throw it on," I said.

"Uh-huh." He glanced at his watch. "We have time. It's

only 1426. You double-time up to your hooch and I'll hold the bus." Darren had a command for the military vernacular before we were even taught it. I met his eyes and didn't have the courage to argue. As I walked away I heard him yell, "Pride, Kelly. Look it up when you're in your room." Wound a bit tight, are we?

Sprinting to catch the bus ten minutes later, we passed a woman on Massachusetts Avenue who screamed, "Go home, baby killers!"

I turned and gave her the finger, and when I stepped onto the bus, laughing, Darren snatched my arm and pinned it effortlessly to my side. "Don't disrespect the uniform like that. Ever. You want to dignify something like that with a response . . . do it on your own time."

Bison Breath finishes in a fury—clearly this man needs to learn the art of nightly self-help—and sticks out his gloves for Big Duke to untie. "Terrific young man. Shame the Corps lost him. I assume you know he's applying for reinstatement in the Corps?"

So that's it. I hop to my feet and bring my arms down and frozen, standing at attention. "Nosir." The Marine rank structure generally limits the subordinate's ability to speak freely, made worse by the fact that I am communicating with a man who was known as Missing Link before he snatched the Vader name.

"I told him that if he's as physically fit as he says—and he gives the battalion a favorable television report here, of course—I'll throw all my weight behind his reinstatement. He's made a remarkable recovery, what with being shot by that lucky Iraqi.

"Anyway, Phillips said he'd look out for us and make sure we get the . . . *right kind* of report. Like we used to get in the old Corps. He's proposing that he be allowed to move around the battalion freely. I've granted permission because, first, we could use some . . . *good press,* and second, we owe him. You especially, Kelly."

I know what's coming now and relief washes through me. It's not the first time Darren Phillips has rescued me, but it is the most important.

The colonel nods at Big Duke and points at a water bottle on his desk. Big Duke grabs it and squirts it into the Bison's mouth until a glove comes up again. Bison Breath pants for a second and continues. "I think Phillips argued pretty vehemently against his colleagues at CNN who wanted to pursue this. One woman in particular, a woman named Thayer-Ash. Consider the matter of last night closed, Kelly. I'm not happy with your personal performance, but your Marines did well. That Somali kid left them no choice. And you'll be happy to hear that NBC has taken full responsibility for having armed guards down there—without press ID cards—and letting them wander off. They've issued a formal apology to the boy's family, the Corps, and Armstrong himself. Phillips said it would look even worse if they tried to blame us. Especially after the fiasco with all the lights on the beach. They're—the media, I mean—catching *hell* back home for lighting you up.

"Anyway, the last thing this battalion needed was some form of . . . *controversy* as we get started here. You never know what the press is going to drum up."

"Nosir, you do not."

The colonel grunts. "Saw you out running with your platoon. Sergeant Major Duncan and I have been talking. Thinking of organizing a boxing smoker once things get settled here . . . maybe invite some cameras. Do some real combat preparation for a change instead of *jogging.* What do you think?"

"Sounds good, sir."

"Does it? Good. Can't have officers fighting the enlisted, though, so we'll have to partner up. How much do you weigh?" He has slipped his gloves off now and is unwrapping the tape job on his hands, the Ace bandages dark with sweat and stitched with hairs. The heat must have the colonel shedding.

"One-ninety, sir."

"Well, well. Looks like you'll be matched with me. I was worried because you look skinnier."

"Haven't got a gut yet, no, sir."

It was meant in jest but he ponders it for a second. "I saw some of your Marines didn't have shirts on during your little run."

"Yessir. I mean, no, sir, they did not." His rank is intimidating enough, but the sheer size of him makes me even more nervous.

"Am I to assume, then, that you missed my speech to the battalion?"

When we set up in the airport, the colonel gave an extensive speech about our mission. The priority after force protection? Appearance. Every Marine is to wear the same uniform—heavy flak jackets and helmets, sleeves rolled down at all times, heat be damned—and act, at all times, as if a CNN camera is pointed at him. The colonel is beside himself with paranoia that one of his own will do something dumb on TV. He believes his career may depend on it and, sadly, he's probably right.

"No, sir. I heard it. I just didn't realize that it applied to workouts as well. It won't happen again." I am left wondering whether shorts and T-shirts are acceptable or if we have to run in our full gear.

"Gosh *darned* right, it won't. And another thing. I don't know what to make of this aversion your generation has to body hair. What do most of those Marines do, shave their chests and legs? They look like little Barbie dolls . . . little Peter Pans."

Sergeant Jesus Montoya and his elaborate shaving ritual invade my thoughts; in field operations he humps a fresh razor and a bar of soap in his pack so he can shave his chest and arms to "feel smooth." In fact, most of my Marines shave their chests and legs like narcissistic bodybuilders— except for Armstrong, who likes to show off his hairy chest and point to his five o'clock shadow as signs of testosterone overload.

Bison Breath has worked himself into a foamy froth and all of the black hairs are pressed flush to his soaked tank top. It's pretty gross, but in a world bereft of women you get used to sights like these . . . and much worse.

"Not everyone has the natural complement with which you have been blessed, sir," I say.

Big Duke laughs sharply and the colonel waits a moment, looks at him, then joins in. "All right, all right, I had that coming. Nothing wrong with manliness, I say." He pauses, grasping the hairs on his chest absentmindedly, and the laughter fades quickly.

It is an awkward moment, and when I realize he isn't going to dismiss me, I say, "Saw you on TV yesterday, sir." CNN videotapes are flown in the day after stateside broadcasts and all the Marines in the camp gathered this afternoon in hopes of glimpsing themselves. The Gunny and I dominated the early images. The colonel got some face time, too, but he was supporting cast.

"Saw you too, Kelly. All over the place . . . you and Gunny Ricketts. *Newsweek* may even put you on the cover, I'm told." He shakes his head and I misread his mood.

"Don't hate me because I'm beautiful, sir."

"I don't *hate* you, Lieutenant Kelly." The reference is lost on him, somehow, and he is suddenly angry. "But frankly, I think you hammed it up a bit, reviewing the tapes. You were showing off and you got reckless. Just like your old battalion commander, Colonel McTavish, warned me you might. We've got no room for hip-shooting in the gun club. Big Duke here thinks you made the right choice, distracting the press, but I'm not so sure."

"Sir, I—"

"Listen, Kelly," he interrupts. "No more slipups. Just do your gosh-*darned* job. Let me take care of the interviews." Big Duke rocks forward a bit and grunts. The colonel looks at him and nods. "But, as Sergeant Major Duncan here says, I can't punish your whole platoon just because I think you're a glory hound. Right?"

"Nosir," I say seriously.

"Right. Okay. We're sending your platoon out to replace an infantry platoon at an FDC tomorrow." FDC stands for food distribution site. Don't ask.

"Simple mission. Remember, Kelly, full uniform the entire time, and no swearing. Got that? NO SWEARING . . . you never know when a gosh-*darned* camera's going to be present."

"Wilco, sir. Is that all?"

B-Squared takes off his shirt, walks over to the window, wrings it out, and I hear the rain gutter splatter on the crispy dirt; amazing, the power of cotton. He flops the rag halfway outside, then walks toward me, caressing his massive chest. He moves in across the threshhold of personal space for some close talking and I try not to flinch, holding my breath in preparation for the mouse rot. "Sergeant Major has something else for you. I'm going to go shower up. I'll inspect your lines at 1800." He nods at Big Duke and a salty droplet of sweat hits my forearm; thankfully, Doc has a chemical attack kit in our foxhole.

"Aye, aye, sir."

When the shower comes on, Big Duke says, "The colonel and I think Armstrong ought to be written up for an award. He deserves it and the colonel thinks it'll be good for the battalion, as smooth as this thing is going. We're well ahead of schedule in this operation. Maybe another Bronze Star?"

This is the last thing Armstrong needs. "He's got one already, Big Duke."

"And?"

"Do I have a choice, Big Duke?"

"Nosir, not unless you want to invite some more questions from the colonel."

"Wilco."

Big Duke claps me on the back and smiles. "Tough position you were in last night, sir. Believe it or not, the colonel thinks you handled it pretty well. But he looks at you and doesn't see a lieutenant who needs praise. He's just keeping you honest."

Keeping me honest. I nod my understanding and head out to give the platoon the good news. As for Armstrong, I think I'll wait until I talk with Gunny before I promise him another medal.

––––––––––

At sunset a cool breeze slides across the beach, giving the country a salty and pleasant smell of tropical plants, faintly Bahamian. The Indian is rippled and when it first nibbles on the sun it begins to sparkle as brightly as the sand. White frigate birds spiral down toward the ocean in formation and buzz-bomb the surface. The horizon erupts when the sun disappears, a floating ocean of red that looks like a thermonuclear backdrop. I catch myself—there is a surreality waiting behind me that requires undivided attention—and walk the defensive lines just before dark to make sure the team leaders have placed in their weapons according to the defensive plan. They have. I creep over to my hole and hear some low conversation . . . which is strange because I haven't given Doc permission to invite a third-bed party into our sleep hole.

I hop into the lair. "What's up, Doc?"

Three small beasts rip out past me and I am so startled that I reach for my rifle and slap it out in front, thumb finding the safety and butt finding the crook of my shoulder.

"Oh! Jesus, sir, you scared me," whispers Doc. "Scared them, too." He points at three tiny Somalis beating a hasty retreat to the hole in the wall.

I find the NVGs in my pack and put them on. "Kids?"

"Yessir. They came right up to me. They speak English pretty good."

It does not surprise me that the kids have found Doc; the men say that he is a "kid magnet" and they're right— while the rest of the platoon is busy hooking itself up to an alcohol IV in some Singapore bar, Doc is volunteering at the local orphanage. Children like him, I think, because they can sense fraud, evil, and lies better than most adults and Doc is none of these things, he is genuine and untainted—which also explains why the kids ran when they saw me coming.

"Yeah, well, don't encourage them. I don't want them sneaking around here at night. Might steal something." It occurs to me that the kids might be reporting back to the Gangbangers—measuring the distance to the wall, sketching the defense, figuring out where the machine guns are—but I dismiss that when one of the kids comes walking up again.

He has an American T-shirt on and when he gets close enough I see a picture of the Marine Corps bulldog. Below the dog in the Smokey the Bear hat it reads: "Bodies Heal, Chicks Dig Scars, Pain Is Temporary, Glory Is Forever! *Marines!*"

"Now . . . damnit, Doc. How'd he get that shirt?"

"I . . . well it wasn't me, sir. 'Sides, teaches a bad lesson to the kids, the message, I mean. Some pain hurts a long time." Yes, Doc, you are right about that one.

"Come sunup, you tell the men that I don't want any more gifts given. It ain't Christmas, yet. Understand?"

"Yes. I'll tell them, sir. It's just . . . while we were digging the holes . . . some of the kids were helping and talking away, sir. You shoulda seen 'em, how cute they were."

"Please, Doc. Spare me."

The kid walks up and squats by the hole. "T-shirt," he says.

"See what I'm talking about, Doc? Damnit."

I turn to the kid. He has a short but wild Afro and definitely isn't starving. He's dressed in polyester bell-bottom pants and flip-flops. He's chewing on some kind of stick. "No. You have a T-shirt. You go. Go."

"T-shirt," he says again. Behind him, more boys poke their heads through the wall. Another one crawls through and walks over casually, his flip-flops smacking on the dirt. We've got our own version of the Maginot Line, here. His shirt reads: "There Are Two Types of People, *Marines,* and Those That Wish They Were." Well, even if the men have gotten these kids entirely too comfortable with us, at least we're waging one hell of a propaganda war. I wonder what their older brothers think. "T-shirt. Pleeese. T-shirt," the boy says again.

"Tomorrow. *Demain.* Tomorrow. Now go. Go."

"'Morrow T-shirt. Okay?"

"Hi, sir!" whispers the Gunny, who has crept over to my hole and is on a knee next to me. He holds up a T-shirt with a picture of the American flag wrapped around the Marine Corps flag. Below it, the caption reads: "These Colors Never Run." He smiles, genuinely relieved, and says, "Heard my little brothers were back. Never got to get 'em the T-shirt I promised! Okay. Who didn't get one?"

"Guns. Tonight's not Secret Santa night—" A deep pop like a big truck backfiring, maybe a mile away, interrupts me. *Choom!*

The three boys scream something that sounds like "Muhammad" and sprint toward the hole, dive through, rolling back to their hometown, Gunny with his hand up and asking for quiet, unslinging his rifle.

"What? I thought—"

"Shhh, sir. Listen."

I cock my head, listening. In the distance . . . *Choom!* . . . more hollow than thunder, abrupt . . . and again, *Choom!* "What the fu—"

"Mortar, sir!" Gunny says. He leaps into my hole and screams, "INCOMING! INCOMING!" It is a foreign tongue to most of us, and I hear one of the Marines in Echo Company tell him to pipe down. "Incoming mortar rounds!" he screams. *"Fire in the hole!"*

The battalion seems to understand all at once that he is not crying wolf and Gunny's words are echoed by most of the Marines on watch. *"Take cover,"* some are yelling. Take cover! The battalion disappears into its holes and the only audible sound prior to the impacts are the screamed warnings and the snaps of chin straps.

With a thirty-second flight time, we have a chance to chat a bit as the 82-millimeter mortar rounds float down toward us. I pull my helmet over my brow and tuck my legs in tight to my stomach. Gunny grabs the two ALICE packs and drags them into the hole, on top of us. He squiggles tight and I feel him breathing right next to me, spooning, an arm snaked over my back. Doc has somehow managed to wriggle his way under both of us. "What're the odds they land in our hole, you figure, sir?" Gunny whispers.

"Zip," I say. "Tell you what. I'll bet you my life savings neither one of us dies." I'm surprised at how easily the words flow considering that I am fighting for control of my bladder.

"What odds will you give me?"

"Million shillings to your one."

"Done," he says.

The first round lands well behind us, somewhere on the tarmac behind the hangar. *Kaa-whump!* It's a thunderous explosion and though I'm prepared for it, I can't help but shake for a second, electrified, nostrils flaring as I struggle to shove as much air as I can into my heaving lungs. The shock wave passes through us the same way the bass shakes you when you enter a technotronic nightclub. The ground rocks and trembles for a moment before it resets, dust and pebbles plinking around us.

"You got that shilling on you, Guns?" I manage.

Kaa-whump! Whump! The other two rounds explode harmlessly five hundred meters to our left, south of the airport, moving away from us like a passing thunderstorm. "Must not have set the base plate properly," says Gunny. "Bounced right after the first round, the dumb fucks. I'm good for it, sir."

Beneath me, I can feel Doc trembling. Gunny stands up and screams, "Guess the welcome wagon just pulled up, Devildogs!"

The entire battalion answers him with a war cry, like a pack of wolves howling.

– 9 –

10 DECEMBER 1992

I'm out of order? You're out of order!
This whole trial's out of order!

I'm awake when the restless glow of the false dawn turns the trees from black to gray to green. The color builds quickly and steadily, filling out the trees I can see above the Swiss cheese wall—lush, robust, and surprisingly alive, waving back and forth with the onshore breeze that's arrived with the sun. I notice a kid's face peeking out from one of the holes in the wall and it gives me a start. I recoil and my canteen cup goes spinning and clanking on top of Doc.

"Time to do some good, Doc. Wake up."

"Roger, sir. You didn't have to dump coffee on me."

"Sorry," I say lamely. "I'm a klutz. It's just bug juice, though."

I wave at the little girl and she smiles and returns the salute before her head disappears, leaving her face behind in my memory. I take a few minutes to think about her life and decide that the death of Said Lahti is both justified and not worth another moment of my time—we're here to stop one of the most brutal man-made famines in history and Lahti was one of the dregs. And if he wasn't a dreg, then he was a stupid, as Red would put it.

The platoon stretches itself awake and I hear the sharp whispers of the three team leaders giving instructions. Thirty minutes later I hop into a Hummer with Armstrong's team and we race off to FDC 3, on the western outskirts of Mogadishu, where we'll link up with the Red Cross and establish a protected food point. Gunny and the other two teams trail us in a five-ton truck lined with sandbags, weapons pointing in every direction, a giant porcupine of steel. The Marines in my Hummer are buzzing with excitement but I'm not as loose—scenarios are flipping through my mind and I'm rehearsing my responses, checking them against the plastic ROE card in my lap. Behind me, Armstrong's telling a joke and everyone is laughing.

"Then this other kid in my class says, 'I have a lesson. I was driving to deliver our eggs to the grocery store and I dropped the basket and they all broke.' So my teacher says, 'What's the lesson?' And the kid says, 'Don't put all your eggs in one basket.'"

I hear Armstrong pause so he can spit some tobacco before he finishes. "Anyways, I stand up and say, 'I have a lesson.' The teacher finally calls on me so I say, 'My mother was flying C-130s during the last year of 'Nam and she got shot down. All she had with her as she floated down into hostile territory was a bottle of Jack Daniel's and a Ka-Bar knife. So she guzzled the Jack and when she hit the deck, she smashed it over her knee so she'd have two weapons. Then she cut the hell out of thirty North Viets with the Ka-Bar and slashed her way clear across to Laos with her broken bottle leading the way, parting flesh from bone as she plowed through, leaving men, women, and children in her wake.'

"'My God!' said my teacher. 'What's the lesson, Jake?' I says to her, 'The lesson is, ma'am,' I says, 'is you don't piss off my mom when she's drunk!'"

An officer can't really shoot the good shit with his men, so much of one's interaction comes from eavesdropping. I chuckle and when the laughter dies I hear Johnson say, "Wish we didn't have to wear these flak jackets, Stretch. Ain't worn one of these since I visited Compton last."

Lance Corporal Terrel Johnson, Armstrong's partner in crime and the crown prince of Hong Kong, is from the Valley but he has the platoon convinced he is living the cliché. To reinforce this he is prone to pop off or throw a punch when his peers are watching. Take the Hong Kong brawl: Armstrong mouths off to seven British military police officers in a pub and when one of them spits back— I think he called Armstrong a "wanker"—Johnson wades in to defend his team leader's honor, flattens an Anglo nose, and later tells me he couldn't stand by while his "Tee El was being disrespected." This is before he asks me to define "wanker" and before he loses a rank stripe and half a month's pay. Truth be told, though, Johnson respects authority and he never fully strays in my presence or Gunny's. He won't admit to the pack that he's a lifer, but he's a career Marine.

"This required gear's awful heavy," Johnson continues. "Hate these helmets, too." The platoon isn't used to wearing all the cumbersome mandatory gear; being silent types they're willing to sacrifice body armor for speed and we patrol at night in soft covers and soft uniforms. Our flak jackets don't stop bullets, and the Bangers don't have artillery to speak of, so Johnson has a point.

"Part of the image," says Armstrong. "Uniformity. All Marines have to look the same. Much more intimidating, too. Here, see how much bigger I look? Look at me, I look like a fucking monster robot. Bad asses walkin' the earth, right?" I hear some open palms slap behind me. "Wait'll they get a load o' us!" Armstrong does not toe the party line, so it is clear he actually likes himself bulked up.

Mogadishu is a maze of narrow streets that crisscross in a jagged spiderweb of impossible navigation. The streets are so narrow that the driver has to keep careful watch lest the Hummer plow into a small house or a stoop filled with inquisitive Somalis. They've come out to greet the engines, little boys up front, backed by their sisters and flanked by their mothers, few older men in sight, and most of them seem to be . . . *laughing.*

Somalia is much greener than I imagined; small trees line the road and larger ones stretch out over the major intersections, waving a windblown greeting. The houses are crammed side by side all the way down the roads, but many of them have courtyards and most of them are actually quaint. The open country may not smell like death, but approaching the heart of Mogadishu it is different. Every other block, we pass small fire pits in which the Somalis burn trash and even human waste, and the mix of pungent smells is washing through the Hummer too quickly to discern but too slowly to ignore. I shudder and pinch my nose.

I am not prone to claustrophobia but I am responsible for the welfare of my men and I am immediately paranoid; I see phantom AK-47s in the clay houses and imagine the mass of people crushing ever closer, all of them shouting and pointing now, waiting to ambush their rescuers. I notice that most of the walls are pockmarked with bullet holes, evidence of a firefight ten or a hundred or a thousand days old. This is a beautiful country that is at the same time wild and full of violent promise.

Somalia's plunge into chaos was rapid. More precisely, its rest from war was brief. It is a country ruled by several violent clans. So it is not governed at all, except for the occasional bullet or machete swipe.

Under the rule of Siad Barre, Somalia received over $100 million in U.S. aid. When President Bush severed the relationship, theft of multinational food aid quickly replaced foreign aid as the salient industry, and circular reasoning ensured that some people starved, so food aid was mandated, so clans stole from each other to pay for bullets so they could steal more food, so more people starved.

Rival clans preyed on the unrest, and when Barre was overthrown, civilians on all sides were murdered because of fraternal bloodlines as the clans fought for power.

Hunger gave rise to entrepreneurship. Private male bandits roamed the land, some working for clans, others working as independent contractors, everyone hunting for food or bullets. On one occasion a young gunman stalked a woman toting a twenty-five-pound bag of rice on her head and, from four hundred meters, shot her dead with his AK-47. This was rare for only two reasons: Four hundred meters is the maximum effective range on a point target for the AK—the Gangbanger was a good shot and cheered his kill—and when he ran over to retrieve his bounty he recognized the gut-shot woman. It was his wife.

The Somalis are a warrior people.

By last September fully half of Somalia's nine million people were severely malnourished or had related diseases.

One and a half million people were in danger of immediate starvation because the food shipments were being looted by clans. Grain shipments were held hostage and fed to the Gangbangers, not the children. Aid workers were extorted daily by all the warring sides. Youths with mortars and antiaircraft guns controlled the airport and were robbing relief flights.

CNN took notice, and after Clinton defeated Bush it became a story of the day. Today there are 2,500 reporters in Mogadishu, up from *nine* in August. President Bush and his despondent staffers saw the terrible pictures of the starving and did what was right: They gave an order to the Pentagon, which alerted our amphibious task force.

The main Gangbanger, Muhammad Aidid, says he controls thirty thousand troops. The other clans have approximately the same numbers. We have about fifteen hundred combat Marines here. It's not a fair fight. Gunny alone could take out half of them.

The estimates of those dying daily from starvation vary from between one thousand and five thousand. Grain is stacked right now in the warehouses of the Mogadishu harbor, a klick up the beach from where I am driving, but the gangs are preventing the food from reaching the starving. The Red Cross is down to giving the lucky ones who stagger in from the wasteland just quarter rations.

I don't mean to sound too righteous, though; what's really important to us is that there are bona-fide bad guys who need to be "learned," as Sergeant Armstrong says. The starving women and children give us reason and good quotes— we all like to play the knight in armor—but we don't need this much motivation to kill. Just orders. We're happy to save lives, but our true function is erasing them.

For a brief time the Marine Corps experimented with

the recruiting slogan "Nobody likes to fight, but somebody has to know how." It was soon dropped. Marines like to fight.

———

I look out the windshield of the Hummer in time to see the camel on its haunches. "Jesus!" says the driver. "They're going to kill it!"

He slows the Hummer and we both stare. Next to the road a man in a polyester disco suit lifts a machete high above his head—my grandfather raising the hammer to ring the bell at the circus—and brings it down swiftly, the neck becoming bright red. The camel bellows and rolls on its side, and the machete comes down again and again, the Hummer rolling past as if in slow motion.

"Just like *Apocalypse Now*," I say.

"That's a dumb-ass thing to do now that we're here. He'll be getting fed soon enough. Maybe that Skinny was a Banger who can't rob for food anymore, now that we're here," Armstrong says. He's poking his head out up front. Armstrong wears his hair in a jagged flattop that juts out from his head like the blackened bow of a battleship, accentuating his long, narrow nose and face. His cheekbones flush when he's thinking to himself because he sucks in his cheeks so that they touch. This facial tic is always followed by a stupid comment. Here it comes . . .

"Too bad machetes ain't against the rules of engagement, right, sir? Then we could have brought him in, or at least taught him a lesson. I'm fixin' to teach that old boy a lesson he won't soon forget."

I want to say, Like the lesson you taught Said Lahti, but that would be awkward considering I'm supposed to write him up for a medal. I turn around to face him and he has his Oakley blades on. I can't see his blue eyes for the black.

His lower lip is crammed full of chewing tobacco. "Just get your team ready. I'll make liaison with the Red Cross rep and get set in. By the book."

"Yessir," he says slowly and just sits there. "Check that chick out, the one over there, walking." He extends one of his long arms and is actually able to put his hand clear of the window. "Put a few pounds on her and I'd fuck her. What about you, sir?"

I crane my head around again and stare at him; the genesis of violence is the spoken word. He contemplates me for a moment, then snakes his head back.

———

I see the FDC in the distance because of the crowd, a huge line of women and children snaking around a building. An aid worker guides us through the foot traffic and in through the concertina wire gate of the FDC. The compound is the size of half a football field, buttressed by two roads that lead into Mogadishu proper. There are several Red Cross trucks filled with bags of grain and barrels of water, and a series of long tables; essentially an outdoor soup kitchen encircled by concertina wire and sandbags, backed up against a small building. A miniature fortress to defend the food. The Somalis are standing patiently in line as if they are waiting to gain entrance to an exclusive nightclub.

I hop out and sling my weapon, then stop dead in my tracks. "Oh my Lord," says Johnson behind me.

Gunny whispers, "Oh, man. This ain't right."

A woman from the Red Cross walks up to me and laughs. "Well. You're the second group of Marines in two days with those looks on your faces. I thought you guys were supposed to be tough."

I glance at her but do not register anything but her Irish

accent, then turn back to face the starving. Television does famine far too much justice. These are real people and it is an overwhelming sight. It is otherworldly, the depth of their suffering. I struggle against the urge to bend over and catch my breath. Gunny exhales loudly next to me and wipes his face. "Sweet Jesus. Let's get to work."

A tiny kid—as small as a baby but perhaps three years old—is lying in the dust on his back, shirtless, his little belly sagging up and down, some form of white drool or vomit staining the side of his face, flies all over him. A woman is squatting barefoot in the dirt, waving her hands over the baby's face. She has no breasts and from here she resembles a praying mantis, her ribs and breastbone so nearly visible that I expect her skin to split before my eyes. There seems to be a sea of overgrown heads rolling precipitously on bones, white teeth everywhere, also oversize, jutting nearly horizontally out of their heads. Against the wall a woman is babbling at me through tears, pointing at a naked child lying in the fetal position, immobile except for the movement of his chest and eyes. Even though it is black, his skin is fragile and nearly translucent in the sun. Eventually the woman stops pointing when it's clear we are just statues, and she begins to gently stroke his head, still crying.

"They . . . I didn't think they'd look so sick," I say. "Why are . . . the stomachs are more bloated than I thought. I didn't think Somalis had that."

"Mostly the children. They have a protein deficiency that causes their stomachs to swell out like balloons," she says.

"Yes. Yes, I saw that on TV, but this is different." I take it in for another moment, expecting to be interrupted, but she lets me stare. The Somalis are in constant motion, swatting flies away from themselves and their babies. I get itchy and irritated just watching. The black dots rise quickly with each swipe, then descend onto their faces again. I feel my throat begin to close and realize that I have not cried since my last beating by the Montgomery brothers. I'll be damned if I'm going to do it here, in front of the men. I'm sure all of us are thinking the same thing, my Marines in a line staring at the Somalis, silent observers of an accident in progress, the Somalis staring right back, trying to engage us in a conversation that our ears do not acknowledge. The most heartbreaking thing of all: Some of the Somalis are smiling and waving, so full of spirit that I wonder how those lifeless bodies can support it.

Finally I look at her and say, "I'm Lieutenant Gavin Kelly. I've got twenty Marines with me. How can we help?"

"Maureen O'Donnell. You guys have done wonders in this country already, just being here. Getting the food out to the needy. I really need four things. First, the most important, guard the people and the food. I don't expect the clans will give us trouble but Somalia is far too unpredictable for promises. Second, I'll need a detail to set up the food lines and distribute it. They get their rations and then exit the compound. The Somalis do *not* eat in here unless they are sick. It'll get too crowded, chaotic. Third, do you have a medical staff?"

"We have a Navy corpsman, yes."

"Good. I'll have him work with our doctor. Finally, I'll need a few of your men for burial detail. We were running behind on the burials the last few days . . . in anticipation of your arrival the clans were raiding everything. There are bodies outside the compound, around the corner. About fifty, I think."

"*Fifty?*"

"Lieutenant Kelly, I've buried over a thousand people since I've been here." She lets it sink in, then continues,

"We allow fifty Somalis within the compound at any time. They come in, grab a ration, then leave so someone else can enter."

"Any trouble with the warlords?"

"Now, or then?" she asks.

"You tell me."

She pauses for a moment and bites her lip. "Well, they're murderous, thieving bastards, I'll tell you that. I was in one of the warehouses by the harbor with Jimmy Henry, negotiating for release of some of the grain, when Hassan Farah—he's the one who runs these streets for Aidid—interrupted the discussion, put a pistol to Jimmy's head, and killed him. Killed him because he said that he was *rude,* didn't respect him. It was just awful. So, to answer your question, no. I haven't seen them in a few days. They'll be back, though, and I recommend you just steer clear. That's the best solution. Not violence."

I ignore the comment. It is, in fact, the promise of violence that has kept them away.

"This country seems awfully green for a famine," I say.

"What no one seems to understand is that this is a manmade famine. Somalia is able to sustain itself, but the warlords just steal all the food so the farmers stopped growing it. Some farmers were killed, too, so now the land sits here, idle."

"Well, if we can get rid of these warlords for them, then people can farm again. If we were allowed to actually fight them, I mean."

O'Donnell scowls and shakes her head as if she is an impatient teacher. "That's pretty naive. I'm sorry to be so blunt, Lieutenant, but you wouldn't want to fight them anyhow. If you did, it would be just like Vietnam. Last forever. They're very, very tough people. Hassan Farah and his like have been fighting since they were five. *Five years old.*

They are capable of a violence that you and I cannot comprehend."

"I can."

"That's not true," she says, almost sweetly, an older sister now. "You have no idea what suffering is."

"I'm not talking about suffering," I say. "I'm talking about a language that the warlords understand, a language in which Marines are fluent. They're punks. The way to communicate with them is through force. As you said, they've been doing this for years. *So have we.*"

She looks at me almost sadly and smiles the way my mom did when Red began to drone on about his wars, as if she is wondering why there are people like me and mine on this earth. "You haven't been here long enough to understand. The clans will just wait you out. You won't have the stomach for it and you'll pack your bags and leave. Then the famine will 'resume its march,' to use your term. Please remember that you've landed in the midst of a civil war. You can't possibly outlast it. Now, after you brief your men, meet me over at that hut. I have something to show you."

I brief the Gunny. I move toward the center of the FDC and am quickly surrounded by a screaming platoon of Somali children. "Water!" some of them are squealing. "Water! Candy!" I unsnap a canteen and make the mistake of handing it to a bloated, shirtless boy with humongous teeth and wild hair, expecting he will share it. Instead, he tucks his head like a fullback and tries to barrel through the crowd. Two or three kids catch him before he runs the gauntlet and they beat and slap him, stomping on his arm now, angrier and angrier, the happy mood of the crowd slipping away as quickly as the water is draining into the parched dirt. I separate the kids, reach down, and snatch up the empty canteen.

Behind the kids I see a shirtless, starving woman pushing a shy girl toward me who's sucking her thumb and shaking her head no. The woman slaps her behind and the girl nods and gimps over to join my fan club, dressed only in an oversize yellow blouse I assume is her mother's; half of her bare right foot is missing and she is forced to do a deep knee bend to gain traction every other step . . . limp, teeter, step . . . limp, teeter. When she gets to the crowd, she reaches up to me and I snatch a wadded piece of paper from her hand and open up the note. It reads:

HELP MEE.

My heart breaks. I mean it. Then, right after the sadness, a deep feeling of shame comes rushing up—all the petty complaints of my life in full, in-my-face context now—and I turn away from them and point across the courtyard. Doc has set up an aid station and the Somalis somehow, right off the bat, recognize him as a corpsman. Women begin rushing over to him, cradling their infants and dragging their children. I watch in horror as Doc works on a baby. I am not sure what he's doing because I am too far away to see precisely what treatment he's attempting and I am too afraid to move up. But I can see that he is crying, wiping the tears away with his rubber gloves, talking to the woman and shaking his head, trying to hug her.

I make my way across the FDC, gently pushing the kids away, and enter the small hut. Maureen O'Donnell looks up from changing a diaper and whispers, "This is a children's shelter I set up a month ago to protect the orphaned. I haven't been able to get here for three days." She parts the curtains and I put my hand to my mouth;

children are strewn all across the dirt floor in varying poses of agony. The stench is thick and I waver, but I cannot pinpoint it. A few of the kids are crying. Most are lying in the dirt, unmoving, just breathing slowly. Many are babies and one of them is lying in its own filth. O'Donnell grabs it—I can't tell if it is male or female—and says, "Help me, Lieutenant."

I walk over and stand there dumbly, the thunderstruck cliché of a man who's afraid of handling a baby. "What do you—"

"Not this one! Start checking the other kids. We need to get some nutrients into them. I want you to check every one of them for a pulse. My coworker has some nutritional fluids coming in IVs. No hard foods." She rushes out into the light with the baby. When the curtain swings closed, I'm in the dark again. Alone.

I wish I had brought rubber gloves, then feel guilty because of the thought. The kids are obviously immobile—the ambulatory among them rushed outside the moment they heard the trucks—but I cannot move either combat boot, not for the life of me. Not for the life of *them*. There are about ten children. It is quiet. A few of them are crying, but it is *quiet* . . . the commotion outside dampened by the walls, my heartbeat blasting up out of my throat and slamming back and forth among the walls.

One kid in the corner is lying on his back, his head twisted toward me, cheek in the dirt, staring at me. I nudge him by his little shoulder and he doesn't respond. I put my hand next to his mouth and feel nothing . . . but he is so small that I may be missing the tiny exhalations. I look around but the Red Cross isn't back yet. I stand up and back away, he's still watching me; I take my helmet off, wipe the sweat from my face, put my helmet on, peer out the curtains, say, "Please, God," walk over, and kneel down again. Please help him. *Help me get through this.* No, that's selfish.

I put my hand gently on his belly but I am not delicate enough and my hand nearly covers his entire torso anyway so I jerk it back. I slide a finger—my pinkie—up his neck and wait for my hand to stop shaking. It does when I apply enough pressure, but I feel no pulse. Some drops of water splash on his belly and trickle down across his little rib cage, disappearing behind his back. Probably just sweat from the tip of my nose, nothing to think too deeply about . . . even though my nose is dry when I wipe it. This child is wasted.

"What are you doing, Lieutenant?"

I turn around and can make out Maureen O'Donnell from behind the cloudy film.

"I just don't know . . . what to *do*," I whisper.

She comes over, looks at the boy, and pats me on the shoulder, her touch dulled out by the flak jacket. Everything dull and buzzing. "Do you mind taking him outside? That burial site is being dug behind the last building, over that way." She hands me a big cotton sheet. "Joseph and I will finish up in here. You just go look after your men after you take him over. Go on. And use the sheet; Muslims wrap their dead."

I spread out the sheet next to the boy and roll him as gently as I can with my combat boot. He flops over onto his stomach and I kneel down again and feel his neck, just to be sure. Then I put my hand on his back and it just sits there. I pull the four corners of the sheet together and lift him off the ground.

I'm carrying the bundle out the door when O'Donnell says, "Don't take it hard, Lieutenant Kelly. We've saved a lot of them today. You should be proud."

I carry the sack through the barbed-wire gate of the

FDC and over to the graveyard where two Red Cross workers are digging with a few of my Marines. I put the sack
down next to one of the corpses. A strong, hot gust of wind
blows across my face and several sheets open up, exposing
the dead children. I hesitate, then fold them back neatly
over the bodies, careful to keep my hands on the cotton
and away from the flesh. Johnson is on the dig but he stops
when he sees me and nods, sagging onto the bowed
wooden shaft, his eyes full of tears. I nod back—I know he
wants confirmation of some shared emotion but I have
scant control over my own at the moment—then walk
back over to the relative joy that is the compound.

I pass a boy who is lying in a pool of blood next to the
hut. A Red Cross worker passes me and I hope he takes
notice. I look the other way and shout some fake orders to
a group of Marines too far away to hear, ignoring the dead
boy. When I turn back, the worker is over with the food
line and the child is still there, against the far wall of the
hut. *Shit.* I grab a sheet out of the truck and walk over to
him. It looks like he's been shot in the head, judging from
the blood pool. *Them motherfuckers.*

I roll him over and the front of his pants have been
pulled down. But it is not a him at all; I pull her pants back
up and wonder why she wasn't wearing a dress.

I wipe the blood from her head. She has not been shot.
More likely, she passed out from hunger and hit her head. I
roll the body into the sheet, fold it over her, and cradle her
in my arms. I am not surprised by her weight, but her
shape breaks my heart: She is all bones, thin rods that jab
into my bicep and a skull that rolls heavily above my left
hand. I move it up, grabbing her head now, and walk over
to the grave. No one is talking. I stand awkwardly for a
moment before a Red Cross guy with a shovel says, "Just
set it down there. We're a little behind here."

Johnson, behind him, uses the butt of his rifle to flip a tiny body onto a sheet. He reaches down and grabs a corner, pulling up so that the child rolls into the center. He notices me and, eyes glistening and lids drawn back almost desperately, he shakes his head. Johnson has hazel eyes that are closer to green than brown; in the civilian world his good looks would be considered exotic and edgy, but in the Marines he just gets razzed good naturedly as a freak or as "Vanessa Williams's illegitimate love child."

I set the girl down on the far end of the stack. Johnson passes me with his stork bundle and sets it down next to my feet. The corpse slips down over a few other tiny bodies and falls into the grave, an arm flopping back and a head rolling. Johnson says, "Oh. Oh, no. Oh, damn," and hops in after it. He hides his eyes from me when he sets the body back on the stack, but I hear him whisper, "We're gonna end this, right, sir?"

"Yes."

"Promise?"

There is a heaviness to his voice that makes me feel like I am out of my depth, that he is demanding something I cannot deliver. Or can I? "Yes," I say.

He raises his head proudly and I can see the trails of tears that are already beginning to dry in white streaks of salt. "*Semper Fi*, sir," he says.

"*Semper Fi*, Johnson."

Above me, there are billowing cumulus clouds splashed across the blue, moving quickly. Someone must be enjoying this day.

———

In the FDC an hour later, most Marines are surrounded by their own personal set of young, screaming fans. Mine are poking me occasionally, giggling nearly uncontrollably. "Marine," I say, and stick my thumb in my chest.

"Marine!" they shout. "Marine!"

"You on recruiting duty here or what, sir?" The Gunny has walked up behind me. My silent-killer skills must be getting rusty.

"Sure have the enthusiasm," I say. "Imagine if you were starving. Would you be this upbeat? And look how orderly the others are." I point over to the trucks where a neat line has formed for the bags of food.

"Makes my DI blood warm. Course, this heat alone will do that. Damn, it's hot today." It was near 90 degrees when we woke up and we popped through the century mark by 0900. I check the thermometer on my Casio but it still reads 106, and has for several hours. The heat has melted the gauge and pinned a permanent reading.

Gunny wipes the sweat from his Rushmore forehead and points at the food line. "I put Armstrong and his team on the chow detail. He wanted security detail, so he ain't pleased. Look at him."

I look across the compound and there he is, sulking behind the chow tables, giving orders. His Marines are hard at work ladling rations into paper cups and organic containers that the Somalis have brought with them. Two are holding children in their arms while the mothers fill up their cups. Doc has set up a miniature aid station under a tree and is wrapping a bandage around a girl.

"Doc seems to be in his element," I say, changing the subject.

"Sir, sometimes I think that boy'd be out of his depth in a puddle. So do you want Armstrong on security?"

"No. Let him do his soup-kitchen time."

I look up and Armstrong is staring at me again. I smile

broadly and wave. Armstrong looks around, realizes I am waving to him, scowls, and shuffles out of view behind a truck.

"You should talk with him, sir. He thinks you're still suspicious and it's making him crazy," Gunny says.

I walk over toward the truck, the older Somalis bowing their heads but the young ones shouting and even laughing. Lance Corporal Johnson is chatting with some of the refugees and forming them up for a picture, a child hugging his leg like a koala. For two weeks before we landed in Somalia, Johnson—like many of the black Marines—could not contain his excitement. "Going back to the motherland, sir," he told me one night on the *Denver*. "Africa. See my peeps. Rescue my peeps."

"Your *peeps*? Those marshmallow bunnies?" It's important to the men that I keep up the officer-geek image.

"People, sir. *People.* You best stay outta the ghetto."

"You too, Johnson," I laughed. "You, too."

Johnson smiles at me when I approach and swivels his hip so the kid in his arms is thrust toward me. "Hey, sir. How's it hangin'? Too bad we can't unfuck the States like this, huh? Help out my people here, first, then my brothers and sisters back home. I went hungry for a long time as a kid. We should land the Marines in South Central next." Johnson grew up the poor child of a successful Northrop line manager.

"Save the working-class-hero speech for someone else, Lance Corporal J. I've read your service record book."

"Oh. Forgot about that, sir. Works on the other guys, though." He winks, returns to ladling rations, and begins to talk to a kid. Come to think of it, a few of the younger Somalis speak a halting form of pidgin English. It must be from the years of foreign aid work rather than the military presence, as is the case in the Philippines.

I pass some Marines hefting bags of grain, move in between the two trucks, and find Armstrong cleaning his rifle. "Should have done that before we crossed the line of departure, Sergeant."

He doesn't look up. "Figured you'd find me here, sir."

His big back is hunched over the M-16. I move around to his front and he looks up. Armstrong's blue eyes glow under the roof of his black eyebrows and black hair. He has a chin that juts out suddenly from his face, and though he has shaved this morning, his beard is already popping through. Mine takes a week to gestate—with cultivation.

"Why aren't you with your men?" I ask.

"Figured you'd ask that, sir. You come to baby-sit me again?"

"I'm not baby-sitting. I'm trying to figure out why a team leader in my platoon is shirking his duty, off sulking."

"No. Sir, you're baby-sitting me. Like you think I'm no good. Like you don't trust me after I saved everyone's asses, and yours, too, sir, no disrespect intended, protecting the platoon and you. And now you look at me like a . . . criminal. Like you want to burn me. No disrespect, sir, but where do you get off?" He stands and leans his rifle against the tire well of the truck. He looks me square in the eyes. With all of his equipment exaggerating his physical advantage he seems bigger than he is.

"Sergeant, I'm not judging you. But I need the truth to make decisions and you lied to me, didn't you?"

"And so did you, sir. *So did you.* Lied to the colonel. Gunny and you was busy back on TV when this went down. I was callin' and callin' on the radio. Who are you to judge, sir?"

He ponders me for a moment, then spits a wad of tobacco

juice onto the dirt. "I was just trying to protect you, sir. They was walkin' down that road. No shit, sir."

"Sergeant, I'm supposed to recommend a medal for you. Think you deserve it?"

"Yes," he says simply, raising his eyebrows in wait.

"It was a courageous thing you did, I'll give you that. And, yes, you may very well have saved our lives. But I don't like to be lied to, and at first you hid those passes. Makes it hard to trust you. You ever lie to me again and you're done. Understood?" If he had a different personality, I might boost his ego a tad now, talk about how he's the best combat Marine we've got, but Armstrong would just take it as weakness on my part.

"Yes, sir. Understood," he says seriously.

I give him my hand and he takes it. "I think we're a lot alike, sir, you and me." I wait for an explanation and he gives it, shaking my hand firmly. "You've sized me up, haven't you, sir? What I mean is, when you walk into a room, you look at the men first—not women—and size them up, see if you're more man . . . if you could kick the piss out of them, if that's what it came to." He has not yet released my hand.

"Sometimes."

"No, sir," he says and shakes his head. "I'm willing to wager that runs through your head first thing with a true rival. So what's your verdict?"

He's still grasping my hand and it is clear where this is headed. Our mutual respect for the Corps puts a natural cap on the escalation, though, so I play along. "I think I'd take you, that's what I think. Be close, though."

He smiles, releases my hand, and says, "I disagree with both statements, sir. Guess we'll never know."

"We could always arrange a reunion tussle, twenty years from now."

"Oh, hell no, sir. I'll be dead by then," he says, laughing, totally at ease. "You ever see *Streets of Fire*? Well, they got this scene where the lead dudes get to square off and one gets to pick the weapon. Know what he picks? Sledgehammers, sir. Sledgehammers! What would you pick?"

"Rifles."

"Yessir, you're a good shot. I'm partial to the knife myself." He wears his Ka-Bar knife on his cartridge belt, behind his right hip. He moves his hand back slowly and deliberately past his magazine pouches and I rest my hand on my pistol holster, my thumb casually tugging at the clasp, an unconscious action that must come from my grandfather. We look at each other for a moment before he shakes his head, smiles, and picks up his rifle. "Wooo. Hot out here. Best get back to the team, now that I've been dressed down. Got some goddamned Skinnies to feed."

"One more thing, Sergeant. This country needs feeding and that's why we're here. That's our mission. So adjust your attitude."

He stares at me for a long time, grinding his teeth, so that his big chin juts toward me like a recoiling AA gun. Bam. Bam. Bam. Finally he says, "Aye, aye, sir. I'll fix it around the men. But Marines ain't made for this type of mission. Fighting the Bangers is fine, but this soup-kitchen bullshit is some sort of Peace Corps thing, not Marine Corps. I'll never feel right about this part of it, just slave labor is all."

"That's pretty selfish."

"Sir, you want to hear an old Corps saying? *'If a Marine can't eat it, fuck it, or kill it, he ain't interested.'*" He turns his back and walks back between the trucks, slapping his hand against the metal as he goes.

"Sergeant—"

A scream rips across the compound, dousing the murmur and the laughter, and when the woman gets her breath she screeches again, this time blanketing silence. I flip my rifle out in front and move toward the truck. Armstrong catches my arm and pulls me behind him in a protective manner, yelling for me to keep my head down, his big arm easily pinning me against the truck. We take a turkey peek, then sprint across the compound—both of us hunched and Armstrong still standing a full six feet—rifles at the ready. All the Marines are in their defensive positions, either flat on the dirt or against the sandbags. I see the Gunny make for the gate and I follow.

Just outside the FDC six Marines are standing in a circle, gawking at someone. "Down and defensive!" I shout. "Now! Disperse!" They shake out the cobwebs and drop to their knees, spreading out.

I push through and Gunny is saying, "Can you help her, Doc?"

"Carotid's totally severed! Even if I tie it off . . . she's gonna die."

Doc is pressing his hand, which I see is wrapped in a rubber glove, into a woman's neck. Blood is seeping through the spaces between his fingers and flowing down to the ground. She is lying flat on her back, kicking her legs forward on the dirt like a dying insect. The dirt next to her head is already muddy. I kneel next to Doc and hear gurgling noises. "Windpipe too, sir. Cut clean in half," Doc says. The woman stops kicking and is still. Off switch.

I wait a few seconds, pull her eyes closed, and one of the lids pops back open. I pull it down and it snaps open again, giving all of us a big wink, enjoying some hilarious secret that we do not yet understand. I give up and say, "Dead, Doc."

"I know it, sir. I know it." He looks up at me and his eyes are watering. "Nothing I could do . . . a wound this bad. Just nothing. I lost another little . . . watched a girl die earlier, too, sir. Right in my arms. Two in one day." He bends over and begins to sob.

I want to pat him on the back but I am not sure what the proper response is and, in mulling it over, I choose to remain frozen. "You did your best, Doc."

Doc lifts his hand and reveals the fatty cut of meat that has been removed from the woman's neck. There are little pulpy white things blossomed in the middle of the wet wound and the sand next to her is bright, shiny red in the sun, not the purplish ink they use in movies. I glance up at the Gunny and he points at Johnson, who is holding a frail Somali woman's hands behind her back. Johnson is twice her size and Johnson is barely six feet tall.

"This girl here did that, sir," Johnson says. "Caught her with the machete . . . standing over the body yelling something. I . . . I can't believe it."

"*She* did *this?*" It is totally startling; I was certain a Gangbanger had done this, the brutality of it, the purity. The woman is just over five feet tall and she's built out of pickup sticks. "Get this body out of the way. I'll call headquarters. Gunny, bring that woman there into the compound for questioning. And tell Montoya to frisk everyone entering the compound. We don't want any more machete deaths."

"Already doin' the frisking, sir," says Gunny. "I'll get her inside. Doc, why don't you and Johnson drag the body inside for me."

There are no tarps for the body, so Gunny has the Marines drop it into the far corner of the compound where it crumples into a death pose, arms and legs askew, head folded entirely back now. Doc grabs some empty grain bags and lays them over her gently—"Donated by the People of the United States of America"—for a grave shroud. Gunny brings the murderer before me. I call for the Somali translator who is assigned to the FDC so I can interrogate the woman, but he's nowhere to be found. We were warned about this: Many of the food workers' bodyguards and the translators assigned to UNITAF forces are actually moonlighting Gangbangers whose underlying loyalties will never be bought or pinpointed.

"Where the fuck is the translator, Guns?"

He shrugs. "Motherfucker musta gone home for lunch, sir."

A small Somali boy, about eight years old and dressed in baby blue dress slacks, shiny black shoes, and one of our platoon T-shirts that dangles clear down to his ankles, the Sharkman logo with "Kill 'Em All, Let God Sort 'Em Out" embarrassing me now that I see it draped over a little boy, scoots out from under one of the trucks and walks up.

Doc makes the introduction. "Remember him from last night? In our hole? He was helping me translate during sick call outside the FDC. He must have snuck in when I wasn't watching. Really cute kid. Speaks great English."

"Yeah, well, growing up here I'm sure that was the way to survive . . . get in good with the aid workers." I squat and stick out my hand. "Hi. Name? What's your name?"

The boy runs around Doc and hides. "Joe," Doc says. "I've been calling him Little Joe."

"Must not like your looks, sir," says Gunny.

"Either that or he hates officers." All the Marines laugh.

The boy runs back around Doc's legs and shouts, "What your name, Marine?" His teeth are as huge as potato chips and just as yellow, popping out at weird angles from his skull, separated by an inch-wide gap that would make

Letterman blush, an impossibly cute smile for all of its imperfections.

"Kelly."

"I Joe," he says. "Little Joe!"

"How old are you?" I hold up eight fingers and shrug. "This many? Years?"

"No. I thirteen."

I stand and ask Doc, "Is that possible? He's so small."

"Yessir, it's possible. Either that or he's lying." The Gunny chuckles and I roll my eyes. I can't believe that I expected Doc to explain stunted growth, this a man who thought you had to cross an ocean to get from New York to Los Angeles.

I hold the machete out in front of our miniature murder suspect, a woman who looks like she may faint from hunger at any moment. She's wearing a bright yellow wraparound skirt and a blue blouse that would be pretty if it were not sprayed with red dots. The machete is a crude device, the wooden handle wrapped onto the metal with frayed twine, but the rusted blade is a foot long, jagged and threatening. Still red. Clumps of wet sand. A black hair.

I nod and ask the boy to figure out what happened. Little Joe talks with her for five minutes, then he says, "Uh, dis lady here, she kill de oder because she was standing, waiting for long time in de queue to get food ration . . . and de oder lady—de dead one—moved in front of her. Thas it."

"That's it?" I ask, astounded.

"Thas it. Made her mad. She go to her bag and get de knife. Cut her down. Thas it."

"You're gonna have to take her to the airport for processing, Gunny. Take the Hummer. I'm going to go make the radio report."

I move away in a daze. Every Somali we apprehend is to

be run through headquarters, but I'm not sure we're setting a good precedent when our first arrest is a fifty-pound female refugee who is a two-day hike from death's door. Behind me I can hear the Gunny saying to Little Joe, "She killed that lady with a machete because she *cut in on her in line?* That's *fucked*—oh, sorry. Excuse me, Little Joe." The boy shrugs and Gunny explains, "That's a bad word. Sorry you had to hear it."

– 10 –

The demon is a liar. He will lie to confuse us.
But he will also mix lies with the truth.
The attack is psychological, but it is powerful.

With Gunny gone in the Hummer to deliver our prisoner to headquarters at the airport, I am left feeling slightly alone. I've had nine months with the platoon; given the arduous training cycle that vacuumed my time before we boarded ships for our six-month deployment, I haven't had the time to form tight relationships with all the men. Marine officers are supposed to keep a professional boundary between themselves and their units, but I was successful, I think, in crossing that line often with my first platoon and I'm hopeful I can do the same with this one. The Corps caste system is designed to excel in combat, but I've listened to my grandfather enough to know that an officer's first responsibility is to relate to his men. In fact, growing up around Red Kelly has left me slightly uncomfortable with even *being* an officer, as if I have betrayed a code and crossed a sort of picket line, cavorting with the enemy now. So while lieutenants like Darren Phillips rigidly kept their walls in place—always quick to correct an enlisted Marine for a half-hearted salute, routinely inspecting the shine on his men's boots, never sharing a beer after hours—I broke down the strictest barriers and was always comfortable sharing a laugh with the platoon.

I move up to the northeast bunker to talk with Sergeant Armstrong, who has been allowed to pull security duty, where he belongs. Much of being an officer is wandering around, supervision disguised as boredom, and I'm eager to make amends anyway. The sun is an hour higher and I am shadowless, just like the barren hinterland itself, withering under a constant solar pounding.

Armstrong nods at me and spits some tobacco juice through the barbed wire. "Pretty fucked-up shit, wasn't it, sir?"

"Yes. Sure was."

"Gunny took her back for arresting?"

"Yes. He's going to run her through processing at the airport, whatever that means. He'll be back soon."

"Well."

He's not in the mood to chat and I'm too hot to fight it. I grab his binoculars, the green rubber coating soft and hot because of the sun, and scan the city of Mogadishu, next to us, then the wasteland to the west. The mirage is thick; I can see only about a mile before the wavering heat blends land with sky, shimmering and dancing. It looks like—yes, two jeeps are headed to the FDC. Could be Bison Breath— he likes to pop up unannounced, which is good practice for a commander. But when the vehicles get closer I see that they are pickup trucks, the vehicle of choice for your everyday East African warlord.

I prop my elbows on the sandbags to steady the picture. For the first time in Restore Hope I see a threat that I am trained to deal with. "Inbound!" I yell over my shoulder, not trying to stifle my enthusiasm. "Man up the perimeter!"

The Marines on the chow line drop their ladles, swivel their rifles forward from their backs, and take their positions on the perimeter. The *plink*s of the M-16 shoulder strap clips jingling on their swivels, the *shaahshaa*s of the flak jackets as they rise and fall with each step, and the *thump*s of sprinting combat boots are infectious sounds and I can feel the hair on the back of the platoon stand up.

"Is this another drill, sir?" asks Armstrong.

"Negative." I stand up and say, "Remember the rules of engagement!" and immediately regret it. I don't want to be a mother hen, especially if this is bogus. "Translator and bullhorn, up!"

"Translator's gone, remember, sir?"

"Then get that kid Little Joe up here."

The trucks stop about a hundred yards from the FDC, then meander behind one of the buildings to our front, rolling slowly, watching. They're filled—I mean college-stunt full—with Gangbangers: all male, all adults, all armed with AK-47s. They disappear behind a building and everything is still. Soon, four of them dressed in various uniforms—blue jeans, khaki pants, polyester disco shirts, a Dallas Cowboys jersey, flip-flops, Nike high-tops, well-polished dress shoes—walk out from around the building, straight toward the FDC, looking quite unintimidating for trained killers. I suddenly understand the colonel's policy on uniformity and am glad for it. None of the Gangbangers has a rifle.

"Here they come," says Armstrong. "Unarmed, too. Maybe they want to get fed."

"Naw, look at 'em. They ain't starving." I sometimes revert to slang when I'm nervous, to sound as rough and tumble as the men I'm leading.

When they are thirty meters from the FDC, Johnson taps me on the shoulder and presents the translator, a

Somali man called Boom Boom who is dressed in a rumpled plaid Sunday suit, dust covering his right side, a big red bullhorn gripped tightly in his left hand. "Found him underneath a truck, sleeping," Johnson growls.

"Not true, sir," says Boom Boom. "Merely getting a rest."

At least Boom Boom has not yet sold the bullhorn the United States government issued. I should probably warn him about the repercussions of losing USMC property—the SEAL platoon lost an entire machine gun to the ocean on the journey from Singapore and they filled out a form and shrugged it off; a Marine in another platoon dropped his NVGs, broke a lens, and almost had his left testicle hacked off for his clumsiness.

"Tell those men to stop where they are," I say.

"But of course, sir."

Boom Boom nods, squints at the four Bangers, rubs his eyes, and squints again. The Banger in the Cowboys jersey—taller than the rest and well built for a Somali—says something to his three friends and they share a laugh. "Sir! That is Hassan Farah!" whispers Boom Boom, pointing at Number 88.

"My namesake?" interrupts Armstrong behind me. "I'll be! Which one?"

"Farah, Farah!" calls Boom Boom. He rushes up to the gate, unlocks it, and half-sprints toward Farah. Boom Boom bows deeply and then the two men embrace, share a double-cheek kiss, and trade some friendly banter, Boom Boom holding Farah's elbow with two hands as if he is cradling a newborn.

"Woooo-hoooo!" shouts Johnson. "Get some of that good shit!"

The other Marines join in and their hoots and hollers fill the courtyard, catcalls overlapping with deep whistles and blending with ya-ya-yas and hiii-caaarrumbaaas.

"Save some of that tongue for me!" shouts Montoya.

"Welcome to the Boom Boom room, gents!" shouts Armstrong. "Step right up, don't be shy, a kiss from the Boom Boom'll send your pecker to the sky! Can I get me an oooo-raaah!"

"*OOOOO-RAAAH!*" shout the men.

"Quiet down, recon," I growl halfheartedly, not trying to hide my big grin. "Pull out your culture cards and read number one, and I quote: 'Somali men greet each other with a hug and a cheek kiss. This is a sign of friendship and is not to be ridiculed by Marines.'"

I point at the group of Somalis, now about twenty meters away, curl my index finger and say, "Boom Boom, get back inside. *Now.* And I don't give a damn *who* he is. Tell him to stop right there."

Boom Boom shakes his head and gives me a weak smile. "It's okay, sir. He just want—"

"Do it!" I say sharply.

Boom Boom babbles for a few seconds and trots back to the wire with his head low. "Best not to anger Hassan Farah, sir," he whispers when he gets inside.

The four Bangers stay put, then Farah in his Cowboys jersey begins to yell.

"What'd he say?"

"He say he want to see what's inside. He say he want some food too. He say he trade for some khat. Sir, I advise to maybe give him some food. Hassan Farah is the man next to Muhammad Aidid! In the Heeber Geeder clan!"

Khat is a mild narcotic that many of the Somalis chew, a leaf that's ground up and siphoned like chewing tobacco. Siad Barre once went so far as to ban the substance, which went over as well as Prohibition did in the States, and now its use is widespread, predominantly within the gangs. The effects of khat are debatable; we were told it lies somewhere between heavy-duty speed and cocaine. I personally believe caffeine is the best proxy, but we've told all the Marines that it's damn near hallucinogenic, to build up the Somali threat a tad, the same way we believed a million Iraqis would charge us in a bid for glory. Right.

"Motherfuckers got to be hopped up to come over here like this," says Armstrong over his rifle. "Old boy Farrah Fawcett has got some *cojones,* don't he? But I bet that Skinny ain't never seen animals like us, though, has he, sir?"

"Easy does it," I say, knowing Armstrong's nickname for Farah will stick. I look down the road but Gunny's Hummer isn't in sight so I turn toward Boom Boom. "Tell him he gets no food and to go away."

The translator relays the message and Farah actually takes a few steps forward, yelling the entire time, pointing at me. "He say you not his . . . not in charge here. His country. He say he jes want food," says Boom Boom, nervous now.

"Tell him to stop where he is." I raise my rifle and align his body in the oval sight, a useless exercise because he is unarmed, but one that nonetheless placates some hidden need. I pull the front sight post up past his legs and stop at his head.

"Sir! You cannot do that!" says Boom Boom.

Farrah Fawcett glares at me, smiles, walks right up to the food line ten feet from me but on the other side of the wire gate, and shoves a woman and her baby down to the ground. The woman takes the impact on her shoulder, and though the baby is screaming, it's unharmed. Farrah leans over the woman, curled up and nestling her child in the fetal position now, and spits a black chunk of lumpy khat on her. It slides down her cheek and splats flat on the ground. Having cut to the head of the line,

Farrah Fawcett stands there waving his buddies over, shoulders back, staring at me. He points at me and babbles.

Boom Boom coughs and says, "Farah say he didn't hear you so good. Would you like to repeat your order? I'm sorry, sir, I'm just translating."

"Shit. See that! He dissed the lieutenant," hisses Armstrong. "I played your part, you Skinny fuck, and it ended with you dyin'! Leave that woman be, you fucker! I'll fucking *end* you."

"Easy now," I say to Armstrong. "He's no threat to us."

"Too bad the chick with the machete isn't there in line. We should have let her stay . . . she would take care of our problem for us." Armstrong is excited. Not angry—that's just a mask for our real feelings. I can tell that his blood is up and he's looking for an excuse, just like I am in the deeper corners of my mind. Given the green light, some Marines will shy away from violence and search for other solutions. Others, like Armstrong, embrace it. "Fucking A, sir. They got some balls, don't they? What say me and you escort them from the line?"

I hear the *click* of Armstrong's safety flipping to Semi and the second line of the ROE card is suddenly in my head. "Be cool, now. They're not armed," I whisper. "Minimum force, graduated response."

"He done wrong, that Farrah Fawcett Majors, pushing her like that. But I'm willing to cut him some slack for his Texas loyalty. That's a pretty jersey, now ain't it, sir? Boys are on the up-and-up, I'm telling you." I hear his rifle click back to Safe.

I step away from the bunker and walk up to the gate, meters drifting to feet and then to inches away from the enemy. We're supposed to kill the modern enemy from cyberspace but I can reach out and choke this one with my hands—what a wonderful world this is becoming. Lance Corporal Johnson is already here next to me, pointing his M-16 through the wire fence at Mrs. Lee Majors, who is staring right back at him, babbling, spitting khat. Farrah Fawcett's three henchmen slink over and join their leader, laughing and smiling now, enjoying themselves. All of them have yellow, khat-stained teeth and mid-length Afros. Farrah is bigger than the other three—maybe just over six feet—and it's clear his henchmen are taking their cues from him. I notice that he has a lazy eye that twitches when he talks—it's all askew and it's pretty freaky, quivering out somewhere over my left shoulder when he looks at me.

"Marine, yes?" Farrah asks.

"Goddamn right," says Johnson. "In the flesh."

Farrah spits some khat bark at Johnson's feet and babbles.

I motion for Boom Boom and move shoulder to shoulder with Johnson. I can feel him trembling—or is that me? "Easy, Johnson. Easy now. What's he saying?"

Boom Boom is hiding behind me and he stammers, "He say he jes like him, black. No better than him. Fighting wit whites. He challenge him. He say like you say, a nigger traitor."

"*What?*" I ask, immediately regretting it.

Boom Boom points at Johnson. "He say this man here a nigger traitor."

I avoid looking at Johnson and am immediately so uncomfortable that my reaction to the statement is reduced to the hope that the translator has made a mistake. Johnson looks at me and exhales loudly. Time to lighten the mood and lighten Johnson's load. "You boys need to watch your dental hygiene," I say to Farrah. "Those choppers are pretty nasty. And that eye . . . *whew.* That's nasty, baby."

Farrah looks at me, smiles—*cocky prick but he knows violence*—and glances around at all the rifles. His left eye flickers and vibrates. Here I am, facing off with a fearsome gang leader in *Africa,* of all places. Of course, I head up a faction of the most brutal gang the world has ever known.

He spits a stream of khat through the wire gate at my boots and a fleck stains the light brown synthetic on my toe. Armstrong, perched in the bunker above, fires his own harassment and interdiction mission with American tobacco and the black juice strikes one of the Bangers on the arm. Superior range and accuracy.

"Have some Skoal, brotha," Armstrong drawls.

The Banger wipes his arm furiously and screams a string of babble but Farrah grabs his arm, lectures him, and picks a long twig from the dirt. He sticks it through the wire and points at Johnson, violating our space. Farah says, "You nigga traita."

I step forward but Johnson is already in motion. He lowers his M-16 down flush to his side and moves right up against the gate, across from Farrah, who looks like he's just been given a birthday present. The sling keeps the rifle tight to Johnson's body, accessible while he unlocks the gate, rears back a leg, and slams it open with his boot. It swings wide and clatters against the sandbag wall, Farah jumping out of its way with surprising speed and nimbleness. For a moment I believe that Johnson aims to bullrush the Skinny, the way he strides forward, but he stops a few inches shy. I'll be damned if Farrah doesn't hold his ground, unyielding, staring back, comfortable in the conflict.

"Cease fire, Johnson!" I hoarse-whisper. He does.

The platoon is quiet and I see Johnson glancing around at his peers, recognizing their stares. He knows the rules of Restore Hope but he also knows The Rules, and the latter are demanding a violent response now. I try to step in and release some pressure, hoping that Gunny will arrive soon. As a white officer I feel the stab of trepidation as I move in to calm a class and race conflict between two black men.

"He's a United States Marine," I say, pointing at Johnson. Then I plop my finger on my chest. "Marine." I point at the light green Marine (all Marines are green, just different shades) next to us and say, "Marine. All Marines."

Farrah Fawcett laughs and jabbers with his buddies. They all laugh. It is maddening not understanding them. He points at me and says, "Yes, you Marine." He smiles, says something to his friends, points at Johnson, and repeats it. "He nigga," he says. "Nigga traita."

My toes curl in my boots, tense. I wait for the "mayor" of this district to go spinning backward from the punch, but Johnson just stands there in his desert camouflage uniform, a statue of virtue, the small American flag on his shoulder glowing bright against the tan blouse and the country itself. I am tempted to let him kick the shit out of the four Skinnies, but with Maureen O'Donnell having joined the audience, that would be the third strike. I've learned that any decision is better than the impotence of inaction, so I move up and put my hand on Johnson's shoulder. His thick muscles are twitching like a racehorse's legs, sinewy and electric.

"Marine," I say. "Number one Marine. Best Marine."

Farrah actually backs up a few steps when I move up and, to make matters worse, he is suddenly deferential. He touches his small Afro and bows his head. "Sir," he says. "You Marine." He actually smiles at me in a completely friendly way, the way the Somalis do in the food lines. I notice for the first time that his eyes are wild and bloodshot, bulging well free of his lids.

"Yes," I say, and thumb Johnson. "Him, too. Marine."

But Farrah simply frowns; he does not comprehend how black men can also be Marines. He shakes his head, and before I can interrupt he says it again, perhaps the most singularly divisive and inflammatory word in the English language. The gall of him. He walks up to us and tries to poke Johnson in the chest, repeating The Word. One of his henchmen—a Somali with a humongous head that's perched precariously on a Wiffle-ball-bat neck—starts to chant, "Nigga! Nigga!" cognizant now that it affects us.

I feel the situation sliding out of my control—if I ever even had any to begin with—and between the ROE and this debacle I feel as if I'm caught in a vise, an impossibly terrible dream from which I will certainly wake if I just close my eyes and count to ten. I look desperately for Gunny's Hummer but the street is quiet—filled with kids and refugees watching the scene unfold, but *quiet.* I am onstage, it's my line, and I'm screwing the hell out of the pooch.

"What'd you call me, motherfucker?" Johnson hisses. "Say that again and I end you."

His eyes flick across the Bangers and then he twists his head to face me—Terrel "Big Dog" Johnson, twenty-four years old, out of Sherman Oaks, California, and the assistant team leader, Team One, First Platoon, First Recon Battalion, is seeking guidance from his platoon commander. And I somehow cannot find any words. I want to get all the Marines together in a circle, arm in arm, like a football team before a game, to show there is no racial divide, but coming from me—now—it will seem false and political. Impure.

Some goddamn African warlord is tearing my platoon apart with words and he doesn't even *speak English*. Johnson snorts loudly, like a bull, and I see that he is squeezing the hand guard of his weapon with all of his might, the veins on the top of his hand bulging and full. He is nearly hyperventilating. The salient question as to what will happen next is instantly replaced by: How many Bangers will he kill? I am trying to come up with a dignified exit strategy for this clusterfuck—Johnson has no fuse left and I do not want to embarrass him, or myself, in front of the men—when Farrah Fawcett looks at him and laughs. Things are happening so quickly.

"You a *NIIGGGAAAA!*" Farrah screams.

Johnson takes the step and we're all going over the falls.

I move to stop him but suddenly Armstrong is there, holding him back by his web gear with one hand and snatching the shoulder armor pad of his flak jacket with another. "Cool out, J.," he says. "Cool out, brother."

Johnson snaps forward in a sudden lunge but Armstrong yanks him back, hard and behind, with incredible strength, holding him easily, Johnson pinned now to Armstrong's back. He starts moving backward slowly and Johnson, who might be strong enough to free himself if he really tried, is putting up what I take to be token resistance. It looks good, mind you, Johnson screaming at Sergeant Armstrong to let him go, that they called him a nigger, that he's going to beat them all down, wrestling against Armstrong's big arm, spitting and spinning, but Johnson is not going full-out balls-to-the-wall psycho here. I realize immediately that he just needed to keep some pride, which Armstrong has maintained for him.

Now boosting it, Armstrong spins around and wraps a big brother's arm around Johnson's shoulders, holding him tight by his gear harness like a wild stallion, moving back toward the Bangers, stopping well short, talking softly to Johnson about maintaining his bearing, not letting these motherfucked get under his skin, that he's a United States *fucking* Marine and therefore the meanest *motherfucker* on the continent. Johnson is quiet now.

"This here Marine is one of the best I've got," Armstrong says calmly. "And he's my brother. All these guys are my brothers. *My brothers.*" He says it with an obvious authenticity that I could never achieve with my rank.

"You ignorant fucks just slip up, just slip up once, and we'll fucking *end* you. Recon. Remember us. *RECON* make you *die*," he says. "And my brother J. here will be the first one to do it. End you ignorant pieces of shit. Backward, uneducated, slave-trading, racist motherfucked."

He turns to Boom Boom and says, "Translate it."

Boom Boom shakes his head and says, "No. That is not smart thing. To make Hassan Farah angry. Very dangerous, yes? For your unit."

Little Joe is somehow next to us and he's not daunted. The boy speaks rapidly and translates, clearly enthusiastic, pointing at the Bangers. Then he turns to Armstrong and says proudly, "I told the men, Stretch!"

Armstrong nods his thanks and spits a long stream of tobacco at the feet of the Bangers. He points to the eagle, globe, and anchor symbol on his helmet. "All that matters is this." Then he takes a finger and rubs it down his sweaty face. "Not this," he says. He walks forward calmly, to within inches of Farrah, and shuts the gate closed in the warlord's face.

It is a stunning performance. For the first time, Farrah Fawcett keeps his soiled suck shut.

Armstrong grunts and faces the man whose hand he's been holding, whose back he's been protecting. "Hey, sir, Lance Corporal J. and I should get away from this gate. You mind, sir? We're gonna go over behind the trucks and take our lunch break. Mandatory by federal law, right?" Armstrong winks at me and I nod. "Back in a flash, then." He and Johnson walk across the FDC toward the trucks. Johnson turns and watches the Bangers the entire time with his arms open wide, welcoming brutality. That or he's lonely for a hug.

Boom Boom says some things, and the Bangers talk back to him rapidly. "Dey say dey meant no insult to you, sir, only de nigger man. Dey say dey want food, is all. They mean no harm . . . Dey won't come in, sir."

"Montoya," I say to my Team Two leader.

"Yessir."

"Put a Marine on these Bangers with a rifle pointing at their faces as long as they want to watch. They aren't invited in. Any attempt by them to force their way in, we will kill them. Shoot them dead. Boom Boom, repeat to them exactly as I said it."

Boom Boom scrunches his face up and says, "But, *sir*, that would be against your rules."

"What rules?"

"Your rules of engagement that we were given."

I hesitate and try to make sense of this clusterfucked situation. Little Joe jumps at the chance and begins to scream at the Bangers with obvious hatred. Farrah leans his face in through a frame of barbed wire and like a snake spits a yellow stream of venom into the boy's eyes. Little Joe covers his eyes and falls to his knees, groaning but not crying.

"You son of a bitch," I say. "You'll pay for that."

High-pitched shouts begin a block away and leapfrog up to us, echoing across the alley, sloshing back and forth. A few boys appear behind the Bangers and wave frantically at them, lookouts screaming warnings of some kind.

Farrah nods his head at me and babbles. Boom Boom says, "He says he'll come visit you real soon, Lieutenant Kelly."

I turn to Farrah and smile. "I'll be looking forward to it."

Farrah laughs and says, "Okay, Kelly Recon. Okay." The Banger with the Volkswagen-size head taps Farrah on the shoulder, both Somalis moving away from the gate now, Farrah never giving me his back even as he quickens his pace and disappears around the building and out of my life.

A few seconds and I hear the roar of a diesel engine, Gunny arriving in his Hummer like an older brother to make things right. The gate opens and the FDC absorbs the Hummer. Gunny's boots swing out and down with a thump, then he stretches his bulk out and swivels his head around, the deus ex machina.

"Why you manned up defensively, sir?" he says. "I miss somethin'?"

I'm telling the story when Little Joe staggers to his feet, covers his left eye, walks right past me, and hugs Gunny fiercely. He breaks down and begins heaving, speaking in stutter-step bursts, pointing at the gate, trying to draw air between his sobs. I notice a big clump of mud clinging to the gap between his teeth.

Gunny hoists the boy up and cradles him in his arms. "Jesus Christ, sir. Did they hurt him? Are you hurt, Joe? What's wrong?" Gunny has five beautiful daughters back in

Camp Pendleton and I am not surprised by how easily and closely Little Joe and he relate, what with Guns's promise to try for a boy when we return.

"That's Farah," says Little Joe when he catches his breath. "Wit de America football shirt. Cowboys. He wit General Aidid. De other one is Muhammad Ali. Big head. He de one wit de morta bomb."

Gunny pats the boy's Afro and I say, "Gunny, you just missed Hassan Farah in a Cowboys jersey. He spit in the kid's face. Khat. There was this other Banger with a huge head. Joe, that's Muhammad Ali who fired the mortar from last night? Muhammad?"

"Yes," Joe says and buries his head back in the expanse of Gunny's chest.

"You need to get cleaned up, Joe. Where's your mommy and daddy?" asks Gunny.

"Dey dead. Killed by de men. Four years."

"Who? *Those* men?"

"Yes. Dey Heeber Geeder," says Little Joe, almost pleasantly now as Gunny pours his canteen down the boy's brow and wipes his eye clean.

"Remember the brief? Hibr Gidr." I say to Gunny. "Aidid's crew of Gangbangers."

"They cut my dad head right off. Right off. Take my mom and lay wit her. Den dey burn her in de fire. Muhammad Ali burn her. You kill them, Kelly?" the boy asks.

It is a startling question from someone so small, but I suppose for a thirteen-year-old who has been on his own since he was nine—who may have seen his father beheaded and his mother raped and burned—it is not that shocking. All the Marines are looking at me. "We'll protect you from Farrah Fawcett. Okay?"

"Farrah Fawcett?"

"That's what we call him. Hassan Farah."

"Farah? Okay. Yes, he de most bad one. I stay in de FDC wit Marines. Okay?"

"Let him stay, sir," says Doc, who has been eavesdropping.

"Okay, Dad, but this ain't an official adoption. That's all this platoon needs."

"Fighting a fucking Farrah Fawcett and a Mortar Muhammad Ali?" asks Gunny.

Joe nods his head rapidly. "Yes. Muhammad Ali. He de one who like to lay wit de ladies. He lay wit my mother, too, dat one. He de one who burn her, too."

Gunny shakes his head and whispers, "Does he mean rape, sir?" I nod. His eyes narrow. "Fighting a rapist who burns women. And we can't erase them from the earth right now?" He turns to Joe. "And he . . . did . . . bad *things* to your mom? You know where they live? Where they sleep?" asks Gunny. He is still burning.

"No," says Little Joe. "No one place, dem."

"Well, we'll get 'em."

I look over past the trucks and see that Armstrong has Johnson gripped by the shoulders, face-to-face, trying to send a difficult message. I lift Little Joe from Gunny's arms and say, "Gunny, why don't you go talk with Armstrong and Johnson? They'll tell you the rest. Johnson and Farrah got into it and Johnson did well. I . . . just talk to him, Guns. There was a racial incident."

We're just about finished feeding the refugees. I've allowed some of the Marines to go play with the kids and Doc and Johnson are swirling like dust devils, recon chasing kids chasing recon, dust floating up, obscuring the mirage on the horizon and the curtain of death in the compound itself.

It's extremely hot; *Africa* hot. I've coated the back of my neck with sunscreen and still the sun seems to be burning through, frying me like the egg in the antidrug commercial, compressing my helmet and squeezing my brain. Doc walks over to me in a full sweat and says, "What's wrong with Gunny, sir? He didn't want to play. He's not in a talkative mood."

I decide to camp out next to Gunny and share the silence until we literally pull the chalks. I want to ask him about the racial incident—and see if he thinks I somehow contributed to it—but don't know how. I unscrew my canteen, take a delicious swig, douse the back of my neck, the water cool as it crackles down my spine and sends a welcome shiver up my neck that evaporates too quickly, and extend the canteen in front of his face. "Kill it if you want."

"Water ain't what I want to kill right now."

A thick knot of flies settles above my head and I swat at them absentmindedly, trying to keep my mind off the heat, waiting for Gunny to elaborate. I study the dog tag in my left boot and notice that Farrah's phlegm is still pasted on a piece of me. It is a full half an hour before Gunny speaks again.

"You know what really gets me, sir?" he says. "It's not the word 'nigger' but who's saying it. In Brooklyn I heard that, what, probably well over a thousand times? And you know who's saying it? Black folks. I've been called a nigger maybe thirty times by white dudes—and never by a woman, by the way, and only a few times right to my face—but I've heard it so many times . . . so—*many*—times. I mean, as a natural way to address a man in the city. On leave last year—you remember I took the kids to visit my mother?—must have heard 'nigger' a hundred times . . . on subways . . . just walking down the fucking *street*. My daughter Jessica asked me about it—she's six and never heard that word except on TV in *her life*.

"There's this basketball court near my mom's house. I'm walking by with my family and one of the kids on the court blocks some other kid's shot, then he screams, 'Get that shit out of my fucking house, nigga!' Right *there* in front of all my little girls! All five! My wife tries to calm me down but I just can't, so I walk up to the chain-link fence and say, 'Hey, men. Watch your language and get some self-respect.' You know how I get."

I nod that I do.

"Kid walks up to me—I mean from me to you, sir—and he says, 'Shuttup, nigga. Get your bitch-ass off my court! That's my nigga, so shut the fuck up, motherfucker!'"

Gunny pauses and shakes his head, exhales, smiles sadly. "It was then that I knew I could control my homicidal tendencies if I had to. Just took my family and walked away."

Gunny stands to stretch, flipping his M-16 behind his back with extended arms. "Sir, Johnson came to the 'motherland' he's been talking about so much to help his own people, and I think he fully expected to be treated with respect and maybe even awe, like Muhammad Ali when he came to Africa to fight Foreman. Ali was treated like a king, not called a *nigger*. Here he is, assistant team leader in a United States Marine recon platoon, and some thieving bandit punk calls him a *nigger*? Please. It's like someone walking up to Jordan and telling him he's shit for a basketball player. What would he do? He'd just laugh, that's how ridiculous it is. I told Johnson the same thing and he agreed, but he was still hurt and embarrassed by it."

"He was this close to snapping," I say.

Gunny nods and smiles. "Kid's from the suburbs. Probably never had anyone call him that in his life. Good thing Armstrong stepped in. From what I heard, it was masterful."

"Yes," I say. "It was."

— 11 —

– 11 –

Just don't feed them after midnight.

The afternoon brings more heat, and I allow the Marines not standing post to take off their helmets and flak jackets so they do not cook themselves, as long as they remain behind the sandbag walls in the rear of the FDC. This runs counter to the colonel's standing order and my men—who've been complaining lustily—know it, so I'm able to soak up some serious loyalty points I may need to cash in someday.

Our reporter walks up to me and asks if we want our picture taken, just a private shot for the troops. Most of the platoons are accompanied by reporters and ours is from *People* magazine, assigned to us, I'm sure, because the colonel didn't want *Time* or *Newsweek* to give us press. This is ironic because the Marines prefer *People* anyway. The Marines all beg for the picture, so we gather behind one of the trucks for the shot.

A van swings by the FDC and beeps its horn. Maureen O'Donnell walks up to me and says, "Well, I'll leave you here for the night to guard the food. I'll be back tomorrow."

"Where are you staying, ma'am?" I ask.

"Hotel," she says, embarrassed. The reporters and even some of the aid workers stay in hotels that are "protected" by various Bangers who are drawing fat paychecks for bodyguard duties, the Restore Hope version of my elementary school years—paying the Montgomerys my daily lunch so they would protect me from their own fists. Incredibly, before the Marines arrived, the UN force was employing over two hundred Bangers as a protection force for the airport compound. Maybe Armstrong is right—we are just cheap labor, sleeping on the blood-soaked ground at night and dishing rations during the day, a much more cost-effective protection force than the Bangers, with a ladling ability to boot.

O'Donnell says, "You may get some drifters trickling in tonight, asking for a ration. No food after sundown, that's our rule. None."

"Just like *Gremlins*. What do they do, turn into monsters?"

"Well, no, the refugees don't. But others do. Good night and thank you so much." She walks over to the van, hops in, and it speeds away.

I see Armstrong standing over by the gate, staring out at the hinterland, no doubt hoping for some hurricane of horribles to blow in so he can shoulder his weapon and take. I debate it for a second and walk over to join him. He turns and nods his head, acknowledging me, then spits some tobacco. Many of the Marines chew, but Armstrong feels compelled to make Texas proud and has a wad in his mouth every minute that his eyes are open. "Afternoon, sir."

"Yes."

He nods over to some Marines sitting by the truck. "Thought we was ordered not to take off our helmets, sir." It is not a challenge—he's curious.

"Circumstances allow it," I say simply. I don't want to get into a discussion of why I am ignoring the colonel's order, especially with Armstrong.

"Well."

A long string of black tobacco juice jets out from the gap in his big teeth and pools in the dirt two feet in front of my combat boots, like spray-can party foam at the end of its flight. Armstrong backs away from the sandbag wall, grabbing me gently by the elbow as he moves back, tilting his head back in a "Come back here I have a secret" gesture. When we are fifteen meters back from his muddy target, he reaches back, a snap as the leather strap is undone, the Ka-Bar blade up in the air catching the Somali sun, Armstrong's meaty hand snatching it by the wooden handle and snapping it forward like a whip, the knife striking the tobacco and skidding across into a sandbag, following the divot.

His face shrinks into itself and he turns red. "Fuck! Angle was too flat. You stay here, sir . . . let me try it again. God*damn*. Fuck!" It is a violent overreaction; perhaps Armstrong is related to Bison Breath.

"Easy, cowboy. No need to show off for me. Your father not give you enough attention when you were young?"

The anger washes from his face immediately and he smiles, relaxed again. "Sir, my old man ain't got nothing to do with this here. He ain't got nothing to do with my actions, period. I mean, I like him fine, but do I look like one of them who relies on his parents' blessin' for who he is? Or even worse, blames 'em for all their problems like them talk-show freaks? Naw, I'm my own man, sir. Just like you."

Just like me. I'm so self-conscious that I take it as sarcasm in the second before I remember that Armstrong knows nothing about me. He does not know that I was, in fact, one of *them people*, and might still be. Armstrong is my physical superior and now it is clear that he is my emotional superior—on one level at least—as well.

After I lost the first fight to Joey Montgomery, the beefy twins attacked consistently for several years, four or five times a year, and I struggled to find the will to fight back. I cried after my first fights, then began to cry during the fights themselves, and by the seventh grade I was crying *before* the fights even began. These were in the days before claiming "Victim!" was chic, however, and the sweaty fists of the Montgomerys found their way through my preemptive tears.

Red Kelly found out about the tears on Thanksgiving when I made the mistake of asking him how to deal with the fear before a fight. My mother had just called us in from the porch for dinner, and I grabbed Red's thick forearm, asking if he could still pull me up. He laughed, switched his Pabst to his other hand, and raised me off the ground, holding his bent arm out parallel to the ground so I could flip over it. When I did—and felt he was self-content—I asked him about fighting.

"You *cry* before you even *fight?* What're you, eleven years old now?"

"Yes, Red."

"Jesus H.! You know when I last cried? When I popped out of my mom's quim!"

"Pop!" my father hissed. He had been eavesdropping and was gritting his teeth with anger, a rarity for a man who never raised his voice. "Gavin, are those creeps bothering you again? I can always call Mr. Montgomery."

"Bullshit," said my grandfather. "They'll just keep pouring it on until you stick up for yourself. And *no*, Tom, you're *not* going to call their father, because this is something he'll face all his life unless he solves it. Pussy has a way of infecting a man if he lets it. Just *fight them back,* Gavin. They're no bigger than you."

"Yes they are, Red."

"Well, okay, so *what?* How long they been doing this to you?"

"Like a few times a year since fourth grade."

"You'd think it was Vietnam for the length of time he's been fighting it. Like father, like son." He glared at my father briefly and tipped back his beer. He has a bulldog's neck and I watched his huge Adam's apple dance beneath the thick sleeve of skin. "You ever consider getting the boy into the martial arts? Or boxing? He may never even make it to the Corps at this rate, and by then he'll be so used to carrying other people's luggage even the Corps will have trouble making a man out of him. Cut the wimp out of him now, I'm telling you. Let's look into the boxing thing."

"How about knife fighting, Pop? I mean, come on. He's eleven, for Chrissakes. And he's also a helluva lot smarter than we were, so the Corps may not even *be* in his future."

"Nonsense," Red said, and looked right at me. "Nonsense! Gavin and me, we been talkin' about the Marine Corps since he was four. Ain't we, Gav? Remember when you were five I gave you that Jap bayonet?" I nodded. The bayonet was hanging proudly above my bed upstairs. "If there's one thing this boy will do in life, it's join the Corps . . . even if it's just for one tour."

My father stepped off the porch, his body tense, and said, "No, Pop. He'll do whatever he wants to do." His voice was thick and I was suddenly terrified that the two men were going to fight over me.

"Don't listen to him, Gavin. That's a man who doesn't understand the Corps like I do. Handing out canteens and boots will leave you bitter. He didn't even win his war."

I had heard Red talk about Vietnam, but I suppose we had never discussed the outcome; it seemed inconceivable that the Marines might have lost a war. I blurted out, "You didn't, Dad? You guys didn't win?"

"No," Red answered for him. "He didn't."

My father moved down the lawn steadily, shaking his head from side to side. "Go inside, Gavin." I did.

By the time I entered high school, I was resigned to my Montgomery beatings, bitter that I lacked the powerful will and fighting spirit of Red Kelly, somehow siphoned off by my father and wasted. To grasp at what little self-respect I had left, I made jokes about the Montgomerys all the time, which invited more beatings, which invited more jokes. Eventually I targeted the most dangerous and powerful actors because those jokes got the biggest laughs. My teachers didn't appreciate it.

Three Somali men walk past the gate dressed for a night at Studio 54 circa 1978, and I take the opportunity to change the subject. "They look like we did in junior high."

Armstrong spits again. "I ain't never looked like that there. Sir, in this world there are the motherfuckers and the motherfucked. And them people is the motherfucked. The whole damn country."

"Who are the motherfuckers? The clans?"

He laughs as if the question is a complete surprise, the naïveté of it. "Nooo, sir, come on," he says and spits. When I raise my eyebrows he continues, "You and me. The platoon. We're the motherfuckers. *Biggest motherfuckers on the planet.*"

————

It is dark now and occasionally, over the hum of the distant generators and the crying and hacking, I can hear the laughter of the Marines on break. I put on my NVGs and see a group of Marines sitting in a circle listening to Boom Boom. Gunny is on watch with Armstrong and the security detail, so I decide to investigate all by my lonesome and stop behind one of the trucks when I'm within earshot.

"I got one, Boom Boom," whispers Montoya. "Peter Piper picks a peck of pickled peppers."

"Oh! That is wonderful, Sergeant. Peter Piper and his peppers? All *P*s!" says Boom Boom. The Marines must be testing the tongue-twister claim espoused on our culture and phrases card.

"Fuckin' A, right. Here's another: She sells seashells by the seashore."

"Hold up a sec, Montoya," Johnson interrupts. "That Peter Pepper one ain't right. It's 'pack' not 'peck.'"

"It's 'peck.'"

"Then tell me what the motherfuck a 'peck' is? See, now a 'pack' of peppers makes sense. Like a 'pack' of cigarettes."

"I'm not talking about cigarettes, dumb fuck. I'm talking peppers here."

"Whatever. How do you know all this shit, anyway, Sergeant M.?" asks Johnson.

"I taught my kid sister these rhymes just a few months ago, that's how. She was having a test in school." Montoya has three or four sisters; this would normally be a serious liability for a Marine but the Devildogs don't tease Montoya about his family after he popped a fellow jarhead for calling one of his sisters a ho.

"Wait a second. Your sister's in the States?" asks Johnson, looking around to share a glance with the other Marines in the circle.

"My whole family's in the States, you idiot."

"But she's illegal, right? So she gets to go to an American school? How do you get away with that?"

"Illegal immigrants can still go to school, asswipe. And I'm not illegal anymore."

"But they are."

"Yeah, and soon my sisters are gonna take your sisters' jobs."

The galley gives out a collective "ooohhhhh daaammmnnn," hoping for some sparks; it's still just a friendly discussion but in the Corps, where a salutation with the wrong emphasis can end in a wrestling match, any chance to escalate conflict and dump fuel on a fire is seized and executed.

"What're you gonna do about that, Big Dog?" one of the men asks. "Your *sisters!*"

"You gonna fight Sergeant M., Big Dog? For what he say about your sistah? I have a sistah!" squeals Little Joe, whom I now recognize, sandwiched tightly in the circle. He's wearing his "Marines Never Die, They Just Go to Hell and Regroup" T-shirt.

"At ease, everyone. At ease," laughs Johnson, smiling widely. "Now, since I was busted down to lance coolie, I got two ranks between me and the good sergeant, so I'm gonna keep this civil. And we all know how M. gets with his sisters. So let me just ask this—M., you're sayin' your sisters are gonna be a lot better than my sisters are at their jobs?"

"Yup."

"I mean, a *lot* better, right, Sergeant M.? They're gonna take over and just outwork the hell outta them?"

"That's what I'm saying, Big Dog."

Johnson stands and I know something's coming. He picks up his helmet, plops it on his head, fastens the chin strap, and says, "Well, I got news for you. You're right—your sisters *are* gonna take over for mine and they're gonna do a *lot* better. Wanna know what my sisters do?"

"What?"

Johnson starts to giggle and he presses the Velcro flat to secure his flak vest. "Porn stars, dude! Your sisters are gonna be porn stars and they'll be a lot better! They'll be fuckin' allll niiigghht, dude! Yeah, got you!"

Montoya smiles and leaps to his feet, chasing Johnson right toward me. I step out from behind the bumper and ask, "What have we got here, gents?"

Sergeant Montoya skids to a halt and actually comes to attention, startled. Johnson's still laughing and he forces his hand over his mouth, trying to apologize to me. He bends double and looks as if he's vomiting, he's laughing so hard at his mediocre joke. The rest of the Marines in the circle hush; a normal person might assume the troops were talking about him, but as an officer it is not atypical to halt any conversation simply by coming into earshot.

"Oh, hey, sir," Montoya says. "I was just testing Lance Corporal Johnson's reaction drills."

He is a terrific Marine and, like the three other Mexican Marines with whom I have served, he's the epitome of the straight arrow. I was surprised to learn in October that he was Mexican (I was tallying the absentee George Bush ballots from the platoon before mail run and came up one short), but all you need to join the United States military is a green card, so I suppose I should have recognized the signs: conduct well above and beyond the call of duty and a relentless work ethic that flirts with a nearly psychotic obsession. I sometimes feel that Montoya—just like Darren Phillips—is so desperate to prove himself that he might one day snap. So I can't wait for his citizenship to come through. Foreigners who fight for the States in a war are often granted citizenship and Montoya is a Gulf War vet, but I've sent three letters to the INS and he's still waiting for a decision.

Montoya wears a wispy mustache that has been struggling for one year to fully emerge, like a weakling sprout. The platoon harasses him consistently over this ugly absence of testosterone, but none of them push Montoya too hard; he has a swift uppercut and a temper that can sear laughter pretty quickly.

A moaning cry drifts up out of the night from behind the wire walls of the FDC. "AAAuuuhhh . . . aaauu- uhhh . . ." Montoya wheels at the sound and shoulders his rifle. The Marines in the circle scatter, running toward their security posts bent over in hunches.

There are some stragglers moving toward the gate, sob- bing in the dark. The shrieks of children begin to echo off the walls as they approach and soon they are at the gate. "Ahhhh! Waaahhh!" They are so loud I can't even hear Montoya speaking to me.

"What?"

"What should we do, sir?" shouts Montoya.

"Grab Boom Boom and the bullhorn."

Montoya returns a few seconds later with the bullhorn but sans Boom Boom. "Must be hidden away, sir. Gunny's lookin' for him. Lazy, fucking, pussy cocksucker." Montoya may struggle with Ye Olde English, but he's got a good handle on USMC lingo. "Should I shout a warning? It's just women and kids."

"No, it'll just scare them."

It's a small group of refugees—maybe fifteen—and they walk right up to the barbed wire and start babbling. All of the kids are crying. "Goddamn hate that crying. Drives me crazy, sir," says Montoya. "Too bad we can't let them in."

"*Waaahhhh! Waaahhh!*" The white noise increases and it sounds as if the entire country is wailing and shrieking and coughing and begging. I put a finger in one ear and nod my head.

Gunny jogs up and says, "Boom Boom's gone, sir. Don't ask 'cause I don't know. Anyway, guess we just got to ignore them. The Red Cross lady said no feeding at night."

The Somalis are pulling at the concertina wire gate now. A woman with a terrible bow in her back yanks her hand away and shrieks because she's grabbed one of the razor blades that dot the wire. She sits down hard and wails with her hands held skyward as if in anticipation of a cooling rain. "That's going to be a tough order to follow, Guns."

The three of us walk toward the gate making shooing motions, saying, "Go! Go! No food. Tomorrow!"

The women are pleading now through their tears and I'm gritting my teeth and clenching my jaw in an effort to block out the noise. "Goddamn. Thought my daughters were bad," says the Gunny, hands over his ears. "Chow hall's closed, people!"

"Screw this," I say. "Imagine you walked for twenty miles for food. Montoya, tell Armstrong to mix twenty rations, please. We'll feed them and get them on their way."

He trots off, rousts Team One, and returns with Little Joe. "Got us a hasty translator, sir."

"Hi, Joe. We feed them, then they go. Okay?" I make all sorts of hand gestures.

Joe talks for a long time with a Somali woman and then says, "She want to stay here. Sleep inside here."

"What do you think, Gunny?"

"Sir, we're not supposed to feed them as it is. Besides, ground's just as hot here as it is out there, and I can't take much more of this crying, you know? We might catch some germ or something."

"Okay. Joe, tell them food but no sleep here. Okay?"

Gunny posts some extra security and when Montoya opens the gate, the Somalis do not rush in Who-concert

style, somehow showing the discipline to queue up without argument. Doc comes forward and guides the refugees
to the food tables, then begins health inspections after
they've eaten. None of them pass. Armstrong's men are
talking happily at the Somalis, the Somalis not compre-
hending but smiling nonetheless, while Armstrong stares
at them from atop a little hill with his NVGs, shaking his
head slowly, bare arms crossed, white-green and engorged
in my goggles.

I hear Johnson giving some excited instructions, and
when the architect is satisfied a flash lights the FDC like
lightning. The white fog comes back green and crisp in my
goggles and I see the picture that will be: Johnson in the
center, Somalis under his arms on either side as if it's a
family reunion. Somehow everyone knows to smile.

"Lance Corporal Johnson!" Armstrong's voice rips
across the courtyard. Thunder following the flash. "Get
away from them freaks and bring your camera here. *Now!*"

Doc walks up to me and Gunny. "They want MREs, sir.
Is that okay?" MRE is the acronym for "Meals Ready to
Eat," the highly caloric vacuum-sealed slop we eat in the
field; imagine the joy on a Marine's face when, on a freez-
ing evening, he tears into one of the rations and finds a wet
omelette staring up at him, trembling with larval life,
packaged in 1969, having waited over twenty years for
some poor bastard hungry enough to eat it. The Corps
ain't McDonald's: We don't throw away fries that are a
minute overcooked.

"You tell me, Doc. Didn't you tell the platoon that the
sudden influx of calories might kill them or make them
explode or something?" I ask.

"Oh. Well, actually, Doc Baker said that that wasn't
true, but I had to pass that word anyway to the platoon so
nobody would feed them. I felt real bad about that, sir,

telling that to the platoon. No, the Somalis won't explode."

I thought that was a bum scoop at the time; just a way to most effectively prevent the Marines from giving away their chow, the same way we tell the men that the AIDS rate in Thailand is 95 percent. Or that good conduct on a Persian Gulf training exercise will bring a liberty port in Australia. Or that a top grade on an inspection will bring more time off. Controlling conduct through misinformation, the Marine Corps way.

"Unburden your conscience, Doc. Have at it, then send them on their way."

He hustles over and many of the Marines donate an MRE, most of them omelette or the dreaded tuna with noodles, the meal I seem to eat every day because, falling last in the pecking order, I am faced with that or the omelette for nearly every meal.

Gunny lines up the Somalis to count them as they exit the FDC in case we have another stowaway, and Little Joe says, "She didn't get no emeree, Gunny. She want two." He points to a woman and her child in line.

"Tell her she can share an MRE with the others, Joe," says Gunny. I consider tossing mine over, but that will only leave me with one tomorrow. The thought makes me guilty so I tell the team leaders to do a gear check before the Somalis depart.

Little Joe gives up on Gunny and starts to plead with me when Armstrong says, "Sir! Hold it up. Johnson's missing his NVGs." He walks over with a very dejected Johnson in tow. Armstrong shakes his head apologetically. "Better check the Somalis before they di-di. That's two fuck-ups for Johnson tonight." He stares at his assistant but Johnson just droops his head.

Gunny blocks the exit and asks up and down the line, but no Somali steps forward. The Somalis stay put, smiling stupidly in the dark. "Should I pat 'em down, sir?" he asks. I nod. He grimaces and begins to pat down the first person in line, a stick figure of a woman, stops and scowls; I nod again, and he continues. He's on his fourth search when he says, "Jackpot," and holds up a pair of NVGs. "She had them in her chow container, thankless wench." He turns to the woman. "Why you do this? Why?" The woman just cowers and holds up her hands.

"Montoya," I say, "have your team do a full search of the Somalis, then get them out of here. No more food . . . tell that woman, Joe. No food, Little Joe. Tell her. Gunny, can you have all the teams get a gear and weapons accountability check, please?"

In ten minutes Gunny says, "Everything's up, sir. Montoya found some spoons they tried to lift, but no more of our gear. Told you we shouldn't have fed them. Ungrateful thieves. Gonna let 'em keep the MREs?"

"Yes. Johnson just got careless. I'm sure Armstrong will make him pay."

"Count on it, sir. Can't afford that kind of mistake. Hate to be in Armstrong's shithouse. Should we get the Skinnies out of here?" I nod. "Including Little Joe?" he asks.

"No," I say. "He stays. Besides, we need a translator."

The one woman is still bitching about an MRE, but none of the Marines feels particularly magnanimous. Gunny herds them out and closes the gate. Little Joe walks up to me and says, "Dat one sad, Kelly. Dat woman wit no emeree wit her baby."

"They stole. They take these." I hold up my NVGs. "Very bad."

"Not dat lady," he says sharply. "You hurt her for de other. She done nothing. Should have taken de other lady's food and gave it to her." He walks back over to Doc to continue his pitch and I feel ashamed.

The salient problem with children is their willingness to speak the truth.

—————

I am asleep when I first hear the screaming, incorporated immediately into some dream that wakes me. " . . . men over there. That's for sure. That ain't hunger cries." The Gunny is speaking to me. I sit up with a start and grab my rifle, tied with some paracord to my wrist to prevent an embarrassing theft. "Montoya says it's from behind that building across the street. Should we check it out, sir?"

"Wait . . . what? Who's screaming?"

"Don't know. A woman. But I heard . . . damn for sure heard some men yelling first. I think it may be Bangers . . . maybe invading some home or something. I know it's dicey . . . but should we at least check it out?"

"We're not supposed to leave the FDC without support," I say groggily.

"Sir, listen to it. This is goin' down *now.*"

I stand, and it is obvious by the pitch and continuity of the screams that something terrible has happened. *"Aahhhhh! AAAhhhh! NAAAAAAAAAH!"* The UN rule book is clear as to whether we should go investigate—we can't leave the compound unless we're under attack—but the Marine Corps rule book always leaves room for initiative. *"WAAAHHH! WAHHHHHH!"*

I think about how impotent and indecisive I was this afternoon when Farah was toying with Johnson, how the men were looking for me to *act,* and when I failed, Armstrong rescued me. "Fuck this, let's go. What team is off duty?"

"Armstrong's. I'll grab him and we'll be on our way."

"Hey, Gunny. Sorry to do this to you, but one of us has to man the fort. Can't have us both get shot."

"Pardon me, sir, but that sucks. I was on duty."

"Well, sorry. If something happens, then the colonel will wonder where the fuck I was again, just like the first night."

He hesitates, says again that it sucks, then accepts the decision. "I'll get Armstrong."

I brief Armstrong, he briefs his team, and I'm waiting on a knee next to the gate when he leads them up to me in a crouch. In my NVGs he looks like a killer robot, face smeared with paint, NVG monocle jutting out from his eyes like a deadly horn, flak jacket and gear harness giving him a square, metallic look, smoke grenades and flares taped tightly to his shoulder straps with black duct tape. I count only five Marines and pull Armstrong aside. "Where's Johnson?" I whisper.

"In my doghouse, sir. Told him he's in the box tonight for letting some Skinny steal the NVGs and for takin' that picture. Told him he'd need to get my confidence back," he whispers.

"Listen. The first team I pick is yours for exactly the opposite reason. The way to get that Marine back on track is to show him you still believe in him. He made a mistake, just like you when you lied to me, and I picked *you*. Get me? We need your whole team."

He nods immediately and says, "Tracking. My bad, sir."

We depart the gate after another brief and spread out, moving quickly in the dark, using a diamond formation that will provide all-around fires, our paths illuminated by the glowing haze of the ambient starlight sucked in and expanded by the NVGs. We pass the building and enter a street intersection. Armstrong gives some hand signals that are passed down the formation and back, arms extending, then the formation shifts into something resembling a flock of geese so that most of our firepower is directed in front of us, Johnson in the lead. He brings his hand up in a fist and everyone freezes. He gives the signal for down, and we do that, then the Marine in front of me tugs at his collar and I know I've been requested up front. I crawl up to Armstrong.

"Bangers at noon, sir. See them?"

I see two pickup trucks with men in the backs, eating. No rifles that I can see. Other people are milling about in the square intersection. Several women are still crying. Occasionally I hear a man yelling something. "Let's scoot around their flank and approach the trucks from the opposite side. Don't want those people in a cross fire," I say. "Remember, no rifles, no shots. Our lives have to be in danger. Understood?"

"If that's the case, sir, we'll never get to fire. When are the Bangers gonna be a danger?" he whispers brashly.

I see Farrah, who is carrying a machete, emerge from the crowd. He walks toward the pickup trucks shouting orders and then the trucks start their engines. "Shit," I say. "No time. Let's move up."

Armstrong and I hop up and the Marines follow us forward, spreading out as they walk, rifle butts finding shoulders and burrowing in tight. "Farrah Fawcett's got a machete," Armstrong says. "That good enough?"

Unfortunately not. "Hold fire," I whisper.

A woman breaks from the crowd and chases Farrah. He wheels around, raises his machete, and cuts her arm off at the shoulder. She bends over to pick it up, then tilts drunkenly and collapses.

"Motherfucker! Can I take him down, sir?"

"He's not a threat to us! Hold fire," I hiss, hating myself.

Farrah spots us and sprints to his truck, yelling. We

drop to our knees and bring our rifles up to our shoulders, the reflection of the laser sights suddenly bouncing off the trucks and the men in them, white in our NVGs. That means all of the Marines have sighted in, pulling their triggers just hard enough to send the lasers forward. Another half a pound of pressure and they'll all be dead. "Hold fire!" I yell.

The trucks gun their engines and race off. I see a few rifles as we speed away, but none are pointed at us. I turn to Armstrong and say, "Take us up."

He shouts some orders and we move forward by bounds, covering the Marines who are rushing, and sprinting like hell when it's our turn. The Marines form a hasty defensive perimeter and Armstrong does some fine-tuning, placing his machine gunner next to the road in case the Gangbangers return. If they do, the machine gun will rip them all to pieces. Several hundred of them.

I move in among the squealing crowd of Somalis and an old man points at a child who is crying, sitting in a pool of blood next to a headless corpse, splashing spasmodically with his hands as if he is in a kiddie pool. He is green in my goggles and when he waves his arms, still screeching, black dots of blood fly toward my goggles but fall short, others sprinkle his face. I glance around the group and a few Somalis come toward me, grabbing me, screaming unintelligible phrases over and over. The one-armed woman struggles to her feet and stumbles over to me in a wicked lean, grabbing hold of my NVGs as she falls against my chest, pulling them down past my nose around my neck, dying at my feet, no longer green and crystalline but black and shiny and real, bleeding out now and lifeless, Armstrong swearing in the background. Everyone is screaming.

"Armstrong! Get someone up here to grab these bodies. We're taking these people back to the compound. Got her *head* cut off. Another one, I mean."

He trots over to me in a hunch, NVGs shifting all around him, taking it all in, then barks out some orders. "Johnson! Police up this dead Skinny! Not that one-armed thing. *This* one!"

Johnson rushes over, says, "Oh. Oh, Jesus Christ, it's got no head. They cut its head off," looks at Armstrong, grabs the corpse by a hand, then under both armpits, drops it, and throws up on the road.

"Sergeant?" Johnson coughs. "I'm sick."

"Forget the body," I say. "Armstrong, just get them in formation and let's get the fuck out of here. I'll control the refugees . . . you got external security." The Somalis drag the headless corpse along easily, but the one-armed body is a trickier portage and they are forced to stop and regrip several times along the route. Eventually they just drag it by the legs, its torso bouncing across the bigger stones in the blood-soaked earth.

When we reach the gate, Gunny puts all the people in Doc's care and says, "What the hell happened, sir?"

I tell him, then request Little Joe. The boy is sleepy when he appears in front of me, stretching and rubbing his eyes. Boom Boom walks up right behind him in his suit, nervous and babbling about where he was told to sleep.

"Sir. De men told me to sleep, so I just wanted a small rest—"

"Look, I don't give a fuck. Just find out what happened," I say.

The translator begins to talk with the refugees and, after about five minutes, Little Joe starts questioning, too, apparently frustrated with the conversation. The translator yells at the boy and slaps him across the face. Joe sobs and sprints into the Gunny's arms, little back heaving when he arrives. Not smart. Gunny's hand shoots out like a bear's and he grabs the translator by the throat, "Touch this boy again and I'll kill you." He lifts Boom Boom off the ground and throws him into a pile of sandbags.

The violence is as ubiquitous as the heat in this country, burning away at life itself, steadily whittling the population.

Boom Boom scrambles to his feet but steps back, gasping for air and gauging the Gunny's intentions. He brushes some dirt from his suit and smiles nervously. "I'm so sorry. Sorry. There has been a mistake. Thought he was just a boy in the camp. He's just a rude boy, sir. Usually I would use a stick."

Gunny starts to move forward and I put my hand flat on his chest. "Go back to sleep," I tell Boom Boom. "You're officially fired."

"*Fired?* Sir, that is impossible. This is my assignment."

"Let me get something straight with you right now, motherfucker. I see you again, I *Boom Boom* the flesh from your face. Understand?!" roars Gunny.

Boom Boom narrows his eyes and says coolly, "As you wish, Marine." He smiles at me, bows, and disappears behind the trucks.

My heart is pounding again, so I rub Joe's head gently and say, "Joe, you're our man now. Tell us what you know."

The boy's tears evaporate. "De lady without emeree, de one I tell you about? De men kill her for it . . . She have no emeree for dem and dey kill her. Farah. Den her sistah attack de men and she get de machete arm." He shrugs as if to say, Cool out, Jack, happens all the time.

"What?" says Gunny, shocked. "They killed a woman— *two* women—for an *MRE?* With a machete? Chopped their heads and arms off?"

"Yes," I say.

"Fucking savages is what we're dealing with. You know that, right, sir?"

"Guess I should have given her that extra MRE," I say, and walk off to make a radio report that I might have avoided but for petty greed.

– 12 –

11 DECEMBER 1992

Aren't you sorry you bombed babies? Are you grateful for the humane treatment of your benevolent captors?

"The woman from the Red Cross tells me she told you not to go feeding people at night, without her," says the colonel. He is highly agitated. Much more effective than a cup of coffee as a wake-up call. In fact, his visit this morning may never be forgotten. Not if he fires me. Big Duke is across the FDC talking with Gunny. Certainly *he'll* understand that we—

"Damn it, look at me when I talk to you, Lieutenant!"

"Sir, they came to us hungry and desperate. I knew how to mix proper rations from watching the Red Cross and they were starving. So I fed them."

"And you gave them *MREs?* I can't believe you'd be that dumb, Kelly. You know what they can do to their stomachs, first of all, right? That amount of calories? Were you at the same medical brief that I attended? So you should have figured out it was for some of the war-lords."

"Sir, I . . . had no way of knowing."

I'm sure every FDC except mine slept soundly through the night. Maybe I'm snakebit. I'm so drained that the ability to argue the case is gone. Rules are rules; maybe we should have stayed in the FDC, even if it meant listening to people die just a few hundred yards away. Hell, we've even got earplugs that would have blocked out the crying. I've become a dog that's been hit one too many times by a rolled newspaper. Now the colonel just needs to raise an arm and I'll cringe.

"It's your *job* to *know*. It sure as heck is! So you effectively set the example for terrorism here. These Somalis were just using you."

"Sir, it was just a tough situation. Sir, *all* of them might have been killed if they came out empty-handed. That woman was killed because she was the one woman who didn't bring an MRE back out with her. And I was too selfish to give her mine."

"He's probably right, Colonel," says Big Duke, who has walked over. "That woman from the Red Cross told me the same thing. It's not uncommon for the warlords to kill for food, especially now that we control the food distribution."

The colonel ponders this and says, "Okay. But it was still stupid to set the precedent for giving up MREs. They aren't chips in a poker match, Lieutenant, and I won't be held hostage by these thugs."

"No, sir."

"And I *really* question your decision to leave the FDC without calling headquarters and arranging some backup support. Instructions are clear in that regard. You might have walked into a full-blown ambush."

"Sir, those women were screaming bloody murder, literally, and we had to act."

"But you endangered your Marines. Haven't we discussed these force-protection guidelines we're under? Never underestimate the enemy, Kelly. You know better than that. Geez, General Bellissimo is sure pissed."

It is a much softer rebuke and his tone is almost . . . *friendly?* He starts to add something but pauses awkwardly. He looks regretful. Maybe he wants to be on my side? Finally he says, "Well, Sergeant Major Duncan and I have to go see Lima Company. One of their squads found a weapons cache last night. We've got the media coming over to have a look-see with us. I'll speak with you back at the airport tonight. Think you can last another few hours here?"

I tell him we can.

They both turn to walk off and Big Duke swivels his head around to face me, winks, and gives me a thumbs-up. Near as I can tell he's not gay, so I take this as encouragement and it buoys my spirits. He mumbles something to the colonel and walks over to me. He has an awkward gait, courtesy of a 7.62-millimeter round that slammed into his hip in 1968. The early sun that has cracked through the trees gives his eyes an icy sparkle and when he smiles at me wrinkles flair up in the corners of his eyes and streak back toward his ears.

"You followed your instincts last night, not the rules, Lieutenant."

"They were *screaming,* Big Duke, and as Marines—"

"I'm not questioning your decision, sir. Force protection is one of the missions, but you and I both know a Marine's not going to sit back and allow murder on his watch. That's what we're paid for. And some of these other rules—allowing these bandits to be armed is one—aren't too palatable, either. You and I know that. And, sir, *some-one else* knows it, too. Clear?"

"Nope."

Big Duke glances at the colonel, who is outside the gate and tapping on his watch, and sighs. "As your command-ing officer, the colonel can't say exactly what's on his mind, get me? He's under a *lot* of pressure from the UN. Bellissimo chewed his ass this morning for you leaving."

"Yeah, but I get the feeling something bad's gonna hap-pen here if we bow to that pressure."

His face gets serious, wrinkles converging, upper lip vibrating. Big Duke is deeply tan, but he seems to darken and I am taken aback, the trepidation skyrocketing when his eyes well. "In Vietnam I saw more than a few men killed because of restrictions. My team was attached to Fifth Marines for the Hue City battle. Supposed to call in air. When I crossed the Perfume River and joined the fight for the citadel in Hue, we were told that we couldn't destroy any 'cultural icons' because the Viets viewed the place— especially the Imperial Palace—as sacred grounds, you know? So we had no proper artillery or air support when we went in there, and guess where the North Viets shot us from? All the places we were told were off limits. My bud-dies, Patrick Jirka, Eric Prinkalns . . . It was just . . . it was just . . . *it—was—just—the worst fucking betrayal and I . . .*"

His voice trails off and he wipes his face. The deep emo-tions have made an M-1 tank of an entrance and I do not know how to react.

"Is it so wrong to hate for so long, sir?" he asks from behind cupped hands.

"I . . . don't know, Big Duke," I whisper, stunned. Lacking anything better to say I whisper, "My dad fought there, too. Or, served there, I mean." I want to take it back as soon as it's left my mouth—the Corps is a tiny place and

I fear Big Duke will have somehow run across my father while drawing a new set of boots or something.

"Huh. Didn't know that. Was he a Marine?"

"No. Well, not a real Marine. He was a supply weenie."

"Sir, every Marine's a warrior. You know that. Anyway, we lost *lots* of good men because of the way we were forced to fight, and the captain I was attached to at Hue, he told me he had no control over the rules. And the anger, sir, the *anger*.

"That was just before an NVA mortar round took his chest away. Oh yeah, sir, the NVA was using mortars but we couldn't because we were concerned about *their* architecture. Hell, you could say the entire fucking *war* was lost because of rules like this. I mean, how many other wars you study in your Harvard history books where you win *every single battle* but lose the war?"

He sneers and then stares right at me. I have never seen a Marine cry and I turn away. He wipes his eyebrows, trailing fingers down across his lids. "I'm sorry, sir. Just . . . it's still hard to take, you know? And there's a point to this. Bet your old man raves just like me, don't he? Right?"

"He didn't . . . no. Not really," I say, embarrassed that my father's been mentioned.

He puts his hand on my shoulder and squeezes it. To a civilian, this might not seem like an important gesture, but to a Marine it is monumental. We aren't too touchy-feely.

"What I'm saying is, in Vietnam at least we got the chance to learn from fighting the enemy, learned from our first engagements, where we screwed some pooches, and we applied those lessons and adjusted, kicked their asses. Same as they did in Korea and World War II before that. Problem in these new wars, sir, is that you ain't gonna have a second chance. A firefight is going to erupt out of nowhere and it's gonna be a one-off deal that the whole country will watch live on CNN and it will involve innocents and it will not be clean. *And you had better be ready.* So, yes, we have some strict rules here, sir, but when the fight is joined, you follow those instincts your old man gave you. Then do the right thing."

He turns away from me abruptly, throws a forearm across his eyes as if he is elbowing the air, and trots over to the colonel, running diagonally with that crazy hop of his, favoring his left leg.

My old man gave me? I am surrounded by my platoon of Marines—most of whom are staring at me now, having watched to see how the colonel would react to the night's events—and still the feeling of loneliness overwhelms me. I should be confident about command, yet here I stand, with the experience of two years as a grunt infantry platoon commander and a war under my belt, and still the heavy cloak of responsibility makes me question whether I am worthy of them, whether I am up to the task, whether I have truly overcome the cowardice that still seems so deeply lodged, whether I will *do right.* Stranger still is Big Duke's last sentence. I have modeled my decisions as the *opposite* of how I imagined my father acted, running away from the mysterious ghost of his failed years in the Corps, not embracing it.

———

I am chatting with Sergeant Montoya, dishing out some rations, trying to clear my head by focusing on finishing this mission, when a raven-haired woman hops out of a jeep in front of the FDC and strides in past one of the guards. Mary Thayer-Ash is wearing cargo pants and a white tank top that's too tight for her. And the rest of us. She brushes off the Marine with a back-handed wave and continues toward us, the Marine yelling after her, aviator sunglasses and her head tossed back, hair billowing. I am stunned and excited, then terrified as she approaches. Darren is following her.

The Gunny stops them, shrugging apologetically across the courtyard, but I yell my consent. Darren grabs Thayer-Ash's arm, whispers to her, then approaches me alone. "Lieutenant Kelly. I was told you'd be here."

I raise my hand at the Marine guard who is still shadowing him, indicating that I'm okay with the breach—though I'm not—and toss my head toward the trucks. "Let's go over there where we can talk in private, dude."

"Don't call me dude. Thought I cleared that up years ago. You need a fresh education?"

Darren's trying to reestablish his familiar territory in our relationship: superiority. And while I have resented this for nearly a decade, I also know that I do owe him much and have not yet outgrown the desire to be more like him.

"Look, Gavin, I'm in a position to help you here, but you have to understand the dilemma. Check? Mary Thayer-Ash has gone into core meltdown over this thing and she's insisting on a big report. You know how we always talked about how perfect Hitler was as an enemy and how we would have loved to get some of The Big War? Well, people like Mary think that My Lai is the example of good reporting, and she aims to expose. She was very close to that Somali you guys offed—you know they were her protectors for, like, two months?—and the surviving brother is going to go on camera. So you need to do what I say."

Darren is wearing a white polo shirt with a CNN logo. His biceps pop out from the short sleeves like cantaloupes, then taper sharply to the elbows before his forearms snap the angles out again. Military-issue aviators, square lenses, quasi-intellectual without putting off either his new peers or his old. His big press pass dangles over his chest. His trousers are old-school military desert-issue and they are rolled and crisply bloused at the tops of his Desert Storm combat boots, just like mine. Of course, Darren first taught me how to do that. He also has a dog tag in his left boot. You can take the kid out of the Marines . . .

"Muhammad Lahti's got no credibility. He had a rifle, for fuck's sake, Darren. And let me tell you something, these Somali warlords are fucking *dangerous.* They know violence. Put a rifle in their hands and the Marine *has* to assume mortal danger."

Darren opens his mouth and removes the shades with a deft snap of his wrist. "Oh, Kelly," he laughs, "don't tell me you're giving this practice squad the same credit you gave the Iraqis before the war. Come on, now. You're dealing with amateur hour again. They fire their fucking AK-47s blind around corners, pray to Allah, and spray. You guys will *eat these punks alive* if it comes to serious blows."

He winks at me and I am left to marvel at the unwavering confidence that even an Iraqi bullet and a medical discharge could not diminish. Just before Desert Storm was launched, my imagination conquered my bravery and whatever sense of adventure I lusted for was crushed by thoughts of body bags and bullet-swept trenches. So I went to the only person who could calm me before we crossed into battle—Darren Phillips.

The first images beamed back from the Gulf were pictures of soldiers sucking down bottled water, spilling it over their burning bodies. What a laugh. I have never been as cold as I was in the weeks preceding the ground war, soaked to the bone every other day in my mud hole in the Saudi dirt. Our desert camouflage utilities were wet the day before we began the hunt and stayed that way for three days, clinging to our bodies with a persistent chill.

On 23 February 1991, the Russians invited the Iraqi foreign minister to hammer out a last-minute peace. Marines like Darren held their collective breaths. Was this to be the mother of all Chinese fire drills? That afternoon the Iraqis set fire to the Kuwaiti oil wells, a certain sign that a fight was at hand. The prevailing winds sent the thick blackness southwest, writhing and foaming on a track as inevitable as the war itself, and when it reached us, the sun just disappeared. I did not see it again for three weeks.

The oil carried a foul smell within its cloud, a smell that I will forever associate with death itself. We would fight after all.

The perpetual fires and their concomitant plumes of black fog gave the battleground an appropriate backdrop. When we finally started our engines and moved forward, I felt I was descending to a truculent and base plane, painted as if it was a movie set. I had read the script and knew the ending. So did the Iraqis. We moved through the daylight darkness knowing our mission was to slaughter the Iraqis even as they mourned their dead.

A few hours before the attack, I found Darren in his hole, studying his map. "You should get some shut-eye, war dog," I said as I hopped into his pit.

He growled. "Got lots to think about. Like how I'm gonna support your white ass when you call for me."

The other lieutenants would have been irritated to hear Darren acting like a big brother again—he was determined to be the superior officer in the group, and though he probably was, he never quite mastered the art of letting that go unsaid—but I was used to his brashness and welcomed it that day. I was nervous, and he was, for all his bravado, a comforting presence. If I was caught in a firefight, he *would* join the fight, just as he had done so often in college.

I shook his hand. "Well, good luck, brother. I may be needing you. This could get ugly fast." The Marines in my platoon didn't seem afraid of the Iraqis, but I was. Many of them were veterans of a bitter war with Iran, and the reports of the Iraqis' willingness to die for Allah jogged memories of Red's stories of brutal Japanese fanaticism.

Darren shook his head and grinned. "Please. Paaleease. You know, the Iraqis have this Baath holiday called 'Day of the Dead' or some shit to honor their war dead. Did you know that?" I shook my head. "Well. Tomorrow we're going to give them about twenty thousand more reasons to celebrate."

"More than that, if they truly believe dying to be a gift to Allah."

He snorted. "What a bunch of bullshit. Guaran-*fucking*-tee you that they'll turn tail when they see what we can unleash."

"Well, I hope so." Overhead, a flight of Harriers roared by, heading north, and we were forced to halt the conversation, so loud were their engines. The United States war machine is an awesome and beastly phalanx, and between the birds and Darren I was looking at two of the meanest animals in the herd.

The flames of their tail cones grew faint and I said awkwardly, "I'll see you in Kuwait."

He grabbed me by my harness and shook me playfully. "Damn, Kelly, I should take offense. You're *nervous*, aren't you? After all my years of tutoring. Oh, me. Listen to me, brother, you get in any kind of trouble, *anything*, and I'll get you out, but you're going to do well. You know that, don't you?"

I told him that I did.

"Good luck, bro. Make me proud."

"Okay, Dad," I said, and stepped out of his lair.

The next time I saw him he was in a hospital bed in San Diego.

Darren grabs my arm and shakes me awake. "Oh, shit, here she comes. Follow my lead."

He turns and we watch Mary Thayer-Ash approach, Nike Air Pegasuses catching sand and sending it in rooster-tail spits as she strides over with those long legs. Darren mumbles, "Just let me interpret, Kelly."

She is livid and looks as if she may break into a run. Strange as it sounds, I reach down and unhook my pistol holster, so crazed with rage was she the last time we saw each other. Perhaps she's come for revenge. I take off my sunglasses. My mother always said that was the polite thing to do and, who knows, my baby blue eyes might help her forget the whole thing. Yeah.

She ignores my hand and says, "You look different without your makeup, Lieutenant."

"I've got a cammie kit in my pack if you'd like me to gussy up before this interview."

"Oh, it's not an interview. Just a question: Did you get away with murder?" she growls.

"Jesus, Mary," says Darren.

I fight the urge to say, *And Joseph.* "I can't discuss it, ma'am. NBC agreed with the findings. It was not our fault."

"You know *goddamn well* it was. You killed that boy in his sleep and you covered it up."

This woman wracks my nerves and I just want her out of my life. I have Somali warlords, murdered refugees, rules and reins that my platoon is straining against . . . and this woman joins the violent mix, accusing us of murder. "That's it. You two aren't supposed to be inside the FDC to begin with—"

"Wait. Wait just one second," she says, grabbing my elbow. She's trying to control her emotions, but it's clear she's upset. Her lips are pursed and her nostrils are flaring. "Just . . . please just answer a few questions. Please, Lieutenant. NBC barely knew the Lahtis. I spent two months of my *life* being protected by them. Now, I know you weren't there. They were asleep—"

"Stay away from me," I say curtly and jerk my arm out of her grasp, walking away. "Were you there?" I ask over my shoulder.

" . . . they were *asleep* and they had their badges on! I know it and you know it! And were *you* there?" she calls after me. "Were you?"

I walk over to the Gunny and say, "Give me two Marines."

He looks over my shoulder at Ms. Thayer-Ash and Darren and says, "Visiting time's up, sir?"

Darren helps us, talking her down out of the rage and coaxing her toward the gate. She doesn't put up much of a struggle, just a "Get your fucking paws off me" when one of the Marines grabs her elbow. She is a proud woman whose walk accentuates her need to be in control of her life and her surroundings, the level head and the shoulders thrust as far back as they will go, and she seems to come into a state of calm indignation. But the truth is that Mary Thayer-Ash is too livid to cap her feelings.

As she walks by the group of Marines on guard duty she says, "Which one of you killed Said Lahti? Which one? I'm going to find out the truth! Speak up now!" I walk behind her, just to make sure nothing happens, and I hear her mutter, "Murderous bastards," as she departs the barbed-wire fence of the FDC. She stops in front of the jeep, turns once more, and screams, *"You COWARDS!"* with a venom so palpable that I expect one of the men may shoulder an M-16.

How did it come to this? Should I have even let her in the compound?

Darren stuffs Thayer-Ash into the jeep, frowns at me apologetically, and shrugs. I watch the jeep depart; fortunately the dust manufactured by the tires rises up quickly and obscures it from our view, leaving me the freedom to concentrate on slowing my breathing. Armstrong saunters up to me in his Oakley sunglasses and spits some tobacco in the direction of Thayer-Ash's jeep.

"What're we gonna do about that crazy bitch, sir?" he asks.

Well I'm all broken up over that man's rights.

Noon. Just a few more hours left on FDC duty. The sun at its apex, hotter today, burning away at my patience and consciousness, bursting the bubbles of sweat that dot my forearms and sucking them dry. I feel an incredible sting on my leg and notice a huge, bright green horsefly as large as a Twinkie twitching with pleasure just above my knee. I swat it as hard as I can and it staggers onto the dirt, crushed out of proportion, twitching for different reasons now. Chalk up Somali kill number one for the kid. Then, amazingly, it flips over and zips away, buzzing me as it passes. *Negative, Ghostrider, the pattern is full.* This is a hard country.

I watch it jag over to the food trucks and feel guilty—that bastard will wreck a child's week if it bites—then happy when I see it light on Armstrong's Popeye forearm, not because it may bite, but because it has just landed on the Grim Reaper himself. Armstrong squashes it instantly and flicks the carcass like a paper football, then settles back into the boredom of the watch.

Like the rest of us, Armstrong is watching, waiting, hoping. *"For you, to justify my love."* Where are you when we need you to give us a boost, Madonna? Actually, she doesn't strike me as the USO type. Who is, anymore? No one gives a flying fuck. The Good War is over, and we're so passé I can taste it. Folks outside the extended military family are neither for us nor—and this part is perplexing—against us. Even the sons and daughters of the peace freaks could care less where we're sent. I've never seen a protester firsthand, let alone a protester who will become a president. Red believes we won The Good War because we were morally superior and the whole country was one. Was it really like that, with everyone pulling for one another? I've never experienced that in a country that is still reeling from a generational fracture that will never heal. Maybe I *do* relate to my father.

Red Kelly marched in *five* parades when he came home—hell, he *still* marches—and his actions were celebrated in newspapers and magazines for more than a decade. When Big Duke arrived in San Francisco in 1969, he couldn't find a taxi willing to drive him to the bus station.

The ship has since come off that terrible heel, but today even *Life* is more interested in which celebrities are attending the Tyson fight than United States foreign policy. As for the military, don't even *try* to name a fighting man or woman who held a rank lower than four-star general in Desert Storm. Apparently, there were none.

My mood has taken a nosedive, but a sulking officer isn't an officer at all, so I reverse the gear and square up again. If there's one thing a Marine does not do, it's feel sorry for himself.

The Marine Corps is a proud guild and would probably be defined as a cult if an outsider were to observe the daily actions of its fanatical followers. We have sacred rituals, secret traditions, and granite codes of conduct that run roughshod over the civilian rules we learned before our heads were shaved. I have seen Darren Phillips rehearsing Marine running songs—guttural chants, really—on a Saturday night when the rest of the battalion lieutenants were going out drinking, I have seen Terrel Johnson arguing with Gunny over the proper way to lace a dress shoe, I have seen Jesus Montoya practice his rifle drill for an entire weekend in preparation for a parade, and I have seen Jake Armstrong interrupt his parade deck brawl with a sergeant from another platoon the moment morning colors were sounded, working his thumb into his opponent's Adam's apple one second, both of them standing rigidly at attention when the crackling bugle notes leaked out of the battalion speaker system the next. I have never felt such an acute sense of belonging and purpose. When they come for me, they'll have to pry me out of the Corps with a bayonet.

I call to Little Joe. The boy squints at me, locks his body, and salutes. He is considering his options: continue watching the Marines' card game or come over and talk with me. It is clear I will lose, but Johnson whispers something to him and he smiles and scampers over.

"How's it hangin', Kelly?"

I smile back. "How's what hanging?"

"How's what hanging?" he repeats, not understanding.

I glare at the Marines, who are laughing, and say to him, "Have a seat. Want a cracker?" I hold up the best part of the tuna noodle MRE.

"You have emeree?" I nod. "I want emeree. Chicken rice."

"Pretty savvy for a kid."

"What is savvy?"

"Smart. You a smart boy."

"Yes," he says, giggling. "Smart."

The sun is raging and the inside of my flak vest is soaked. I've drained three quarts of water already and I crack another water bottle, drink three quarters of it, and hand the rest to Little Joe. It sounds weak, but I'm afraid of his germs. The sweat has salted my sunglasses with vertical jail bars and I wipe them with my T-shirt. I lather some more sunscreen across my neck and face and the boy says, "I want that."

"You don't need it, Little Joe. You're black. Sun doesn't burn you."

"I black?"

"Yes." I point at the Gunny. "Like Gunny. Black. I'm white. Gunny's black." I point at my face. "White." Then I hold up his small arm and place it next to mine, pointing from one to the other. "White. Black."

He runs over to Gunny and says something and the Gunny laughs and picks him up, tossing him into the air. In his arms Little Joe looks no larger than a five-year-old. I hope he doesn't break; the paperwork would be unbelievable. Gunny is walking over to me, smiling, when a Marine guarding the gate begins to scream.

The Marines in the card game hop up and dash across the compound, and when I sprint past their table a moment later with my rifle, the cards are fluttering and swirling around me like snowflakes.

"Yo! Stop right . . . hey! Stop or I'll shoot!" It's Armstrong, yelling at someone in front of the compound.

Armstrong sits up on a knee and levels his weapon at something. "Drop her, motherfucker!" I wait for his gunshot but it doesn't come. "I said *drop her.*"

I'm up by the bunker in an instant and see Farrah Fawcett, Mortar Muhammad, and four other men dragging two women to a truck. The women are not crying: No, they're putting up a hell of a fight, thrashing and spinning. "Farrah Fawcett in that Cowboys jersey and those others just walked up and snatched them, sir. I wasn't sure what to do at first," says Armstrong. "Got a bead on 'em, sir. Can I put one down?"

"No. We've gone over this, as—"

"We didn't go over a rape in progress, sir! *Not a rape.* Not like this. We can't just let them take them."

"We're still red. They are *not* imposing mortal danger. Hold fire. You might hit the women, anyway." This is an impossible position. We kill the six Bangers and we face courts-martial. We let them go and, well, that speaks for itself, the impotence of it. I am starting to think that in this, the epicenter of violence, brutality is the only way to achieve peace; it is a dismal thought.

"Let me shoot!"

"Hey! I said *no.*"

"Shit, sir! They're getting away!"

The men toss the women into separate trucks where the rest of the snakes pounce, pinning them under their coils, writhing and smothering. Farrah Fawcett, in his Cowboys jersey, stands up in the far truck and lets out a junior varsity war cry, pumping his fist in the air, a haughty end-zone celebration. The trucks speed away in a cloud of dust, more men standing and hooting now.

I put one of the Bangers in my sights and think about it. Man, I want to shoot so badly I can taste it.

"Fuck!" screams Armstrong, who takes off his helmet and slams it into a sandbag. It spins precariously for a moment, then falls into a mess of barbed wire in front of the bunker. "WHAT THE *FUCK* ARE WE DOING?"

I turn to him in a rage and put my finger in his face, "You get your fucking helmet on and report to me by the trucks. Were you just going to shoot them all?" I'm angry at myself just as much as I am with him.

"I . . . *yes, sir, I was.* They kidnapped them two girls. I say we kill them all . . . *let God sort them out.*"

"You heard the lieutenant, Armstrong!" Gunny booms. He's standing right behind us, thank God. "Get your helmet and get off the post or hell will be paid—in full—to me."

Armstrong regards him for a moment, nods, and says, "Aye, Gunny."

———

It takes me a while to come up with some words so I can chew Armstrong's ass. The fact is, I'm angry at the whole situation—not just his burst of recalcitrance—but Marines don't question orders and, more than that, I'm expected to lash into him. Gunny expects it, Armstrong expects it, and the platoon expects it. When I work myself into a fake lather, Gunny leads me across the compound, behind a truck where the other men won't hear.

Armstrong stands when we approach and comes to attention. He's the one who's supposed to be full of trepidation but when I see his face, *I'm* suddenly the nervous one. As I walk up to him, I am left wondering how it can possibly be that a lieutenant of Marines is shy of conflict, a trait so embarrassing that I am tempted to resolve it quickly and violently when I next get the chance. Am I making the right calls when the blanket of pressure comes, or are they the decisions of a coward who's leaning on strict interpretations of the rules of engagement as a means of saving both his career and his own skin?

"Sergeant Armstrong, if you can't live with the rules of engagement, I'll send you home! You understand me, Marine?" I have a headache caused by this helmet I've been wearing for nearly twenty-four hours, and the screaming is making it worse. The band is tight and it's making me crazy.

"Yessir," Armstrong says coolly, looking right at me. I

need to work on my bad-cop tactics, I guess. Perhaps I can take a tutorial from the colonel.

"You're unreliable right now. I know it's hot, but you have to keep your cool. This is the second time you've been warned. You lose your shit again and you're outta here. Do I make myself absolutely clear?"

Armstrong flicks his eyes to Gunny, then down at his boots, then back on mine. He mumbles, "It won't . . . I just wanted to apologize to you, sir. I lost my cool and it won't happen again. It's just . . . I thought this was a war and I was wrong."

I just nod—so sick of the whole situation—and dismiss him.

"NOW GET OUT OF THE LIEUTENANT'S FACE, ARMSTRONG!" Gunny booms, having drawn his bow over a minute ago. Both Armstrong and I jump a few feet.

We'll need about six hours back at the airport for everyone to cool down before the Gunny and I debrief this operation and rebuild the group. This is anything but a war, war as I know it, at least. It more closely resembles my father's, what with all the restrictions. My first war was not Red Kelly's war, but it's the only one I've got. And I miss it. All of us do. In that 100-hour fight the narcotic of power—in its purest form—washed across all of us, whetted our appetites, and rekindled genes that had been deemed outdated and unnecessary. For four days we were kings. No matter our personal circumstances back in the States, we shared a family's pride. I do not have a brother, but in 1991 I had forty-two of them—my platoon. Like many people my age, I was searching for my place in the world, a problem compounded by the fact that, as a newly crowned butterbar lieutenant, I had no confidence as a platoon leader and struggled against a lingering fear that I was, beneath my flak jacket and gold bars, a coward. But when the call came, I shouldered my rifle and charged forward with the rest of the Marines. *And I belonged.*

I have been waiting for that next fix ever since.

————

My platoon was at the end of the column going through the breach, a strip fifty yards wide that the engineers had plowed through the minefield and berms on the Kuwaiti border. We were silent at G hour, watching the vehicles at the head of the column roll slowly toward the lane, behind the tank plows. Two thousand meters to our front, Iraqi artillery fire began to impact with deep *whumps!* I felt the shock waves expand, rolling the ground, sending vibrations up through the rubber soles of my combat boots and into my bones. I stood on my toes and tried to see the destruction, but the sky was too black. I cringed and looked around at my men, totally panicked. *They'll kill us right in the breach! Why doesn't the battalion commander try another avenue? No wonder we ordered ten thousand body bags! Fucking Iwo Jima all over again!*

"Jesus! I think that's Iraqi arty, T-Bone," I said to my radioman. I had broken an unwritten rule a month earlier when I'd first used Corporal Tommy Bonneger's nickname to address him, but I figured, what the hell, we've shared a soggy foxhole for three months and we're going to *war*, for Chrissakes. The bond between a platoon commander and his radio operator is deep and symbiotic—both are a step removed from the internal social structure of the platoon (the officer because he should be, the RTO because he's viewed partly as a sycophant for spending so much time chatting with the zero)—and T-Bone and I were each other's best platoon friends. And without a true mate to watch his back, a Marine wanders in purgatory, damned and lonely.

"*What?*" screamed T-Bone, mouth agape, staring like an excited kid at the flashes that rippled the horizon. T-Bone was, at twenty-one, a year younger than me. He had blond hair, a sharp wit, and an easy laugh—all three of which had apparently done him justice at Rutgers before he'd dropped out.

"I said I think that's Iraqi arty!" I screamed.

"Nosir. Iraqi eighty-two mike-mike mortars. Not even fucking close, are they?" He smiled.

"No!" I forced a laugh. "Not even fucking close!"

"Here we go, sir. That's G hour."

A long whistle sounded and the first vehicles revved their engines and roared through the breach. I stood still and waited like a spectator at the Indianapolis 500—riveted because I felt tragedy loomed. But nothing happened. Marine tanks spread out on the other side of the minefield and vehicles began to pour through the gap in the abandoned Iraqi line. Not a shot was fired. Soon after, the Iraqi mortar barrage stopped altogether.

A thunderous cheer rose from the hundred-odd vehicles around me. "They're through!" a Marine yelled. "*Die camel jockeys!*" screamed another. I pumped my fists with the rest of the posse, suddenly feeling as if I was part of a Superbowl team in the tunnel, waiting to sprint onto the field in front of the cameras.

The engines of my platoon's five-ton trucks turned over and began to rev. The drivers popped the air brakes and they hissed loudly, like giant serpents, *ppsssssssssss!* I let out a startled yell and jumped away from one of the trucks and into the arms of two of my men, both wearing masks of horror, I was sure, not because of the sudden hiss but because they were following a coward into war.

"You okay, sir?" they shouted.

I nodded, leaned into the center of the circled platoon,

and shouted, "Let's get it on!" *Hail, Mary, full of grace . . .*

I rolled toward the pass through the berms in the Hummer, ahead of the two trucks carrying my platoon. As we approached the lane, I saw that there were bright red trash cans marking the entrance on either side, with big, black arrows providing direction if anyone became confused. Two ground guards stood next to each can, waving us through, and it reminded me of the same superfluous exercise to which drivers are subjected by traffic cops standing under green lights. I mean, where else was I going to take the platoon? Straight over the berms, mines, and concertina? The Marine Corps: designed by a genius to be run by twenty-two-year-old idiots like me.

Suddenly I was on Kuwaiti ground. It was light enough so that when I passed through the minefield I saw big anti-tank mines, surrounded by hundreds of fist-size antipersonnel mines on either side of our vehicle, just outside the lane. They were the devils that had tormented Big Duke in Vietnam—and exploded thousands of lives—and we were just waltzing through, staring at them as kids would point at sharks in an aquarium.

T-Bone was manning the .50 machine gun, standing up through the vehicle's sunroof. "See anything up there, T-Bone?" I yelled up. There was no answer from him so I grabbed his knee. He poked his head down inside and pulled a Walkman headset out of his ears.

"Sorry, sir. Had my Walkman on. Playing Morricone. Theme songs from Eastwood's spaghetti westerns. It's surreal. Keepin' my anger up."

"What are you so angry about?"

"Fact the Iraqis are preventing me from going home. Fact they ruined my Christmas. Fact they made me sit in that hole, waitin' for them to leave Kuwait."

George Bush needed the baby-tossing stories to galvanize the country, not the military. We had plenty of reasons to hate Iraqis, homesickness leading the charge, followed closely by foxhole misery and female deprivation.

I pulled his sand goggles an inch off his face and let the elastic yank them back in with a snap. "Take off that fucking Walkman and pay attention up there."

"Yes, sir. I was paying attention, though. I wasn't fuckin' off." He handed me the Walkman and poked his head and torso back out into the air.

The platoon closed behind the main convoy and sand began to fill the inside of the Hummer, so great was the torrent of dust ripped up by the convoy. I could not see and told the driver to swing out early into our position on the right flank to escape the sandstorm, covering my mouth and nose. My Hummer, trailed by the two big trucks, swung wide to the right of the main convoy, taking up our designated position close to the Kuwaiti coast. Our mission was simple: Stay parallel to the main convoy two kilometers to our left, following the tracks of the tanks that had already cleared our sector an hour before, acting as right-flank security.

When the dust settled I scrambled to find our position on my map. There were no landmarks that I could see, and ahead of the Hummer lay only desert and the black sky that seemed to hang down like a curtain. We had driven for fifteen minutes when Private First Class Tulowski, who was driving the Hummer, said, "Uh, sir, uh, we have a problem here."

Tulowski was a chubby, blond Marine from Chicago known only as "Tubs" to the other men. He had struggled to meet the Marine weight standard and had actually been recommended for early discharge, when Saddam rolled south. "We might as well keep that food blister with us, Lieutenant," my platoon sergeant said at the time. "He might shed some of that weight. Besides, he's a big target and he'll get popped before we do. Probably explode all over the place." Marines have a low tolerance for fat people—whom they view as undisciplined—and Tubs was the platoon outcast. That's why my platoon sergeant had assigned him to me, loner number two.

"What is it, Tubs?"

"Sir, the tank tracks I been followin' lead up that big dune. Looks too steep for the five-tons."

I looked up at the rise and agreed. "Swing around to the right, over there, then turn back. We'll just go around it."

We swung around the rise and the dusty contrail of the main convoy disappeared. Out of sight of the friendlies, I felt alone and uncertain. "Turn back toward the main column when we get around this dune."

"Heard you the first time, sir," Tubs said.

To our front, some specks that shone green against the smoke appeared; I thought at first that they must be glow sticks marking something, perhaps a mine. But the distance was too great to discern glow sticks and they grew larger and larger. Maybe they were fireflies about to smash into the windshield and leave glowing, green smudges so we could claim our first kills of the war.

Suddenly they were climbing above us and well right. Before I recognized them the tracer bullets zipped past the Hummer with a series of loud cracks. *Craack! Craack!* More green blips appeared, and they seemed to move slowly at first, then flew by in a rush. Tubs stomped on the diesel pedal and tried to drive under them. He screamed, "Sir, they're *shooting* at us!"

"Stop!" I yelled. "Reverse! Don't give them a sitting target. Use the dust for cover and get back behind the hill." The Hummer shuddered and twisted to a violent halt. A cloud of dust from the skid washed over the hood and billowed up lazily, obscuring our view. I gripped the dash and pulled my face close to the windshield. The tracers had disappeared but the snapping of the bullets was somehow closer. *CRAACK! CRAAACK! CRAAAACK!* I couldn't see the phosphorous burn because I didn't have the angle—the bullets were on target now.

T-Bone popped his head down and said, "Lieutenant, I think someone's *shooting* at us! Are they friendly?"

"Green. Firing south. They're Iraqis. *Kill them!*" The .50 went off on the roof and the entire Hummer shuddered under its recoil. I could see that T-Bone was firing way too high, just like the Iraqis. In fact, I thought for a moment that he was firing at Baghdad itself, so great were the trajectories of the red tracers I saw.

We emerged from the dust cloud behind the friendly side of the dune and I called my company commander for tank support.

"Bravo Six, this is Bravo Three! We are taking fire!" *Someone just shot at me! Someone just tried to kill me! Some fucking Iraqi tried to KILL ME!*

"Roger, Three, we've had some sporadic fire over here, too. What's the sit? Over."

Is everyone on this battlefield calm except me? "We're tucked in safely behind a big dune. I think it's a small trench that the tanks must have bypassed. Maybe one heavy gun. If we can get some tanks over here, we can direct them. Over."

"Roger, I'll have Bearhug roll over to your platoon freq. Keep me appraised and keep the men out of the trench. If you have to, just bypass it. There'll be more pockets of dug-in troops like them farther up the road . . . Tankers blew through and must have left some survivors. We're going to keep moving with the main effort. Remember the CO's order: '*Keep the men out of the trench.*' Six out."

I stepped out of the Hummer and saw the platoon

deploying on automatic pilot, just as we had drilled so often. Marines were sprinting into defensive positions, dragging LAW rockets and shovels, shouting crisp orders. The five-ton trucks had wheeled sideways, acting as natural barriers. Sandbags were being stacked around machine guns. When I had started screaming orders during a training attack on a Camp Pendleton range, T-Bone had told me that the "best thing you can do is stay out of the way, sir." Now I understood.

T-Bone and I scrambled up the dune and I pulled out my binoculars. All I saw initially was a black stripe on the brown desert, about a thousand meters away, as if someone had spray-painted a section of sand fifty meters long and two meters wide. Then pieces of the strip began to move, about twenty bodies in all that I could see, and the shadow took on the depth of a trench. They must have been overlooked by the slew of tanks that had charged out ahead of us and, indeed, we would have blown by them, too, had they not panicked and fired.

Now they would die.

"Bearhug, this is Bravo Three," I called on the radio to the approaching tanks, faint contrails of dust to our west that announced their onrush with a low, metallic rumble. "You should have our five-tons visible behind the big dune to your southeast, over."

"Roger, Bravo, we see you. Do you have eyes on the objective? Over."

"Affirmative. About a klick due north of us. Just some troops moving around in there. We'll open fire when you're about thirty seconds out to pin them down, and you can roll right up and shoot them if they don't surrender, over."

"Roger, sounds good. Keep their heads down. But we're not going to shoot them . . . just watch, over."

Magically, there were Marines on their bellies next to us on the crest of the dune, snapping in. The machine-gun teams raced to set up their guns on the reverse slope, *thud*s as they slammed their tripods into the sand, *klank*s of ammunition boxes opening, *kalick*s of ammunition belts being snapped in place. One thought: *This is for keeps.*

I pointed at the frenzied men and turned to T-Bone. "I don't think they can range the trench," I observed. "Waste of ammo."

The Marines close to us looked at T-Bone as if waiting for him to plead the case. He whispered, "I know that, sir. But the Marines . . . just want to *shoot*. Get in on it, you know? Everyone wants a piece of this one. And we got plenty of ammo in the trucks. Come on. Whaddaya say, sir?"

I looked past him and all eyes were on me. I realized that for the first time as a platoon leader, I was truly responsible. And it felt great. "Okay, listen up! Your target is an area target about a klick away. Watch for the fifty-caliber rounds. Don't shoot more than one magazine each! If those Iraqi rounds start to get close, I want everyone pulled back from the crest." Mixed in with my terror, I felt the need to war, to brawl with a distant enemy in a fixed fight, to prove myself, and I would not deny my men the same.

Everyone grinned.

I crawled over the crest and set up on my belly with my binoculars, then shouted at the machine gunner and began to walk his rounds on target. A glowing red ember leaped out of the barrel and snapped past the platoon, over the dune, curving slowly to the earth. The tracer burned itself out after about eight hundred meters, but a half second later I saw a cloud of dust kick up behind the trench. The Iraqis heard the bullet and ducked for a second, then popped their heads out again like Whack-a-Moles.

The .50 erupted again with each correction I shouted, and soon spirals of dust trickled up all around the trench. The Iraqis were taken by surprise and were looking skyward, as if the rounds were coming from an aircraft.

When the tanks were five hundred meters from the trench, I gave the order to open fire. The eruption was deafening; I had never heard our weapons chatter without ear protection. The ground trembled and escaping gas from the M-16s flicked tiny sandstorms across the berm. Against the black sky the red tracers looked like nuggets of fire as they rocketed forward, seeking flesh. I could see that the Marines on my left were looking over their sights, which annoyed me briefly before I realized that given the distance, it was as good a method as any to use with a rifle.

Besides, they just wanted to watch the destruction.

The Iraqis disappeared into their trench. Splashes of sand shot up all around the trench like pebbles striking a pond, and the tanks swooped in close, unopposed, firing their machine guns at the trench, too. I saw something moving in the hail and focused my binoculars. Someone at the far end of the trench was waving a piece of clothing on the end of a plank. I gave the cease-fire signal and it was passed down the line quickly. In fewer than five seconds, our platoon stopped firing and I was pleased with the fire discipline. In fact, I was awed by the entire experience, the power in it. With a simple command I had rained death on an enemy force, then, just as quickly, stopped it with a wave of my right hand.

"You see them, sir? Wavin' that flag?" yelled T-Bone.

"I see 'em. What do you make of it? Surrender?"

"It ain't white, though."

"No, but maybe they don't have anything white to wave." I grabbed the radio handset. "Bearhug, this is Bravo Three. Do you see that guy waving the flag? Over."

"Negative, over." The tanks were at the far edge of the trench and I saw the lead had a giant plow mounted to its front. Using the same principle as snowplows, these tanks cleared lanes through mines so the rest of us could breeze through.

"Hold your fire, Bearhug. I think they're going to surrender."

"We're not going to fire. Just gonna bury them and be done with it. I do *not* see this white flag. Where is it? Over."

"Sir, it went down!" T-Bone yelled.

I keyed the handset again. "Bearhug, this is Bravo Three. The flag's gone now, recomme—"

"Bravo, this is Bearhug. *We don't have time to screw around next to this trench.* They could pop a Sagger in us *right now.* Sing out if you see a white flag, but we're setting down the plow. We're vulnerable here, over."

The tanker was right, of course. He couldn't just stop and present a fat and immobile target right next to the trench. I looked through the binoculars and saw that the lead tank had lowered its toothed plow and was caving in the length of the trench, burying the slow ones alive and squeezing the rest of the Iraqis toward the far end like toothpaste in a tube. The plow scooped plunging waves of sand up and slammed them down into the trench. A few Iraqis hopped out and sprinted away. They were cut down by machine-gun bullets and danced before they fell.

Because of the distance I felt I was watching an old kung fu movie, the sound effects delayed and exaggerated. The Iraqis were dead on the ground a full second before *pop! pop! pop! pop!* drifted up past us. Only five meters of trench was left uncovered when the flag, a pair of trousers, was waved again. Two Iraqis scrambled out of the end and the second tank immediately gunned them down, destroying their bodies in two red puffs. "Oh! Cool! Y'all see that!" someone yelled.

Then the trench disappeared.

"Did we bury them ragheads alive, sir?" asked T-Bone. "Sure looked like it."

"Yes," I said.

He smiled and shook his head. "Wow! We got them good, didn't we? So we on the move again?"

"Affirm."

"Hell, we did 'em a favor ... sent 'em to meet Allah in all their glory, fighting the Great Satan, right? The Marines did good. So did you." He clapped me on the back and slapped my open palm. "Man. So did you, sir. That was fuckin' *great*."

I was excited about the new acceptance, tasting the fact that I had done as well in combat as the other Marines. Just like Red. "Well, let's go find some more!"

———

Just before our scheduled relief arrives, the two Gangbanger trucks return. "Farrah Fawcett's headed this way, sir! Same trucks!" That's Armstrong, yelling out from behind his binoculars. His voice is tempered this time, steeled in preparation for the disappointing probability that they have not come in search of a fight. I clamber behind the bunker and offer up a simple prayer: Please let them have huge machine guns mounted on the backs of the trucks, pointing them at us, firing wildly, maybe even killing a refugee or two so we can really look like Prince Valiants.

I can see the Bangers now, waving at us and shouting again, most of them standing up. No weapons. Are they smart enough to have figured that out? Is that why they're showing their empty hands, waving them?

"Draggin' something, sir. Two somethings. Want to take

odds?" asks the Gunny, who is also peering through binos.

I raise my binos and see the ropes stretched taut, the Bangers in the trucks leaning back, holding on like a tug-of-war, a spray of dirt ripping up behind each truck like a waterskier's wake. How can human beings do this? My quick vision: destroying both truckloads of the enemy, appearing in a highly charged court-martial, acquitted in a national celebration of values. What would you have done, they would say, if you had seen them dragging two bodies behind the trucks?

Which gives me an idea . . . What if I shout, "I think they're still alive," open fire, kill the Bangers, and *then* discover that the women were already dead? Deadly force would be allowed, given that state of mind. *I was just trying to save the struggling women behind the truck, sir.*

I'm too slow. The trucks make a hard-right turn fifty meters in front of the FDC and the Bangers drop the ropes. The trucks keep going, Farrah Fawcett with both hands raised like Michael Irvin after a touchdown. Centrifugal force sends the two bodies our way, cartwheeling and tumbling across the dirt road toward us, stopping well short of the concertina wire in a shower of dirt that eventually blows past me in the form of dust.

To dust.

"Goddamn them," says Gunny quietly. "They must be the two girls they captured, sir."

Armstrong, next to me, spits out some tobacco. I wait for his comment so that I can light him up but he stays silent. He looks at me, raises his eyebrows, and spits again.

The Somali refugees in front of the gate just stare; there's no crying or screaming. Little Joe talks to a woman with four tiny children who are crawling across her feet like ducklings. "Dey want to come back inside, Kelly," he says. "De ladies were kilt because dey didn't give Farah no food. De ladies laugh at Farah. Dey told him you Marine protect dem and he get angry."

This is not war as I know it. I think of Big Duke's war— my *father's* war—steeped in restrictions the nation has pledged to remember and avoid. I am beginning to understand why my father refuses to discuss a war he fought in handcuffs.

– 14 –

You can get farther with a kind word and a gun
than you can with just a kind word.

"Reasonableness and proportionality," says the colonel.
I'm sitting at a table in the U.S. forces hangar at a pre–press
conference battalion staff meeting—everyone in the room
has rank over me except Big Duke, and he doesn't count
because he's more powerful than all of the captains. We're
listening to Bison Breath pontificate about the day's
events. There is reason to be proud—resistance has been
scant and the food lines have been opened completely.
We're pushing the food out much more quickly than was
anticipated, the Marine Corps way. Give us another week
and we'll have this famine thing licked entirely. Glancing
around the round table, listening to the other knights
debrief Bison Breath with clear confidence and deadly
serious understanding—and mastery—of their profes-
sion, jaws rigid and brows creased and sloped, I'm filled
with intense pride to be part of this gun club, a wondrous
sense of belonging and camaraderie that I never want to
lose, and the sharp sting of paranoia that I may be
discovered.

After this commander's brief we've been invited to stay for the important one; following this meeting B-Squared will hold his first press conference. And it's going out worldwide. So we're supposed to voice our gripes now, in private, *in-house*. The colonel has just answered my critique of our rules of engagement concerning this afternoon's kidnapping fiasco; apparently I'm the only commander at the table who had a bad go at it with Farrah Fawcett and the Bangers.

"But, sir, the idea that they can roam around with weapons, even small ones, is crazy. We should be able to confiscate AKs, not just heavy weapons."

"Lieutenant Kelly," B-Squared sighs, "that's not up to us . . . that they, the clans, I mean, have the right to bear small arms. We're here to open up food lines within the guidelines given to us. Marines don't question orders; we comply with them."

I think about staying quiet, but after the incident at the FDC I'm too confused to suck this up. The rules of engagement are a chaotic version of bureaucratic combat theory. On the one hand, with force protection as an overrider, Marines have to sit behind sandbags, keeping warm and safe, while the people we're here to feed—to *save* from starvation—are cut up by machetes. What the hell are we paid for? On the other hand, we cannot fully protect ourselves because the warlords have a right to bear arms. We fire only when a weapon is raised, and by then it will be too late. One of my men might be killed because of this insanity, and when he is, they'll scream force protection. If he shoots first, they'll scream murder, just like they wanted to do with Armstrong. Are we here as Marines or food-aid workers?

"I know it, sir, but the ROE still need to be more specific . . . the rest of them, I mean."

"How so, Lieutenant? I just told you—"

"Sir, we had that case today—"

"Let me finish. I want you to explain why you fail to grasp the words 'reasonableness' and 'proportionality.' What more do you want?"

"I want to know—"

"I mean, Lieutenant, come *on*. We can't map out every scenario for you, now can we?" He looks at the other captains, feigning surprise that these words, mine, are coming from a Marine officer, and they nod approvingly, better attuned to the king's emotional warning signs than I am. "I need to know that you have *judgment* out there; that's why you're an officer, for crumb's sake."

I do not capitalize "crumb's" because I am not sure to what he is referring. I would have preferred "fuck's," the default noun, verb, and adjective of most jarheads. "Sir," I say, "I don't want *every* scenario. I just want you to tell me what a proportional response to rape is. And murder. And, sir, what's a reasonable response to savages who drag bodies behind their trucks? Or cut heads off over an MRE?"

The colonel sighs heavily and shakes his head, glaring at me. He's acting impatient, but I know he doesn't have a real answer. No one does. He looks at the captains who surround me and says, "Anyone want to answer the lieutenant's question?"

Some captain who cannot contain himself for fear, I'm sure, of being preempted, bursts out, "Was there a trial, with proof? Was there? Because we aren't equipped to mete out proper sentences and enforce them."

"That's not quite right, sir. I'm equipped to dish out capital punishment," I say. "We all are. I think rape and murder are punishable by a gunshot. Period. I think if you cut a woman's head off, you die. That's what I think. I think if you kidnap a child—"

"You're generalizing here—"

"—if you kidnap a child we should be able to stop you. And if you continue to resist, based on what I know, I should be able to kill you."

There is a brief silence, and one of the captains across from me actually growls his support, the way Marines do. "Errrrrrr," he rumbles and nods. If you want to research the missing link, come visit a Marine base and you'll find plenty of us. Please don't feed the animals, though. I nod back my appreciation, but my initial debate opponent clears his throat.

"What I was *trying* to say before you interrupted, Lieutenant," continues the first captain, angry now but keeping his bearing in check, sitting upright and rigid, his teeth grinding but his hands clasped placidly atop the table like a costume prop, "is that, of *course* these things are upsetting. But we have to look at the big picture here. We're trying to stabilize a country, not tip its balance with more violence. Our mission statement is clear—feed them. That's it. We're not nation-building. From what you said earlier, you don't know if anyone was raped, you don't know who killed the first woman, and you don't know how those other two died. Do you?"

"I know enough—"

"*Do* you?"

"—to know right and wrong. I know what I should do the next time I see him. What would you do, Captain?"

"I . . ." He shakes his head and gives an exasperated sigh. "This is *not* the United States. We aren't a police force, and we're sure as hell not a judge and jury. It could have been a domestic dispute, for all you know. This . . . violence that you're speaking about . . . has been going on for hundreds of years here. What would I do? I'd capture him and turn him over—"

"Except there are no authorities here to turn him over to," I interrupt.

"*Then I'd sure as hell prevent this stuff from happening in the first place,*" he spits out.

"Gentlemen, cease fire," Bison Breath says. "Lieutenant Kelly, what you did out there yesterday and today—with the exception of giving away MREs and taking that patrol out—what you did the *rest* of the time was right. You protected those people as best you could under the circumstances and you didn't go doing anything dumb, like starting a firefight. You protected your men. You were never in danger. Since you were out of reach and couldn't stop the . . . *abduction* . . . you were right to stay put. To open fire might have been the dumbest thing you could have done."

"Sir, that's the first time you've said anything positive to me in two weeks, and that's also the first time I think I really screwed up, failing to stop all that *shit* out there today. Because that's what it was, sir. It was *shit* and I was *shit* as a Marine for letting it happen. We keep backing down and they keep pushing. Sooner or later they're going to turn on us, like they did on the Pakistanis a few months back. They gouged out eyes and ripped out hearts. I don't want that happening to my people, sir. I want to come down hard on those Gangbangers now. They grab somebody, we light some up. Smoke them—"

"Lieutenant Kelly, I do not want another word out of that gosh-darned mouth! Understood? NOT ONE!" His voice swells to a roar and the room is immediately silent. A piece of wood cracks like a thunderclap. Even the reporters gathered outside the hatch stop talking. If you think E. F. Hutton commands an ear or two, try a 220-pound Marine lieutenant colonel who is able to lift the end of a long, heavy table with one hand and slam it down while still pointing at you with the other. The captain next to me slides his chair back in horror, recovers, bows his head.

"Yes, sir," I mumble.

There aren't any more questions.

"Let's take ten, gents, then I'll see you back here for the press conference," the colonel says, almost apologetically.

I push past one of the captains and walk quickly toward the center of the hangar, careful to turn my head when I move past the group of reporters who have gathered for the conference. I'd love to seek Darren out, but my nerves can't take the prospect of Mary Thayer-Ash. I'm darting around a Hummer when I feel a strong grip on my elbow—it's Big Duke and he steers me into his office, from the looks of it formerly a pilot's locker room.

"Got one thing to say to you, sir." He glances over my shoulder, out the hatch, so rapidly that I just barely see his eyes shift.

"Colonel Capiletti watching, Big Duke?"

He smiles, looks down, and shakes his head. "You're on the edge, sir. I like you." Then he looks up at me. His teeth are white against his tan. There are flecks of gray in his blue eyes, which are dancing. He takes off his cammie blouse—he's going to change into a pressed uniform, I'm sure—and his brown T-shirt is dotted with sweat. His dog tags are dangling on the outside.

"Yessir, the colonel wanted me to talk to you. He is not your enemy, Lieutenant. He's just doing things his way. He's a good man, you just can't see that from where you're standing. And you don't exactly help your own cause. So don't put your relationship in the way of the platoon . . . You don't want to stop getting missions, do you? Be stuck in here all day?"

"No. In fact, this is what I dread most, back here." Marines don't enjoy watching others fight; we like to be first.

"Yeah, well, sir, that's where you're headed. You've already been placed on the mission shit list. That was supposed to be a simple mission out at FDC 3; guess you just have a knack for finding trouble. I been doin' so much lobbyin' for you—mostly because I think Gunny Ricketts and some of your men are the best we got—so much lobbyin' it makes my head hurt. So help yourself a little more, learn the difference between a winnable fight and one where you're just banging that head of yours against a wall. Okay, sir?"

"Loud and clear, Sergeant Major. Play the game."

He narrows his eyes and I can tell I've overstepped my bounds, rank an inconsequential aside. He takes an iron out of his locker and fills it with water, then plugs it in and smooths his blouse flat on a desk. "Don't take this talk for something it ain't, Lieutenant. Most of what you said makes sense . . . and it might shock you to hear that the colonel would *agree* with you, off the record. He's just as frustrated with his situation. But he's got orders to follow, sir, and so do you."

"And I'm just watching out for my men, Big Duke."

"When caring for your men clashes with authority, sir, authority wins. That's the way it is—the Marine way. Mission accomplishment comes first."

The Marine Corps wartime priorities were pounded into my head during officer training—mission accomplishment must take priority over the welfare of the Marines—but Restore Hope is not a traditional battle set and I'm struggling with the delineation between betraying my men and betraying the mission. I grit my teeth and spit out, "Authority could get my people killed. When I'm out there, I have to make the call, not headquarters, and sure as hell not people in Washington. Who are they to judge moral right on the battlefield? Who are they to judge the choices my men make?"

Big Duke looks at me levelly. The iron begins to hiss and he applies some spray starch to the blouse as preparatory fires followed by a main assault with the iron, expert strokes nearly obscured by the steam billowing up, causing him to sweat even more, his T-shirt soaked now. "Well I got news for you, sir. You *do* make the call out there, and the reason the higher-ups and, yes, even Washington bureaucrats, are watching so close is that *your* decisions can affect the *entire country.*

"Take a look around you. Understand your environment. In baseball you got a warning track. In football you got a line of scrimmage. In the modern military you got a rule book and a CNN camera over your shoulder."

"That doesn't change the fact that I have an obligation to my men."

"Yes, but in my opinion you go too far, sir. You also have an obligation to enforce law. You know the main problem I seen with young lieutenants? They want to be *liked.* They want to be *popular.* Some college holdover habit the Corps wasn't able to exterminate, I guess. Well, sir, your job ain't to be popular. Your job is to run that platoon according to the rules. It may be lonely as hell sometimes, but that's what the Corps expects. Understood?"

"Wilco, Big Duke," I say, giving him the radio code for "understand and will comply."

"Good. We best get back to the brief." He strips off his sopping T-shirt and I notice a familiar tattoo on his left pectoral—a skull-and-dagger hybrid of the popular recon tattoo. It is my father's. The Marine Corps is a small community and I debate the question; I am caught between the need to know my father better and an overwhelming dread that Big Duke will spit on his memory and forever associate me with a loser. I decide to keep the inquisition limited to the tattoo.

"Is that tattoo from Vietnam?"

"Yes it is, sir." Big Duke glances down and reveals the entire thing by stretching his tan chest. It is the same tattoo, all right, except beneath the skull there is just a single slash instead of five. My grandfather has long hypothesized that my father passed five inspections of his supply hut in Vietnam and rewarded himself with five blood stripes, a theory I somehow came to accept as truth. "It's an old First Battalion tat."

"First Supply Battalion?" I ask seriously.

I do not know much about my father's role in Vietnam but I *do* know he was a supply jockey. We were at a Sox game in 1977 when a man called out to my father and rushed over, excited. My father brushed him off gruffly and dragged me off through the crowd, but not before my grandfather and I heard the man say, "Tom Kelly! Remember me? Eric Chehab? We worked together in that supply hut in Da Nang." Red Kelly walked over and introduced himself, and I remember my father looking over his shoulder as he carried me away, cursing under his breath at my grandfather, who stayed behind to soak up whatever details he could. There weren't many: My father served with the man for a month while he was waiting for a court-martial to convene, and he had heard that my father had received an Other Than Honorable discharge, but the man never heard what the charges were to begin with. Red Kelly knew; in REMF billets like supply—surrounded by the temptations of expensive equipment and a thriving black market—there was generally one reason for a man being charged and sent home, a sin that went unspoken in our house but for which my father was blamed nevertheless. Theft. Stealing from your own team-mates.

"First *supply*? Sir, are you serious?" Big Duke laughs. "You are, aren't you? Hell, no. This is a *First Recon Battalion* tattoo, same unit as you're in right now, for Chrissakes. Don't you recognize it?"

"I recognize it. Looks different from the one we have now, though."

"Yeah, well, it was a hybrid my platoon used."

"Your recon platoon? Can anybody get the tattoo?"

"I suppose."

"What about the slash?" I ask, pointing at the blood stripe.

"That? Oh. I was just a youngster then." I have embarrassed him for some reason and he puts on a fresh T-shirt.

"So what's with the slash?"

"Not important, sir."

"Indulge me."

"Between me and you, it's some macho stamp we used to get."

"Fathered a kid in Vietnam? Killed someone? What?"

He exhales and his eyes look right into mine. His are twinkling in the fluorescent glow of his makeshift office, powerful but sad at the same time. "Like I said, it's nothing to be proud of. It's really not important."

"It is to me. I read somewhere that someone had five slashes . . . always wondered about that."

"Well, I don't know what book that was in because it was kept to our own platoon. Five? No. No way. Well, I take that back. There was maybe one who had that many. Not public knowledge . . . but yeah, maybe one guy . . . you said you read . . ."

His words slow to a crawl and then cease altogether. He looks at me and frowns, considering me, staring harder, eyebrows slanting, shaking his head ever so slowly from side to side. Then his eyebrows rise and his mouth opens. "My God. You've got his eyes . . . You're Tom Kelly's boy."

"My father was a supply sergeant."

A Marine ducks his head into Big Duke's office and I barely hear him in the background, telling us that we are wanted for the press brief. Big Duke nods his understanding and just stares at me, smirking and nodding now. I hear the hum of the lights overhead. I hear the blood rushing toward my ears.

"Yeah, your old man spent some time in a supply shack. But most of his time was spent in the bush. On recon patrols."

"Tom Kelly? From Boston?"

"*Keee-riiist,* sir. Yes. Are you really that surprised? Because you look shocked. You know how small the Corps is, let alone how tiny the recon community is. Compound that with this fact: I ain't never seen a crowded battlefield. So if you were recon in Vietnam, well, chances are I know you or heard of you. Yessir, I knew your old man. Real good."

"He was *recon?*"

Big Duke clucks his tongue. "If your father didn't tell you about his Vietnam service, I'm sure as hell not going to violate that wish. We best get back to the briefing room, sir."

"Well, how come he was both supply and recon? What'd he do wrong?"

Big Duke leans close and whispers, "Sorry, sir, we'll talk later. We're late. Now let's get going."

———

"Total Grain Distributed" reads the sign over the colonel's head. Below that, there are village names as column headings, with the various units making up the row labels. "I want to draw your attention to this," the colonel says, pointing at the "Total Tons" box. It reads 195. "This, ladies and gentlemen, embodies our mission."

Bison Breath smiles and the room comes alive with *clicks* and *whirrs* as the cameras shoot him. He has changed into a pressed set of camouflage utilities, pristine as he swivels in the glare of the spotlights. General Bellissimo has positioned himself on B-Squared's flank so that he won't be cut out of the frames. Lieutenant Colonel Capiletti taps the sign with his pointer. It is a massive sign, as overstated as the flag in *Patton*'s opening scene, easily ten meters long. "One hundred ninety-five tons of grain, well ahead of expectations. Very, *very* well done, gentlemen. The whole world is watching you with pride, including me," he says, waving to the captains standing against the wall, patting himself on the back at the same time.

The captain behind me whispers, almost giggling, "He had Marines painting that sign all day. Gave them all sorts of hell . . . had them redo it three separate times. Lieutenant in charge is still punch-drunk."

"Welcome to the party, right, sir?"

"Me, too," he whispers. "Colonel caught two of my Marines with their flak jackets open outside the hangar. Evidently he went crazy. He called me over for an ass-chewing but two reporters showed up so he had to put it off."

I tune in to the colonel again. I have not missed much. The long and short of it is that more battalions of Marines are on their way. Today we own the city; in a week we'll own the whole goddamn country, if we choose to. "Questions?" he asks.

A few reporters lob softballs. They are easy questions and the colonel is doing well.

"Colonel, what have you concluded—" a woman yells, shouting down the others. "Excuse me! Colonel Capiletti! What have you . . . What are the results of the Said Lahti investigation?"

I turn around to face her and Ms. Thayer-Ash stares right at me. *Man looks into the abyss . . .* Some of the other reporters are rolling their eyes and one is even shaking his head. She must be as lonely as I am. "Ms. Ash, I'd be happy to discuss that off-line. We've already discussed the—" I hear the colonel say.

Thayer-Ash is the only reporter left standing. "No, Colonel, you *asked* for questions. Is this an unfair question? Will you guarantee me access to your investigation report?"

"Well, I . . ." The colonel has just been yanked out of AAA ball and put into The Show, but he's not ready. "There's no written report, per se . . . but I can insure you . . . excuse me, *assure* you, that it was thorough. NBC took full responsibility, as you—"

"Vincent, permit me to interrupt, if I may," says General Bellissimo, stepping right in front of the colonel. "Ms. Ash, you and I have discussed this but I will repeat what I told you so everyone will be clear on my policies. I was very, *very* disappointed with the . . . *act of violence* on the beach. Said Lahti should not have been there with his rifle, but I was also disappointed with the hasty actions of the Marines. It was justified, as the Marine investigation concluded—that was out of my authority—but I was disappointed and I made that clear to Vincent here. We are both confident that we will be able to avoid such unpleasantries in the future."

I see the colonel share a glance with Big Duke and it's clear now that they shielded me. Thayer-Ash continues, "But, General, isn't it correct that bodyguards and even *warlords* are allowed to carry personal weapons? They don't wear press passes, but you don't send Marines after *them* unprovoked. General, Muhammad Lahti maintains that he was asleep at the time he was attacked."

"Colonel, if I may?" says Big Duke, ignoring General Bellissimo. He stands and nods to the reporter. "Miss . . . Ash, is it?"

"Thayer-Ash."

"Ms. Thayer-Ash, let me make something totally clear, ma'am. *Totally* clear. We have zero tolerance for war crime, which is *exactly* what you're inferring."

"Colonel, I was just—"

"I'm a sergeant major, ma'am. I work for my thousand bucks a month. Please let me answer your question," Big Duke says, winking at the colonel. His voice is gravel, and in combination with his smile, which melts right back into a serious stare, the room falls silent, listening.

"Essentially, what you want to know—what we all want to know—is if the Lahtis were asleep when Gunnery Sergeant Ricketts and Sergeant Armstrong came upon them. They were not. There's no proof one way or the other—though I would doubt if they could have slept through that welcome—but a Marine's word is gold. Our foundation.

"I know about your man. I know he was a personal friend of yours. No one wanted him dead, least of all the Marine who took his life. To believe the surviving brother's story, we have to believe that a man like Gunnery Sergeant Ricketts is lying. Jarius Ricketts, Ms. Thayer-Ash, is one of the finest Marines we have in this Corps. He has a perfect record and the highest perfor-mance-evaluation marks possible . . . on *every single report.* He has fought in three conflicts and was awarded the Bronze Star in the Gulf War. He was a Naval ROTC instructor at UCLA. He was the most highly rated drill instructor we had at Parris Island, a stressful job, as you probably know, that requires the strictest emotional discipline, where only our best Marines are sent. He's also got five daughters and a terrific wife.

"So, to believe your man, to reach the conclusion that he was asleep, with a big, glowing, press identification card, which, by the way, no one has seen, we have to believe that Gunnery Sergeant Ricketts is a *liar* and a *murderer.* I think not. Neither did NBC or our investigating officer. Under Colonel Capiletti's direction, the investigation was totally thorough and fair. And it is closed.

"That is not meant, of course, to infringe upon your rights as reporters. But I would ask you to recognize that these young men have had to *kill,* something that they did not want to do—believe me, I know the feeling—so please respect their privacy."

Big Duke thanks her, then turns to the colonel and says, "Thank you, sir."

Ms. Thayer-Ash is positively bristling. Her eyes are black, reflecting the lights overhead. She looks around the room but no others respond—including other reporters—so she goes it alone. It's impossible not to admire her tenacity in the face of so much repellent. "This is ... just ... In two *days* you decided this? That's premature, isn't it, Sergeant Major? Colonel? I mean, did you examine radio calls, time of death, testimony by reporters—"

"Miss Thayer-Ash," says the colonel, his confidence restored, his voice booming and earnest. *That's it, sir.* "Time does not an investigation make. We had all the facts we needed. And the salient fact is that this is just an inch short of a war zone, Somalia. It is a *very* dangerous place, as I am quite sure you are aware. We need people like Gunnery Sergeant Ricketts in the field, making the kinds of decisions he did today. When he was confronted by armed warlords yet controlled the situation."

"Then assign me to Lieutenant Kelly's platoon," she says. "General? That way I can see for myself. Form a fair opinion. Just trail along for a few missions."

Bison Breath is stunned and his mouth opens; he is a fish out of water. There is an awkward silence in which I actually hear the hum of the cameras, and finally he says, "I think that's fine. You'll go tomorrow. Lieutenant Kelly?"

"Sir?"

"Stay after the brief."

"Aye, aye, sir."

I glance out of the corner of my eye. Ms. Thayer-Ash is scribbling in her notebook. She's certainly savvy, having achieved this assignment by appealing to Marine instincts: hand-to-hand, in-your-face combat. I'm terrified about tomorrow, all prospects of television stardom long since vanquished. Mary Thayer-Ash carries the most powerful weapon on the battlefield—a camera—and tomorrow she's riding shotgun with me.

———

Dusk. Some annoying bird or insect is squeaking three-round bursts over my head, *eeeeyaaah, eeeeyaaah, eeeeyaaah!* Little Joe is sitting in my foxhole, thumb-wrestling with Doc. I am trying to get some intel out of the boy and am irritated that Doc doesn't recognize my angle. Problem is, if I send Doc away, the boy will follow. He has grown symbiotically attached to my corpsman.

"Doc," I say. "Hold it up a sec."

"We got one more match to go, sir. Got to win by two and Joe's up one."

"Must win by two, Kelly," Little Joe laughs. "I beat de Doc."

They clasp hands and work their thumbs around again

for a minute before Doc, to my complete frustration, pins him. "Arghh!" shouts Joe. "Got me, Doc!"

"Shhh. Pipe down, Joe," I whisper. "Quiet. *Damn it, Doc, I need the boy.*"

He looks up at me in the disappearing light and his face brightens, having interpreted a critical secret. "Oh! I got it." He winks at me. "Well, that's it, Joe. No more for tonight."

"Nooo! I want to beat you, Doc!" the boy screams again. "NOOO!"

"Shhhh! Doc. Doc! *Doc!*" the Gunny whispers. "Finish the thumb war. *Finish it.*"

"But we're tied."

Gunny looks up at me and smiles, shaking his head. "Doc," he says, "you've reached rock bottom, and now you've started to dig." He leans in and whispers in Doc's ear.

Doc and Little Joe play two more matches and Joe jumps up and down, the winner. "Now I get emeree. I want chicken and de noodle."

Doc rummages through the box of MREs and tosses one of the plastic bags at Joe. The boy rips it apart and squirts his package of peanut butter into the chicken noodle mush. Then he crushes his crackers and dumps them into the stew, followed by his iced-tea mix, nondairy creamer, and salt package. "Damn, Joe," says the Gunny. "You cook like the lieutenant does. No sense of flavor."

The boy just smiles and stirs his concoction. "I love you, Doc," he says.

Doc takes a seat and grabs the boy, lifting him onto his lap.

"I think you mean you *like* him, Joe. You like Doc," says Gunny. The word "love" strikes fear deep into the hearts of Marines, and with it a terrible awkwardness, especially in the spoken form. To hear another man utter it is more terrifying than a gunshot.

"Yes," the boy says. "I like you and I like de Lootenant Kelly. I love de Doc like my dad." He takes a huge spoonful of the 1969 chicken stew and gulps it down greedily.

"Don't eat your spoon," I say. Doc laughs suddenly, like it is the best joke he has ever heard, and Little Joe joins him, cackling away in the night, biting down on his spoon now. Gunny starts in, a hearty laugh, and I am the party pooper, staring at these lunatics, the designated driver.

"Joe. What do the Hibr Gidr clan plan? What do they say about the Marines?"

The boy looks at me, still laughing, and shouts, "Dey say dey can kill you when dey want, the heeber geeder. Dey say Marine gonna die Somalia!"

"Joe, what else do they say? Farah and the other Hibr Gidrs?"

"Farah pay a million shillings if dey kill a Marine. Most for recon."

"Mostly recon? Us? How does he know recon?"

"I tell my friends who you are."

"Great. How? How are they going to try?"

"Dey get two million shillings if dey bomb de Marines. Dey gonna try for de two million. Maybe tonight."

"Who's gonna try?"

"Muhammad Ali, wit de morta bomb. He try soon."

"Thanks, Joe. You're a good boy."

"Yes," he says, smiling. "I be Marine and go to America. Yes? I don' want to go back outside dere. Doc said." He points at the wall.

I look at Doc. *Who made this stupid promise?* Doc shrugs and shakes his head.

"You have to go home tonight, Joe. Sorry."

"I don' have no home," he says. "I stay here and help Marines."

"No. You go outside the wall tonight."

"Noo," he whines. He begins to cry. "I stay here. I stay here wit Doc! I stay here, Kelly!"

In the span of two minutes, I have confronted our most lethal adversaries: the word "love" and tears. "Gunny, you handle this mess," I say and walk off to check the lines.

———

The murmur of the battalion has faded and everyone, including the command post, is observing the Corps' strict night-discipline rules: red-lens lights only, 50 percent security in all foxholes, and only silenced grunts during self-love exercises, no groans allowed.

I get up several times during the night to check the lines. I pass one hole and can hear snoring so I lean in and whisper angrily to the Marine who is on watch. It's Johnson. "Hey! Just what are you doing, Johnson? I can hear whoever that is a klick away. Wake him the fuck up if he's snoring."

Johnson loves comic books and I can see he is covering Spider-Man with his hand, hiding the fact that he was reading on duty with his NVGs, a serious no-no. "Sir, I . . . yessir," he whispers, looking down.

"What's the problem?"

"Well, sir," he whispers and points at the body lying at the bottom of the hole. "I already did that once and he told me he'd kill me if I did it again."

"What? Who the fuck is it? Armstrong?" I am thoroughly pissed and prepare to give the sleeping Stretch Armstrong a rousting he'll never forget.

"It's the Gunny, sir," he says, nervously and with reverence.

I chuckle and pat him on the shoulder. "Anyone can die, it takes courage to live. Better let him sleep, but I want you to pinch his nose like this." I reach down past the two white doughnuts on Gunny's eyelids and cut off his nasal air supply. His mouth opens and he gasps like a fish, silent, until his brain realizes he has to switch valves. He eventually inhales with a great, sucking sigh and I release his nostrils when he's breathing through his mouth. Johnson smiles and I turn away, laughing to myself.

I crawl back to my hole and in the slowly pulsating green haze of the NVGs I see something small curled up beneath a poncho in the bottom of the hole. "Joe," I say.

The hump stays quiet.

"Well, the least you can do is push over if you're gonna sleep here."

The little bundle is sliding magically closer to Doc when I hear a mortar's *choom!* in the distance. I scream, "Incoming!" but the call has already been relayed by the sentries. Thirty seconds later three rounds crack well to the west. Clumps of dirt from the edge of the hole splatter on my poncho.

Near the gate the armored reaction force turns over its engines and revs up.

"De tanks gonna try to get Muhammad, Kelly?" asks Joe, not a stitch of fear in him.

"Maybe."

"Dey won't. Too slow for Muhammad trucks. Next time, I tell you when he gonna bomb."

"How will you know?"

He pops out from beneath the poncho, scrunches up his face, and punches me in the shoulder, chuckling. "Everybody know! He tell everybody to listen. Hear?"

When the reaction force rumbles out of the gates chasing echoes and shadows, I am able to hear Somalis in the distance. Cheering.

– 15 –

12 DECEMBER 1992

Ripley: Hudson! This little girl survived longer
than that with *no* weapons and *no*
training. Right?

Hudson: So why don't you put her in charge?

The colonel has sent us on a bunny-slope mission, a simple day patrol in Mog to make nice-nice with the indigenous pop, the mother of green-dot assignments. A poor
man's parade. The villages and warehouses in the hinter-
lands are the sweet spots where the rest of the battalion is
headed today, to feed people, search for weapons, and
enlarge our web. Recon is stuck taking Ms. Thayer-Ash on
a benign walk, so chosen because the chances for me to
screw it up are zero. Well, as close to zero as the colonel
could manufacture.

I am supervising the prepatrol inspections behind the
hangar when I smell cologne in the second file. I walk up
to Montoya and his scent is so strong that I close my eyes
and fan my face. The other Marines are chuckling.

"Gunny, I think we have a situation here," I say.

Gunny stomps up and pinches his nose, grimacing. "Whoaa! Where do you think we're going, Montoya? Some Mogadishu nightclub?"

"That reporter's coming, ain't she, Gunny? The hot chick from CNN? I figured a little douse of Polo Sport might help the cause."

"Unless she's a lesbo, she ain't gonna go for that shit," says Armstrong, standing at attention in front of him. "Real men don't wear that shit."

"Real men got two nuts, too, Uniballer."

The platoon bursts into laughter, including Armstrong.

"Should we make him jump in the shitter, sir?" giggles Gunny, holding Montoya by his scruff. "That'd douse this sweet smell pretty quick."

"No. Considering the mission, I'm not worried if they smell us coming. Even if it's over a mile away. You three team leaders conduct test fires, please. Then we'll roll. Dismissed."

The teams fall out laughing and walk over to the firing range, Armstrong locking Montoya in a playful headlock. When they're out of earshot, I say, "I thought Armstrong was keeping the one-nut thing private, Gunny."

Gunny chuckles. "Naw, sir, he was discovered onboard ship. Don't ask me how."

"I won't." I turn to watch Armstrong in a crouch, circling Montoya for an attack.

"He ain't wired right, that's for sure, sir. That's what you get with them fatherless kids, you know? Prone to violence, just like young elephants without big males."

This surprises me; I make it a habit not to gossip about the personal lives of my men but this is a case that simply arouses too much curiosity. I remember going over Armstrong's record of emergency data with him, and two parents were clearly listed. "Armstrong told me he gets along fine with his old man. He was bragging that he was his own man."

Gunny laughs and we both regard Armstrong, who wrestles Montoya to the ground to prove a point, then helps him up and claps him on his flak vest. "Sir, between you and me? That man doesn't have no father. Or any parents to speak of, for that matter. That tractor story? About it rolling over and crushing him? Total bullshit, along with his football stories. Jake Armstrong had his pelvis shattered and lost his nut when his father threw him off a two-story roof. When he was *seven*. Nearly killed him. Was sent to foster care after that and hasn't seen his parents since. Ran away from his foster home when he was twelve and has lived on his own ever since, taking small jobs to afford a roof and food while he went to high school. But he's the one you'd want most on your side, ain't he, as fucked up as he is?"

His voice is distant; I'm thinking back to my conversation with Armstrong, when he refused the opportunity to sell out his father, to blame him, something I would have embraced until . . . when? Just now? Armstrong had every reason to point a finger and he didn't. As it turns out, I have *no reasons* yet . . . I shake the thought from my head. "No, Gunny, I'd pick my grandfather first. Then you. Then Armstrong. Then maybe my own father."

He claps me on the shoulder and says, "Thanks, sir. Your grandfather must have been a helluva killer, drafted in front of me, the supreme war pig. And I didn't even know your old man served. Was he a Marine?"

"Yes. A recon Marine."

We saunter over to the firing range and I hear someone yell, "Lieutenant Kelly!"

Mary Thayer-Ash struts over, Gregory backpack slung

over both shoulders, bottle of Evian (don't get me going on the fact that we use a supplier with a French connection) in her hand, Ray-Ban aviators that have been out of style since *Top Gun* was released on video. The Marines are just about to test-fire—the last thing you want on patrol is a weapon jam when you actually get to shoot at someone—so I hold up my hand in the stop mode. The reporters know better than to walk onto a hot range, even Ms. Thayer-Ash. She keeps coming.

"Hold up!" I yell at her. "Hey! Wait one!"

"One what?" she yells and keeps coming. My Marines look over their shoulders at her and now my hand is forced.

"This range is hot, Ms. Ash! Stop right there." She's not in any real danger, but range protocol is range protocol, and I own the makeshift range.

"The whole country's hot, Lieutenant. Nice to see you've finally figured that out."

"Daamnn," Johnson whispers behind me, drawing it out. I glare at him but he just winks.

She walks right up and smiles. "Ready to go, boys?" The platoon grumbles a happy response. Yes, it's an early Christmas in Somalia. Maybe Montoya's cologne will start working.

"We're conducting a test fire here and you've just screwed it up. Please go back behind the firing line," I say.

"Are your weapons broken? I'm sure you'll need them in case a famine-stricken child threatens you."

If she were a man, things would be so much simpler. I just shake my head. "Step back, Ms. Ash."

"It's Thayer-Ash, with a dash."

I'm tempted to ask her what her child's last name will be if she runs into another dual citizen. Three generations from now, he may be John-Jacob-Jingle-Heimer-

Schmidt-Fonda-Thayer-Ash. "Sorry. Thayer-Ash. Where's Darren?"

"Just me today."

"No cameraman?"

"Just me. Building some rapport with the boys here."

I shrug. "Fire when ready, Gunny. Ms. Thayer-Ash, please step back here with me."

The Marines fire a quick string, an eruption of jack-hammers, and Thayer-Ash brings her hands up to her ears too late. It's pretty funny really; rifle fire, especially twenty of them at once, is shockingly loud if you're not prepared, and she hops up and cringes, hands streaking to cup her ears, dropping her water bottle. I try to repress a smile but fail. In her eyes there is hate again; she's as bad as old Bison Breath with that thin skin of hers. "WAIT HERE!" I shout. It's questionable if she hears me with her bell rung.

I walk over to the firing line, unsling my M-16, aim at a tree stump, flip the selector switch forward with my thumb and fire two rounds. The rifle bucks hot and fast and I smell the cordite. It never fails to excite me, the power of it, the sharp kicks against my shoulder and the tree bark flying. It's hard to explain precisely *why* shooting is so exciting, the answer hidden somewhere between my belief that it reinforces my membership in the American warrior clan and the fact that shooting is one of the few things I'm really good at. I walk back over to her and pull out my earplugs. "Next time I'll get you a pair, ma'am."

———

Montoya's team is on point and they lead us out of the gate on foot, past some grunts who are pulling security duty. I'm sitting in the Hummer with Gunny and Ms. Thayer-

Ash, about twenty meters behind teams one and two. Normally we wouldn't dare put both leaders of the platoon in the same vehicle, but the colonel wants me to monitor their conversation.

As we exit the compound, Little Joe dashes out from behind a rotten tree and falls in right behind Montoya's team, next to Doc, carrying a big stick as if it is a rifle and wearing a T-shirt that reads: "When in Doubt, Empty the Magazine." I let it slide: He's a good kid, we need an interpreter, and, frankly, he's the best intelligence asset the battalion has.

"Ms. Thayer-Ash," Gunny says. "My instructions are clear. I'm supposed to be absolutely frank with regard to the night incident. Normally we wouldn't do this, but you were a friend of his, I understand, so word came down to fill you in entirely. Let me first say how sorry I am. It was just the last thing we wanted to have happen but, unfortunately, he left Armstrong no choice."

While the Gunny is filling her in in the back of the Hummer, I am watching the Marines fan out to my front, moving through the outskirts of Mogadishu with real precision. They're covering every alley and roof, moving by bounds, sprinting across open alleys, weapons and eyes pointed in a variety of directions—left, right, up, down—a Death Star formation rolling into downtown for some meet and greet.

We roll slowly down a long, narrow road lined with small, square, Mediterranean-style houses. There are sidewalk fires smoldering and occasionally a gust from the hot wind sweeps the putrid smell of human waste and charred rubber into the Hummer. All the Somalis come to their doorsteps to watch the parade. I might have changed the route at this point but this was the patrol route given us and the alleys to my right and left are too narrow for the

Hummer. Besides, all of the streets and paths are a tangled clusterfuck of urban engineering in which I would just get lost, the design making as much sense as the whole god-damn country.

Along the way I see my Marines breaking the rules, toss-ing an occasional applesauce package or bag of M&M's to the audience. All of the handouts are met with cheers and everyone is smiling. One Marine tosses a jelly packet too far and it sails into a burning trash hole. A little boy hops into the fire in his bare feet and retrieves the packet, hop-ping up and down but still smiling when he's back on the dirt.

"You see that, sir?"

"I saw it, Gunny."

Little Joe has taken to deciding who gets what on the patrol, running up to certain Marines and ordering a handout. He's developing quite a Napoleon complex, run-ning around with that stick of his, the great Somali liaison. He's a cute boy. If this scene doesn't thaw Ms. Thayer-Ash, I don't know what will.

After an hour in the heat, I see Montoya's hand go up and dance, signaling for a security halt and a water break. All of the Marines move to covered positions and take a knee, Montoya and Armstrong tuning up the formation, grabbing an occasional Marine and shifting their position so all the avenues of approach are covered. "Security halt, Gunny. Ms. Thayer-Ash, you can stay in the Hummer, in the shade."

"Where are you two going?"

"Outside. We're in a temporary halt. It'll only take a moment."

"Pshh," she grunts, and hops out of the Hummer, next to Gunny.

Gunny is trying to get Ms. Thayer-Ash to move a safe

distance from him, just in case, but she's stubborn and I can hear her arguing mildly, questioning the benefits of dispersion. I hear him begin to explain it and realize it may be a match made in heaven, the two of them suffering from a permanent case of verbal diarrhea.

Something is different. Not altogether eerie, but askew nevertheless. It's the Somalis themselves, closer than I have ever seen them get, either a newfound bravery or a clearer understanding of our restrictions. No longer hiding and laughing from the safety of their homes, they're surrounding us now. Boys, mostly, and a few women. No obvious Bangers.

Some of them are quite bold, taking quick runs at the Marines, turning at the last moment, birds defending their nest or bats swooping in for a mosquito feast, all of them cackling. Others are laughing hysterically and throwing little sticks, just playing. I resolve to end the food handouts.

One little boy in a Nike "Just Do It" shirt rushes up to Johnson and pulls at his gear harness. He can't weigh more than seventy-five pounds. It is the first time I have seen a Somali move within arm's reach of a Marine. Johnson, smiling, says something that I cannot hear and peels the hand off his canteen gently. The boy moves away, but his friends start screaming something at him. He turns, grins almost shyly, moves back toward Johnson, walking this time, Johnson immobile, the boy rushing at him now, Johnson standing, the boy hanging on to his rifle sling, Johnson spinning him around like I used to do to my kid sister, the boy releasing and tumbling to the dirt, Ms. Thayer-Ash kneeling in front of me now with a camera that I missed earlier, the boy running back at Johnson in a rage.

Several of the boys are grabbing at the Marines now, tugging at their uniforms and pulling at their gear. "Hey,

kid. Hey! Get off me! Get the fuck offa me! Joogso, jiifso!"
a Marine yells. Montoya looks at me and shrugs, so I give
him the signal to move out. A boy rushes up to him and
snatches a canteen from his cartridge belt. The boy gets
about five feet before the canteen is yanked out of his
hands by a string; Montoya has dummy-corded his gear to
his body for this very reason. In the swarm of Somalis I
think, *Gee, what a terrific troop.* Montoya pulls the canteen
back by its string, sticks it in his pouch, and gives the hand
signal.

Johnson is trying to move forward, holding his groupie
back by the shoulder, when another boy opens one of his
magazine pouches and runs off with thirty rounds of
5.56-millimeter ball ammunition, property of the United
States government. Johnson screams and Armstrong is on
the thief, taking the magazine back, wagging his finger in
the kid's face, tossing it over to Johnson with a gruff
rebuke.

The boys are swarming now, grabbing and poking, trying to steal something? Or just playing? A kid rushes up to
me and swats my shins with a stick. I snatch him by his
wrist, shake him violently enough to scare him, and release
him. But he isn't scared. The kid hisses at me and joins a
friend who's making a run at Ms. Thayer-Ash. The two of
them split up when they get to her; one grabs her camera
and the other holds on to her hair with both hands and
pulls her to the ground. I push a kid in front of me and he
bounces back on his butt, stands, and rushes for my cartridge belt. The two boys on Ms. Thayer-Ash are clawing at
her fingers, trying to wrestle the camera away, kicking her.
One of them buries his fingers in her eyes. The other drives
his head into her chest and bites. Even with all the commotion, her shrill scream turns the heads of my Marines.
Gunny leaps past me and tosses the two boys back like

Cabbage Patch dolls. Ms. Thayer-Ash stands, crying, and puts her arm around the Gunny. Some guys have all the luck.

"Back in the vehicle, Ms. Thayer-Ash!" shouts the Gunny. She actually does what she's told; that Gunny, what a charmer.

"What did you do to them?" she asks me, huffing and puffing back to the Hummer, blood streaming down from a nick below her eye. She's absolutely terrified, muddy tears branching back toward her ears as she runs.

"Who? The kids? Nothing. They just started to get a little wild, I guess. Tried to steal some gear."

She says something else but I don't hear her over the engine's noise. Gunny lifts her into the back and I trot out in front and take up a spot in the center of the formation; I need to get this under control. *Now.* I give a signal to Montoya and the platoon is moving again, using speed as security.

The kids follow, shouting and laughing, Montoya leading us all down the road like the Pied Piper. The platoon is now configured like a bomber formation, the flank securities pushing back the kids who are darting in like fighters, the Marines inside them keeping their eyes out for bigger threats, ignoring the kids entirely.

The chatter rises and I realize that the boys are yelling at Little Joe, who is still walking behind Doc in the center of the formation, carrying his stick, screaming back at them. Four of the boys, led by Johnson's new buddy in the Nike shirt, sprint inside our formation and shove Little Joe down before we can react. Doc grabs two of the boys by their arms and Little Joe picks up his stick, stands, and smashes it into the face of one of the attackers. Red spills out of the boy's cheek and nose and the air is filled with a singing shriek of pain.

"Ohh, Joe! Why'd you do that?" shouts Doc and he kneels over the wounded boy. "Sir, I think his nose is broke and his eye is . . . I don't know. It may be shoved inside him. It's gone. We gotta get him back to the battalion aid station. Sir!"

Some more kids run over and wrestle Little Joe to the ground, clawing at his eyes. We are still dispersed for combat: spread out to the point that Marines on the edges of the formation can't stop all of the Somalis now shooting the gaps. I begin to peel the boys off, shouting for help, tossing them backward into the dust, probably a little too hard because I am nervous. The first one is so light that I literally toss him backward over my head like a shovelful of snow. A Somali woman is in front of me now and her arm moves—it is so fast that all I can do is duck my head and hope that it is not a machete. Something thumps against the side of my helmet and I hear the shatter of glass. A bottle. I keep my head down and find her with my helmet, pushing it into her stomach and sliding it north, finding her chin with a *thud,* pinning her arms to her sides with my hands. She is writhing back and forth like a fish, screaming, and I feel kids punching me in the legs and pulling at my rifle.

"Riot formation!" I yell. "Close ranks! Riot formation!"

For the thousands of hours we have practiced our standard combat tactics, we rehearsed this particular exercise—count them—two times, both times on the flight deck of the *Denver.* The formation is a coplike phalanx pressed shoulder to shoulder, last used by military units in the Civil War, so foreign to the modern battlefield that we laughed our way through the exercise. Timewaster, we said. Goat rope. "Great way to lose a bunch of Marines at once, all this is," said the Gunny. "One grenade takes out the whole platoon. I wouldn't be caught *dead* in this formation. You use this in combat you'd *be* dead, riot or not."

Yet it takes less than a minute before the glimmers of order and control break through the chaos, our internal batteries recharging, confidence rising, hearts slowing as our shoulders touch and we form two unbroken ranks. The street is narrow and the two lines of Marines wall the Somalis off completely. Somalis trying to move through us are met with compact shoves from the M-16s. The three or four Somalis trapped behind the men—including the screeching woman whom I am holding—are passed forward, shoved and squeezed through the ranks, spit out on the other side as if bounced from a bar.

The boys and the two or three screaming mothers contemplate the situation. Some of them pick up rocks and begin to throw them, but the boys are not very strong and the rocks just bounce off the flak jackets. Others take off running down a side alley to our front.

Doc is already moving past me with the injured boy cradled in his arms, but for some reason I am compelled to say, "Get him in the Hummer, Doc." It is a superfluous order but it feels good gaining a semblance of control again.

"Yessir," he says.

Gunny walks up to me and raises his hands, What next?

Ms. Thayer-Ash is next to him, breathing hard, eyes darting around. No wonder the Gunny is so quiet; he doesn't want to give her anything to report. The injured boy gives me an easy out. Without him, it would be tough to reconcile canceling the mission. Though we're not equipped for a riot—and the mission itself is just a hot walk in the sun— Marines like to complete their tasks. I imagine the story Ms. Ash would broadcast if we were turned back by a bunch of ten-year-olds. Of course, the headline would be much, much worse if we were to force our way through the patrol route, punching and butt-stroking with the M-16s. *If you lose, you lose. If you win, you still lose. You can't win!*

"Tell the driver to turn around. We're heading back. This mission is over. That boy needs to get to the aid station. Get Montoya's team on front security in front of the Hummer, with me. Armstrong, you keep the ranks closed here as rear security. Gunny, you watch his back. Remember the ROE and keep your heads up. If any shots are fired we need to disperse immediately. Those boys are already on their way around our flank."

The Hummer does a squealing three-point turn and I am trotting just behind Montoya's team up front. I can hear the Somalis shouting at us from the houses—and hear the rocks *donk* off the roof of the Hummer—but to my front I see the occupants of the tiny houses that make up either side of the alley spilling onto their stoops, smiling, holding their hands up in mock salutes to block the sun, still unaware of the fiasco that took place two blocks behind me.

"How's he doin', Doc?" I yell into the Hummer.

"His eye's real bad, sir."

"Almost there."

Two hundred meters from the airport gate a group of boys darts out of an alley and walls off the street, arms cocked. Most have bottles or rocks in their tiny hands.

"Slow up," I say to the platoon. "Just press forward at a walk. When we get close we'll use the riot steps."

The Somali boys are patient enough to understand the strength of their arms and wait until we are within twenty meters before they begin to throw. The whites of our eyes. The Nike leader throws first, then the others follow suit and reach down for more rocks. They operate in much the same way that we do in an ambush, sucking the enemy into the kill zone, the leader firing first. Rocks fall among us but are no more forceful than hailstones. One hits a Marine on his head but it bounces off the helmet harmlessly. My head is tucked down chin to chest, my helmet protecting my face, watching the boots of the Marines to my right, following the cadence of Montoya, who is shouting so we move in lockstep. A rock bounces off my thigh. The boys are yelling and laughing loudly; they mean more fun than harm. Somalis sure have one wild sense of humor, boy! Ha, ha.

A bottle crashes on the hood of the Hummer but does not break. It bounces up against the windshield and shoots back across the hood, over the grill, and under a tire. It explodes with a loud *pop!*

"Shots!" shouts Montoya. "Get down! Anyone see it?"

The Marines kneel and raise their weapons, looking for the rifle. I hear the sharp clicks as safeties come off.

"Only a bottle!" I yell. "Keep moving forward! Just a bottle breaking!"

I glance up and a rock sails right next to my face, over my shoulder.

Nike Boy bolts straight for us under a barrage of covering fire, slips between Montoya's legs, and is up on the hood of the Hummer before I can stop him, trying to clamber over the vehicle. I grab him with one hand—I don't dare release my grip on the M-16—and yank him close to the windshield, hoping that Thayer-Ash isn't taking pictures. The kid tries to bite my hand and then rakes his fingernails down my forearm. I jerk my hand from his body and he makes a grab for my pistol holster. I slap him hard across the face and he falls back, slides down the front of the hood, bounces off the bumper, and disappears under the moving Hummer.

"OHMYGOD! Freeze!" I scream and hold up the hand signal for the driver, a clenched fist. "Stop!" I kneel down fully expecting to have to extract his body, but the boy is still full of life. In fact, he has scrambled clear under the vehicle and out the other side. "Coming at ya, Gunny!" I scream.

"Got him, sir!" I hear from behind the vehicle. "What should I do with him?"

"Is he okay?" Still yelling over the vehicle.

"Marine die Somalia!" I hear the kid scream.

"He's fine, sir," says Gunny.

"Let him go, out through your rank!"

Gunny sets him down but Nike Boy runs back toward me instead. Trapped now between the two lines of Marines—the houses lining the sides of the roads—he runs back and forth like a separated bait fish, frantically searching for an exit from the predators come to kill him. He's screeching and jabbering. I chase him around the Hummer once and it's like Rocky trying to chase that chicken before he's in shape, the kid darting and cutting.

"Montoya," I pant, "open your rank and let the kid out!"

He does and Nike Boy buzzes back toward his gang like a hornet that's finally found the crack in the window. The boys disappear and we double-time to home base.

We're about fifty meters from the front gate when Gunny yells, "Can you hurry up there, sir? These kids back here are throwin' rocks at us again and the backs of my legs're sore."

– 16 –

There can be only one.

A thunderhead blocks our view of the afternoon sunset but the lightning sparks crisp and flat across the broiling sky. The black clouds are trying to capture the heat lightning for themselves but their underbellies flicker with anger and rumble a few seconds later as if raging for having given off any light. The squall announces its arrival with a gusty wind and a pop in the humidity that you can nearly chew.

"Should we break out the ponchos, sir?" Doc asks.

"If it ain't rainin', we ain't trainin'."

Doc looks at me for a second before he says, "Is that a yes?"

I nod and watch him get out of the foxhole, walk over to the hole-in-the-wall, and whistle.

"What's up, Doc?"

"I want to get Little Joe situated before the storm so he doesn't get you all wet by screwing up the ponchos when he climbs in to sleep, sir."

"How thoughtful of you, Doc."

A Marine sprints over to my hole holding his helmet to

his head with one hand, his blouse flapping in the wind. "Lieutenant Kelly, Colonel Capiletti wants to see you in his office, sir. In PT gear."

"PT gear?"

"Yessir."

"Let me guess. Boxing?" Bison Breath probably wants to beat the hell out of me because of the patrol.

"He was punching his bag when I left, sir," says the Marine. "Two reporters are in there, too."

He trots off and I begin to strip out of my camouflage utilities, dreading the upcoming visit but hustling for three reasons: A lieutenant doesn't keep a colonel waiting, I don't want to give Mary Thayer-Ash any more time to spin her version of the patrol, and the fewer seconds the platoon sees me naked the better. Familiarity, after all, breeds contempt.

"How'd you know it was boxing, sir?" asks Doc when he walks back over with Joe snuggled tightly to his side.

"Just a lucky SWAG." A SWAG is a scientific wild-ass guess, not to be confused with a JAG (judge advocate general), a MAG (Marine air group), a CAG (commander, air group), or a FRAG (a delicate subject for lieutenants, best left unmentioned). It gets much, much worse.

When I hear the dull thuds of his fists on the heavy bag, I feel my stomach boil and foam. I struggle to remember exactly what happened on the patrol and how I might have acted differently.

I knock three times and scream, "Lieutenant Kelly reporting as ordered, sir!"

"Get on in here, Kelly!" Bison Breath shouts enthusiastically. Something is amiss.

I open the hatch and mutter, "You have got to be fucking kidding me," under my breath.

"What's that?" he asks. I am not in any danger; eavesdropping would be impossible considering how hard Darren is punching the colonel's heavy bag. *Thump! Thump!* The colonel waves me in, smiling, and returns his hand to the back of the bag. Darren nods at me, crouches into his fighting stance again, and throws a series of savage combinations to impress me. It works. He backs up to rest, feints right, then steps in again and blows the bag into Bison Breath, rocking his head and twisting his hips with each punch, B-Squared screaming, "That's it! That's it!"

Bison Breath holds his hand in front of Darren's face after everyone in the room—including Mary Thayer-Ash—has had ample time to marvel at Darren's stamina. *Thump! Thump! Thump!* "Nice work, Phillips!" Bison Breath says. "For a wrestler, you've got great hand speed."

"Maybe you missed your true calling, Darren," says Thayer-Ash.

"No I didn't. I was a Marine once," Darren pants.

The colonel says, "And we're trying to fix that and bring you back."

"Listen, guys, I have some editing to do," Thayer-Ash says. She turns to me and I hold my breath. "Lieutenant Kelly, I just wanted to tell you how impressed I was with your platoon out there today. The restraint. I wanted to say it in person. Thank you." She extends her lithe hand and I take it. She nods gravely, excuses herself, and leaves the office.

I exhale.

"Don't get too comfortable, Kelly," says Bison Breath after she's gone. "She still hasn't given up on her Lahti killing theory. Still wants to interview Sergeant Armstrong and the other Marines."

"Oh, don't worry, sir. I'm not comfortable at all."

Bison Breath reaches into his sea bag and tosses me a pair of boxing gloves and a head protector. "Phillips told me that you two used to have a pretty serious athletic rivalry going. I thought I'd put that knee of his through a real test."

"I don't think it was much of a rivalry, sir. Phillips beat me in most everything." I stare hard at Darren and he meets my gaze, not embarrassed at all about setting me up like this. Some things never change.

I first met Darren in the predawn nausea before our first ROTC *Semper Fi* workout, freshman year. The Marine Corps falls under the Department of the Navy, chafing reins against which jarheads have strained since our inception in 1775. So while the baby squids in our ROTC unit were sleeping soundly, the fledgling Marines were running up and down the banks of the Charles three mornings a week, screamed at by a drill instructor determined to prepare his future officers for the "rigors of hell that is life in my beloved Corps."

It was unusually cold for a fall morning and I could see my breath. I could smell it, too—130 proof from the party in the Yard the night before. I approached the bus stop rubbing my hands together, trying to concentrate on the dark lines between the red bricks of the sidewalk so I didn't lose my balance, and nearly stepped on a black man in a gray sweatsuit who was doing push-ups. Steam was rising from his glistening bald head and his face was illuminated by a streetlight that reflected his image in a wide pool of sweat that was swelling underneath his nose. He'd been there awhile.

"You must be Gavin Kelly," he panted, still pushing.

"How'd you know?"

He twisted his head enough so that I saw his white grin, then shook it slowly, as if he was surprised by the question. "Hell, man, do you know how many Marine options there are from our Harvard class in the unit? Two. Me and you."

"How'd you find that out?"

He stood and threw his shoulders back. We shook hands and it hurt. He looked to be about six feet and an efficient 185 pounds. "Called the secretary at the ROTC unit," he said. "My name's Darren Phillips. You and me, Kelly, we're going to have to stick together for the next four years. This place doesn't exactly enjoy having our kind around."

"Our kind?" He was an aggressive conversationalist, as if he was lecturing, but I was compelled to follow his lead.

"Military. Marines especially. Let me illustrate. You're familiar with Memorial Church?"

"The big church in the Yard where we had that beer bash during Freshman Week?"

He rolled his eyes. "That church was built to honor the Harvard men who died fighting in World War II. About seven hundred of them. But something changed in the 1960s. You know how many died in Vietnam? *Ten.* Shirking personal sacrifice, students burned the ROTC building as a substitute sacrifice instead. And the ivory tower's been trying to rid itself of the military virus since then. You know the commissioning ceremony used to be held on the steps of the church every year? Guess where the newly christened officers were pinned last year? In the basement of the fucking *science center.* So like I said, we're a team."

"How do you know all this stuff?"

"Part of the research I did for my final high school paper, 'What Happened to Duty?'"

The bus rolled up Massachusetts Avenue and screeched to a halt. Its lights threw our shadows on the Yard wall. I hoped the ride was brief so I wouldn't have to listen to too much more from the freshman I'd just met—his few sentences gave me plenty to think about—but he grabbed my arm and asked, "You're not *riding* down to MIT, are you?"

"I was planning on it."

He shook his head. "No. Let's get in the habit of running to workout. Besides, man, you don't want to show up for workout smelling like a still. You need to sweat some of that poison out."

"Why would you run? These workouts are supposed to be tough enough as it is. If we run down to MIT, that's just extra work."

He laughed and started to trot. I followed, lacking an exit strategy that would salvage pride. "That's *exactly* why we're going to run down there every time. Come November, we'll be in the best shape in our class. And by winter—and for the next four years—we'll be the hardest two motherfuckers in the entire unit."

Darren looked plenty hard already. At the time, of course, I didn't know he was an All-Prep wrestler who would make the All–Ivy League team all four years. My goals were far more modest—join some coed intramural volleyball team where I could meet some tall women. But, as I would do so often for the next six years, I followed his lead.

I rarely beat Darren in our workouts—every single one finished with a race or some other competition—but he brought me something that had proved so elusive until I met him: confidence. And he showed me what true determination meant. One winter evening we were racing through a stadium workout—sprinting up each one of Soldier's Field Stadium's thirty-eight sections, lunging up the steep concrete steps, legs and lungs burning—and I asked Darren if he wanted to stop. The sun had set and I could no longer see the sharp edges of the steps. Darren grunted and continued the race. A few minutes later I heard him yell in pain. He began to limp and I passed him easily, gaining speed as I approached one of my few victories. When he gimped up the final section, I saw that he had scraped most of the skin from his left shin. "I'm going to need stitches, Kelly," was all he said. When the nurse removed his sneaker at university health services, there was so much blood in it that she had to pour it into a wastebasket.

Bison Breath ties my gloves snug and escorts Darren and me out behind the hangar to a patch of grass next to the tarmac. A few Marines who are cleaning their rifles nearby catch the scent of a future kill, like vultures, and saunter over. The wind is slicing in from the sea and I hear the deep rumble of thunder. I'm in a bad horror movie. "I'm still pretty tired from that patrol, sir," I say.

B-squared grunts and sticks a mouth guard in past my lips. "Well, Phillips here has been working the bag for a while. Besides, with that bum knee, he shouldn't be able to move at all."

"Sir, ith thith your mouth guard?" I manage.

"Yes. I've used it, if that's what you're asking me."

I don't know which is worse, the prospect of losing a fight to a reporter with a plastic knee or tasting the residue of mouse rot the mint-flavored mouth guard cannot stifle. The colonel outlines the rules—three rounds, three minutes each—and when he karate-chops the air between us, Darren closes in quickly, head rolling, stretching his neck, arms loose. I meet his eyes and they're flicking from my hands to my eyes and back again. A predator. I toss some hard jabs to keep him from my body but he ducks and bulls his way close, grinding his head against my ribs. He slams two lefts into my body and catches the side of my head with a swift uppercut that rocks me sideways. I stumble onto the tarmac, where one of the growing crowd of Marine spectators catches me, spins me around, and gently pushes me back into the arena.

"Keep your left hand up, sir," he whispers to me. It's Big Duke.

The first spittle of rain hits us, but to my dismay none of the crowd leaves. If anything, the crackling of the lightning just charges up the ring of Marines and I hear one of them say, "Fuck the rain, this's gonna be good!"

I bend my knees and try to keep my feet light by bouncing on my toes, but it's just a poor man's imitation of what I've seen on television. The Marines teach the endgame of fighting—grabbing a rifle and smashing it into an enemy skull, slashing a throat with a bayonet and sticking it in deep, stomping the heel of the boot into an enemy's nose—but they do not teach its art. Darren closes again, almost gracefully, and blocks two of my jabs. I catch him with a hook that snaps his head back, but his thick neck absorbs the blow and he counterpunches with a tight hook that crushes my rib cage and robs my air. Rain is bleeding down the headgear over my face and I have to exhale to keep it out of my mouth.

I lunge for Darren, grab him, pull him in close where he can't hurt me. He tries to shove me back but I need time to catch my breath so I slow-dance. I can hear his consistent breathing, almost mechanical, efficient, like a machine, raspy and heated.

"I feel sorry for all those chicks you brought home," I gasp.

"I know you miss each other, gentlemen, but stop dancing," says the colonel. "They teach you that at *Hahvahd?*"

The crowd laughs. Darren shoves me hard and when he leans forward I slap a jab right in his face. It stuns him and he stumbles backward. I try to widen the opening by throwing a fierce combination, so I never see the hook coming. It's a vicious counterpunch that could dent a redwood and it impacts the side of my head with such force my vision goes black.

When I wake up Darren is leaning over me, asking if I'm okay. I'm on my back. There are clusters of stars that are bursting around his face like sparkling fireworks. "I've had plenty of these," I hear Bison Breath say. "So everyone relax." He face dips right in close and he says, "Kelly. Can you hear me?"

"Your breath is a natural smelling salt, sir."

"What city are you in?"

"I'm in hell, sir."

Everyone laughs and the colonel lifts me to my feet and into Darren's big arm. My best friend walks me back into the hangar, conciliatory now, dissecting the fight, telling me how one of my punches stunned him and how I should have followed it with another. I notice that Montoya is part of the audience, and when our eyes meet he clenches his fist and nods; I'm not sure if this is a promise of revenge or a message of bereavement. I turn away and pretend not to see him, embarrassed.

When I get to the colonel's office, I sag into a chair, totally defeated. My head is pounding. *Boom. Boom. Boom.* I hear the colonel dismiss Darren and when I look up the colonel and I are alone in his office. I know what's coming now—the colonel will fire me and I'll be replaced on the spot with Darren. The world has come back to its proper axis.

The colonel pats me on the back and kneels down, untying my gloves. "I figured it was a good way to test the strength in his knee," he says apologetically.

"We've sparred before, sir. At the basic school. He beat me there, too, but he didn't knock me out. I'd say the knee is fine."

"Don't tell him, yet, but I'm confident I'll be able to get that waiver signed off on. Get him back in the Corps, where he belongs. Man's one of the most squared away I've ever seen." He takes a water bottle and squeezes a burst across my head and shoulders. "When I was interviewing him, he said he got all that determination from his mother. Other than that, he refused to discuss his background. Was she a single parent? Did Phillips grow up under tough circumstances?"

Normally I would never discuss another man's personal business, especially Phillips's, for fear of being pummeled, but this is exactly the kind of stereotype that Darren rages against. "Sir, his mother raised him alone because his father was killed in Vietnam. He was a platoon sergeant with Echo Company, two-twenty-six. He was killed during a hellacious NVA attack on his trench at Khe Sanh. So, no, she wasn't a single mother. She was a widow. And Phillips never met his father, just a few Marines who talked about him. He's still searching for others who knew him.

"As for the rest of his background, that's just Phillips's inherent personality, sir. He grew up comfortable. Went to the best prep school in the country, St. Paul's. He just doesn't believe that we're products of our environment, that's all. He's Mr. Self-Determination. So he doesn't discuss circumstances because he holds them to be irrelevant. He's all about the future, sir. He sets goals, and when he achieves them, he doesn't celebrate but looks ahead. But when he fails, well, he becomes obsessed. Like he is now."

"I'll say! I notice he runs around the tarmac every day."

"Yes, sir. And you can be sure that *he* notices that you notice."

The colonel nods, pondering Phillips, then stands suddenly. "I want you to know that I'm . . . that your platoon did well today, Kelly. Today's . . . *conflict* . . . with those boys is exactly the type of action the Corps is going to have to get used to facing. And the next time they'll have pistols."

"Which is exactly why we should liberalize the rules regarding deadly force, sir."

The colonel reddens and immediately I know I've overstepped my bounds again. "No, Kelly, the rules have been set and we'll obey them. You see, it's comments like that that make me wonder about you. You enjoy talking about Desert Storm around me because I wasn't lucky enough to go. You—"

"Sir, I don't—"

"Don't interrupt me, Lieutenant," he says softly. "The fact is, Desert Storm is *not* the war we'll be fighting in the next few decades. It'll be Operations Other Than War, just like we're doing here. And they won't be clean. And they'll have restrictions that don't make sense. And *we'll by God carry out our orders as best we can.* Understood?"

"Yessir."

"These wars will be confusing and frustrating, just like this one here. But Marines don't complain. They adapt. Phillips tells me that your grandfather is Red Kelly?"

This is all I need. A comparison to Red, a relationship that I've managed to keep secret for three years. I'm going to get Phillips for this, though I'll need a gun or a machete. "Yes, sir."

"Well, if you're trying to live up to him and his wars, don't. Ours are going to be vastly different, Kelly, Desert Storm notwithstanding."

Phillips, you asshole! You're the one who's chasing a ghost!

The colonel tosses a magazine at my chest. It flutters to the ground at my feet and I pick it up. It's a *People* magazine. "Page thirty-eight," he says. I open it and it's a full-page picture of my platoon at FDC 3, a full team wearing

T-shirts without blouses, all of us holding up weapons and smiling. Armstrong dominates the back row; he's holding his Ka-Bar knife aloft and wears a maniacal grin, a titan among boys. Underneath the picture, the caption reads: "The elite Marine recon platoon takes a break after feeding a village."

Uh-oh. Fucking reporters promised it would be a private picture! Can't trust the press!

"Sir, I . . ."

"One step up, one step back, Kelly. Do you know that *Headquarters Marine Corps* is demanding an explanation for this gosh-darned band of rabble? That platoon of, of . . . *banditos* is bringing exactly the kind of unfavorable press I warned you about! This *isn't* World War II. Marines do *not* dress like this! Uniforms are *critical*.

"This is strike number two, Kelly. When the situation goes bad, like it did today, you perform well because you can think. And because you're surrounded by great Marines. But when you get reckless, you make us all look bad. I haven't made up my mind about you after eight months, Kelly, but after just a few meetings I *have* made up my mind about Phillips. Think about that. He's consistent. And he'll be a superior officer when we get him back in. You think about that. Dismissed."

I come to attention, execute a wobbly about-face because my balance hasn't returned yet, and stagger out of the hangar and into the heat. It sears my body and squeezes my pounding head. Only after I've stumbled for a hundred meters do I realize that it is pouring rain. "Oh, I do think about it, sir," I say to no one. "I think about it all the time."

Red's was a much more brutal war; he was attacked by a legion of fanatical warriors, we *chased* most of ours back to Iraq. On Iwo Jima the Marines lost 6,825 men—one man in three was a casualty—and killed nearly all of the 22,000 Japanese defending the rock. In Desert Storm America lost 148 men and women—a quarter of them to friendly fire—and took over *200,000* prisoners. So while Red and his killed every living Jap they saw, shooting first and questioning later, today we ask questions first, then more questions, then *more* questions—keeping our eyes glued on the guys with the AK-47s and the cameramen behind them—before we press the trigger. This assumes, of course, that our rifles are loaded in the first place; in Beruit, Marines were asking permission to insert magazines of ammunition even as the car bomber swerved past their barricades, on its way to destroy 247 Marines and sailors.

Maybe the colonel is right. It's a complex world filled with clusterfucked countries hosting goat rodeos. It's not clear and crisp. Never will be. But is it really any harder for a warrior to deal with? Not once the shooting starts. My job is to make sure we get off the first round . . . and aren't hung by the information age for the opening shot. Do I really envy my grandfather and his wars? I think about Red's stories and shake my head. No. I do not. I want to do right by him, but I do not want to *be* him.

———

In just three weeks on Guadalcanal, Red has established quite a reputation. Such is the crucible of combat: In one brief and furious moment, skill and character—everything you've ever done and hope to do—intersect violently with fate. And in an instant you are a hero, or a goat, or just plain lucky, or dead.

Red wipes his brow and resumes digging. Here's how it works: Clark designs the position and draws it up and Red digs the fighting hole. "It's just the most efficient use of time. You're stronger and I'm smarter," says Clark. Red cannot find a flaw in the reasoning so he has been the digger since D plus one.

As the BAR man Red's job is to send bursts of bullets across the front of the Marine line, three feet above the ground, to cut down any Japs making their way through the wire to the holes. Not the greatest job, but it beats the hell out of roofing in South Boston.

Red is digging just inside a sandy tidal plain, in a tree line, and when he finally folds up his shovel, he hops into the bottom of the lair. The ocean puts him to sleep. Red sleeps first, that's part of the deal he negotiated with Clark and he's proud of it. Clark takes the 1900–2400 shift and Red watches after that until the sun rises.

"Kelly!" Clark whispers. Is it three minutes or three hours later? "The LP says they're comin'! I already called the captain." LP stands for . . . what? Oh, yes, listening post, Red remembers.

Red sits up quickly and grabs the spare Browning Automatic Rifle that Chehab used to own before he was stabbed, unwraps it, and places it neatly next to his own BAR. Then he says the Lord's Prayer as he stacks the grenades in front of the hole. Red knows that right there, at that moment, there are thousands of other prayers emanating from that one island in the Pacific, shooting up to the stars like radio waves, requests all similar to his.

The Jap mortars fire first, deep pops half a mile away. A mortar round has a thirty-second flight time, and there in his hole in the darkness, Red listens to his last piece of silence—and peace itself—as it slips away. When the rounds get close, they *whoosh* and Red knows they are going to impact on his right, near the center of the line. Close.

Red grabs his weapons and pulls them into the hole, on

top of him. The mortars are crashing all around now, deep
booms, *whump! whump!* Lucky salvo, Red thinks. No way
the Nips have a spotter close enough. *They're just giving the
shock troops cover to move in close.* The fighting hole—the
whole island!—is rocking from side to side like that terrible troop ship that brought him here. Clark is yelling
something, but Red can't make it out.

The rounds begin falling farther behind him and Red
glances up, half-expecting to see a Jap standing right there
looking down into his hole. But all he sees are the leaves
cut down by the whizzing shrapnel, drifting slowly down
into his hole like snow in the moonlight. Red wonders
when it snows on this island.

Time to get ready! Jap bullets are snapping into the jungle now, through the trees, *craack! craack! craack!* Red pops
up and shoulders the big rifle. He sees the muzzle flashes
on the other side of the sandy clearing that separates the
combatants. Clark stabs the machete in front, snaps his
bayonet on, and sights in behind his M-1.

Red grabs his arm. "Let 'em get close."

"Stay together."

Red nods and adjusts the BAR. Green flares burst with a
hissssssss over the lines. He squints to the front and there
are hundreds—thousands?—of Japs walking across the
tongue of sand.

"We don't have enough people!" screams Clark.

"We got plenty of bullets," Red says.

"*Banzai!*" the Japs scream.

The wall of flickering bodies leaps forward and charges
across the sandy clearing, splashing in shin-high water.
The green light of the flares makes them look like alien
beings, which they pretty much are, being from Japan and
all. The Marine line explodes and Red sights in and
squeezes the trigger, too. The BAR bucks and steadies,

boom! boom! boom! boom! The world is not as it was. Now it is just a metal rainstorm, a roar that tilts the earth, a descent to the foundation of fear itself. All the branches and leaves to Red's front disappear. And so do the Japs.

Red can tell which ones have been hit by his BAR; Clark's bullets spin them around or crumple them right where they stand, but Red's actually lift them from their feet and jerk them back suddenly, as if they are being yanked by the leash of hell.

But there are so many! After several hundred rounds Red's BAR is glowing hot red. "Grab me the spare!" he screams. Clark fires off the rest of his clip and sets his M-1 down, frantically reaching for the other BAR. Red grabs two grenades and throws them through the broken and lifeless trees. *Kaahhh-wump! Kaahhh-wump!* The heat waves knock him back and make him cringe. His ears pop and begin to ring. Shrapnel zips through branches and *kahdiiiings* off trunks. Red hears screams following the explosions; *real* close now.

"My fuckin' hand!" That's Clark, whose hand is smoking as he hands Red the fresh BAR. He must have touched the burning BAR, Red thinks. I can't wait to make fun of him after this is over; usually *I'm* the one who forgets the little things we learned in boot camp. When Red shoulders that horse weapon, there are Japs *all over* the place, hung up in the wire ten yards in front of the hole, screaming at him. Red holds the trigger down and traverses the big weapon back and forth. Pieces of the Japs disappear and they no longer have human form.

The flares burn out and the light evaporates with them.

"Just use the grenades and get me ammo!" Red screams. Clark tosses one and reaches down for another magazine. Red ducks inside just in time; the shrapnel shock wave from the grenade blast washes over the hole and sucks away his breath. When Clark pops his head up again, a Jap sticks a bayonet into his face. Clark manages to grab the rifle, but the Jap decides that this one needs a bullet and he blows Clark's face off.

Red snatches Clark's M-1 and pulls the trigger. Nothing happens. The Jap is screaming. Red's arms are quaking. As the Jap tries to pull the rifle out of Clark's head, Red sticks Clark's bayonet deep into the Jap's neck. Blood shoots out all over his face, blinding him. He curls under Clark's body in the hole and paws desperately at his eyes.

They are screaming all around him now, a horde of devils. Red feels a poke in his back, like someone is tapping him, so he freezes. Then something pushes into his flesh, grinding across a shoulder blade deep into the meat below his armpit. Red rears up and spins, twisting the rifle out of the Jap's hands. He feels the rifle dangling off his back, the bayonet solidly embedded in his lat, and when he faces the Jap he feels like a wounded bull facing a matador, the *banderilla* bouncing.

The crazy Jap does not run, though, and he leaps into Red's hole with a yell! His face is greeted by Red's fist and his head snaps back. Behind him Red sees Japs scrambling over the corpses hung on the wire. He grabs the machete. There is suddenly a Jap standing over Red and he shoots Red in the collarbone. Red grabs the Jap's rifle, absorbs a second bullet with his guts, and when the Jap refuses to let go of the rifle, Red cuts his arm off at the elbow with the machete.

There are three Japs ringing Red's foxhole and he cuts the unconscious one open—the one he punched, sport!—so there's plenty of blood to go around. Then he stretches out and grabs the Jap who shot him—he is just sitting on the BAR staring at his severed arm—and drags him into his hole. The Jap begins to scream and claws at the BAR with his good arm, but Red is too strong and like a moray eel pulls both the Jap and the machine gun into his lair, where he decapitates the offender.

Then, as if he is folding the top of a carton, Red pulls all of the bodies on top of him and waits in the bottom of a hole that has so much blood in it, when he shifts to put pressure on his back wound—the collarbone bullet isn't going to kill him—he hears it sloshing against the sides.

Please, God, let me live, he prays. And He does. And Red does. Well enough, in fact, that just two years later, frustrated with his new job, his new *life*, Red manages to get himself back into the fight, the flashbulbs lighting him up when he steps up into the train with the others, all of them young and green, some of them so timorous that they have tears in their eyes. *Tears! In public!*

PART III

Any man in combat who lacks comrades who will die for him, or for whom he is willing to die, is not a man at all. He is truly damned.

—WILLIAM MANCHESTER, *Goodbye, Darkness*

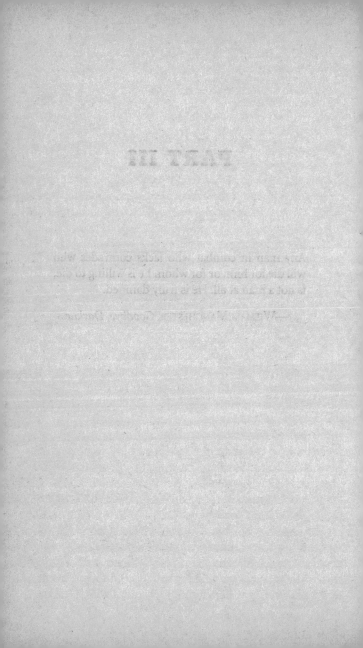

– 17 –

24 DECEMBER 1992

Call the FBI. Call the CIA. Call the Pentagon.
Find out who won the game!

The day before Christmas and all through the night not a
Marine is sleeping when the mortars take flight. We've been
in Somalia for two weeks and the mission has become surprisingly banal—pop in the earplugs so the crying and the
begging don't fray *every* nerve, feed as many refugees as
possible, and buckle your chin straps for the biweekly
Mortar Muhammad attack. I've followed the colonel's
orders to the letter; my salient goal is to leave Somalia with
the platoon intact, as soon as possible. Awards don't matter.
Good press doesn't matter.

The Gulf War started slowly as we built forces for six
months, but it concluded with a violent sprint to the finish. Restore Hope announced itself with ruffles and
flourishes but now we've downshifted and there's a fear
that we may be kept here indefinitely, what with the elec-

tion and a new administration coming in. Desert Storm was so clean—we had a clear mission, and when it was accomplished we went home. The mission was never to kill Hussein; it was to rout him from Kuwait and it was clear and achievable. The mission here is just as clear and it has also been attained—so every additional day in this hole is just another risk. Time to hand the entire thing over to . . . well, I don't *know* who, but it sure as hell shouldn't be us.

There are over ten thousand Marines in Somalia right now and the famine is over. To kill the germs we unleashed the world's deadliest virus and now we've fully infected the country; open food lines stretch out like a cobweb all across the country. There's been talk of running the country for a few days just to get the experience—perhaps I'd be the equivalent of a state governor—but the international community might frown on a nation annexed by Marines. The mission accomplishment feels good, and I'm proud to serve with a group for whom success has come naturally—albeit with extreme hardship—for over two centuries.

Americans have better things to worry about than Somalia now, and our growing restlessness is at least partly attributable to the fact that no one back in the other world cares. The television reports have relegated us to minute seventeen, and we're slipping quickly, a back-page story that no longer sells.

This is partly explained by the mission: It was interesting at first, feeding the walking dead, the images. But, hey, these pictures have become old hat, there's no longer a story that can rival the growth of baby boomer assets in the market today and, by the way, did I mention it's my turn with the kids this Christmas?

I am sitting on a cardboard MRE case at FDC 7, a makeshift courtyard in the northwest corner of Mogadishu proper, talking with Darren. The colonel has relegated my platoon to permanent second fiddle and the best way to escape Restore Hope with a decent fitness report is to shut my mouth and smile every day I draw another field mess-hall assignment.

"There are fewer than *thirty* reporters left in Somalia, Hoss," Darren says, "and five more are leaving after President Bush's visit. Mary Thayer-Ash was supposed to leave yesterday, but she managed to lobby for another week. She's desperate for a big story, especially since I convinced her to call off the dead bodyguard chase."

CNN refused, in the end, to air a piece on Said Lahti's death. I know this because Darren reported to the colonel that his recommendation was responsible for the blackout, but the likely truth is that the piece was a loser from the moment NBC took the blame for employing armed body-guards.

"She's with another platoon today. Problem with following you and your boys, Kelly," Darren says, "is there's no story left in feeding people. When Mary's story was canned, she hoped to do a piece on the little riot you-all had, but there was no footage, and without pictures you got nothing. Nobody writes anymore. Then she proposed a vanilla piece on feeding the starving . . . but with an inside angle, you know, reactions from your Marines and real-time interviews that others can't get. They told her that it's old news, find something else or fly home. She's going fucking *crazy* looking for a good story."

"Where is she?"

"She's out with a grunt platoon looking for a weapons cache."

He raises his big arms up to stretch and I see a flash of metal in his belt. "Don't tell me you're carrying."

He glances over his shoulder and pulls out a 9-millimeter

Glock from his waistband, overly careful to keep its barrel down and his finger away from the trigger as a signal to me that he hasn't forgotten proper Marine Corps carry procedures. "Smuggled it in a camera case in my duffel bag. A former Marine can't be empty-handed in a place like this, check? Besides, you get into a fight, you'll need me, Kelly. Or have you forgotten I'm a stone killer?"

Even here—as a civilian reporter in Africa—he considers himself my superior. Darren won the Bronze Star in Desert Storm for leading his platoon in a small skirmish against dug-in infantry. He's always avoided telling me the actual story; my hunch is that he feels guilty for being awarded a medal for getting shot while I got nothing but a savage lecture.

"You put that thing away and keep it there. A Somali sees that, he's likely to steal it or kill you for it. I'm serious."

He swipes at the air with his paw and says dismissively, "I can take care of myself, Kelly. You got enough to worry about with your platoon, though I do have some comments about setting up security in this FDC the way you do. Why don't you put a fire team up in that northern bunker?"

I hop onto the hood of my Hummer and watch the Somalis in their disco clothes grab sacks of grain and dance off with them, laughing. *You can laugh, you can cry, having the time of your life.* I'm not going to give Darren the satisfaction. "Reporters don't have comments, Darren. Only questions that stem from a lack of understanding." Standing here above him, one hand on a hip, the other resting lazily on the butt of my issued pistol, I feel refreshingly superior. Twenty-one Marines around me, *my* men, are feeding a nation and there he sits, a civvie, on the outside looking in, reporting on the men in the arena, a critic, paid to describe and explain to the world what *we* are doing. He has become what he most despised.

A woman screams somewhere outside the compound and my empty hands move instinctively behind me and return with my rifle, spinning it up and into my shoulder. I am already off the Hummer and on a knee next to Darren. "What was that?"

"Woman screamed, sir," says Doc. Thanks.

"I think it came from that building. The last white one on the right before the next road. Fifty meters," pants Montoya, pointing his weapon at the house. Our FDC is situated at the end of a narrow alley lined with tiny houses packed tightly on both sides. The front and rear walls of our perimeter are a composite of barbed wire and sandbags, with houses providing the protection on the flanks. I've inherited the position from a grunt platoon and they have done a terrific job of preparing this defense for an attack. My Marines are moving to their assigned posts, breathing heavily and hoping.

"Want me to go out and check it, sir?" Montoya practically pleads.

"No one leaves the compound. And get down behind that sandbag."

A small Somali crowd gathers in front of the house down the street and a small girl, maybe eight, tugs at an old man's arm, trying to pull him into the house. He holds his ground, shaking his head, peeling her fingers away and backing up. She is crying.

"Gunny!" I scream.

"Already on it, sir. Got Team Three off serving duty and ready to go if we need a moving force. All the Somalis in the FDC are on their faces and frozen."

The girl breaks away from the crowd and runs up the

street to the barbed wire, screaming and crying. She's wearing a wraparound piece of bright blue cloth fashioned as a skirt, a torn blouse, and sandals that flip-flop loudly as she approaches. "Marine!" she screams. "Marine! *Marine!*" She blurts out some unintelligible Somali phrases and grabs the gate, shaking it and screaming, drawing blood where her left hand has grabbed a spike in the wire.

"You'll hurt yourself," whines Gunny. "*Stop,* honey, stop it. No! Bad girl." He rushes up and tries to pry the girl's hands from the gate. "Sir?"

"Open the gate. Someone grab Little Joe for translation."

"He's right here, sir," Montoya says.

Joe walks up and says, "She say her mother in wit de men now. In de house now."

"What men?" I ask.

"De Heeber Geeder. Sound like."

Gunny swings the gate open and hugs the girl but she pushes him back and grabs his belt, trying to pull him out of the FDC and back down the street. She loses a sandal but continues to yank, digging her bare heel into the rocks and leaning back, Gunny following her slowly, saying, "Sir?"

"Hold up, Guns. And get down, for fuck's sake! We're not supposed to leave the FDC. This could be an ambush."

In the distance the crowd parts and four Bangers walk out of the house and stand in the middle of the street, smiling at us. Their AK-47s are slung behind them. They raise their hands and wave at us to signal peaceful intentions. One of them's dressed in a striped dress shirt and even back here I can see that he has a massive head. "Hey, Marine!" Mortar Muhammad shouts. "Recon nigga!"

Like the rest of my platoon, I am on my knees sighting

in. The rear aperture of the M-16 is a circle in which I have enclosed the fuzzy outline of a Banger. I tilt back slightly and the front sight post rises and steadies in the middle of the enemy. "Let's go get 'em, sir," says Armstrong. "I think that tall one there is Mortar Muhammad Ali."

"We've gotta stay in the compound. And we don't even know what they've done."

"Dey lay wit her mother," says Joe. "Right now."

"*Quiet*, Little Joe."

"Dey lay wit her mother *now*."

"I said *quiet*, Joe." Fuck me.

"So they're rapin' her in there, sir!" says Armstrong. "We on standby again?"

"Tell me you're not going to just sit here, Kelly," Darren says, pistol in hand, peeking over a sandbag. "'Cause if you are, I'm going myself."

I put my finger in his face. "*You'll* do what you're told. Stay here in the compound. Team Two, stay here on security. One and Three, listen up, I'm going to give a brief order. We're going in."

"Fuckin' A," Armstrong says.

Darren grumbles something about making fast decisions in rapidly deteriorating circumstances and disappears behind a truck. Down the street two more Bangers stroll out of the house and many of the Somali villagers run inside, all the Bangers waving at us now, a siren's call to arms. A woman pokes her head out of the doorway and screams something. The little girl answers and sprints away from Gunny, back to her house. Somalis pour out of the house and point at the Bangers, waiting for me to act, as statuesque and telling as the tragic photograph dated April 4, 1968. One of the Bangers casually slashes the barrel of his rifle across a woman's jaw and waves to his friends. Two of them enter the house again, the others laughing and waving, one stepping casually on the chest of the fallen woman.

"They're goin' for sloppy seconds, sir," says Armstrong.

"They're instigating this either to show off or to suck us into a kill zone down that alley," I say to the team leaders who have appeared next to me. "Either way, we need to surprise them in the act. Those lookouts see you coming down the alley, they'll give one of two orders: Prepare to open fire or run, and both are bad. So you need to sneak around, flank them. Get over the roof and use the other alley."

I point in time to see Darren clambering onto the roof of a house butted against the FDC. "Let's go!" he shouts in a hoarse whisper when he rolls flat on top. "This way's good and they can't see us. Let's run across the roofs!"

"What the fuck does that clown think he's doing?" hisses Gunny to no one in particular.

"Get down from there!" I hiss. "I have a plan!"

On the roof Darren pulls out his pistol and waves us up. "I got one, too, Kelly. We can hop from rooftop to rooftop this way. They can't see me. Other alley looks clear, too. Let's go!"

I want to pop him in the knee again for upstaging me, I really do. "Gunny, take teams One and Three and get over this roof and into the next alley. Circle up unseen and surround that house. I'll get Phillips off that roof and back here, and give you fire support down the alley. You get to go this time."

"Wilco."

"Yellow smoke if you need the Hummer. Rest of the signals per SOP. Montoya, you got my back while I get this asshole." I stand to chase down my best friend, but he's already preparing to jump to the next roof.

"He's going to get himself killed," Gunny whispers.

Darren crouches a third time, and as his legs extend into liftoff I see his left knee buckle. He twists awkwardly in midair and manages to get his forearm onto the tin roof of the next house, the rest of his body dangling straight down. He swings his leg up once, twice, and he manages to hook the toe of his boot in the corrugated metal, but the roof has a slight angle and he begins to slide down toward the main alley where the Bangers are lazily standing watch. He accelerates as he nears the gutter lip. *Oh, no.*

"Cover him, Montoya."

"Got him, sir."

Darren makes a violent lunge just before he reaches the gutter and manages to get some of his leg up onto the tin, but it gives way and bends deeply. His pistol flies back toward the FDC as he tries to free his right hand in time to stop the inevitable. It clatters into the middle of the street. He grabs the lip of the gutter as he shoots past and rips the entire makeshift pipe from the lip of the roof in a series of loud pops like exploding packing bubbles, Darren falling now, arms pinwheeling like a duck-shaped weathervane in a stiff breeze. He lands on his back with a loud thud and grabs his knee.

The Bangers erupt, screaming a series of warnings, and run away from us, sprinting down the alley. The two who just entered the house come tearing out a second later and follow the first four. "Forget the flank, Gunny! Just get down to the house!"

"Sir, that was Mortar Muhammad Ali! Should we chase him down?" asks Gunny.

"Negative. Have Marines scattered to the winds if we try to chase them," I say in a rush of words.

I open the gate and run to Darren, grab his arm, and begin to pull him up. "Get offa me!" he shouts. "I'm good.

Go with your men." I look back at the FDC and Montoya nods and gives me a thumb.

I follow Gunny and the teams in their careful but hasty leapfrog down the alley, rifle barrel moving with my gaze, legs moving only when I'm covered. I enter the house behind Armstrong's team and a woman grabs me immediately and pulls me into a small room. The Marines are standing still in a semicircle, staring at a woman lying on her back on a dusty wooden table. The little girl is shaking her mother's shoulders. One of the Marines looks up at me and says, "They beat her up pretty good, sir. We're gonna need Doc."

Armstrong unrolls a hasty stretcher and we carry the woman back inside the wire walls of the FDC. Her daughter follows alongside, holding her mother's hand. The woman stares blankly through her good eye without shedding a tear. The right side of her face has been crushed by a rifle butt and is concave. Her eye socket has been shattered and her cheekbone is visible. A large, purple bubble of fluid has risen out of her forehead, swollen, full of blood. Perhaps she is in shock.

We set her down behind the Hummer and Doc takes over, cracking cold packs and wrapping the woman up like a mummy. Her jaw has been splintered and several of her teeth are dangling out of her mouth. Her daughter whispers in her ear and the woman pulls her in against her breasts, holding tight. Doc has left some space for her left eye and it wells and drains over her nose, the tears absorbed immediately by the white bandage, streaking it a bluish dark.

She whispers to her daughter.

"You're gonna be fine," says Doc.

"Did they rape her?" Armstrong asks.

"Don't know," says Doc without looking up.

"Ain't you going to look down there and check?"

Doc looks up at him and glares. "Have some respect, Armstrong! She doesn't want me looking down there, and, frankly, it's the least of her problems." Doc turns to me and says, "We really should get her back to the battalion aid station, sir."

We are packing up the Hummer when Little Joe walks up to me and says, "She Darod clan . . . fight wit de Heeber Geeder. Now de men lay wit her after dey kill her da. Wit her daughter, too. Dat why she run to you, Kelly. Dey already lay wit her."

I pick the boy up and set him in the Hummer. I brush him playfully on his head and he smiles, but my frustration has already mutated into a yearning for revenge. What was it Armstrong said? *What the fuck are we doing?* My blood lust is rising and I am at once reminded of Desert Storm. When I was in that Iraqi trench with the other Marines, I was awash in the terror that was so familiar to me as a kid, a fear so overwhelming that it froze my thought process. Almost. Some long-dormant gene—too long!—awoke and stuffed the fear down just enough, a lust for battle that had been passed on through my grandfather, and injected into me. I felt the urge to war alongside the Marines plunging into the trench around me, screaming, raging forward to maim those who would seek to harm us, and, for the first time in my life, I joined the fight without hesitation and relished it—the electric instinct to kill.

————

Two hours after our first Iraqi contact, my infantry platoon was still trailing behind and right of the main convoy and losing ground. One of the five-tons couldn't get past the third gear and it was limping along at fifteen miles per hour. The convoy was nowhere to be seen and our FM radios couldn't range them.

"Is that Objective Eastwood, sir?" asked T-Bone, leaning down into the Hummer.

"I think so," I said.

A burning oilfield, hidden in a low bowl on a flat expanse of gray dirt, lay in front of the Hummer. From the rise on which we were perched, the smoke obscured everything in the depression, as if we were on a mountain staring down into the clouds.

Tubs turned to me nervously. His face was wet and clammy, pale complexion whitening as he spoke. "We goin' down there, sir?"

"What do you think?" I was debating a western run to the highway and the main convoy; although it would have delayed our arrival, it was also the safest route. After all, we'd found our firefight already.

"I don't know, sir. Looks pretty dangerous. That five-ton is barely crawling."

T-Bone leaned down from his perch and shouted, "What gives, sir? Let's get on down there! I want to fire this thing again. We're goin', right?"

"Hell yes, we are," I said and nodded to Tubs.

We rolled down the hill and were soon below the thickest ceiling of smoke. When we reached the bottom of the bowl, the tank tracks we were following suddenly crisscrossed in all directions; clearly the tank unit had begun to maneuver at this point. I could see all the well towers spitting continuous fire and smoke into the air, some more than others, and as we moved forward I noticed that the weaker flames had their origin in the hulls of Iraqi vehicles, trickles of grayer smoke compared to the jet black streams from the well heads.

"Jesus Christ, sir. Heck of a battle here, huh?" Tubs said. "Look at all them burnin' vehicles!"

It was an eerie landscape and my apprehension grew; maybe we should roll back up the hill and get over to the highway. There were burning Iraqi vehicles in various stages of death. Every vehicle looked like the military models I had built as a boy after I finished them off with rubber cement, lighter fluid, and matches. Charred bodies hung out of some of the hulls, last, desperate lunges for cool, and there were many others strewn about in the sand. I saw body parts, but they were not grisly because they had been charred. Hunks of flesh left too long on the barbecue. The smell of oil filled the cab, but when I rolled down the window it worsened.

I turned my head and looked out the windshield. "Where are the tank tracks?"

Tubs looked around quickly and said, "Well . . . I don't know, sir. I been concentrating on weaving through these vehicles. Guess I lost the friendly tracks."

"Shit!"

"Should we turn around, sir?" His tone plowed upward through several octaves and it unnerved me.

We approached a slight rise and I felt the butterflies move in my stomach. My grandfather once said that human beings, like animals, can sense fear, and that understanding when to embrace paranoia kept him alive in his war. I fought the urge to scream, to turn and head for the highway.

The rise to our front flashed several times, as if a bevy of paparazzi was waiting to bathe us in light. Green streaks cut through the black air all around us; several bullets struck the hood of the Hummer with ringing *clangs,* the flashbulbs winking furiously now. The noise filled my eardrums, louder than the most savage thunderstorm, and I couldn't hear myself screaming orders. *Boom! Boom! Boom! Boom! Boom!*

The Hummer shuddered and came to an abrupt halt, then lurched to the right, shaking and quivering, as if a jackhammer was pounding on us. The windshield shattered and a hurricane of glass seemed to be washing through the cab. And sheer terror, swelling with every breath, as if the air itself was laced with fear, drowning my thoughts, literally shaking my bones. I wondered how the Iraqi rounds were rocking us so violently, then realized that the recoil of the .50 machine gun on the roof was the culprit.

I opened my eyes. There were no more flashbulbs from the Iraqi position, just explosions of sand and red tracer ricochets from friendly bullets. *Saved our lives, T-Bone.*

"Get moving!" I screamed at Tubs.

"Can't, sir!" He pressed the Start button several times and the smoking engine gave a death groan. "It's stuck, for some reason." He tried again. "Can't get it going!" His voice rose to a panic. "CAN'T! CAN'T!"

"Get out!" I told him. Tubs stared at me and his eyes were the widest I have ever seen in a human being. "Now!" I yelled. He rolled out onto the sand on his stomach, without his weapon. I grabbed his M-16 and hopped out of the Hummer, scrambled around the vehicle, and threw his weapon to him. Rounds *craaacked* into the Hummer and *piiiinged* when they ricocheted. Fire superiority dictates a firefight and I knew that the next few seconds would determine the outcome of this duel—if the Iraqis pinned us down from a covered position, we'd be chewed apart.

"Help T-Bone!" I screamed, trying to add more words but unable to; I was so mortally afraid, my throat closed and cut the sentence in half. Heat slaps where the bullets tore open the air prodded me down flat on the rolling ground. *Craack! Craack!* Sand swirled in razor jets and shot into my nostrils, mouth, and eyes. My hearing was pummeled by the thunderclaps, louder, *louder, LOUDER.*

The world was not right; its axis had been twisted, the rules had changed, and I was unprepared. I had been afraid before—when the Montgomerys beat me, when I crashed my dad's truck, when Darren and I flipped a kayak in the San Clemente surf and could not right it—but this fear was so overriding and alien that I was no longer sure if I could function. I couldn't think of a tactically sound response to the wave of steel. I couldn't think of an attack, I couldn't think of a defense. I could . . . not . . . think . . . period. *It's not supposed to be like this!*

But then I saw Tubs. Something changed in him—I mean it, his face morphed, his body swelled. He narrowed his eyes, grabbed his rifle, and sprinted up toward the Iraqis in a series of short rushes, firing wildly. Tubs Tulowski, Mr. Weight Control, a man who had once been duct-taped to his rack and photographed for the *Silence of the Lambs* fat-body picture board, sprinted *forward.*

I shouldered my weapon and shot at the flashes of fire from the Iraqis' AK-47 barrels, bright orange-yellow against the backdrop, depressing the trigger as fast as I could, trying to hold the weapon steady while the entire world seemed to be shaking. When I reached into my pouch for another magazine, I saw that the Iraqi fire had ceased.

Snap decision: T-Bone was at risk sitting on top of the vehicle in the open, but his big machine gun had gained—and maintained—fire superiority over whatever Iraqis were on the rise, and we couldn't give that up. Plus, Tubs was still crawling forward, exposed. T-Bone stayed.

"Hey, T-Bone!" I screamed up. "Go to the sustained rate and save some ammo! You see anybody?"

He glanced down at me briefly, then turned his attention back to the rise. He slowed his rate of fire, squeezing off a three-round burst every ten seconds or so. "Yeah, I can still see a few. Better not give them our backs or they'll get brave! Can you toss up another ammo can, sir?" he yelled. "I'm almost out. Think I got a few a them fuckers!"

I reached into the Hummer and hefted out two big boxes. I had no breath in my lungs and my arms felt weak. I was swinging them up, keeping my eyes on the rise, when three Iraqi torsos popped up and the clatter of their AK-47s erupted again. Sand jumped all around them and one of T-Bone's tracers evaporated an enemy head like a bursting watermelon.

One Iraqi managed to shoulder a rocket-propelled grenade, but he tried to aim it, and something—a round from either Tubs or T-Bone—jerked him backward just before he fired. His shoulder and upper chest disappeared. *Must have been T-Bone.* The rocket took off with a *shoosh!* and sailed over the Hummer in a tall arc, followed by a white contrail that burned out near the apex, then tilted over and fell into the sand three hundred meters away with a soft splat. It did not explode.

I shouldered my weapon and squeezed off another magazine. Something hot pierced my neck—a 7.62-millimeter bullet—and exited from my lower back. I screamed, "I'm hit!" and rolled onto my back, next to the Hummer. I slapped my hand over the neck wound and waited for help, shocked. Shot! Shot by an *Iraqi!* In the neck! Blew out my kidney!

T-Bone stared at me in horror and then hopped down from the Hummer. "Where're you hit, sir?" he panted.

"My neck and back! Oh, FUCK! Oh, man, it hurts!"

He pulled my hand from my neck in a struggle—I was afraid to let up on the pressure—and pursed his lips. "Roll over."

I spun around and felt him lift the soaked T-shirt carefully off my lower back. T-Bone clapped me on the shoulder and said, "I think you'll live, sir." I turned to look at him and he was smiling, holding up the metal jacket of a .50 caliber, one of his expended rounds. "Just hot brass that got down your shirt, sir."

I smiled dumbly and followed his eyes down to my trousers. I had urinated sometime in the last twenty seconds. I tried to turn, out of shame, but T-Bone grabbed my arm and held me in place. He scooped a handful of loose sand and tossed it on my crotch, where it stuck like sugar on a cookie. The stain was gone. I looked up at him to thank him but he had already shrugged it off.

"What we got up there you think, sir? Part of a trench system?" My authority, in a sentence, was restored.

Of course, I didn't need authority at all. The platoon's two trucks had skidded up alongside and those Marines were charging into the fight as if they were desperate not to miss it, shouting, cajoling, encouraging, the entire platoon moving as if it was an orchestra . . . no . . . wild dogs dragging me along by their collective leashes, *Devildogs*. My job was suddenly simple—give them a steering nudge or two, and let them go to work. The strings of red tracers looked wonderful.

One of the trucks had two flat tires and its engine block was on fire. The Hummer was completely shot to hell, too.

"We got a *big* problem, Lieutenant!" my platoon sergeant said when he joined us from his sprint. "There's two armored personnel carriers motoring this way from behind that there ridge. Iraqi."

"*What?*"

He nodded. "Coming on strong."

I heard the rumblings of metal, mashed together at first and then separate; engines *revvvving,* treads churning and *clinking* over the teeth of the wheels, the *whirring* of hydraulics. It was a horrifying and alien sound, people coming to kill you in giant steel death machines. Our infantry rifle platoon would be smashed apart by armor.

"Load up! Let's get the fuck out of here!"

My platoon sergeant shook his head. "Not with just one broken truck, we won't. Those APCs will catch us right quick and blow us sky high, we try to load up in that one shit-hole five-ton!"

I glanced around the flat, gray field. "But there's no cover here. What'll we do?"

"Any air available?" he asked.

"No," I said quickly, absolutely terrified. "Too cloudy. What else?"

I waited for him to answer, but he shrugged and licked his lips. "I . . . well, I don't know, sir. You're the platoon commander."

You're the platoon commander.

"We'll have to take the trench. Use it for cover. Consolidate whatever rockets we can find in there. We know they've got RPGs."

"Take the trench?"

"We'll get killed out here in the open. Keep whatever 203 gunners you can find with you and set 'em up on that low rise with the machine-gun teams. They can act like a mini-mortar section—try to clear the trench ahead of us as we go. When we've gained the foothold, you guys come in and concentrate on the APCs."

"Inside the trench we won't have the angle to hit with the machine guns."

"Then just keep the fires over the top of the trench and kill anything that pops up ahead of us as we're clearing. Hell, look at those Marines. They're there already!"

The Marines were crawling on their bellies, firing wildly in an attempt to reach Tubs, each shot leaving a signature of stirred sand as the escaping gas blew hot and fast into the earth. The friendly fire crescendoed when the platoon locked in on the Iraqis who had Tubs pinned down, and the barrage blew them back into their holes, enemy torsos replaced by geysers of sand and ricocheting red bulbs.

T-Bone and I sprinted up to where the lead Marines were crawling and I tucked in behind two men who were about to toss grenades into the trench. "We goin' in, sir?" one of them screamed, and I barely heard him for the *deeeeeeeeeee* in my ears.

I nodded and they released the spoons from their grenades with quick flicks of their wrists, initiating the four-second fuses inside, counted to two, and tossed them over the crest. There was a deafening *whump!* and a cloud of dust rose on our front. My ears exploded and sang high and distant. Sand pebbles plinked down and the earth reverberated.

A massive dust cloud rolled over us and I held my breath. *Please let me live.* T-Bone shoved me forward and I wiggled into the cumulus cloud, thick with dust and swirled white and yellow where some of the Marines must have tossed smoke grenades. Every Iraqi weapon in the trench line seemed to fire at once. I felt the wind from some of the rounds as they zipped overhead, well high, whip-snapping the air as they went. I pressed as flat as I could and writhed forward, hugging the ground and, indeed, life itself. I dug my helmet into the sand like a plow, hoping to deflect a determined bullet as the hail ripped all around us. We can't survive this, I thought. *I've killed my platoon.*

We would leave this world as we arrived: on our hands and knees, terrified and helpless in the dark.

I flopped into the trench and smelled cordite and then blood. Even in the thick murk, I saw that my face was inches away from two Iraqi bodies contorted in violent and awkward death sprawls. Two other bodies were folded neatly inside the walls, in the sitting position. Both had been struck by the .50 right in the face. The sides of the hole were black with blood and one of the corpses was still draining like an ebbing volcano, the blood spilling steadily over the torso. Now I understood just how fragile flesh was in a squall of steel—a tiny round, just a few ounces of metal, could rip through bone, blood, flesh . . .

The visibility was improving and I felt T-Bone slap me on my back, urging me forward to make room for all the Marines pouring into the trench. I could see two or three Marines in front of me, crawling into the narrow, four-foot-high smoke alley ahead of me, firing continuously. I hustled forward and was soon straining over the sights of my weapon, afraid of so many things—on so many levels—that I became a machine.

I could not account for the other thirty-five members of my unit, but they were in there with me, fighting the same fight. I was not leading, but I was not following, either. I felt an acute sense of brotherhood and the desperation not to let any of the men down by chickening out. So I just followed the instincts that the Corps had pounded into me: When in doubt—or unable to even *recognize* doubt because you are so scared—shoulder your weapon, close with the enemy, and kill him. *And don't stop until they're all dead.*

The trench line doglegged sharply and the Marine in front of me pointed at his weapon and screamed, "Almost outta ammo!"

T-Bone and I took the lead and skipped grenades around the corner. When the blast broiled around us and the tiny rocks found their way up into the underside of my chin, I lunged around the corner with T-Bone, firing into the cloud. We saw a dark shape moving and we both emptied half a magazine into it and pushed forward. An Iraqi with half a face came charging toward us and we fed him the other halves of our magazines, then screamed for replacements. Four or five Marines charged over us and we pulled in behind them when we had completed the magazine change.

I stood to catch them, but T-Bone grabbed my harness and jerked me to my knees from behind. "Stay down, you fucking asshole! That's stupid, sir! The worst thing you can do to this platoon is get killed! Stay low!"

I looked up at him, nodded dumbly, and crawled forward in a deep hunch. I put my boot into an Iraqi's chest cavity halfway down the dogleg. It stuck briefly before I twisted my ankle and pulled it past his ribs. I've got a big foot. I stepped over six more corpses—two blackened and twisted by grenade blasts, contorted and torn apart, the rest shredded by bullets—and arrived at the next corner, where the lead Marines were changing magazines, one man at a time.

I turned around to check on T-Bone and saw that he was standing up, waving at a group of Marines coming up behind him—also running straight up instead of crawling—and screaming at them to get down, *get down, GET DOWN!*

An RPG *shhhooooshhhed!* out from behind a cloud in front of me, just a few feet above my helmet as it rocketed over, and slammed into T-Bone's head. It did not explode but it knocked him flat on his face, the white plume of exhaust still roiling and puking when I arrived at his side screaming and screaming and screaming again. I grabbed the green metal atrocity by its fins and tried to pull it out of his head but the cylinder was still flaming and I scorched my left hand entirely, leaving my fingerprints forever behind on that heinous stalk of steel. I was moaning for T-Bone when I pulled my flak vest off, wrapped it around the tube, put my boot on his back, and strained so hard that something popped in my stomach. It didn't work. The bulbous head of the RPG had penetrated his helmet and skull. When I rolled him over, the tip of the fat, radish-shaped warhead had popped his head wide open and was pushing out of the middle of his forehead, stretching his skin like a miniature rhino horn. His eyes were wide open, but the warhead had split his skull so savagely that the eyes were three feet apart, like a hammerhead shark's. T-Bone's head had been folded open and was as flat as if it had been crushed in a vise.

I jerked my head at the three Marines gawking at me. "He's dead! Get moving! *Kill them all!*"

I turned away from T-Bone and followed the Marines back into the fight. The loss of him was so sudden that I had no time to digest it, it just *was.* But later, when the shock left my body—at about the same time the APCs fled the firefight when the Marines began firing on them with grenade launchers from the cover of the trench we owned—I went back to T-Bone's body and tried to wrest out the arrow again. But my arms were weak and my legs gave way. I collapsed against the muddy wall and tried to come up with my next act.

I was still sitting in a hunch when a Marine handed me the radio handset that was still connected to T-Bone's backpack. "Don't you hear them calling for you, sir?"

I shook my head and grabbed the handset. I gave a rambling situation report and after my company commander dispatched an armored rescue force, he paused and then said, "I might as well give it to you all at once. I'm afraid I have some bad news about Lieutenant Phillips. He was shot in the knee. He may lose his leg."

The Hummer starts its engine, so I lift Little Joe off the hood and set him down. He scampers around and hops into Doc's arms before the tailgate shuts and the Hummer departs for the battalion aid station, the field medical tent back at the airport terminal. I grab the radio to call for another vehicle and am reporting the incident when Darren limps up to me. He'll talk about his reasoning, but there's no chance he'll apologize. Not to me.

"How's the knee?"

"Fine," he says. "Look, before you start in on me, Kelly—"

"Excuse me, gentlemen," Gunny interrupts. He pulls a Glock pistol out of his belt and hands it to Darren. "I believe you lost this, sir. After your failed flight. I recommend I never see it again, neither . . ."

Darren shakes his head and reluctantly reaches out and grabs it. "Thanks, Gunny. That damn roof—"

" . . . because if I do I'll beat you over the head with it. I really will. I know you're a friend of my lieutenant here, but I just have to say this. You royally fucked up today and you let those men get away to rape and kill again. You. Because you tried to play Rambo. *You. A fucking reporter.*"

Gunny takes a step toward Darren and his chest is heaving. He extends a finger and drives it into Darren's breast-bone. "Your Marine days are done, sir, so remember that the next time you try to stick your nose where it don't belong. You stay put and keep your mouth shut around us. And you do exactly what Lieutenant Kelly tells you to or you and I are going to have serious issues."

If these men fight, it will be *Clash of the Titans 2*. Gunny stares at Darren for a long moment before he nods at me and says, "Excuse me again, sir. For interrupting, I mean." He walks back to the perimeter, where Armstrong greets him. Gunny nods his head and looks over his shoulder at Darren, eyes still narrowed.

It is as strong a rebuke as Darren Phillips may have had in his entire life, a B-52 bomber of a scorching that has left him obviously shaken and embarrassed. He stares after Gunny and when his mouth opens I am sure he's going to give a stupid response that will cause a minor nuclear det-onation within the FDC. But he shuts it and turns to me, his teeth clenched and his nostrils flaring. Glassy eyes. "Goddamn this knee. It's not supposed to be like this, Kelly," he hisses. "Not like this."

"You're the one who fucked up today," I venture.

"I know I did! Okay? I'm sorry. I fucked up today and I'm sorry. I really am!" He tries to fight back tears but loses, his lip quivering and his teeth grinding. He turns away from me and wipes his face, swearing silently. I have never seen him like this and I do not know what to say; Darren Phillips has never, to my knowledge, explored the range of emotions hiding below his low boundary of boredom—rock bottom for him. I don't think he has ever been disap-pointed in himself.

"It was totally unacceptable. Are you going to report it to Colonel Capiletti?"

"Of course not, Darren."

"Can we talk in private?"

I nod and lead him into one of the empty bunkers. He's grinding his teeth and when he looks at me his face is wild and raw, clearly pained. "I just wanted . . . to prove myself in front of you guys. To show you that I could make a good officer."

"Darren, what are you talking about? You *were* a good officer. The best in the battalion. You didn't get a Bronze Star for nothing."

"Yes I did, Kelly," he whispers. "Yes I did. I wasn't shot by an Iraqi. That was just a cover story my platoon made up to salvage my honor. I shot myself." He twists his head and it's the first time I've seen him break a stare out of shame.

"*What?*" I consider a follow-up but am too stunned.

He looks up at me and his eyes are narrow slits. I'm thankful the anger is pointed inward. He nods rapidly and I get the feeling that he is about to unveil some horrible burden. "You remember that tiny blond Marine in my platoon? Henry? The Marines called him Doogie Howser, USMC?"

"Yes." I still can't believe what I'm hearing and I'm doing everything I can—that is, *nothing*—to hear the rest of this.

"It was right after you destroyed the first trench. I'm thinking, 'Kelly got his. Damn! It's got to be me next.' We roll up on trench after trench, but all the Iraqis have vanished. When we finally see some who are still alive, they come running at my platoon waving white flags. So I'm supervising the arrest when a lone holdout begins firing his AK-47 from under an overturned truck. Inaccurate shots. Way high. See, he doesn't have the angle.

"So someone gets the idea that Doogie should be the one who gets to kill him. You know, like a frat initiation? Everyone's cheering him when he kneels down and aims his 203. The first grenade sails high and explodes in the truck. The Iraqi answers with two erratic shots. People are razzing Doogie now. 'Whiskey-Delta, weak-dicked motherfucker,' and Doogie's face gets beet red. He was uncertain at first—you remember how *nice* that kid was—but now he's pissed. His next round impacts just short and he lets out a sharp 'Fuck!' He slams the breech open, pops in another round, and slams it shut. I'm telling you, that kid smelled blood.

"His next round is in the air—I'm watching the black canister arching forward—when the fucking Iraqi stands up, waving his shirt. The grenade blows his chest apart. I mean it, it opens it right up, bone and guts spraying everywhere. Doogie looks up at me with these huge eyes, right? and says, 'I didn't see him surrendering before I shot, sir. I swear to God.' He wants *me* to forgive him for something *I* ordered in the first place!

"I feel this . . . this . . . *guilt.* He's shaking and he can't get the breech open on the 203. I kneel next to him and say, 'You did *exactly* what needed to be done, Henry. That sniper was firing at us and you got him. Thank you.' He smiles broadly and some of the guys begin to clap and congratulate him. I grab his jammed weapon and I guess I'm so nervous I forget my rifle's not on Safe. I'm straining against the tube and it breaks. My hand goes flying into the trigger housing of my rifle and the next thing I know I'm missing a kneecap. Careless! That's not like me! You know that. I mean, *you of all people know that.*"

I nod that I do, and it is true. His words are shocking and I have the eerie feeling of a confessional. In a prison. I mean, this is *Darren Phillips.*

"My platoon sergeant screams for the corpsman," Darren continues in his whisper. "With the platoon standing around gawking, he tells them all that we're brother

Marines and to forget what just happened. Forget what they just saw. Forget what they heard. Then he tells them what *really* happened—an Iraqi dinged me just as I wasted him.

"My Bronze Star is a lie, Kelly. You deserved that, not me. I know the old man thought you were foolish to attack that trench—that you didn't follow orders when it came to entering the oil field—but all of us admired you. *All of us.* Especially me. You listening to this? Because I may never say it again."

He smiles and wipes his face, crying again. Then he exhales loudly and meets my eyes. "You were the better officer, Kelly. Whatever it is, you've *got* it. You were better than me then and you're better than me now. I'm sorry for today. It won't happen again."

– 18 –

Arthur: Now stand aside worthy adversary.

Black Knight: 'Tis but a scratch.

Arthur: A scratch! Your arm's off!

Black Knight: No, it isn't.

Arthur: What's that, then?

Black Knight: I've had worse.

Christmas Eve in Somalia: As a way of erasing the bitter memory of the rape that occurred on our watch this afternoon, Gunny and I are dining together this evening. We open our MREs, lay out the different packages on the edge of my fighting hole, and clang our canteen cups together in a toast. "Merry Christmas, Guns. Can you believe we got the omelette and tuna noodle meals again? More paranoid leaders might think the MRE lottery is fixed."

The platoon divvies up the chow by means of a blind lottery, and by sheer coincidence we have landed the two worst meals in the selection. For the hundredth time. In a row.

Gunny grunts and squeezes the egg juice out of his meal pouch. "And peace on earth. Well, maybe not the *whole* earth. I mean, I got to stay employed for another six years before I get that pension."

"No. You could go join the post office. It's a federal job, so you'd keep your time in service. And you'd look mighty cute in them shorts."

"Just be tempted by all them housewives, though. Never finish the route."

I laugh. "Oh, I think you'd finish, Guns. You aren't the slacking type."

Gunny should write an MRE cookbook. He combines the egg with some mix of Tabasco and pepper and I'll be damned if it isn't the best meal I've had in two months. For dessert, he mixes some cocoa beverage powder in with the nondairy creamer and some water.

"Tastes just like pudding," I say.

"Thank you, sir. We aim to please."

"I hope Kim realizes what a terrific wife she has."

He coughs and I can tell there is something he's been meaning to tell me. "You hear Doc is going to adopt Little Joe?"

"*What?*"

"No shit, sir. He's adopting him. Got the paperwork and everything. I didn't want to tell you before because . . . I just wanted to be sure. And get this: Joe has a sister named Tamir."

"*And?*"

"And . . . Doc's adopting her, too. The whole fucking Sheik Ali Baba family, what's left of it."

I whistle softly and Gunny grunts. Marines are like whales in that we can communicate with clicks and whistles. Twenty minutes later he says, "He'll be good to them. Kid's got a heart of gold. And a brain made of one, too. I . . ."

Choom!

". . . Mortar Muhammad!" Gunny stands up and shouts, but this time other Marines have beaten him to the punch and everyone is in a hole this side of ten seconds.

Choom!

"Christmas fucking Eve!" shouts the Gunny. "Godless bastard!"

The reaction force is quick this time, and before the mortars impact the AAV engines are roaring. I picture the colonel rushing to get his gear on, torturing the poor lieutenant who actually commands the armored vehicles.

The first mortar round impacts harmlessly behind the hangar but the second hits it square on the roof with an ear-shattering *Kaaaaa-whump!,* as loud as a close lightning strike. The ground rolls like the moving bend in a whip or an ocean swell, and when the shock wave hits the hole, our meals go flying and splatter all over us.

"Jesus Christ!" I yell.

"Happy birthday!" screams Gunny over the echo, smiling.

———

At 2300 hours I wake up with a start and it takes me a second to get oriented. A foxhole. A rifle. The rustle of ponchos. A little boy who complains that I've been shifting around when I'm asleep. A man staring at me with his NVGs, asking me if I'm okay. Doc. Somalia. *Shit, I'm still here.*

I sit upright in the dark and realize that the rape is bothering me too much to sleep. We could have stopped it if we had acted earlier. If *I* had acted earlier. But when we returned I learned that General Bellissimo had summoned Colonel Capiletti to question him about our leaving the compound in the first place *and instigating the assault*. I've avoided Big Duke for two weeks, but I have to talk with him, even if it means that I'll learn that my father's court-martial was initiated on charges of thievery.

"You seen Big Duke wandering the lines, Doc?"

"Yessir. Saw him over in the hangar about ten mikes ago."

I grab my weapon and plop the helmet over my head. "I'll be over there if you need me."

"I thought we were banned from there, sir?" asks Doc. The Air Force and a few Army units have arrived in country and every Marine has been relegated to a fighting hole. Worse, we hear that the other services have humped in some snacks and treats with their air-conditioning units and microwaves but that Marines have been totally banned from entering *their* hangar, even for a head call, for fear of violating sensibilities. The Marines don't normally give up ground so quickly—we were the first ones here and might have told the Force to go squat—but you don't generally want to raise the ire of men flying overhead with bombs. Besides, we get to talk about them behind their backs this way, IBM wanna-bes.

"Desperate times call for desperate measures," I say.

I strut into the hangar and some airman with a Beatles haircut says, "Merry Christmas. Can I help you?"

The air is sweetly cool and has a manufactured scent to it. I resist the urge to run over to the air conditioner and stick my head in it. Behind him, a sign reads: "One shower per person, per day." My Marines haven't showered in sixteen days. "Yes. You can start by addressing me properly and finish by telling me where the ice cream is kept." Word has leaked that the Force has flown in Popsicles. It's 2300, the oven is on High again outside, and I'm on a mission from God.

"I don't know of any ice cream. Uh, sir, I mean."

I see Big Duke talking with a senior airman, and when they finish their conversation I walk over to him. "Here comes trouble," he says. "Where've you been hiding?"

"I've been around. I'm looking for Popsicles."

"Ahhh," he laughs. "Just talking about that before you walked up. I was seriously warned by my counterpart. Those Popsicles are strictly off limits. They didn't bring enough for everybody. Yeah, those Popsicles kept in the freezer next to the colonel's old office are strictly off limits." He smiles and tilts his head, contemplating me, then walks over and claps me on the shoulder. "How're you doing, sir? I mean, how you *really* doing?"

I've been waiting for the question and I'm relieved that he asked. "I don't know, Big Duke. I just don't know anymore. And I'm talking about my performance, not my disposition. How do *you* think I'm doing? People are getting attacked on my watch. Women are getting *raped* on my watch."

"So you want some advice?"

"You asked me how I—"

"So you want some advice?"

"*Yes.*"

"Here it comes. Why did you leave the compound to try to investigate today?"

Big Duke has been waiting for this, maybe for two weeks. He folds his arms while I mull over an answer. "That's the thing," I say. "I know General Bellissimo is up in arms about me violating his order, but I feel wrong for not violating it sooner."

"That wasn't the question I asked, but I'll address the point. How'd you find out about that? Did the colonel chew your ass for it?"

He's like a wall and all my comments are being pounded right back into me. "No. It's just scuttlebutt."

"Yeah, well, sir, the colonel *did* get an ass-chewing from that Italian . . . *general* . . . but he never mentioned it to you, did he? He never chewed your ass. He never even mentioned it to you. Think about that. Think about what message he's trying to send. Now, *why'd* you leave that compound?"

"I felt it was the right call."

"Lieutenant, is that the best you can do?"

"I was angry, okay?" I hiss. "And so were the other Marines. All of us. I feel like a fool out there behind sandbags. What am I supposed to tell the men when they ask why we're sitting by when a rape is occurring?"

Big Duke holds up an index finger and nods angrily, so I shut my mouth. He motions for me to follow him behind the air conditioner, where he has to boom his words to be heard. Big Duke prefers it that way. "You have the same tactical sense as your father, sir. But as an officer, you're expected to think on a different level. Tactics aren't enough. What are you supposed to tell your men? Tell them you're following orders and they'll goddamned well do the same. So temper that blood lust you inherited from your old man before you do something stupid like he did."

He turns to leave but I grab his elbow. I feel like I'm seconds away from unearthing a terrible and embarrassing secret, but still I cannot stop, greed and hurt overpowering fear. Geraldo must have felt this way leading cameras into Capone's vault. "Big Duke, how do you know him? I mean, I think you may have the wrong guy. My dad isn't what you'd call gung ho. You served with him?"

I'm wearing a carefree smile and it's a mask.

"Yes, sir. Your father was a remarkable officer."

"My father was a sergeant."

Big Duke looks surprised. "We already got into this, Lieutenant. Did he talk to you about the war? Because if he didn't, I won't."

"He talked about the war, just not about rank. My grandfather was a sergeant, so I guess he left it unsaid." Big Duke is pondering me, so I bait him. "My father said his performance was better in the supply shack than it was in the field. He said he never did anything worth talking about. He said he was shit for a Marine."

He takes it. "Bullshit. Your father was my swim buddy in training. I swim like a rock and those wiseass SEALs let me drink half the pool. But they didn't want a death on their watch, so they signed my card and told me to stay away from the water. Your dad was like a sea lion. So he's fast-tracked to corporal. Once we're scuba qualled, we're shipped from Coronado to Quang Tri. Maybe we should have challenged the North Viets to a swim race, as much good as it did. Anyway, after three months up at the DMZ, he's a sergeant and scoring kills on every patrol.

"I'm still a lance criminal and scared to death on the patrols, and more scared when we get back to the compound. See, that secretary of defense—the one who said he was so fucking smart he didn't have to listen to anyone—well, he ordered us to build a fence along the DMZ. I'm telling you! In nineteen dark sixty-seven we honest to God strung wire and bulldozed a goddamned highway along the demilitarized zone. 'McNamara's Wall,' the press called it. Hell, it was 'McNamara's Killing Zone' for Marines."

Big Duke's speaking rapidly now, the air conditioner

roaring behind him with condensation beading under its metal lip like the sweat and funk I've worn for two weeks, eventually snapped away with the rest of the heat by the intake vents.

"Picture this, Lieutenant—thick bush to hide in, full of Gooners, and we're chasing them from one valley to the other. We're not making much headway, but neither are they. We sort of cancel each other out. They can't break through to the populated area along the coast, and we can't root them out of the mountains.

"Then one day we stop going on offensive ops and start to build a highway. So of course the Gooners crept to the edge of the jungle and saw us poor bastards in the open, all because of that fool's brain fart. When they came in it was like those sharks that ate the crew of the *Indianapolis*. They came first with snipers, then with mortars, and finally with those damn rockets. Day after day they hammered us. And why not? There we were—fully exposed, hiding behind a strand of barbed wire. Unable to move back, and ordered not to move forward across the sacred demilitarized zone. Shit!

"Recon had it easier. We could go out beyond the wire, and I swear I felt safer. On patrol we were less exposed. The rear was getting pounded. We were coming up with all kinds of excuses to stay out on patrol, not to return. It was crazy.

"So the colonel takes to posting our kills each day. You know, to keep up morale. 'You should see the other guy' kind of thing. We're taking maybe ten to twenty casualties a day. Only recon can go out, and we're scoring maybe five to ten a day. Not good. Except for your dad. When he goes out, it's bigger jobs. He's sly. He registers for an hour in one sector, then goes away. A day later, he comes back, settles in, waits and waits. The Gooners don't get the word about the impacts yesterday. They start to stir. You know, the standard movement by threes and fours. No big targets.

"Most patrols would pop them once they see over four together. In the heat, most of us went on automatic. Four Gooners? Fire mission. Simple as that. We'd get a couple. The others di-di. Next day, same thing. Three-day patrol. Six kills. Not bad, not good.

"Only your dad's always thinking. He had this sense about things. He could spot the replacement units. Something about how they moved, even in small groups. So he'd wait with his registration points, watch a group pass, and wait and wait. Then he'd see another small group and he'd call all hell in—105s, five inch, eight inch, even 155s and 175s. HE VT all the way. He'd say it was a battalion.

"On the recon freq, we'd laugh. We called it 'Kelly's Battalion.' It was so predictable. He'd bullshit the FSCC and they would smash the area. But son of a bitch, maybe half the time behind that small advance guard there *would* be a larger unit, maybe a platoon or a company. And he'd call six, ten, even fifteen Gooners in one sighting. Result— ten, twenty kills. Once he scored fifty."

"Fifty? On one patrol?" I burst out. Shame is coursing through me now, taking a solid foothold, systematically routing the surprise and rooting out the bitterness. All those times I laughed with Red about my father's reticence . . . I want to spit, but my mouth is dry because of the hot air.

"He caught a battalion in a small valley. Steep sides. The silly bastards probably set in there to avoid naval guns. Kelly found them and called in two-thousand-pound air strikes. He never let them out. When he was extracted a day later, the division commander promoted him to second lieutenant, on the spot. We in recon were the heroes, not because we were any better but because we were the only Marines on McNamara's Wall permitted to hit back.

"When we'd come in from a patrol, the construction troops would kiss our asses. I mean, they were good guys with a shitty mission. They could only take it, they couldn't hit back. So they'd come around our bunkers. We had a little beer, no ice, but they'd offer us their two cans a week. They'd sit around as we swapped our stories. Our usual BS, but to them, we were the givers, not the takers. We were all Marines. It made them feel better.

"There was this one kid. My age, around nineteen. Kemper? Lemper? Something like that. Farm kid. Ran a dozer. Big muscles. Kept saying he should be in recon. He'd come around our bunker every night just to listen to our horseshit. Kept leaping to attention every time your dad walked by. He volunteered every morning and every evening to join recon. I swear, if your dad had told him to go out on patrol alone to prove he was recon, he would have done it.

"Finally, your dad agreed to take him out, just a local security patrol. We weren't as restricted back then; you had the balls to get in it, we'd cut you in. Kemper was so damn happy and excited. He was like a big puppy, bounding around, asking what he should wear, carry, memorize—that sort of thing. Hell, we all knew all the patrol would do was snoop and poop out a klick, set in, maybe spot a few Gooners and return. Local walkabout security stuff. Still, to Kemper this was the Corps come true.

"So naturally he gets popped. One of those damn rockets comes whooshing in just at dusk. He's still out on his dozer in the middle of the open trench—you know, one-more-push-up-for-the-Corps sort of effort. Nowhere to hide. It was a mess. No real body to recover. Just some parts. Your dad is painted up, locked and loaded, outbound. Only he's delayed because his chopper is diverted to get Kemper's parts out of there. The colonel was a bug about that. All KIA out of the area immediately. So your dad's team, already on the chopper, was ordered out to collect, bag, and ship out what remained of Kemper.

"This took maybe thirty to forty-five mikes. Then Kelly's released to his patrol. Bad, bad decision by the colonel, but he couldn't have known—your dad was so quiet. But I learned something about him."

Big Duke fixes his eyes on me as if he is trying to push a message into my brain. The air conditioner is still raging but I do not hear it, I'm leaning in so hard for his next words.

"We call it overidentification with the men, sir."

"Are you talking about *me?* I thought this was about my father."

"It's about a Kelly, sir," Big Duke says evenly. "And you're making the same god*damned* mistake."

"What happened?"

"Your father went out splashed with Kemper. I mean, blood on his hands, on his utilities, stuff in the treads of his boots. Bad, bad scene. So he's out there with four other Marines, and they're all shaken after scraping up Kemper. I mean to tell you, that was one good kid. So his team's in the bush, north, near the Z. It's dusk and they're on one of the few high spots. And what comes over but another rocket. More death incoming. Launch point—no more than six klicks away.

"Only one small problem. They're two klicks south of the DMZ and the launch came from three miles inside

North Vietnam. Now there is no way a United States Marine is allowed into North Vietnam. That would upset the North Vietnamese. They can kill us, but the president of the United States and the secretary of defense of the United States have declared North Vietnam to be the one place the United States Marines cannot—repeat—*cannot* go. This rule is iron-clad.

"Guess what? His men start saying, 'Let's do it, screw the rules, payback is a motherfucker, let's get some' . . . all the whispering you're probably hearing out there at the FDC. And that you would *definitely hear* if one of your Marines was shot by one of these Somali savages. Right, Lieutenant?"

It is not an accusation and I want to be honest with him. "Those words might even leave *my* lips, Big Duke."

"And that's what I'm trying to get through to you, sir. You *cannot* do that. A Marine platoon is not a democracy. The Corps is a series of dictatorships because that's what works best to *protect* a democracy. You understand me? Do you?"

I'm struggling to process it all so I just nod to get him off my back.

"So what does your father do? He leads them in. Of course, he doesn't tell anyone. He just wades across the Ben Hai. We called it Shit Creek because the bodies stank so much it'd make you puke. He is definitely north and knows it. He starts laying into them: naval guns, arty, fixed wing. He was on a roll. Smoke-a-Gook. Tom Kelly never talked much, but on the Prick 25 he was a terror. Real sarcastic. If the gun crew didn't have shot out in two mikes, he'd come up on the net and tell them to slow down, he couldn't keep up with their lightning speed.

"This day he outdid himself. The Gooners never expected us to come north. They read the papers. Now here they are with no fighting holes, slack local security, and they're getting whacked. We are *unloading* on them motherfuckers!

"Only, nothing good lasts long. After a few salvos, the Viets figure out that there is an OP out there somewhere. So they send out patrols and your old man goes polar. He has to. He doesn't have the time to calculate resections. So he sends his azimuth and range to target.

"Big mistake. We are also diverting alpha strikes going north. Who knows—Navy or Air Force aircraft getting frags while airborne. Makes no difference which service. Both had to keep records. It was the system. Kelly was probably into his second hour of fire missions when Saigon was notified where he was.

"I don't blame them. Hell, even four-stars have to obey orders and Kelly's coordinates were definitely north of the border. I'll hand it to the colonel, though: He didn't back off. He kept diverting flights as long as your father was seeing targets. Then the inevitable happened. There's little real high ground near the Ben Hai and the Gooners figured it out. They were on our freqs as much as we were. They could hear Kelly clear. Now he's sending shackles, but still—it just took them a while before they could believe he was on their turf.

"They sent at least a battalion. It was Howard's Hill all over again, Gooners pouring up the hillside after him. Kelly's troops started stacking bodies and no Sparrow Hawk, no Bald Eagle would do for that TRAP. Not against a battalion. The only thing to it was a frontal move. Your dad was another mile or so on the other side of McNamara's dumb-ass road.

"The whole regiment was on alert by now and every company wanted to go. Three thousand pissed-off Marines on the move. The Gooners aren't stupid. They like to set things up, not duke it out when they have no edge. We hadn't moved a klick when the pressure against Kelly went slack. We smoked a few going in, but the rest just di-di'ed. We went in about ten in the morning and were back with Kelly's patrol right about dusk.

I think maybe we lost two or three to snipers and we snuffed maybe two or three platoons that didn't get the word. We brought back beaucoup AKs, belt buckles, pith helmets, some flags, stuff we could send home as souvenirs.

"It was Kelly who did the real damage. The FACA recorded twelve secondaries during the fire missions. One went on for three minutes. We went a week after that without a single Katusha-122 incoming.

"Of course they slapped a name on the rescue, called it 'Operation Gaylord' or some fool thing like that. So they kind of buried that we went in to pull out a recon team that had broken orders and kicked the bejesus out of rocketeers. They buried your father, too. Broke him back to sergeant the next day. Made him the supply NCO and sent him to Da Nang to hand out boots while he awaited court-martial. No more Corps.

"That was it. All for Kemper or Lemper or something like that. Damn, I can't remember his name. But your dad sure gave him a send-off. Overidentification, lieutenant, over-identification. Keep that in mind when you're out there."

"Tell me about the tattoo."

He sighs. "We gave each other blood stripes for snatching prisoners. Dangerous as all hell job, though, waiting in ambush along some trail to grab a North Viet tail-end Charlie as he walked by. The rest of the team would smoke the others after that, or try to, but the snatcher—men like your old man—was in just a *world* of danger. Not for the faint of heart, you know, sir?"

I shake my head, *no, not for the faint of heart.* My world-view has changed in Somalia and I am repulsed by the naïveté of my suspicions.

"Anyway, your father snatched a whole bunch of them and five of them are probably alive today. Some are not. He'd wait next to a bend in the trail, nab the enemy, hand-cuff him, and drag him out to the LZ. And sometimes you had to kill the enemy if he fought you or was struggling too much and you couldn't move him out of a hot area fast enough."

I nod and turn away from him. I'm overheating and the damn air-conditioning intake is sucking away my breath. "I should be getting back to the platoon, Big Duke," I say to my chest.

"Hey, sir," he calls after me softly, "hang around a second. I told you all this because you're going to keep getting tested here. You're not going to believe this, but the colonel is close to approving that night patrol you and Gunny Ricketts requested. Maybe you'll get some after all."

Given Little Joe's intelligence, Gunny and I have requested that the platoon be allowed to meet Mortar Muhammad on his own turf one of these nights by patrolling in some likely spots for his firing points and writing any firefight off to coincidence. Somewhere beneath all my confusion I am thrilled, but it is all I can do to nod at Big Duke without crumbling. I avoid his eyes and step into the cool of the hangar. The sweat is snaking down the backs of my legs.

"I'm usually on the battalion tac net during the day—if you want to check in or just talk or anything like that, sir," Big Duke says to my back.

It is just information overload at this point. My father is a recon Marine. He loses Kemper because of stupidity from the top. He must have been pounded by Red the same way I was about looking out for his men. My father strikes back and is busted out. He loses a career, we lose the war because we walk away, and he's a castoff. No wonder he doesn't talk. No wonder there's that silent edge to him. Overidentification with my men? Maybe. I sure don't identify with Bison Breath.

– 19 –

31 DECEMBER 1992

> You want Capone? Here's how you get him. He
> pulls a knife, you pull a gun. He sends one of
> your men to the hospital, you send one of his
> to the morgue.

New Year's Eve and I'm all gussied up, makeup caked to
my face, outfit inspected three times over, pockets full of
party favors, all my accessories meticulously prepared—
250 rounds of 5.56 millimeter, four grenades, a Ka-Bar
knife, two canteens, a medical kit, a pair of NVGs, and my
M-16 of a girlfriend, already well lubricated in anticipation of this evening's fireworks. *Tonight we're gonna party
like it's 1999.*

I hold up a clenched fist and the men stop, on their
knees now, scanning with their rifles. We are an hour shy
of midnight and I'm setting the platoon into an ambush
position behind a series of small mounds overlooking a
dead-grass field. I hold my arms out in an iron cross and

the team leaders align their men, placing them in covered positions and assigning sectors of fire. We picked out our seating arrangements on our leaders' recon thirty minutes ago and it takes but a few seconds to set in. I find a nice spot behind one of the bigger mounds and begin to carve out a firing position. In my NVGs I watch the action of the ambush and revel in the ability to execute some traditional tactics. Now if we could only revel in some executions . . .

A rank smell wraps us when the breeze picks up and I see that some of the Marines are covering their mouths with their undershirts to prevent the horrible thickness from penetrating their lungs. It's a nauseating smell of rot and death—a devil's mix of sour milk, dead mice, defecation, week-old fried eggs, and Jim Beam—and I start breathing only though my mouth. Next to me, Doc loses his battle and vomits quietly in the muck. Flies rise up out of the night and in seconds they are buzzing around my face in a thick knot. I suck three of them into my parched throat before I figure out that I have to pull my undershirt up over my face.

We've set up in the middle of a freshly dug graveyard a hundred meters long.

Gunny shrugs and pinches his nose, then slashes across his throat, but I shake my head. It was difficult enough for Big Duke to lobby the colonel for this ambush, even while armed with Joe's information about the upcoming mortar attack, and the colonel himself has gone out on a limb in approving it. If Bellissimo realizes that this is not a patrol but an ambush and therefore an act of *war*, well, then the colonel has seen his last promotion.

Why Gunny and I picked this spot on the map: optimal distance from the airport, good cover, many avenues of escape, high ground overlooking the airport. No way we're missing this lottery ticket.

Fifteen minutes becomes an hour that melts into three. The moon arcs toward the ocean and then disappears. The flies come in waves with the wind and the stench, the friendly ones sinking their fangs into my neck, the irritating ones crawling down my blouse and buzzing next to my lower back. I feel a steady tug on my finger seconds before I hear the low grumbling of engines; I return the signal by sending to the signaler two quick jerks on the fishing line tied to my left pinkie, then tug gently on the line that connects my right hand to the next Marine in the formation. You don't want to jerk on an initial "alert" signal on the off chance that you'll startle a Marine awake and perhaps induce a lunge for a weapon. The platoon is awake now that the silent signal is racing back and forth, and I hear the smooth sounds of rifles moving across dirt and into shoulders. I untie the fishing line and glance to my right; Doc's already awake, trying to signal me, reeling in an empty catch, and five meters beyond him, I see the Gunny adjusting his NVGs. Beyond him, only desert in my eyes, but two full teams in my mind. The platoon stretches a full hundred meters across for proper dispersion and coverage. We're in silent mode and on automatic pilot now, controlled only by training and rehearsals; the platoon will fire only after the first round leaves my barrel or the Gunny's, assuming we are not busted.

Two trucks roll slowly into my vision, lights off and Bangers crouched in the flatbeds. They stop fifty meters away, what we call a close ambush. Hushed, urgent whispers float across the graves and I see three Bangers pulling a large object from the back of one of the Toyotas. I am so excited that it takes me a moment before I find the threads of the goggles with the 10X magnifier, screwing it on with my hand shaking—not nervous—up to my eyes, and there it is, an 82-millimeter mortar. If you think voyeurism is titillating, try it with a grudge and a rifle. I see Mortar Muhammad himself placing in some security, the dark outline of his big head clear when he silhouettes himself against the trucks. *Smile, you son of a bitch!*

I am so excited because under our ROE we are allowed to engage any heavy weapons straightaway, no warning or threat required, you see it, you kill it. *Ba-da bing!* For the first time in this war we're going to be able to act as we have been trained: as killers.

I see Gunny waving frantically, hand-signaling for permission to fire, and I signal to wait one. "Vader, this is Sharkman, over," I whisper with my hand covering my mouth.

The five seconds trudge by until the radio crackles, "This is Vader, over."

"Get the six on the hook. We have Mortar Muhammad in our sights and we are about to engage. Over."

"Wait one, Sharkman, over."

It's more than one, but Vader Six is on the hook pretty swiftly. I give him a quick brief and there is an uncomfortable silence. This is bad news. I glance up and see that Mortar Muhammad has his base plate set up, four Bangers now struggling to connect the big mortar tube. My earpiece says, "Sharkman, I have your position. Hold in place and do NOT fire. Too big a risk, you out in the open. I am riding out with the reaction force to your pos right now. I say again, continue to observe. Over."

Ladies and gentlemen, welcome to the Restore Hope Goat Rodeo! The first goat out of the gate, Lieutenant Gavin Kelly! On the lasso this evening, Lieutenant Colonel Vin Capiletti!

"Vader Six, this is Sharkman Six. We are covered and concealed. If they hear the reac force, they'll egress. Over."

"Sharkman, this is Vader. Vader Six has already departed.

He'll be communicating with you on this net. He wants you to hold fire."

Here it is: The Colonel wants credit for this kill and to get it he's willing to risk giving Muhammad a few more days. I peer out across the field again and the 10X is so powerful that Mortar Muhammad's torso fills the scope. I watch his mouth moving and follow his extended hand to the Bangers setting up the bipod. Is it so wrong to hate someone with all of your being? No, I decide, Mortar Muhammad, burner and raper of women, needs killing.

Gunny is so frustrated with my vertical index finger that he crawls over next to me. He leans in right next to my ear, cupping it with his hands, breath uncomfortably hot, and whispers, "Sir. They're settin' up aiming stakes and everything. This salvo's gonna be accurate. Let's waste 'em now! What the fuck are you waitin' for?"

I tell him and his head bobs down so suddenly it looks as if his neck's been snapped.

In the distance, about a klick, I hear, carried by the sea breeze, the engines of the AAVs. Mortar Muhammad's head snaps up, there is an argument in a foreign and wild tongue, and the Bangers begin breaking down the mortar and stacking their rounds back into the trucks. Gunny starts to whisper again but I grab his forearm and nod my head.

"Vader Six, this is Sharkman! We can hear track engines coming and the Skinnies are breaking down the mortar. They're about to take off! Request permission to fire, over."

"Sharkman, thiiis is Vaaderr, overr," comes the colonel's jarred voice. The track engines nearly drown out his voice entirely: the preferred circumstance in all situations but this one.

"Negative. Negatiiivve. Wee will . . . we willl pursuue themm. Getttt a good—to follow them, overr."

I unkey the handset and look at Gunny. No way in hell the tracks are going to be able to run down those pickup trucks.

Gunny leans in close and whispers, "This is why you get paid the big bucks, sir. Decide!"

I listen to the colonel's radio voice asking me if I have copied his last. In our kill zone one of the truck's engines turns over. I see the Bangers struggling to load the mortar into the back of another. They *cluuunk* it up and roll it inside the flatbed, then shut the stern gate and clamber up. Another engine rattles to life.

"Bangers're startin' the trucks, sir!" whispers Gunny.

"I hear them, for fuck's sake!"

"Reeepeet," shouts the radio. "I ammm tell . . . hollldd in plaaace."

Thirty-two thousand dollars a year. *The big bucks.* I raise my rifle, pull it tightly into the crook of my shoulder and my neck, push down on the butt with my cheekbone, put a pound of pressure on the trigger, walk the laser across and center it on Mortar Muhammad's chest—other dots lighting up both trucks now that the Marines have seen mine, zipping around like fireflies—and squeeze.

A sharp *snap!* of lethality, the glowing tracer zipping forward and vanishing fifty meters later in an alien gut, the recoil rolling me back, the smell of the burn, the night torn open and erupting like a volcano before I can center the laser on my target again, tracers crisscrossing the field and ricocheting up into the night, filling it. When I find him, Mortar Muhammad is slumped against the side of a truck, holding his stomach. The first truck in line is still moving forward, but I'm not worried; Team One has the left piece of the kill zone and Armstrong won't allow an escape. Instead, I calmly put the dot on Mortar Muhammad's fat head and send a round at him at over a thousand miles per hour. The tracer looks white in the goggles, but when it disappears his head explodes in a black splatter of dots that grease the entire truck door. I have never spoken with Mortar Muhammad but I feel like I know him. I feel . . . fleeting satisfaction, then confusion as to why I don't feel bad, then nothing except the electricity and life itself and nostrils sucking in the smell of death and my hair standing up and rigid and the urge to find another target.

There are other dark shapes fleeing the truck and I start firing rapidly now, working the trigger and the laser across my kill zone, aiming low so the rounds will skip across the deck and send a shrapnel storm of pebbles into anyone smart enough to have gone to ground.

There is a pronounced lull—magazine changes—and the firing resumes its grand finale and crescendos, complete with flaming engine blocks and plinking shell casings. *Stars and stripes forever, baby.* As if to punctuate my thought, the M-203 gunners in the platoon launch several salvos of grenades into the kill zone right on schedule to flush out any remaining game. But the *caarunch! caarunch! caarunch!* is only answered by screams.

"Cease fire! CEASE FIRE!" I scream, giving the hand signal as well. The crackling dies, replaced piecemeal by a growing echo of my order.

"Accountability check!"

Armstrong, Montoya, and the Team Three leader scream that they are fine. The only things I see in the field are two battered trucks, one of them rolling slowly around in a fiery circle, still running, and a few bodies.

Gunny taps my arm and I realize that he has been

yelling for a while, losing the battle to the ringing in my ears. I pull out my earpiece and shrug. "We killed them, sir!" he screams. "Little birds leavin' the nest!"

I smile and nod. I am more nervous; I have the pleasure of calling the colonel. I stuff the hearing aid back into my ear. "Vader, this is Sharkman. The trucks started to depart and my team opened fire on them. We are waiting on the result, over."

"Whaaat? Whaat the . . . ck did youu just say? Over. I gave strict—do that. Whaat is—Sharkmann? Overr."

"Vader, you are coming in broken, over."

"Don't giive mee that. Youu —rd mee!"

The radio goes static and a moment later the reaction force roars around the corner on the other side of the field and grinds up to the kill zone, guided in by the small fire in the grass next to the flaming truck that's still rolling.

"Get down behind a mound and stay down!" I scream.

I hear the up-gun turrets of the AAV hum, then a .50 machine-gun burst hammers the truck and I hear a few ricochets snap overhead. Silence. Then doors opening and shouts—in English this time. It takes about fifteen minutes before I hear the radio say, "Sharkman, this is Vader Actual. Signal us and come on in."

I peek over a grave and flash twice with my red-lens light. There is fire everywhere. I get the proper answer, but before I can organize my troops a spotlight illuminates the kill zone.

"What the fuck? Is that a TV camera?" Gunny asks.

"Looks like he wants to record my execution."

I take the dead-man's walk over to Bison Breath and stop behind Mary Thayer-Ash and her cameraman; they've got Bison Breath in their sights, standing next to the big 82-millimeter mortar that someone has assembled for the picture, one of his big arms draped comfortably across the top, swelling his forearm to tree trunk proportions. It will make for a nice picture. He speaks for about two minutes about the danger that the mortar had posed and how he had to act quickly to grab it when he could. I might skate out of this yet.

When he's finished his brief, the colonel waves at me, pretending to have just noticed me though I saw his eyes snake past me several times. "Kelly! You-all did a superb job guiding us in."

"I . . ." I glance at Ms. Thayer-Ash. Her microphone is stabbing the space between B-Squared and me. Big Duke, next to Bison Breath, winks. What the hell. "Thanks, sir. Looks like the reaction force got one of the trucks."

"Damn right. Well, I understand from the sergeant major here that we had a little mix-up on the radio. It was so gosh-damn *noisy* in the AAV that I was having trouble hearing. Then I got cut off. I thought you were telling me that you wanted permission to just attack the trucks when they were stationary. I didn't realize that they were leaving the position. We arrived in time to stop one of them from escaping—the one with the mortar. Looks like your men got the first one, though. Well done."

He steps closer to me and puts his face in mine—maximum effective close talking. It's an act for the camera, the chummy relationship he's struggling to indicate, but I'm in no position to critique his acting. It's really good. "Well, we sure got them today, didn't we? That big mortar captured." He turns to Big Duke and I take a deep breath; the last thing you want to do when B-Squared is in your face is inhale. It is totally erratic behavior and if I didn't know him better I'd say he was drunk.

"Sergeant Major," he laughs. "Looks like we have something new for the board, eh? Maybe have to start a new category for 'mortars.' Let's put it up on the board ASAP."

The colonel shouts out orders to the reaction force and Marines are running everywhere. Big Duke lingers just long enough to give me a friendly shot in the arm, right between my bicep and my shoulder. The physical abuse is just out of control in this place.

I walk over to assemble the platoon and notice that Armstrong is sliding his hand slowly across the bullet-ridden door of a Banger pickup truck. "Get your team and saddle up, Armstrong. You take the point. We're walking in."

"No lift from the AAVs, sir?"

"Nope."

"Hmm," he says absentmindedly, stroking the Toyota. "We diced this Japanese truck up pretty good, didn't we, sir? And the reaction force tells me they got eight bodies KIA."

"Eight. Yes."

"Three got away. Shame." He sighs and smiles at me, walking up now and putting a hand on my shoulder. "But the night's not a total loss, sir. I was worried these trucks here were American made. Now *that* woulda been a shame."

– 20 –

30 JANUARY 1993

Licensed to kill gophers by the government of
the United Nations. Man free to kill gophers at
will.

We have a week left in country, but the world's interest in
Restore Hope—including our own—vanished weeks ago.
What was page seventeen news is now nonexistent. Armstrong read the platoon a clipping the other day that
asserted 80 percent of Americans had no idea that U.S.
troops were even *in* Somalia anymore. *Somalia? What's
that? Oh, wait, is she a great big fat person?*

In the month since the ambush, I do not know where
the days have gone or what I have done. Maybe we've
entered some kind of dog-year's time warp—every day in
Somalia is the equivalent of seven back in the other world.
The initial mission to vanquish the famine was completed
in the first few weeks, but just when we started to believe
we'd get to go home, Somalia's strain on our leash only got

tighter. We've learned that the new president is considering extending the mission from famine relief to rebuilding this poor, broken bastard of a nation, long ago relegated to life support. We're to become part of a new foreign policy that vastly increases American military participation in UN peacekeeping around the globe, rescuing nations from themselves.

General Bellissimo loves the new effort and thinks it's possible to rehabilitate his old colony—he told us as much two days ago in a speech when he announced that he would assume full command of all forces in Somalia when the UN takes total control tomorrow. Strange as it sounds, the American warriors left in this rat hole are going to fall under his command as part of the new policy of participation. All the Marines are itching to pull stakes before someone worsens that bad decision and makes us wear those robin-egg-blue helmets. "Operational control"—a term vague enough to allow the colonel to approve the ambush—was one thing, but "command" is another. Granted, the U.S. military has served under foreign chains of command before (Army units under Montgomery, Marine units under the Army) but picking your commander in a war is vastly different from a UN assignment in a peacekeeping mission.

"Yo, sir. Check out them Army boys," says Armstrong, pointing to a group of shirtless men on the edge of the tarmac, next to the ocean. They've set up a volleyball net and have quite a game going, judging from the screams and the slaps. They're in good shape so I figure they're Rangers or Airborne; no way pilots are that ripped. They're also tan, which tells me they get to play a lot.

"What about 'em?"

"Can we play? I'm bored. I mean, I've been bored for three weeks, but watchin' them drives it home, you know?

Plus it's hot as hell and this fucking gear is driving me fucking crazy. Six weeks now wearin' this heavy shit."

I lean against the edge of the foxhole and look up at him. Truth is, I'm *dying* to take off this thick flak vest—or at least crack the Velcro to allow some of the steam to escape—but Big Duke has been on uniform patrol lately and I don't want to shift the burden of my command to him. "No. We have to keep the gear on."

"Army has the authority to dress down when it's appropriate." He takes off his helmet, smooths his tall, black flattop, and replaces the helmet with a thunk. "My team's cookin' like a big ol' steak."

"You're a Marine."

"I know it, sir."

"Then you also know that our policy is firm."

"Well."

How many days have passed like this—sitting in a dank hole under a pounding sun, baking like a veal cutlet, watching the Indian for signs of our brother squidleys come to rescue us from this armpit? "Anything else, Sergeant Armstrong?"

He spits close to my hole and squats his huge body down next to me like a mountain gorilla. He pulls a tin of chew from his trouser pocket and raises his eyebrows but I shake my head no. He snaps the top with his flopping index finger—all the dippers have this habit—and puts a gumball-size plug under his upper lip. "Nosir. Just that with most of the other guys sick, I figured I'd hang out with you a bit for conversational exchange. Become more familiar with you so I could breed some contempt." He winks.

Most of the platoon has contracted a violent form of dysentery and every few minutes a Marine leaps from his hole and half-sprints toward the shit trench with his entrenching tool and paper in one hand and his rifle in the other. I had mild diarrhea yesterday but the pork patty MRE stopped me up. Naturally Armstrong hasn't been affected with anything but a patience vacuum. "So we outta here in a week?"

"That's the scoop," I say.

"Not a minute too soon. Only language these mother-fucked understand is violence and we think we can learn 'em a democracy? Shit. Where we off to next, sir? Bosnia?"

"Home."

"If you got one," he grunts.

Two Somali boys slither through a hole in the wall and come walking up to us with scowls. "Marine, gimme food!" one shouts.

"Uh," I stammer, "you boys . . . aren't supposed to be in here."

The kids cock their heads—they don't speak English as well as Little Joe—and one of them screeches, "Marine! Gimmee Emmereee! M en M! M en M!" He saunters up to me and grabs my flak vest by the shoulder pad, tugging and screeching, some terrible harpy come to haunt me. I slap his hand and he immediately head-slaps my helmet.

"GET THE FUCK OUTTA HERE, YOU MAGGOTS!" screams Armstrong. He's so loud that when I look around, cringing and expecting to see the colonel, I see that the Army guys have stopped their game. The kids dart away from me and dive through the wall.

Doc lifts his head up from below my boots, at the bottom of the hole where he's been sleeping, Kevlar for a pillow. His face is pallid, beaded with sweat and clammy; Doc has been hit hardest by the bug. He weakly props himself up on an elbow and whispers, "Jake. You can't be that way. You gotta be nicer to the kids. Open your heart."

"I don't gotta do nothin', Doc. Why the fuck you think everyone's sick in the first place? Puking and shitting everywhere? 'Cause they been touchin' them little disease-ravaged freaks, is why. Me and the lieutenant, we're fine because we never touch 'em. Ain't that right, sir?"

Now that I consider it, Armstrong may be right: I never touch the children like the other Marines. I take it as an indictment and change the subject. "You better get up, Doc. We need to distribute the next set of Imodium tablets and get ready to roll. We cross the line of departure in four hours."

We've been tasked with roadblock duty and I've delayed it as long as possible to give the platoon time to heal its guts, swapping schedules with some of the grunt platoons. We were supposed to roll yesterday morning and I bought us thirty-six hours. But I'm not about to report recon as combat ineffective for a second day because of a little stomach bug.

"Mary Thayer-Ash's comin' to film, ain't she, sir?"

"How'd you know?"

Armstrong jerks his thumb and I see Montoya sitting in his hole with a poncho draped over his head, lathering his chest with foam. Then he pulls out a razor and starts his primping routine, quick strokes, eyes darting around, washing himself with Evian when he's finished, to nourish that pristine skin.

"We see you, M.!" shouts Armstrong. "Hope she loves that silky skin!"

Montoya gives him the finger and ducks out of sight. To find his cologne, I'm sure.

———

CNN's ranks have thinned to—count 'em—five people, and since Mary Thayer-Ash's regular crew has flown back to the other world, Darren has volunteered to remain with her to man the camera. Thayer-Ash has wangled a reluctant agreement from her superiors to remain in country for the six days that our battalion is still here in an attempt to piece together a story of interest, building on her mortar footage and filming the turnover of responsibility from the United States forces to the UN.

Recon is on another rink-a-dink mission but Ms. Thayer-Ash is shadowing us because the platoon has a nose for trouble and the Hibr Gidr have begun to talk of retribution against our platoon alone for our night action. Recon, Little Joe says, will die Somalia.

Squawk! That's the sound of the Somali chicken in Armstrong's hands as it struggles to free itself.

"Even their chickens are skinny," he pants. "Texas chicken'd kick its ass."

"Gunny," I say. "Please go tell him to get on with the search."

Gunny laughs. "Yessir. Pretty impressive, though, catching that thing."

We're manning Checkpoint Daffy, a vehicle inspection site three klicks north of the airport along the MSR—the Main Skinny Route. Our mission: to stop and search for heavy weapons in all the vehicles coming into Mogadishu proper. Armstrong's team is searching a large bus full of Somalis. We have to empty every vehicle that drives up and search its indigenous pop. In this case the bus is filled with animals and some of them have escaped. The Somalis are yelling and laughing and my Marines are trying to round up the assorted chickens and goats that have disembarked.

The Gunny and I are standing behind the roadblock watching the animal cyclone, and I'm not just talking about the Marines. The MSR is lined with row houses, so we've set up a sandbag defense and have placed a few rolls of razor wire and some tire spikes to our front. Once the vehicle gets the green light, we pull back the wire and allow it to pass.

I'm standing comfortably behind one of the bunkers thinking about what a goat rope this is, no pun intended. Mogadishu's sprawling maze of streets is accessible from several other roads—most of which are unwatched—and the desert country itself. So any smuggler will simply drive around us. But because intelligence pegged this on a map, here we stand acting out the Restore Hope version of the Maginot Line.

Twelve Gangbangers arrive just as Armstrong finishes with the bus; they come sauntering down the street, chanting something, Farrah Fawcett in the lead, still wearing his Cowboys jersey. Nike Boy is with them in his "Just Do It" shirt—Bangers take their sponsorship deals seriously; it's clear that this kid wouldn't be caught dead in Reebok—and carrying his own AK-47 now, a squire who has been promoted. They are about a hundred meters down the narrow road, shuffling dust like a herd of cattle as they approach—okay, small dogs—when they turn down one of the narrow alleys and disappear.

Gunny gives the order to man-up all the security positions. We remain on full alert for an hour, but when they do not show themselves, we slip back into the routine, which today includes some private time with Mary Thayer-Ash.

I stare at her. Her hair is pinned up in her CNN baseball cap and from where I stand, I can see the sweat beginning to bead on the back of her neck, brown from the sun, thin and sinewy, glistening. She listens intently—you already have that anchor's nod down, don't you, Mary?—then throws her head back and lets the wild laugh loose. She's an attractive woman for whom I feel love-hate. Well, lust-hate.

Thayer-Ash is interviewing Gunny but he's not talking. She begins to nod, as if he's sparked her interest, occasionally moving her microphone next to her mouth, then sticking it in the Gunny's face. Strange. These must be for the requisite close-up shots of the assiduous reporter. I am not disillusioned; with her face I'd put it on the segment as much as possible, too. Tell me the thirteen-year-old Nielsen boy won't stay tuned to *that* shot.

My turn is at hand. I sneak over behind Darren to wait for her call and eavesdrop on the last part of Gunny's interview.

"Gunnery Sergeant Ricketts, I'd like to ask a few more questions about things I was unclear on. If I may? Can you explain how you feel being sent here? And, if I can elaborate for a minute, I understand you have a family back home. Can you explain how you feel being sent by the government to Somalia?"

"Ma'am," Gunny responds, "I already answered this. Doesn't matter how I feel. A Marine does what he's told." For some reason, he's impatient.

"Yes, but . . . okay. All right," she says. "You're curt. In your old neighborhood back home in Brooklyn, are there people who need your help, too? Does it faze you at all having been sent here when there are problems back home?"

"I don't remember talkin' about *problems*. And, no, it doesn't faze me." He's short with her and I wonder what happened earlier in the interview.

"But certainly you have an opinion on your mission here? On being sent here by the Bush administration? Are you happy? Sad? Some of the Marines mentioned that they felt like political pawns sent here by people who didn't have a clear understanding of what they faced."

"None of mine."

"Excuse me?" she says.

"None of my Marines said such a thing."

"Well, no. Others. At the airport, I mean."

"May I say something off mike, ma'am?"

"Oh," she says, smiling. "Sorry. Yes. And don't call me 'ma'am,' Mister Reticent."

"Excuse me?" he says.

"Sorry. Taciturn is probably more appropriate."

Gunny frowns, not understanding either word and taking them as insults. "Look, I just want to say how unprofessional I think you are, Miss Thayer-Ash. You're enforcing a double standard and . . . I'm just so sick of reporters doing that."

"I don't—"

"Let me finish."

Both Darren and I stare, unmoving, unsure of what's coming but anticipating a crash nevertheless.

"All your questions to me and Johnson—I overheard that interview—all your questions had a different tone for us than they did for the rest of the Marines. Now why is that?"

"I'm not sure I know what you're trying to say," she says.

"No. You don't. You're treating me and Johnson differently, and the funny thing is, you don't even *know* you're doing it. In fact, I bet it just makes you bristle, hearing me say that. A reporter's worst fear, having the race card played back on you now, isn't it? You're asking me questions as if I was forced into the Marines because I didn't have any other choice in life. It's like . . . you feel *sorry* for me. Like you want to apologize to me for having been placed in the position of 'political pawn,' or whatever you said."

"Gunnery Sergeant Ricketts, I . . . you'll have to explain. I mean, I'm sorry if I offended you but—"

"There you go again. Apologizing to me." He's angry and he starts shaking his head. "Look, let me give it another shot. I first noticed it in the Gulf. Reporters would ask the white Marines how it felt to be fighting for their country, how proud they felt, if their families had a military history—all that happy patriotic horseshit that I happen to believe in. But you know what they asked me? How I felt fighting for oil, being sent to the desert by a Republican administration, poorer segments of the population—read 'black'—sent to fight for the rich. And here you are, doing it again. Everything you asked me has a veiled reference to some ghetto culture that has forced me to join the Marines, where I now languish fighting for a country that spits on me behind my back. Well, fuck that. Pardon my French, but fuck *that*.

"I'm happy to be here. Poverty didn't force me into the Corps. Pride did. I know you'll never do a report like that because it isn't in vogue—I'm sure that sounds monumentally cheesy to you—but that's how I feel. So chew on that the next time you ask your fucking questions."

Gunny unslings his weapon and walks off quickly toward the barricade, shaking his head as he goes.

Ms. Thayer-Ash looks at us and it is clear that her confidence is shaken. I wait for Darren to speak but he's silent, pursing his lips and slowly nodding, as if he had given the speech himself. Or wanted to but didn't.

"Take cover! Kid's got a rifle!" someone yells.

I pull Darren down, hard and flat. He shrugs me off and crawls over to cover Thayer-Ash, who is thoroughly confused.

"It's that Nike kid who started the boys' riot last month. What do you want to do, sir? About that kid?" Gunny repeats. He points down the road.

I scoot up behind the sandbags and take a turkey peek. Nike Boy is standing in the middle of the road, sixty meters away. His head is turned sideways and it looks like he's talking to someone in the alley to his right. He's still holding an AK-47.

"Wha . . . who's he talking to?" I ask when I get to the sandbags.

"I think it's Farrah Fawcett back there behind the building, encouraging him. Some sort of initiation. I saw the Cowboys jersey."

"Encouraging him to do what?"

"Shoot at us, sir. He's—look."

Five Bangers walk out into the street from behind a house and begin to wave at us, laughing, occasionally nudging Nike Boy forward. All of them have AKs.

"Skinnies are all hopped up," says Gunny. "Look at those crazy fuckers. Bet they're—"

"Easy!" I say, loud enough for the platoon to hear. I can hear the brief rustles as the Marines put their weapons in their shoulders and sight in, gaining comfortable firing positions. Darren has his camera propped up behind a sandbag as if it is a weapon, which it is. If someone smokes Nike Boy without cause, I'll be sent for a permanent tour in the valley of the motherfucked, desperate and dateless to boot.

"All hopped up on khat, sir," says Gunny. "Look at them dance for that camera."

The Bangers dance for a minute, smiling and jumping, then begin to shove Nike Boy forward, yelling at him. He walks a few steps toward the barricade, looking at us, then hesitates and turns his head. Farrah Fawcett makes a shooing motion with his hands but the boy remains immobile.

"Don't do it, kid," whispers Gunny.

Nike Boy shakes his head and Farrah Fawcett picks up a rock and hurls it at the boy. It bounces off his back with a loud thud—my God, it's quiet now—and the boy screams.

"Leave him the fuck alone!" yells Gunny.

The boy drops the rifle and grabs at his back where the rock hit. Farrah rushes up to him and slaps him in the face, babbling at him, now shaking him violently. Then he steps back and strikes the boy with a large cane he must have been keeping behind his back.

Gunny stands full upright and I yank him back by his harness, behind the sandbags. "Goddamn them," Gunny says. "Look. He sees the camera. Maybe that's why."

The Skinny points in the direction of Darren but it's not clear to me he even *sees* the camera. The boy nods and picks up the AK-47, wiping tears from his face. He tosses the sling over his back. Farrah joins the rest of his posse and they retreat back to the alley, leaving the boy alone on the road. *I got a bad feeling about this.*

"Fire only if your life is directly threatened," I say for the camera. "Use deadly force only if absolutely necessary. Looks like they're trying to force that kid into a fight."

Nike Boy walks into the middle of the road. I can see three Skinny heads peeking around the corner of the alley, including Farrah's, watching the scene. A gust rolls down the street and sweeps a bunch of chicken feathers up, swirling them past the boy. He walks forward again, boldly this time, smiling all the way. The big rifle is just about as tall as he is; his body is bent back in an effort to keep the muzzle out of the dirt, little hands gripping the barrel, back and arms taut, pulling back in counterbalance, walking forward as if carrying an anvil.

"Hello, Marines! Hello, Marines!" he shouts. "Hello, America!" He is staring right at Darren.

Gunny says, "Sir, better get that camera off—"

"On it," I say.

I can hear the boy continue to shout things in pidgin English. "Darren!" I yell. "Put the camera away! This kid's feeding off it. He's—"

"Leave it," I hear Thayer-Ash say, then see her head poke out from behind Darren so she can meet my eyes. "We have permission to be here, Lieutenant Kelly."

"They *want* him to be filmed. It's for the kid's good. Turn it off."

"You *gave* us permission—"

"Turn the fucking thing off, Darren!" I scream, raging now.

He brings the camera off of his shoulder and clicks it off. I hear Thayer-Ash yelling at him as I turn to Nike Boy. The kid is looking right at me. "Hello, Marines!" he yells again, smiling. "You recon!"

"Drop your gun!" Gunny yells. "No good! No! No!" He starts to fumble for his phrases card.

Nike Boy smiles, glances back at the peering heads, and faces us again. He leans back and brings the weapon up.

"Don't!" Gunny again, desperate now.

The muzzle rises slowly. It pauses at his shins and for a second I think that he may not have the strength to do it, but the boy catches his breath and pulls again. The barrel catches the sun as it comes up and it flashes momentarily, white and shiny, fading just as quickly into metallic black as it begins to level at us. In my rifle sight he is clear at first—a ten-year-old boy wearing a Nike T-shirt and flip-flops—but when the end becomes inevitable I shift my focus on to my front sight post and center it on the fuzzy black mass in the background. Two pounds. One.

It is a single shot that takes him down, twisting him so violently that the AK-47, stretched on its sling, spins around his body several times. A single red jet paints the side of the nearest building in a thin line of blood once, then the dirt road in a dark oval, then the wall again.

"I just winged him!" someone on my left yells. "He's okay! I just winged him!" It's Armstrong.

The boy spins twice, Red yanking the cord on his old outboard, and lands on his back. His chest is rising and falling so rapidly. Blood squirts out of his arm in a series of jets, like a water fountain twisted on and off, the red turning black as it is swallowed by the earth next to him.

"Sweet Jesus. You didn't have to shoot him," says Gunny. "He was just—"

Gunfire cuts him short. A few of the rounds thump into the sandbags but most snap well high. One of the alley Bangers has done a spray-and-pray, the Skinny version of the drive-by shooting. Another AK-47 appears from around the corner of the alley and it spits out a full magazine in our direction. All of the rounds whip over our heads in a crackling of tiny sonic booms.

"Sir, that boy's hit in the axillary artery and he's going into shock. We need—"

"Not now, Doc," I say. I turn and yell at the platoon, "If you see another AK-47 from that alley, shoot it! Montoya! Your team's got the corner building."

There is a pause. I sight in at the alley corner. A mass pops out from behind the house. I allow my eye a millisecond to focus on the Skinny and recognize the rifle, then I bring the front sight post up, focus on it, and center it on the blur. I squeeze the trigger. The smell of gunpowder . . .

the ringing starts again. The M-16 bucks gently into my shoulder, then my body weight rocks it forward, back to its original point of aim where I see the mass is still there, though lower, and I fire again. Before he can shoulder his weapon, the Skinny is hit by at least fifty rounds from the platoon. He goes spinning into the dirt, all broken arms and legs.

I am a killer again. Or am I? Perhaps I missed. Perhaps the other men killed him, not me.

I am glancing over my sights, scanning, when another Skinny darts out into the road and grabs his buddy's body. He shakes and quakes for a second before he sprawls forward, collapsed over the first one in a shape that is no longer a human form. Dust rises behind him in what looks like a smattering of tiny fires. The sound effects continue for a second more because of the walls, then the echo of firecrackers dies. "Reloading," Montoya says.

The window of the corner building next to the alley flashes and bullets rip into the sandbags. This Skinny can aim.

"He's in the building!" Gunny shouts. "Front window." It is hard to hear with the ringing but Gunny is coming in, Lima Charlie.

"On it!" Armstrong screams. A volley of friendly rounds shatters the window.

"Sir. The boy," Doc says.

Nike Boy, on the street, is still breathing. The blood isn't spurting anymore, but I'm not sure if that's good or bad.

"Give me some cover fire when I get out there!" I shout.

"No! You can't go out there!" Gunny screams. "They'll shoot you!"

I glance at Darren for . . . what? Permission? Approval? Dominance? But he's filming and doesn't see me. I sprint through the narrow hole in the wire.

I am not a sprinter and my legs feel weighted down. I simply am not fast enough to pull this off. I can hear the 5.56-millimeter rounds zipping over my shoulder, protecting me, and realize that I can hear the difference when a 7.62 millimeter passes me going the other way. Running to Nike Boy I feel like a blind man crossing a twenty-lane highway.

When I reach his body he's twitching a little. His blood is a very bright, apple red pool on the ground around his right arm and head, but the droplets that shot out farthest are just dark dots in the sand. His arm is broken just below the shoulder and behind the shredded meat I can see the white splinters of his bone. I consider dragging him by the good arm but a Banger has drawn a bead on me—rounds are snapping right in front of the boy—so I grab his foot and drag him to the side of the road, the AK-47 bouncing along behind him, its sling still wrapped around his torso. I yank him into a doorway and bend down to pick him up. I notice a big hole in the side of his neck. He's been shot again, this time by Bangers. The rounds continue to kick up dirt just to my front, but when a green tracer skips by it's clear that the Skinny doesn't have the angle to ding me now.

I flip the boy over my shoulder so that if someone shoots me in the back they'll hit him first. Between the body and the flak jacket I might stand a chance of stopping a bullet. I start to sprint back to the barricade and see that Armstrong is standing outside the wire, waving at me. I recognize the hand signal and dive face first into the dirt road, Armstrong raising his M-16 as I'm going down, the boy spilling out of my arms and tumbling forward. There is a furious explosion of bullets.

"Let's go!" screams Armstrong, standing over me now, pulling me to my feet. I grab the boy again.

We sprint through the hole in the wire and Doc is there to greet us. "Give him here, sir," he says.

I bend forward and the boy flops into his arms. He makes a wheezing sound.

"Popped all three of 'em, sir. Good thing you ducked. They jumped out of the house behind you when you started back," says Armstrong, panting.

"What?"

He points over the sandbags and says, "Them Skinnies, sir. They was gonna shoot you. Got 'em for you."

I peer over the sandbags and see three bodies sprawled on the side of the road in the same spot to which I dragged the boy. "Thanks," I reply lamely to the man who has just saved my life. Without Jake Armstrong there is no Gavin Kelly—I'll never forget that.

"Sir? We got something here, sir," Gunny says, pointing out front. He's pissed at me. "Hold your fire, everyone. This one ain't armed."

A pair of hands waves from the alley in the distance, twisting back and forth slowly. Forearms appear, then elbows, then shiny blue-and-gray sleeves, a head and shoulders. When he's confident we're not going to shoot, Farrah Fawcett walks out from behind the house and steps into the road with his hands raised. He's shouting but I cannot hear him for the ringing in my ears.

Behind me I hear Doc say, "I'm so sorry. I'm so sorry."

Ms. Thayer-Ash is bent over the boy.

"The bullet must have bounced off his arm and went into his neck. I'm sorry." Doc looks up at me and says, "Nothing I could do, sir. Just tore him up inside, from the look of it." He has tears in his eyes. Darren is still filming.

"Damn," says Armstrong. "I just meant to wing him. I

hit him right . . . hit him in the arm, right where I aimed. He just got an unlucky bounce. He was raising that weapon. Damn."

"That wasn't yours, Armstrong. They hit him in the neck."

Armstrong nods at me as if there is a strong bond between us, friends for years. "Well."

"Sir, we got more company," says Gunny.

The boy's wrists are bent forward like a begging dog. Ms. Thayer-Ash unwraps the cotton shirt she has tied around her waist and puts it in front of her face. She wipes her brow and eyes and then puts it over the boy.

"Sir!" says Gunny.

I turn back and kneel on a sandbag, keeping my M-16 in my shoulder. There are at least ten people on the street now, mostly women and kids, all of them holding their hands up as if they are part of a religious revival movement, moving closer. The two bodies next to the alley are gone. Farrah is twisting his head back and forth, yelling instructions as they move forward. When the group reaches the three bodies on the side of the street the women move up front and block my vision, stacking themselves in front of the Bangers.

"Everyone check fire," I say. "Keep cool. Montoya, radio Vader and have them get the reaction force up here now. Armstrong, close the hole in the barricade."

A moment later the women and kids part in the middle for the arrival of their king. Farrah Fawcett comes walking right up to the barricade with another man. Farrah speaks very rapidly and the second Skinny nods.

"He say dat de boy have no bullet in de gun. He jes want to say hello to Marines, dat boy you kilt. He don't have no bullet. He show de CNN," says the translator who is staring at me. Must be my stellar command presence.

"Should I check it, sir?" asks Doc.

"No," I say. "Doesn't matter." I point at Farrah Fawcett. "Tell him that *he* killed that boy. *He* sent him out to die. Maybe next time Farrah will be brave enough to do that himself, instead of sending a boy to die."

The translator babbles and Farrah just laughs and shakes his head, smiling. "Nigga recon!" The rest of the crowd walks up and gathers behind Farrah, chanting something similar, and he quiets them.

His translator points at me. "Farah say you de coward, hide behind wire and sand. He say de people here want de boy's body back. He say you coward for kill de boy. He say why you not come out and fight like a man?"

It is a fair question. I imagine opening the wire and walking out to him, beating him to death and grinding his Dallas Cowboys jersey into the ground. I always hated Dallas, cheerleaders notwithstanding.

I kick my boot up and set it on a sandbag, the sole facing Farrah. This is a serious insult for Muslims, the Skinny equivalent of telling him his mother wears combat boots. Farrah yells something and the women around him start chanting again.

The translator says, "You insult him!"

"Tell him he is not a man," I say. "Tell Farrah that he is only a dog, and I do not waste time with dogs. The recon platoon could kill him any time we want. He is not a man in Allah's eyes. He is a dog." This is the Skinny equivalent of saying that, while his fat mother was still in her combat boots, I fucked her brains out.

Farrah Fawcett moves to the edge of the barbed wire and speaks rapidly, spittle flying out of his mouth. I smile and laugh, not waiting for the translation, and it further infuriates him. I stick my tongue out and wag it from side to side. I mean, who knows? Finally Somalia is starting to get fun.

"He say you kilt his friend Muhammad Ali, you will die, Marine. All recon die."

"People have been telling us that for two centuries, you dog."

The translator steps back, incredulous. "You insult me!" He begins firing off words and his English goes all to hell. "Farah kill all of Marine, you die here Somalia! Marine. All Marine recon! You kill de boy! Farah say he do what he want, he in charge Somalia and he kill you and take who he want, de girls! And you see him! He kill you!"

"We'll be waiting, you dogs. *You dirty dogs.* Marines will be waiting. We always have been, always will be." I try to spit on Farrah but I'm too terrified to find wet.

"Armstrong!" I say.

"Yessir."

"Spit on both those men."

"With pleasure, sir."

He sucks up a savage hock of chewing tobacco and saliva and somehow propels the glob right through the wire and onto Farrah's shirt. There is much screaming. The women and kids begin throwing rocks on command and we hunker down for another barrage, waiting for the reaction convoy. Armstrong turns to me in the middle of the medieval mortar barrage and says, "Hey, sir. That was fucking *awesome,* what you said. Got him totally riled up. That kicks ass." He slaps me on the knee like he's my best pal.

I just shrug and lean into the sandbags. A rock bounces

off my helmet with a thunk. Armstrong is still excited and he's saying something about how we kicked their asses, Johnson grunting and responding, "Fuckin' A."

The shirt has blown off the boy and he's lying in the street behind us in his dead-dog pose. Somehow a few flies have fought the wind well enough to execute landings on what is left of his bloody neck. *Another glorious day in the Corps.*

– 21 –

1 FEBRUARY 1993

> You don't frighten us, English pig-dog! Go and
> boil your bottoms, son of silly person! I blow
> my nose at you, so called Arthur-king, you and
> your silly English kniggets!

It is extremely hot, my Kevlar helmet preventing the steam from escaping, cooking what little hair I have on my head. If I turn my head too quickly, the helmet spins on the leather band of sweat, grinding into the top of my pointy head. At this rate I'll be bald by the time I'm twenty-six. Plus, my chin strap is too tight. It is digging into the razor-burned flesh between my chin and my Adam's apple, chafing it raw. The back of my neck scrapes against my flak jacket with every right step, for some reason, so I am crooking my head at an angle. To the Somalis who are laughing at me now I must look like some overgrown canine walking diagonally, as dogs are prone to do when they are tired. I'm carrying a full combat load of ammunition as mandated by the colonel after it was clear that our honeymoon with this hell hole and its people had ended. Somalia. Bane of my life, fire of my spite. So. Mal. Ia.

We have three days left in this hole. The Marines are dragging ass in the windy heat—imagine kneeling down in front of your preheated oven and opening it every ten seconds—and we've still got two klicks to go on the patrol. We're on a daytime security walk looking for . . . what? Warlords? Weapons? Love in all the wrong places? I'm so hot I can't even remember. Left foot in front of my right foot in front of my left foot in front . . .

"Black folk are supposed to be used to this heat, but goddaaamn," says Gunny. "This gear's eating me alive, sir. Should we take a security halt?" Gunny doesn't like the terms "rest stop" or "break."

"No, Guns. Let's just take it in from here. Maybe two klicks to go. We're out of water anyway."

He grunts and lets himself drift back to his position in the formation. We've got two more blocks to circle before we head back to the airport, and I figure I can pass the time by debating with the translator who requested our platoon for today's mission—Mr. Boom Boom Assan, back in the platoon's employ in a fresh, white linen suit now that it is clear that Little Joe—and anyone else in our employ—is imperiled. None of the other translators will walk with recon anymore, so if Boom Boom's looking for my forgiveness, fine, I'm too tired to care—or even remember why we shit-canned him to begin with.

My *God,* it's hot in this gear.

Boom Boom holds me gently by the arm. Only affection I've had in five months, so, hey, take what you can get, right? "So I was saying, sir. It is a custom. That is all.

Otherwise women get wild and cannot control. Devil-girls, yes?"

"So you rob them of their pleasure buttons? That's fucked," Armstrong says. He's walking right flank so he can eavesdrop. I'm debating Boom Boom on the merits of female circumcision.

"Is not *fucked*, as you say," says Boom Boom sternly. "It is our way. Simple operation. No pain. You not understand." Boom Boom gets irritated and uncomfortable when he's forced to talk to anyone but me. I suppose it's a class thing. He sighs and turns to me. "Sir. You certainly see the reasoning? Cannot have the sex against Allah's wishes."

"No, Boom Boom, that *is* fucked. Look, let's talk about something else. How 'bout those tongue twisters you're so good at? I got one: How much wood would a woodchuck chuck if a woodchuck could chuck wood?"

Boom Boom's eyes light up and he says, "That is *brilliant*, sir! The delicacy of it! I have one I learned from some other Marines last—"

"I got a better one here, Boom Boom," Armstrong interrupts. "Listen up to this one here. There once was a chick from Nantucket, whose boobies were so—"

"Incoming," Gunny half-whispers, bored. A rock sails into the formation and thunks off a helmet or a flak jacket. Unfortunately, the only nonlethal weapons we have been issued are our fists, so the Marines have had to employ them often, more swatting and smacking than punching. Still, an open-faced slap is not a term of endearment, even in this whirlpool of violence, and we aren't the heroes we used to be.

"You die Somalia, Marine!" yells some kid. Yeah, yeah, yeah. What's new, pussycat?

Armstrong walks over to him and the kid is smart enough to recognize a serious threat when he sees one. The kid bolts and Armstrong calls after him, "Who's gonna do it? 'Cause I been waiting. Believe me!" He tries to spit some tobacco juice but he doesn't have the saliva and it trickles down his chin and weaves a wild track around his stubble. He tilts his helmet back, wipes his brow, then wipes off his chin. "Little Skinny fuck," he says.

"At ease," Gunny says. "Goddamn, you got thin skin, Stretch. You're as bad as my wife." Gunny chuckles to himself; he has a lot of fun with his wife when she's not around.

"Sorry, Gunny," Armstrong says. "Guess the heat is starting to get to me, is all."

"Thought you was from Texas, Stretch," Gunny says, laughing tiredly.

"Don't have kids screamin' at you all day in Texas, Guns. They do and you beat 'em down. Pretty simple. Darwinistic, you know?"

Gunny just grunts and Armstrong takes his place in the formation.

Boom Boom has become more and more animated next to me, talking rapidly with nearly every grown Somali he sees on the street. He is stopped by one woman and when I turn around he is so far behind that I have to wave him up to rejoin the formation. "What's going on?" I ask. He just shrugs and smiles. I've been too casual. "What are you saying to them?" Forceful this time.

"Nothing. *Rien.*" He shakes his head and I half-expect it to spin off that thin neck. "She is a friend, dat girl."

"Okay, Boom Boom. Just stick with me." He smiles dumbly and I say, "Stay with me. *Avec moi.* All time. You're starting to piss me off again."

"Yes," he says, and turns to yell something at two women in a building. They shout back at him and he jogs over to them and screams something back. Hell hath no wrath like a lieutenant scorned, but I'm just too hot to care. Besides, poor bastard's most likely catching heavy flak for making a buck working for the U.S. government, an occupation in the Mog that is akin to beating seal pups for a living.

Now that the UN has taken over both hangars all I can think of is those cold sodas they're selling at the airport. I plan to buy a few cans each for the men when we roll in for the debrief. Ice-cold Cokes. Mountain Dew, the cans dripping from the bucket of ice water. The prospect of the wet chill, well, we'd kill for it now. Of course, we'd kill for a lot less if the Bangers decided to show.

Some kids rush out in front of us on the street and block our approach, gathering stones as they set up another poor man's defense. *Les misérables.* "Oh, fuuuuck me," Gunny says. "Not today. Not now."

Fifty meters to my front, Montoya, on point duty, turns to me and shrugs. The kids begin to launch rocks. One of them is wearing Nike Boy's old shirt; I can see the holes and the rusty stain. The cycle of violence continues. He grabs a tin can and sprints right at us, screaming his hot head off. A miniature Stretch Armstrong.

"You best get out of the way unless you want to lose your life, like your buddy!" Armstrong yells. Then he mutters quietly, "Ought to bust that little punk up, that'd get the whole mob under control, decapitating the leadership."

"Form up for riot!" I yell. "Montoya! Close up the first rank and when we drive them back, open up into patrol formation again."

The Marines around me are moving, pieces of a death

machine closing together and snapping into place. The boys are especially recalcitrant today; we close to within ten meters and still they refuse to yield.

"Sir! Sir!" Boom Boom screams. He gently grabs my elbow and points down a narrow alley to our left. "Go dat way. Go around dem. Go AROUND!" He makes an *L* shape with his hand and forearm to illustrate the point. We can shoot down the narrow alley, pop out on the other side, and outmaneuver the boys. No need to scrap. "Go. Go," he says urgently. "Hurry!"

Gunny walks over to the alley entrance and says, "Good to go, sir," with about as much enthusiasm as he can muster. It feels like a hair dryer is blowing on us on High.

"Hold up, Sergeant Montoya," I say.

"What's up, sir?" he asks, agitated. The first rank is taking the bulk of the rocks and he's eager to move, as if he's being forced to stand under a hornet's nest.

I peer down the alley. It's quite long—maybe forty meters—and very narrow. There are no side streets. Boom Boom is right. If we double-time down the alley we can flank the boys' ambush in less than a minute and be on our way. As an added bonus, the entire alley is in the shade.

"Let's hop, sir," says Gunny. He's got his eyes on the prize, too. On the right side of the alley is what looks to be an abandoned, three-story warehouse that's blocking the sun. "Those kids are itching for a fight today. Whaddaya say? Let's scoot down here and move past."

I shrug and wave to Armstrong. "Stretch, take the lead down this alley. Montoya! You got the rear now. Keep the boys occupied and then follow us."

Johnson moves into the alley first, followed by Armstrong and the rest of the team. I am about to follow when I notice some movement behind us, on the other end of the street from where we came, and see a small boy—it's Little Joe— running toward us.

He's yelling now and waving his arms like E.T. Must have come to fight with the boys again. "Hold up," I say to Armstrong, who is already in the alley. I turn to Doc and growl, "I thought I told you to leave the boy at the fucking airport. He could get himself killed out here."

"I did, sir!" Doc yells. "He must have followed us."

I put my hands on my hips and my war face on; Joe's about to get a lecture to remember. I notice that most of the pedestrians have retreated into their homes or . . . somewhere. The street is practically deserted now. Boom Boom is telling me to go ahead, that he'll bring Joe up behind us, but I do not want to leave the boy in his care, especially around the other tykes.

"Kelly!" the boy is shrieking. It's curious. I cannot hear him well for Boom Boom's babbling so I put a single finger in the translator's face—*shut up so I can think*—and strain to hear Joe. "No! No! De men! Heeber Geeder!"

I look at the empty street again, then at Boom Boom— who is shaking his head and moving toward Little Joe, shouting, *"Quiet, boy!"*—then at the warehouse. It is three stories high, three rows of windows on each floor, some of the upper ones missing. On the ground below them, broken glass twinkles in the sun.

"AMBUSH RIGHT!" I scream. "Get 'em out of the alley, Armstrong!"

Gunny just scowls and looks around, confused, but Armstrong is acting already, pushing his men out, yelling instructions.

"Disperse!" I yell and throw myself against the alley corner, pointing my weapon at the warehouse. Gunny drops to a knee and raises his rifle. A grenade catches a window pane on its way out of the upper floor and sails into the alley with a *clink! Three seconds*. I aim for the remaining windows and spray an entire magazine of bullets into them, hoping to create some glass shrapnel that will keep our ambushers away from the windows and a firing position. The glass crackles and snaps, high-pitched *tiiiings* and *caaaah-laaangs*. Some stray droplets from the glass squall rain down on Armstrong's Marines as they run out, dancing and glittering when they bounce off the Kevlar helmets.

"Grenade!" Gunny screams. *Two seconds*.

Gunny is firing over my shoulder into the first floor and a skewer explodes my eardrum just before it goes numb, singing faintly. I eject the clip and slap a fresh one into the M-16, eyes still on the building, grabbing Gunny's gear harness and yanking him around the corner and out of the blast radius. Armstrong sprints abreast of us but Johnson times his dive prematurely and he skids on his face, sliding as if he is stealing a base, right in the middle of the alley's entrance.

One second.

I roll forward in a crouch and start to spring across to cover him but Armstrong hits me with a jab right in the center of my chest. The punch knocks out my wind and sends me flying backward into Gunny's arms, safe, lungs burning, no view of the alley now but a front-row seat for watching Armstrong dive across his man, putting himself closer to the grenade. One of his big arms snakes across Johnson, who is trying to crawl away, and pulls him tight into his chest, spooning.

I feel the blast in my stomach and lungs. A deep *caah-whump!* and a torrent of dust, my eyes closed for a moment as the wave of pebbles sloshes by, some of them burrowing between my lips and into my mouth. I stick my rifle around the corner and stitch a new magazine of bullets into the windows I imagine. Dirt scoots up my nose, into my brain, and I sneeze.

When I open my eyes, Armstrong is jerking Johnson to his feet and they are sprinting to safety. The back of Armstrong's flak vest is shredded and a thin wisp of smoke glides out of the Kevlar as he runs. He's dripping blood. I hear him assigning security sectors as he leaves. It is clear to me now that Armstrong is the true warrior in this platoon, and if we were in ancient Rome, he'd be the one giving the orders. I'd probably be bringing the water to the men.

"Doc! Get over to Armstrong!" I scream.

But he's already moving past me, across the alley, arguing with Armstrong, eventually yelling something back at me. My bell is still reverberating and I turn to Gunny and point to my ear, shaking my head.

"Just caught some shrapnel in the ass, sir! Superficial! Flak vest stopped the rest, I guess!" Gunny yells.

I glance over his shoulder, down the main street, and see Boom Boom tearing ass past Little Joe. I slap a new magazine into my weapon, shoulder it, and consider popping him. Screw these rules. He led us into an ambush. But I let him go. Joe runs up to me and the Gunny grabs him and slams him against the house, out of sight of the alley. "Dey in dair, Kelly. Heeber Geeder gonna kill you! Kill recon, everybody say!" He is panting and pointing at the warehouse.

"Okay, Joe. It's okay. You stay right there," Gunny says. He then points at the warehouse. "Fuckin' translator leading us into a deathtrap!"

"Get on the hook and call for the reaction force. We'll cordon off the building and wait for the cavalry. Infantry are better at room clearing. If they come out, we'll fucking waste them."

"*If* they're armed, sir."

The main warehouse door, about ten meters away on the street side, opens and I raise my rifle. All around me I hear the quick, metallic rustle and the patient silence as the Marines sight in. Someone inside the building is yelling. There is silence and he yells again. Gunny asks Little Joe to translate.

"He say he gonna come out. He don' want you to shoot. He have no gun. No gun."

"*Hubkaa ohig toogan jarta!*" I scream. Silence. Then, jabbering from the dark doorway again. My ear is starting to come back but I look to the boy to see if I've missed something.

"He don' understand you, Kelly. He say he coming out. He say he have no gun so you can't shoot him or de men."

"The *hell* we won't. *We* decide if he lives or dies, now." Little Joe just cocks his head and I wonder why I am spouting off to a thirteen-year-old boy.

Armstrong is yelling and I ask Gunny to amplify his words for me. "He wants to know if they're cleared hot for payback, sir. Platoon's got a serious itch it wants to scratch."

"*Payback's a motherfucker, Guns.*"

Gunny asks me which ear is good. I point to my right and he grabs my harness, pulls me to his head, and says, "You didn't hear Armstrong just now, *but I did.* Felt the energy in the entire platoon. This is what I'd term a Volatile. Fucking. Situation. More than anyone, *you* have to remain in control—*retain* control—because the men will be looking to you. If the Bangers aren't armed, we can't shoot. Right, sir? *Right, sir?*"

I'm staring at his collar insignia, allowing my eyes to blur the eagle, globe, and anchor, and the words fill my head, my consciousness, blowing everything else away. My need for revenge has peaked, a base and virulent instinct that demands to be fed, so powerful! *African warlords tried to kill my men.* But Gunny is right. As much as I want to shrug off the rules that we're wearing, I have an obligation. I am immediately filled with shame for forgetting Big Duke's words so quickly.

"Everyone hold fire! If they come out with weapons pointed, kill them. But no weapons means NO SHOTS!"

It is a surreal scene, my men flopped down around me with their rifles off Safe, in an African country, staring at me, Armstrong's mouth moving, volume on Mute.

"You shut that suck, Stretch!" the Gunny yells. "And do *exactly* what the lieutenant said!"

Armstrong's mouth moves again, his eyes narrow, pointing at Doc, who is pressing a bandage into his ass. "Yeah, yeah. Keep cryin'!" Gunny shouts to lighten the mood. "Don't worry! If they discharge you, the lieutenant and I will recommend you for *Buns of Steel 2* video!"

"You tell him to get his hands up when he comes out," I say to Little Joe. "Or we kill him."

The boy screams at the door and the door screams back and the boy screams again. It is clear that the last little bit is not a translation.

"He coming now," the boy says simply. "You Kill Farah now, yes?"

"Hold fire!" I yell. I am so sick of that phrase.

Farrah Fawcett struts out of the building with his hands above his head, smiling. He is still wearing that Cowboys jersey. Either he has a bunch of them or he's got the same laundry habits that I do. "Tell him to lie down," I say.

For a moment I train my rifle on his head; so simple, a curled finger and the black fuzz behind my front sight post will turn red, be gone from this world, and we will all be the better for it. Ends justifying the ultimate means.

"Tell him to have the rest of his men come out of there with their magazines in one hand and their rifles in another." Little Joe just cocks his head. "Like this," I say, and remove the clip from my rifle, holding it in my other hand. "Hands up." I turn to Farrah Fawcett and demonstrate it, a flight attendant on a doomed airplane.

Farrah stares at me, chewing khat slowly like a cow relaxing in the sun, his elbows casually propped on his knees. Occasionally he leans forward and spits between his legs. Farrah says, "Okay, Marine Nigga Recon. Okay." He speaks for about a minute and the Bangers begin to file out of the building, AK-47s in one hand, thirty-round banana clips in the other. Most of them are wearing knapsacks. Farrah Fawcett strips off his jersey and stuffs it into a trouser pocket. He doesn't want to get it dirty. He brushes away some pebbles and lies facedown. The boy yells some instructions and the rest of the Bangers lie facedown next to Farrah Fawcett, a long line of punching bags.

"Must be twenty of them, sir," says Gunny. "Come to fucking ambush us! I'm gonna kill that goddamn translator. Wasn't for Little Joe here, we'd be fighting our way out of a shit sandwich in that alley. I mean, I am going to *kill* that translator."

Armstrong rushes over in a hunch to ask for instructions. His Oakleys have vertical streaks of salt that appear to jail his lenses and the eyes behind them.

"How's the ass?"

"Ain't nothin', sir. Whatabout those motherfucked, there?"

"Take your team and search the Somalis. Rest of us will cover you. No rough stuff. Just flexi-cuff them, check their knapsacks, and we'll process them. Go."

Armstrong takes his team and breaks them into a search element and a cover element, then circles around the Somalis on the road so he does not get in our line of fire. Johnson reaches down and grabs the first knapsack and says something to Armstrong. Johnson spills the pack and about ten fully loaded magazines clatter on the ground. A few grenades. Presents for their Yankee friends. Farrah Fawcett snakes his head around and in an instant Armstrong brings his foot down on the Skinny's head, grinding it into the deck.

"Sergeant Armstrong!" I scream, angry that I sent him in the first place. "At ease! Back your team off totally. Now! Replace Montoya on security." I turn to Montoya, who is across the road, and yell, "Montoya! Replace Armstrong and do a hasty search of the Bangers!" It's very hot out here.

"Called him a nigger again, sir," says Armstrong. "This little fuck called Johnson a nigger. Tried to ambush us. We gonna let that slide?" He's still pushing Farrah's head into the dirt. The other Somalis are straining to watch, now, and two of them begin to stand before Armstrong's men shove their M-16s into their backs, forcing them back on their stomachs. One of the Somalis gets on his knees and I hear the solid thump of a Marine's boot strike his ass.

"Try that again and you're a dead man," the Marine says.

"Damnit," I say under my breath. "Get him away from them before this goes bad, Gun—"

"Sergeant Armstrong!" Gunny yells. He uses their full titles when he's pissed at the Marines. "Stand down and move back. Stand down! Get your foot off the prisoner!"

Armstrong is pushing harder, if anything. "What are we gonna do, Gunny? Let him go? Let . . . this . . . mother . . . FUCKER . . . *GO?*" He pushes harder and harder, twisting his boot back and forth, then releases. For a moment I am so relieved that I am willing to forget the whole thing, let the incident dissipate in the mirage, write it off to the heat. But he raises that big boot and brings it down with all of his might into the lower back of Mrs. Lee Majors, who screeches and rolls over, holding his kidneys.

The Bangers try to stand and Marines are kicking them back onto their faces. Some of them are using their rifle butts. All of the Marines are yelling now. I stand and rush forward but Gunny snags me by my web harness and says, "Stay here and cover, sir. Let me." He runs up to Armstrong and grabs him around the waist, pulling him backward, screaming at him.

The Somali boys rush forward now, punching and grabbing at the Marines, human dustdevils. Montoya's men are in the fray, trying to contain the boys while keeping their weapons aimed at the Bangers. Armstrong's men are slamming their feet into those Bangers who are trying to stand. Team three begins to rush up but I yell for them to stay back; we need at least one security element in place to keep eyes on the surrounding avenues of approach.

Chaos brims at the top of this intersection and then spills over. Marines, kids, and Bangers in a huge blender. I charge forward to help and it's like opening a storm door and stepping out into a hurricane. Gunny is still holding Armstrong back. Two boys grab Gunny's rifle and try to unfasten his sling. Gunny swipes at them with a big backhand and both of them go down and do not immediately get up. I scream at the rest of Armstrong's team to keep their rifles aimed at the Bangers at all costs, then pull a boy off Johnson, who has the muzzle of his rifle jammed into the back of Farrah Fawcett's head. A boy approaches me, smiling, and when I nod at him he flings a rock into my face. My nose cracks and I stumble across the row of Bangers and trip over one. The Banger on the ground next to me reaches for my pistol and I elbow him in the face and spring to my feet, stomping on his head now.

Everyone is screaming. Everyone is fighting. A boy next to me picks up an empty AK-47, struggles to bring it up to his shoulder, and pulls the trigger. There is no magazine but there *is* a round in the chamber and the *crack!* startles every-one: the boys, the Bangers, and the Marines. Thankfully I don't hear a scream follow the bullet.

"Sniper!" someone yells.

"Where? Where!"

Some of the Bangers manage to scramble away in the cyclone of bodies, first crawling, then running. "Let them go!" I scream at a Marine who has raised his rifle. "Let them all go!" We are seconds away from a massacre.

The AK-47 boy is still pulling the trigger but without a magazine he is not a threat. A Marine smashes the butt of his rifle into the kid's face and he sprawls back, screaming. I should have had the Bangers clear the extra rounds from their rifles in front of us, then stacked them in a guarded corner somewhere. *Dumb.*

A boy rushes at Johnson with, what, a flashing . . . a *knife?* I try to reach him but am too late. The boy sticks the metal deep into Johnson's ass and darts back into the crowd.

Johnson reaches back and yanks the dangling blade out, screaming, "Somebody stabbed me in the ass!"

Armstrong's five men can't possibly control the twenty-five Bangers on the ground with all of the boys jumping on them. "Montoya!" I shout. "Do whatever you have to short of killing them to get these kids out of here. Now! If you can't control the Bangers, let 'em go. I want these weapons—"

Someone crashes into me and I fall down on top of one of the Bangers again. Armstrong and the Gunny are wrestling with each other. No, they're wrestling with two—three—boys over an AK-47, Armstrong pulling the tangled bunch of them over me, tripping backward, wresting the AK-47 from the boys with one hand, then dropping it, falling now, still holding on to his weapon with the other hand.

Montoya moves in and kicks two of the boys. Hard. Hard enough so that they stay down and give us some breathing room. He and his men wade into the crowd, kicking and punching. I hear him yelling not to use the rifles on their heads. A small hand shoots over my shoulder and yanks the sunglasses off Armstrong's face. The boy sprints through the crowd, an AK-47 slung over a shoulder, and turns the corner into the alley. I am yelling, "Forget him!" when Armstrong stands and gives chase, his M-16 leading the way. "Let him go!"

Armstrong ignores me.

Gunny and I run over and turn the corner in time to see Armstrong, halfway down the alley, rifle in his shoulder. I hear two rounds from his M-16. *Crack! Crack!* I cannot see what he's shooting at, but beyond Armstrong I see a cloud of dust rise over his head. He walks forward casually—a walk on a summer day—and bends down.

"What's up?" I yell.

Armstrong stands and slowly wipes off his sunglasses. He puts them on and shrugs. "Just getting my Oakleys back, sir." He walks toward us and tries to push us back.

"You don't want to see that. Neither of you. Kid tried to kill me . . . pointed the AK at me."

So this is it. Clarity. The pinnacle of my training, and, ultimately, my breeding. My upbringing. Man stares into the abyss . . .

"What have you done?" Gunny asks. For him it is the sudden, jarring disillusionment that puts weakness in his voice. I'm woozy, too. "What in . . . what in *God's name* did you do?"

I am still too afraid to speak. I trust Gunny's question is rhetorical, because I know the answer. Any hope that the boy survived died with the second shot. Behind me I can hear the dull roar, the noise I heard often before cresting the hill to pick up my sister from the playground, the shouting, the soprano screeches of children, never knowing whether it was pure joy—which it always turned out to be—or if the schoolkids were all being murdered.

Gunny stands on his toes and looks over Armstrong's shoulder, down the alley, but Armstrong jags his head, blocking the view. "Gunny, please. Let it be. You'll only hurt yourself."

"What? The *hell* I will! You killed that boy, you ain't getting some civilian sentence, either. They might even shoot you, Marine. *I* may even shoot you."

Gunny tries to move past but Armstrong puts up an arm. "*What!* Guns . . . you? Sir, tell him. Tell him to let it go. You better." Armstrong puts his hand on the trigger housing of his rifle but I get the sense that he's not using that as the threat. There's something else.

Gunny looks at me and I shake my head. "Stay here with him a sec, Guns. I'll check on the boy."

I run up to the body and kneel down, looking back. Armstrong is talking with the Gunny, arms held out in front of his chest, palms up. The forgiveness dance. Not this time. The boy is so dead that it is hard to believe that only a minute ago he was running. The M-16's 5.56-millimeter rounds are light by design; they travel so quickly that they leave only tiny entrance wounds, but once they get inside the body they bounce off bones and meat, zinging around wildly, tumbling out of control. Sometimes they exit, sometimes they do not. In this case, it is clear that the boy was shot twice—once in the lower back and once in the head— but even as I roll him over I cannot find the exit hole from the round that stung him in the back. The head wound . . . well, it's obvious where that bullet went because the boy has no face.

I am swiftly approaching the valley of the mother-fucked.

His groin is bloody and I have to assume that the second bullet bounced off a rib and spun out down there. I take the AK-47 out of his hand and run back to the Gunny. "Wasted."

"Goddamn you, Armstrong," hisses Gunny. "God *damn* you. I stuck up for you . . . for *you*. Now you know what my main mission's gonna be? To—see—you—*fry*." He pokes his finger into Armstrong's chest. "Killing a child."

Armstrong backs up and his face flushes in anger. "*Child*? That little fucker tried to kill—"

"Don't give me that fucking horseshit!" Gunny shouts. "DON'T YOU DARE." He grabs Armstrong's weapon and yanks him forward.

Time to play good cop for a moment to avoid another death. "Hey! We'll deal with this back at the hangar. We'll go through it by the numbers. Right now we need to get back."

Armstrong is hyperventilating now, a cornered animal. "Sir. I just wanna say that if you or the Gunny tries to burn me . . . you'll have a big, fucking problem, is all . . . from the first night."

"*Us?*" shouts the Gunny. "I stuck up for you!"

"And lied. Both of you."

"What? Oh, I see. Bring it on, son. The lieutenant and me against *you?* Please. Bring . . . it . . . *ON!*"

Gunny, Armstrong, and I walk out of the alley and things are relatively quiet, but that's why I called for Montoya in the first place—Mister Cool. The only men in the alley are wearing the American flag. Montoya says, "Got those kids out of here, sir, without hurtin' anyone. Had to let the Bangers go or there was gonna be a slaughter, though, with everyone running around like that. Crazy. And that Farrah Fawcett cut Joe's face pretty good with a blade."

"You did great, Montoya. Thank you," I say.

Little Joe comes running up to me with a huge bandage on his cheek, still crying. "Farah say if he want to, he kill you whenever he wants. He say he was just in dat building playing. If he want to, he say he come cut all your"—the boy points to his throat and I give him the word—"troats when you sleep. His men here kill your men, Kelly. Your recon men. He know your name. Stretch Armstrong, too."

"They came loaded for bear, sir. You see all those rounds?" asks Montoya.

"Yes." I stare at Armstrong and Gunny for a while before I realize that Montoya is speaking to me, something about moving out. "Right. Yes. Montoya, take a few men and grab the body in the alley. We'll have to hump it back."

"Body? What body, sir?" Montoya asks. The few Marines who are talking fall silent. I take a breath. "Sergeant Armstrong killed one of the boys in the alley."

"*You waxed one, Stretch?* What'd he do?" Montoya asks.

"Ask the lieutenant. He saw the whole thing," says Armstrong.

There is silence again and the hot breeze is making me feel sick, swirling all the dust into my nostrils. I can barely breathe. Damn flak vest is crushing my lungs again. "Just get the fucking body, Montoya. Armstrong, take point and get prepared to move us out."

Montoya returns a few seconds later and says, "Saw the blood, sir, but no body. Skinnies dragged it off. We followed the tracks for a bit—a lot of blood—they lead down a parallel street. Want us to go get him?"

"God, no. We need to di-di, right now. Kids probably dragged him back to his home. Move out. Keep your eyes open."

We are four hundred meters from the airport gate when the Gunny whispers, "It's gonna be his word against ours, sir. And he ain't got no proof about the first night . . . that we knew, I mean. You don't think they'll reopen the investigation, will they?"

"No. Not without proof. Especially because it will be messy for the colonel. And the Corps. But . . . I don't know. I still think what he did that first night was right."

"I'm sorry I dragged you into this, sir. Protecting him, I mean. But you have to understand that that was the right call on that first night . . . given the circumstances. I ain't gonna do the same for him in his court-martial, though."

"We made the choice together. *I* made the decision. As for Armstrong, I don't think we have the proof to court-martial him."

"*What?* He killed that—"

"He killed a boy with a rifle who he will say pointed it at him. He will also say that he had no way of knowing that the rifle was not loaded."

"It had no magazine."

"No, and it didn't have a magazine when that other boy fired it, either. The round was in the chamber. Armstrong will say that he had no way of knowing it was unloaded. No court-martial will be convened. So the question is, in the face of his blackmail threat and no possible penalty from higher up, what do we do about this, Gunny?"

Gunny walks in silence for a hundred meters. We are steps from the gate when he bursts out, "It's not such an easy call, sir. I mean, if he *does* manage to convince someone to open the Said Lahti thing again, well, then we're looking at twenty years *at a minimum* for obstruction of justice. I got five little girls, sir. *Five.* I couldn't do it to them. And I won't be locked up like some animal. That ain't civvie time, either."

The Gunny is right, of course. In the civilian world we might get a light sentence, or plea it out entirely in exchange for testimony, but not in the Marine Corps. It will become an international incident. And where do the bad boys of the military serve their time? Fort Leavenworth, Kansas. An added bonus: Civilian murderers at the Fort get two hours of recreation time and four hours of visitations a week; military prisoners rise at 0600, work all day with just a half-hour recreation break, and are permitted a visitor every other week.

"But this has got to stop," Gunny continues. "I am so disappointed in myself for defending him. Makes me sick. Giving away my integrity for a goddamn *murderer.* He's going to burn for this, sir. And we have to do our part here on earth."

"Agreed. We do what's right. Thing I'm thinking of will hurt Armstrong the most."

"I'm thinking the same thing, sir. Colonel may not convene a court-martial but we still have authority within the platoon. You want to fire him, or should I?"

"Joint exercise. He's finished in this platoon—we'll relieve him after I tell the colonel tonight—and I'll give him a double-signed fitness report. Armstrong's career as a Marine is over."

I nod at the gate guard and as we pass into the compound Gunny whispers, "I'm so sorry for this, sir. Sorrier than you'll ever know. But it's going to get worse before it gets better."

The sunset emboldens Jake Armstrong's eyes and they start to glow when the liquid seeps into them. His entire face seems to converge on his nose, tightening inward, quivering. His eyes are suddenly red and he grits his teeth. Gunny's just given him the word. "You two don't about-face right now—I mean *right fucking now*—I'm taking you down—both of you! You can't *do* this! I'm the one who's kept this platoon together, kept it *alive,* for fuck's sake. I saved your *fucking life, sir!* Twice! That kid shot at me."

The Gunny shakes his head and hisses, "It's done. Here's the official letter, signed by the colonel. I have nothing else to say to you. The colonel wants you to report to him. He's taking you into headquarters company. Now."

Armstrong's shaking, he's so angry and hurt. "The *REMFs!* ME! You're finished, Gunny. I mean it. You don't tear up that letter right now you're comin' with me. Both of you! It's . . . *This place has no rules and I was just tryin' to keep things right.*"

Gunny grunts. "Get out of my face and get your ass over to the colonel. I think he's going to make you a mess crank or something. You'll be serving me breakfast tomorrow. The entire platoon. Dismissed."

He balls his hands and Gunny says, "Please, try it, motherfucker," and Armstrong says, crying now, "I *am* a motherfucker . . . and you're going to get yours. Kiss your career good-bye. And your precious little career, too, Lieutenant Do-Nothing." He spits on Gunny's boots and strides over to the colonel's hooch.

Gunny turns after a moment and says, "What's the old man got in store for him?"

"Don't know . . . maybe make him his driver. Or make him the battalion poster boy."

– 22 –

4 FEBRUARY 1993

Mayor: And I don't want any more problems like you had last year in the Fillmore district. That's my policy.

Harry: When I see a man with intent to commit rape, I shoot the bastard. That's my policy.

Mayor: Intent? How did you establish that?

Harry: When I saw a naked man chasing a woman down an alley with a butcher knife and a hard-on, I didn't think he was collecting for the Red Cross.

The sun rises fast in Africa for some reason, severing the night and our dreams as quickly as it can, as if reminding us of what a hellhole this place really is. It's been a long two days since Armstrong's departure from the platoon—what with Lance Corporal Johnson's near mutiny before he grudgingly accepted his meritorious promotion back to corporal and the team leader billet that came with it—and I'm ecstatic that we're leaving tomorrow, happier still that the colonel is keeping our platoon hot and safe behind the airport walls so I can't trip any more mines.

There is a leadership gap in the platoon that neither the Gunny nor I can fill; Armstrong was the best and the bravest warrior, and the tribe is still unsettled, casting narrow glances at Guns and me even as we tried to explain our decision for the third or fourth time last night. "Nothing— not these fubared rules, this fubared country, or even the ambush—excuses Armstrong. He shot a kid who stole his sunglasses," I said last night when it was clear the platoon needed another meeting. "Let me say again: stole his sunglasses."

"Kid had a rifle, sir," said Corporal Johnson, the platoon's new mouthpiece.

"Yes. And that *kid* was running away. Sergeant Armstrong was not in imminent danger. We all know that," I said, glancing around for a friendly pair of eyeballs and finding none.

"Stretch said he was getting shot at, sir. Said you could tell by the position of the body."

"Yes, Sergeant Armstrong said that. But the Gunny and I were there, too. We saw the body before it was dragged away. Look, the decision stands. He's out of recon."

"He saved my life from a grenade, sir. Probably saved me from losing another stripe when that Farrah called me a nigger, too. Saved your life, too, sir. Right? Hell, he probably saved a bunch of reporters' skins, on that first night," Johnson continues.

"The. Decision. Stands."

"Well," said Johnson, borrowing his idol's vernacular.

"Well," I said, and then dismissed the platoon.

Montoya and Johnson stayed behind with me and the Gunny. I raised my eyebrows and Montoya coughed. "Uh, sir, uh. You saw how confusing it was. How dangerous. It was *wild* out there. Jake shouldn't be burned because of this." Montoya glanced at Johnson, then just kept staring at me, licking his lips.

"Look. As a Marine he had to be able to switch it on and switch it off. Yes, it was wild during that wrestling match, but he failed to throw it back into low gear when that kid snatched his glasses."

Montoya nodded silently, but Johnson persisted after grimacing at the sergeant. "I got two points, sir. One, that kid was armed and nobody knows except Jake what happened. I mean, what *really* happened in that alley. So we were just . . . we want to know why he wasn't taken at his word. Second, how's a Marine supposed to 'turn it off' or 'downshift' when he's—"

"THE LIEUTENANT DISMISSED YOU!" roared Gunny from out of nowhere. "MAN, I'M SICK OF YOUR BULL-SHIT! GO!"

The two men jumped back and I watched them walk in silence back to their holes, Johnson shaking his head and mumbling something. I was left thinking that I had screwed up again, this time choosing the book over the man too hastily, one of my *own men*.

This morning the feeling of regret is stronger. Who knows what happened in that alley? I dismissed Armstrong's version immediately. Perhaps I missed something. I tap the sleeping man at my feet so we can go over the shooting again. Gunny has moved into my hole per Johnson's request, swapping with Doc, and he wakes quickly, slides his flak vest over his cammies, stuffs his helmet over his big head, and sticks his arm through the shoulder sling of his weapon.

"Morning," I say after five minutes. Gunny's not a morning person.

"Yup."

"Just a day and a wake-up, Guns. You feel like breakfast? I heisted a pork patty meal."

"Not if you're cooking, sir."

It's meant to be a joke, but neither of us laughs. I hand him the heavy plastic MRE package. "I feel like the platoon is broken because of what we've done, Guns. I mean, if you think about it, we just put Armstrong in a very, very bad position. He's meant to fight, not scrap his way across a confusing set of rules that say he can shoot his ambushers one minute and must let them go the next. I . . . I don't know."

Gunny doesn't answer right away, which is just my luck, considering he is the only person besides Big Duke that I can talk to about this. He cuts a slice of C-4 from the block the engineers traded him, impales it on the tip of his Ka-Bar, and sticks it into the base of a tiny firepit he's constructed with some rocks. He lights it and it glows bright blue and soothing, then he sets his metal canteen cup on top of the cooking block and covers it with his green government-issue notebook to prod the water into a boil.

He's ripping the thick plastic cover of my pork patty MRE with his teeth to get at my coffee packet when he says, "*We* haven't done anything, sir. It was *Jake Armstrong* who done something. And it was wrong. Period. And no excuses about this *fucked-up* country or the fact that minutes before he killed that boy we were *fucking ambushed* and that Armstrong stopped a grenade with his *fucking back* changes that. He put us in the position. We had to choose between doing what was right, and doing what was right for him. And no man's that good. No man's got enough personal capital to buy his way out of shooting a boy."

"I feel strange about it."

"You don't think it burns me? Well, it does. It's *killing* me, sir. I known that man for four years. Like you, I owe him my life. But we did right." He's pissed and his hands are shaking when he tears the foil packet open and dumps the contents into the water.

"I'm having second thoughts about rushing to judgment."

"Yeah?" he says shortly. "Well, don't. We done right."

"The platoon doesn't think so."

He slaps the top of the cup and it douses the thirsty sand and goes tumbling across the dirt. He leans right into my face and hisses, "I don't give a fuck *what* the platoon thinks. I mean, God! Grow up, sir. You're the platoon commander! I'm the platoon sergeant! You want to have a *fucking vote? We* are the law."

The light catches his eyes and his pupils shrink, the sun coming back at me as tiny white circles in his brown irises. His eyebrows pop up and back and his shoulders come back into level. He shakes his head and sighs, then clasps me on the shoulder and chuckles. He knows I'm shaken.

"I'm . . . *damn,* I'm sorry, sir. You know better than to ask for rational answers from me in the morning!" He smiles and I try to fake one. "Look. Like any family, this platoon's had its ups and downs. We are in a down. But in a wake-up we're bound for home and then, after a few weeks, the Marines will understand we did the right thing. And you know what, it's not important that they agree. What's important is that *we* agree, and even if the family's in a down, the heads of that family—you and me—have to stay together. We did right."

I nod and sneak a glance over his shoulder, looking to change the subject. Gunny's right, of course, and I'm embarrassed that I've allowed myself to be emotionally whipsawed. I point at a crowd of Pakistani soldiers standing in line for food near the hangar. With the UN takeover we are no longer allowed to eat in—or even go into—the makeshift chow hall in the hangar. The Air Force has somehow cut a deal but the Marines have been relegated to lurker status, trying to stuff down cold pork patty rations while the aroma of eggs and bread drifts over to us. We spent yesterday shuffling around the compound like beggars, erecting a tiny shantytown to manufacture our own shade. You'd think with the colonel's Italian ancestry we'd get a break, but he probably knows that the best Marine is an angry Marine.

"You want me to raid us some chow?"

"No, Gunny, I'm not hungry," I tell him.

Gunny grunts and gazes over my shoulder at the ocean. He sighs. "Me neither."

He hops out of the hole and picks up the canteen cup, tosses it into the foxhole, and sighs again. He looks at me and shakes his head sadly. There isn't much to say. There is much to say.

"You know your buddy Phillips is out with Armstrong today."

"*What?*"

Gunny nods and spits. No saliva comes out. "Colonel made Stretch a driver. He's showing the UN one of the convoy routes through our old sector. I guess Phillips and Mary Thayer-Ash are trying to get some last-minute footage or something. Doing a story on the UN turnover and convinced the colonel to let them accompany a food convoy. Armstrong knows that section and he's leading the convoy."

"That's unbelievable."

"No. Sir, I've seen so much trash here that something

like that's just become par for the course, part of this goat
rodeo landscape."

I watch Gunny walk toward the hangar and I feel alone.
I settle deep into the hole and try to gnaw some nutrients
from the patty between sips of bottled water. The patty is
hard as a rock and after thirty minutes of sucking it like a
Popsicle I've finally made a dent. A shadow slips over me
and rain starts to fall; I look up and I see that it's just Big
Duke who's trotted over after a run and is sweating his face
off.

"You mind backing up, Big Duke, I'm getting wet."

"Thought that pork patty could use some salt. Sorry."
He lifts his shirt to wipe his brow and I see my father's tattoo again.

"You never did tell me how you got that slash."

"I got my slash by grabbing this NVA officer type. Was
pretty proud of it then but now . . . nah."

"The war?"

"No. The *tattoo*. The war, shit, I'm very proud about
that. Very proud. Never should have left the South Viets in
the lurch. See, men like me and your dad, we'd go back and
fight it to a finish if we could. Ask your old man next time
you see him."

"Big Duke, I told you he won't tell me. He disassociates
himself totally from the Corps. He didn't come to my commissioning ceremony, the Gulf War parade, nothing. You
think my father would go back to Vietnam today? To fight?
No way. Not my father."

He leans down into the hole and whispers, "Tom Kelly?
In a heartbeat, sir, *in a heartbeat*."

"I don't know."

He hops in the hole, grunts, and sits right next to me.
"Well, then, you don't know your old man all that well
when it comes to his war. You ever consider that maybe

Tom didn't go to your commissioning because he was embarrassed by his court-martial? Figured he wasn't honorable enough? Let me ask you a question: Did you invite him?"

"I told him about the ceremonies."

"Did you *invite* him, sir?"

"I don't know what you're saying."

He exhales loudly and shakes his head. "Let me try again. When's the last time you thanked him for fighting in Vietnam?"

I just shrug. I'm not sure if I ever have and I sure as hell know Red never did.

"Because if you didn't, who did? Probably nobody, sir, *probably nobody.* So next time you see him, you tell him Little Duke Duncan and the boys been trying to find him and that he shouldn't have gone into hiding. We always looked at Tom Kelly as a hero—his court-martial didn't mean nothing to us except the fact he got burned for making us all feel a bit better about what we were doing up at the DMZ. And, sir, you tell him all the boys just wanted to thank him. Can you remember that?"

"*Little* Duke?"

He shrugs. "I didn't like my old nickname, so when I got enough rank I changed it."

"You really think he'd go back to fight?"

"Let me ask *you* a question now, sir. Let's say you lost half your platoon to the Somalis tomorrow because of restrictions on how you could fight. The Gunny. Let's say Gunny Ricketts was shot and hacked to death. Dragged all over the streets. Then the next day you were told to leave, that the war was over. You get home and people are embarrassed for you. Ashamed. Avoid the subject. Some even hate your fucking guts. Colm Callan—your dad knows him—when he flew into San Francisco with that hook for a hand of his, a woman asked him if he lost it in the war. When he said he had, she said, 'Good. You deserve it.'

"Twenty years later, if you didn't feel the fire burning white hot to right that wrong, well, then I'd say you shouldn't be in command today. I'm . . . I hate to use the word 'bitter,' but goddamned if I don't think about all the things that went wrong every day. The Marines I lost. The anger. Every day! Every *goddamned* day."

He spits out the last few words through gritted teeth and hops out of the hole, leaving me reeling, searching my memory for the pieces with which I might have solved this puzzle myself. There are a few. When I was eleven I went fishing with my father, my grandfather, and my grandfather's friend from The Big One.

We were into bluefish immediately, and I struggled against mine fiercely, pride pitted against survival. My rod bowed wildly each time the fish jerked and ran, and my grandfather peppered me with comments. "Keep that rod tip up. I said keep it up! Get it up! Keep pressure on him, Gavin. Show him who's in control." I think he was worried that I would lose that fish in front of his friend, and when the comments became obsessive my father tried to interrupt and was rebuked.

"Stop babying the boy," Red said, "or he'll end up a real brownnoser when he grows up."

I reeled continuously, until my forearms burned. I placed my palm flat on the handle and tried to push it around in a circle, slowly grinding after every yank of the rod, praying that the fish would die. But he did not and I quit.

"You don't *ever* quit nothing," Red hissed, glancing back at his friend. "Not if you're a grandson of mine."

My father was suddenly in front of me, grabbing the

line and yanking. "You got him, Gav! Just a few more feet! I can see him!" He started to pull, hand over hand.

I reeled in the slack, incredibly grateful, noticing the blood that was beginning to drain down the line as my father tugged and tugged with his bare hands.

My grandfather gaffed the bluefish. It was a big blue, close to twenty pounds, and my grandfather held it away from his body as it thrashed around. Blood and saltwater flew in all directions, and for a second I was happy because I thought my grandfather might drop him. His forearms were too strong, though, and even with one hand he was able to control the eruption.

"Back up, guys," Red told us. He pulled out a billy club and smashed it across the blue's head with a *crack!* The fish quivered and jerked the gaff right out of his grip and onto the deck, thrashing its way into the fuel line.

"I'll be god*damned*," he said. He tried to snag the gaff but it was snapping back and forth on the deck too quickly, cracking and bouncing as the fish flapped its way toward the center console.

My father hopped over the fish like a bear stalking salmon, just watching its movements initially, gently pushing my grandfather back. He yanked the bluefish up by the gaff and brought the bat down in a blur, nearly tearing the fish in half at the gaff point. I'd never seen my father move like that, and haven't since.

He turned the gaff upside down and the fish slipped into the box. He shut the lid and told me, "You're on guard duty, sport." He was smiling.

I sat on the fish box, smiling. A few minutes later the box thundered to life, as if the fish were digging itself out of the grave. I leaped off the box and ran into my father's arms, screaming. My grandfather said, "Some guard!" He was in a good mood after the battle.

Didn't he realize that this particular fish could not be killed? "It's alive!" I screamed.

Dad nodded and smiled. "They're tough fish, bluefish. Don't like to die easily."

"Unlike some Japs we've known," my grandfather's friend said, laughing.

Red joined in heartily. "A lot tougher! That fish is a lot tougher!"

I laughed, too, though I did not get the joke. If there was one. When it was quiet, my grandfather, who had been drinking steadily, said, "Bet them Vietnamese wasn't tougher than the Japs, just Tom's hippie generation didn't want to fight 'em, is all. Wanted nothing to do with 'em."

They were silent for a time before my father said in a voice so low that it was nearly a whisper, "That's not true. I'd go back now if we could bring everyone back to life and do it right. Gavin, grab another bunker and get us another fish as nice as that, will ya, pal?"

I never heard my father talk about Vietnam and I assumed he hated the war. But maybe the war itself did not bother him. The bitterness did, the sting of betrayal by those who prevented him from winning and those who hated him when he returned. How could that have happened?

When the Gulf War veterans were honored with a ticker-tape parade immediately following the war, the Vietnam veterans led the march and many Marines invited their fathers. I invited my grandfather instead. But that parade wasn't for me or for Red, it was for the veterans who didn't get a parade for their war. Or even a thank-you. It was for my father.

———

Joe shakes me out of my daydream when he bursts into the compound screaming his head off. Gunny is somehow at my side—how long has he been here?—and he intercepts the boy, hefting him onto a hip. Doc hears his future adopted son's screams, too, and he comes sprinting over without his flak jacket, but I let it slide considering how wild the boy is.

"Kelly! Kelly, Farah gon' kill de"—Little Joe has reached out and is yanking on my shirt—"get de recon! Get de recon!" He is uncharacteristically out of breath.

"Whoa. Easy—"

"You, recon, come wit me! Gunny! Get dem! You come wit me!" He squirms out of the Gunny's grip like a crazed snake and pulls at my arm.

"Slow down, Joe." I pat his head. "Speak slow. Sloooww."

"What's wrong, Joe?" asks Doc.

"Dad! Farah gon' kill Stretch!" screams Joe, spit flying.

"*What?*" Doc, Gunny, and I say together.

"He tell de men dat Stretch Armstrong recon now drive de truck dis morning to FDC. He gon' kill him for Stretch kilt Muhammad Ali and Muhammad Lahti and Yusef Malim and Hassan Akimi! De whole Heeber Geeder gonna wait for him."

"*Who?*" says Doc. "Who's Hassan? And how'd he find out—"

I put my hand over Doc's mouth. "Must be Nike Boy and the kid from yesterday. Hassan and Yusef, I mean, who Armstrong shot. And another fucking translator must have leaked where Armstrong was going to be. I didn't know the colonel would make him a *driver,* for Chrissakes. Gunny, where's he going?"

Gunny shrugs.

"Joe? *Where did Farrah say he was going?*"

"I don't talk to Farah . . ."

"The *other* men. Where do they say Stretch goes?"

"De FDC."

"*What* FDC?"

"Laido! He go to Laido, Kelly. I run to Heeber Geeder street right now to watch dem. Dat where he gonna do it. I go now. Right now. You go der?"

"You stay here where it's safe!" Doc screams, too late. The boy leans forward and tromps right over toward the wall. Doc runs after him. "Hey! Joe! I said stop right there, young man!"

But the boy dives through the hole.

"We outbound, sir?" asks Gunny.

I grab my rifle and nod. "Grab Montoya's team and have the Hummer ready to go. Fully loaded. I'm going to go tell the colonel."

"If they go for Armstrong, you know your buddy Phillips ain't gonna sit by and watch that happen."

"No," I say. "He sure as hell won't."

I sprint into the hangar and the Italian sentry tries to stop me by extending an arm. I slap it aside and listen to his shouts as I'm barreling through the chow line. It's a beautiful language. In my moment of panic I am finally experiencing total understanding. I did wrong and now I'll pay for it. And, *If You let me out of this, let Darren—and Armstrong—out of this with their lives . . .*

I run through a group of screaming Pakistanis, crash into a Bangladeshi's tray and spin free, then sprint to the opposite side of the hangar where our battalion radio operators are still set up. They are in constant communication with the convoys and the helicopters that watch them in case they get lost.

"I need to get word to the convoy headed to Laido. Can you raise them, please?" I ask one of the Marines on radio watch.

He doesn't even look up from his magazine. "Nosir. Haven't had them up since they got into downtown Mogadishu. Comms suck when they're in the city. Anyway, that's the Italian's convoy, really."

I need to play this coolly. "Corporal, there are Marines leading the convoy. I said to try to raise them. So *try*. I want you to tell that convoy to return to the airport immediately. Got me?"

He drops the magazine and nods. "Why, sir?"

"You just do it, Marine." Tick. Tock.

"Colonel Capiletti's signed off on this, sir?"

"YES."

"And the Italians are good with it?"

There are two Italian radio operators next to this Marine so I grab him by his collar, push my face next to his ear, and whisper, "I said, Marines need our help. Okay?"

He nods. "Aye-aye. I don't think we'll have luck reaching the trucks while they're in the city, but I'll try the helo. We've got a Huey monitoring all the convoys. You're talking about Convoy Bravo, right sir? Going to Laido?" He points at the big map on the board. Convoy Bravo's route is outlined with a highlighter. "I'll call the helicopter and see if they can raise them."

"Good man."

He picks up the handset to a radio and says, "Talon, this is Vader. Is the Charlie Bravo still at Fantasia? Over."

"Vader, this is Talon," says the pilot. "We are not over Fantasia at this time, but we assume they're still loading up at the port. Over."

"Talon, I need you to get an urgent message to the convoy . . ."

"Lieutenant Kelly!" someone behind me barks. It's the colonel.

"Sir," I say. "I need to speak—"

"My former office. Now!"

I grab the map off the board and turn to follow Bison

Breath. "Sir!" says the radio operator, too loudly. "Sir, I need that map. And should I still give the order to withdraw?"

"What are you doing, Kelly? What order?" asks Bison Breath.

"We've got to stop Convoy Bravo, sir. I think the warlords are planning an ambush."

"*Ambush?* Where did you hear this?"

"The little boy who hangs around my platoon, sir. He—"

He starts walking briskly across the hangar and I fall in behind. "Now just a minute. We get three threats a day. Hell, the *CIA* sources have been promising an attack on the compound from day one. So far, not one of these threats— not one—has come true. Now you just gave an order to stop a convoy without my permission—a convoy I set up as part of the handover, to get the UN comfortable—on the statement of a Somali *boy*? How in the hell—"

"Sir, it's good scoop. He saved our lives in that alley. Same kid. We need them out of there."

The colonel's still striding and I assume I'm being dragged to the carpet to be chewed out for running into the Bangladeshi. "Look, Lieutenant. Like I said, we get threats about every convoy. We can't go suddenly canceling one of our most important ones because of a boy's rumor. I sent Sergeant Armstrong to show two of the Italian officers that good route we've been using. Can't cancel this one. It'll look terrible."

"Sir! Phillips and Ash are with that—"

The colonel sticks his finger into my chest. "*You* better start thinking about *yourself*, mister. There is a very serious allegation waiting in there for you. And I'll be damned if I can explain it."

I see the Hummer waiting for me at the gate, Gunny raising his hands, so I stick up an index finger. My legs feel heavy and my mind shuts down. I fall in behind the colonel, fighting the urge to grab him and beg for mercy, beg him to give me a chance to get Darren and Armstrong before he finds me guilty of . . . *what?* Here we go, baby. All the way. Go straight to jail. Do not pass go. Do not collect $200.

Before we enter his office I grab Bison Breath's arm and say, "Sir. Please. This kid knows what he's talking about. Please recall that convoy. Or let me go get them. I've got a vehicle waiting."

Colonel Capiletti squints at me and nods his head. "You feel that strongly about it? We're going to look like we're backing down to ghosts if we do that. Look, I still have a radio in the hooch. I'll ask the general to monitor, and if it's dicey I'll request extraction. It's his show now, unfortunately, and his sector."

I'm thanking the colonel when he knocks on the hatch, requests entrance, and steps inside. When I step in behind him my heart—which has been thundering along as if an animal is trapped behind my breastbone—stops. I mean it; it just stops. General Bellissimo stops a conversation and stares at me as if I'm a child molester or something. A woman in a CNN cap is sitting down, staring at me, smiling sadly. There are two other American civilians—reporter types—and two senior UN officers, one Italian and one Pakistani.

"Sit," says the colonel.

"I'd . . . rather stand, sir."

"*Sit down, Lieutenant Kelly,*" says General Bellissimo.

Go straight to jail.

I check my watch and force myself into the chair, careful to check for electric wiring and duct tape. I imagine Gunny sitting in the Hummer, revving the engine. He's a smart man. Money on the fact that he has realized I'm in hock; he's already gone. Then again, he'll have to finesse his way past the gate guards ... and without bars on his collar, an unscheduled departure may be a tough proposition. I hope he's found a way to leave without me.

"Sir, do you mind if I monitor Convoy Bravo's tac net? I have some information that the convoy is in jeopardy and I may have them return to base," says Colonel Capiletti, already walking over to the radio.

"Information from whom, Vincent?" asks the general, still staring at me.

"A reliable source, sir."

"Nonsense! We have informants throughout the clans and I would know such a thing."

Colonel Capiletti ignores him and switches on the radio, quickly punching in the appropriate frequency and turning up the white-noise static volume. "You're probably right, sir," he says as he walks back over toward me. With his back turned to the general, he gives me a quick wink that is immensely settling in this shrinking room, teeming with the enemy, brimming full of people who are trying to crush me. But Colonel Capiletti is not one of these. No, he walks abreast of me, does a crisp about-face, and stands at parade rest, his elbow nearly resting on my shoulder like a giant bodyguard.

General Bellissimo regards my colonel for a moment before he speaks. "Lieutenant, I just received some information that concerns me greatly. I thought it best to talk to you before I do anything formal. Miss Casey?"

The general points at the woman in the CNN cap but Colonel Capiletti interrupts. "Well, let's be clear here, Kelly. You are under no obligation to speak. We're just after a reasonable explanation. Understand? An *explanation*. Miss Casey."

She coughs awkwardly, caught between a Bellissimo and a Capiletti. "I'm Jackie Casey and I'm in charge of the remaining CNN crew here in Somalia. I . . . I'm sorry to bring this up, really. But I have no choice. I . . . well, Lieutenant Kelly, I got a long note this morning from one of your sergeants . . ."

Do not pass go.

"Probably Armstrong. I relieved him for cause two days ago, Ms. Casey."

"Yes, from Jake Armstrong and, yes, I know you relieved him, Lieutenant," she says with, what? Sorrow? "I know you did." She looks at me and sighs sadly.

Do not collect $200.

"But I can't ignore these." She holds up two plastic bags; each one contains a fluorescent press badge. Damn it, Guns! You never should have trusted Armstrong to destroy them, you should have done it yourself!

I have entered the world of the motherfucked.

She sighs again and shakes her head. "Normally I'd have ignored the note . . . it was so obviously *venomous*." She looks at her shoes and bites her lip. "This is difficult. Specifically, Sergeant Armstrong alleges that a Gunnery Sergeant Jarius Ricketts ordered him to cover up the Said Lahti killing when he saw Said was an official part of the press corps. He writes that Ricketts grabbed the press badges off Muhammad and his brother and told him to destroy them. He says that he thinks you knew about the gunnery sergeant's actions and condoned them. Armstrong goes on to write that he was feeling guilty about his actions and approached both you and Ricketts. Then he says you fired him to make sure he had no credibility when he decided to come forward.

"But Armstrong didn't destroy the passes like Ricketts told him to. He kept them bagged up instead. He writes that if we send these badges to a crime lab, they'll find two sets of fingerprints: his and Gunnery Sergeant Ricketts's.

I . . . boy, it sounds like he's covering his tracks, but we just want to be sure. I have informed NBC, of course. Eric. Bill." She nods at the two American men, both of whom are giving me snake eyes, then holds up the plastic bag in case I missed it the first time.

The colonel coughs and says, "An explanation, Lieutenant. Give us an explanation."

When I'm silent, he tries to help. "Is this just a disgruntled Marine, or what? You've been tracking all the problems you've had with him, right?" He is nervous, too, and he's sweating. It's his watch.

"Ah, yes, Vincent. Problems that would cause you to recommend him for an award, yes? Bragging to me about him? This is the same man?" asks General Bellissimo sternly.

Colonel Capiletti turns his head slowly and says, "Yessir. It is."

I am trembling, the jolt to my nerves so severe that I struggle to maintain my balance, even seated in a chair. I'm a circuit breaker that's snapped, a nuclear reactor that's tripped. They stare at me as my mouth starts to form a word, and even I don't know what it is.

"Vader, this is Talon, over," the radio says. That's the helicopter calling.

"Talon, this is Vader, go ahead, over," the radio answers itself. We are listening to the radio operator's conversation with the helicopter that should be, by now, hovering over Armstrong's convoy. All heads turn and watch the green box.

"Roger. We've got a crowd forming about five klicks north of Fantasia. They're burning some stacks of tires, it looks like. Lots of women and kids, but lots of males with rifles, too, over."

Colonel Capiletti strides over to the radio and cuts in.

"Break. Break. Talon, this is Vader Six. Repeat, this is the *six*. Are they formed up or just milling around? The indigenous males?" He's watching me as if I'm supposed to read some secret message.

"Vader Six, this is Talon. They are not organized, just setting fires to bunches of tires along the road. But this is the first time we've seen so many men with rifles, over."

"Vincent," says General Bellissimo, "may I remind you that they are *allowed* to walk around with small-arms rifles and that there's no law against those tire fires. We've seen it dozens of times. Now. Where is this little . . . *event* taking place?"

The colonel crooks his finger and I practically leap up, unfurling the map as I approach the men. I point to the area and Colonel Capiletti says, "Golf five, sir."

General Bellissimo stares at the map. "Very well. Italian sector. I'll have a few vehicles on standby," he pronounces. He turns to the Italian officer in the corner and says, "Giacomo," followed by a string of graceful Italian. The man nods, snaps his shiny black boots together, and walks out of the hatch, shooting me a nasty glance as he passes.

I feel Colonel Capiletti's hand press a folded piece of paper into mine, beneath the desk, and when the general tells me to sit again, I say, yessir and turn my back so I can read the colonel's note:

Go get your people.

"Now, Lieutenant," says Bellissimo. "As I remember it, you were about to tell us something?"

Colonel Capiletti steps in front of me and says, "Sir. I'd like a moment with everyone before we proceed. With Kelly out of the room. We have to make sure we're following the proper steps according to the Uniform Code of Military Justice and I'm not sure we've thought this through. I also request you order that convoy to turn around right now."

Bellissimo considers it and finally says, "Lieutenant Kelly, you are dismissed. As for your second request, Vincent, I will turn my convoy around if I deem it necessary, no need to panic."

I reach for the hatch and before Bellissimo can change his mind I'm out and running. I run Big Duke over and he pushes me off with a huff. "Jesus, sir. You knocked the hell out of me."

"Sorry, Big Duke. I got to make an emergency head call. I'll be right back."

"Don't let me stop you, sir. You're sweating all over the place. You look terrible." He glances past me to the Gunny and the Hummer. "Got any room for an old man?"

"It's my fight."

"Yes, it is."

I nod and smile weakly, push past him, then sprint as fast as I can toward the Hummer. I hop in the passenger seat and find a stack of loaded magazines and some grenades and duct tape waiting for me.

I look at the Gunny and nod. That's all he needs. *Punch it, Chewy.* The Hummer spins in the gravel and sand for a second—Gunny's given it too much gas—but then the wheels catch and we jerk forward, shooting out of the gate and onto the pavement, where we gain some speed, Gunny laying on the horn now, passing trucks and cows, blasting toward Mogadishu's red-light district.

I plop four of the grenades into their nylon pouches and tape the other two to my harness, then I stuff the magazines into their holding patterns and toss the rest into my right cargo pocket so I have access when I'm flat on my stomach.

"What took you so long, sir?" asks Montoya. "Gunny wanted to leave but we knew how much you'd bitch if you missed this!"

In the back of my Hummer is a sight that would warm the heart of any good gang leader—which I am, really, a lieutenant in the roughest gang in the world, with a death list to its credit that's big enough to replace the population of Connecticut. We're going to bang, and I've got seven fully loaded, armored beasts sitting with me, one giving me the thumbs-up, the others simply nodding. Hell, I've even got a doctor with me. You think Crips, Disciples, or Bloods show up at their gunfights even half as prepared?

"This frequency correct?" I ask, holding up the handset of the radio.

"Yessir," says Gunny. "You heard the Gangbangers are gathering around, lighting tires?"

"Heard that. There they are, in fact." I point at the jet black plumes rising above the city two miles in front of us. "Remind you of anything?"

"Let's just hope it's as easy."

I fold the map and try to focus on the web maze of street names with my hands waving like I'm trying to fan a big fire. The Hummer is a powerful vehicle, but that doesn't make for a smooth ride. "Go straight past the K-Four and down Lenin Road. We'll go until we get even with the smoke, then make a right at the first plume and cut them off."

Gunny screeches around the roundabout and nearly smashes into a bus. I smell burning rubber and then diesel fumes from the bus. "Move!" he yells, leaning on the horn. The air blasts don't do a thing; I'm sure brights will be ignored just as much as they are in the States. Gunny gives the bus some distance, then plows the front of the Hummer into the tailgate. It comes to a skidding halt on the right side of the road and crunches up against a plaster wall, eradicating it. The Hummer fishtails slightly, ripping a huge chunk of tin from the back of the bus, and shoots forward through an intersection, where it strikes a donkey.

Somehow the beast is up on the hood, sliding toward us. It crashes through the windshield and I duck my head. The Plexiglas explodes. Gunny slams on the brakes and I'm thrown forward into the dash. My helmet clunks against the heater and bounces back against the seat's headrest. Dust and sand fill the cab and it takes a second before I can see the Gunny, so thick is the cloud. "You okay?" I ask.

"Good to go. Helmet dinged up, is all. Montoya?"

"Everyone's alive back here, Gunny. I always said New Yorkers can't drive. What'd we hit?"

"A horse," he says.

"Donkey," I say. The cloud has dissipated enough and the animal is gone. "Where'd it go?"

Gunny leans back and kicks out the remainder of the windshield with a shot that would do the dead mule proud. I brush off the glass and check for cuts. There's a piece of hairy donkey meat on my lap but there is no human blood. The flak vest and helmet have saved me. Colonel Capiletti's order has saved me.

An old man's head appears in my window, screaming at me. He grabs my nose and twists it. How rude.

"What's he want?" yells the Gunny, revving the engine again.

"You killed his mule."

"The United States government will pay you for your horse, sir!" he screams. The Hummer lurches forward and we pick up speed quickly, rumbling down Lenin Road, an inauspicious name for a street down which some young capitalists with rifles are cruising for action.

"VADER, THIS IS TALON!" the radio suddenly bursts out. Panic is an easy read over the airwaves. Everyone gets into the zone. "We see a barricade being put up in front of the convoy! Repeat, some indigenous personnel have erected a *barricade* in front of the convoy! There is a large crowd gathering in front of it. Request instructions, over."

Thankfully it is Colonel Capiletti who answers, not Bellissimo. "Talon, this is Vader Six. Can you set your bird down if necessary? Over."

"Negative, Vader Six. The buildings are too close together!"

"Tell the convoy to take the alternate route, over."

"Roger, Vader. *Break. Break.* Charlie Bravo, this is Talon, over!"

"Talon, this is Charlie Bravo," says Armstrong, who could be yawning. "Copied all about the barricade and we're taking the alternate route. I have a truck with civvies in it following me, over." He can hear the helicopter but he can't hear Colonel Capiletti's broadcasts. His is the only calm voice on the net.

My Hummer is about a mile from the convoy that Armstrong is trying to steer. *Just give me five minutes. Please. Just five and You can have the rest of my life.*

"Talon, this is Charlie Bravo," says Armstrong's radio voice, still calm. "We've run into another barricade here trying to get off the MSR. I'm going to dismount and try to get these two trucks turned around. Road we're on now is too narrow to turn around in. I've also got two reporters with me. We'll have to back everyone out."

"Charlie Bravo, this is Talon. Copy. We'll hover above you. Watch the crowd on the MSR. I say again, watch the crowd. They're . . . Watch it! THEY'RE MOVING TOWARD YOU! OVER!"

"Copy."

I feel as if I'm listening to an eerie 911 tape playing back scenes as a terrible tragedy unfolds.

"*Break. Break.* Talon, this is Vader Six." Colonel Capiletti is back on the net. "You tell Charlie Bravo to abandon those food trucks, get in that pickup truck, and get the heck *out* of there. Now! Over." Good call, sir.

"Roger that. *Break.* Charlie Bravo, this is Talon, over." No response. "CHARLIE BRAVO, THIS IS TALON!" Again, silence. "Vader, Charlie Bravo is outside his vehicle. He cannot hear us!"

Gunny puts the accelerator on the floor and the Hummer begins to shake violently, the *Millennium Falcon* flying through the asteroid belt, swerving violently to avoid trucks and pedestrians, the horn blaring. I realize he is shouting, but I can barely hear him over the wind. "This is goin' down right now!"

"Sharkman Six, this is Vader Six. If you can hear me, I assume you are heading to Charlie Bravo. You tell me what I can do to help once you get there. Helo can't land because of the buildings, *so you get in there and get them the hell out of there.* Over."

"Wilco, Vader Six!" It's a shame, because I now believe that if this were an actual war the colonel and I would get along, I was just too callow to see past the by-the-book personality.

"Almost level with the Huey, sir!" shouts Gunny. I can see the helicopter hovering on my right, dust and swirling paper filling the space beneath the skids like a pillow.

"Roger. Make your next right. We're a half mile away."

Gunny applies too much brake too quickly—I meant to say your next *available* right—and the Hummer goes into a long skid and with a crash hits a house. Three or four yellow bricks clink on the hood. He throws the vehicle into reverse and almost hits the little girl who has come out to see the spaceship. When the Hummer backs up, it reveals a gaping hole in the plastered side of the house. A woman's head pops up for a moment, scowling, and disappears. He throws it into gear again and we go tearing down the alley with about a foot of space on either side of the wide Hummer. Branches are *click-click-clicking* against the sides as we drive. Large, green trees line the street and I can no longer see the helicopter.

"Lost the bird, sir!"

"Keep going this way. We'll hit the MSR and we'll see them!" I shout. "You okay back there?"

"Last time I go car-jacking with the Gunny, sir!" says Montoya.

"Do not separate the team. Stick together! This might get ugly!" I shout.

Montoya leans his head forward and says, "That's what we're counting on!"

Ahead of us three children are kicking a tin can in the middle of the road. Gunny blares the horn but they just stop playing and stare. The Hummer scrapes its left side on the alley wall, the mirror snaps off, and the vehicle shudders and screeches. The kids stay put. I flip the safety off and stick my M-16 out the window, pulling the trigger twice. When they hear the gunshots, the kids scatter. The Hummer blows through a second later and I hear the *carunk* of the squashed can.

The radio comes to life again, but it isn't Armstrong. Are they already dead? "Vader, this is Talon! THE CONVOY IS ON FOOT AND THEY ARE SURROUNDED! One of the trucks escaped. But one of the Marines went back to get the two reporters—who *stayed back to film*—and now they are surrounded in the middle of the intersection! They've got that Range Rover at their backs, up against a house. Do we have permission to fire?"

"Is the crowd armed, Talon?" shouts Colonel Capiletti.

"Negative. There's a bunch of women up front, some kids even . . . wait. Yes! There are armed males in the back."

"You do *not* have permission to fire with unarmed civilians in that crowd. But if you are fired on, you may return it."

"Roger. But soon this crowd will be so close we can't risk a gun run."

"Roger that. Sharkman, you close?"

"Half klick, sir!" I shout into the handset.

"*Break. Break.* Vader, this is Talon. I count three good guys at the site. The rest got away. Looks like a Marine and two civilians. The Marine has put the reporters on the roof of the Range Rover. One female. They've got a camera . . . yeah, he's still filming. Black guy from CNN. And it looks like the—is that a pistol, Bobby?—THE FEMALE HAS A PISTOL!"

Damn it, Darren, she's going to get herself killed.

The alley jogs to the right and Gunny slams into the wall and mashes down on the brakes, skidding around the corner. We're suddenly heading into a wall of fire; the Somalis have barricaded this alley, too, and the flaming roadblock slides steadily toward the Hummer. Gunny turns his wheel the other way and we careen into the opposite wall in a wild fishtail.

"Oh!" he shouts.

The Hummer spins and we hit the barricade right side first, brushing through the flames initially and then coming to a sudden stop. We've hit something solid. The left wheels come off the ground and for a second we are going to flip over but the weight distribution saves us; the wide Hummer teeters for another second, then crashes back down on all four tires, right in the middle of the flames. Smoke fills the cab and I smell burning rubber and oil.

"Get us out of here!"

"Hang on!" The Gunny throws the Hummer in reverse and we limp out of the fire, grinding against a wall, dragging a string of flaming debris. I look up and see the Huey again when the smoke clears, hovering half a klick away. One quarter mile. *One minute.*

I pick the handset off the floor and someone is screaming his lungs out. My stomach wants to come out of my throat. "REPEAT," says the radio. "THE FEMALE HAS SHOT SOMEONE WHO WAS CLIMBING UP ONTO THE TRUCK. Oh . . . she shot again! SHE HAS SHOT TWO PEOPLE WHO ARE ATTACKING HER! THE CROWD IS ALL OVER THEM. *ALL OVER THEM!* REQUEST INSTRUCTIONS!"

"And most of the crowd is not armed, Talon?" shouts the colonel.

"Affirm. Most are unarmed. Women and kids, too. Only shots fired were from that reporter. She—MORE SHOTS FIRED! MORE SHOTS FIRED! MARINE FIRING WARNING SHOTS, IT LOOKS LIKE. MARINE WARNING SHOTS! SOME SOMALIS ARE MOVING AWAY AND OTHERS . . . PEOPLE ARE SWARMING ON THE TRUCK NOW!"

I toss the handset at my feet. "Bring it up against the side of that house!"

"We best try another route, sir, that fire will—"

"Do it, Guns!"

The Hummer hops forward and comes to rest against the side of the corner house. I look at the burning barricade. Behind the flaming tires I can see a tangle of barbed wire, a cart, three big piles of concrete cinder blocks, some metal rods, and an old truck. It's not a textbook roadblock, but it worked.

"I'm going over the roof of this house, onto the MSR," I say.

"*What?* Sir! We'll need the Hummer to get them out of there. Last thing we want is a running gunfight on streets we don't know!"

"No time. Take the Hummer and find another route in. Otherwise clear the barricade with the team and meet me up there under the helo, with the Hummer."

Gunny jerks his head back and says, "Montoya!"

"Yes, Guns!"

"You heard the lieutenant. Meet us up by the helo! We need this Hummer in there."

Montoya slithers into the front seat and Gunny pushes me out the passenger door, locking his fingers and boosting me onto the tin roof of the house next to the barricade. When I reach down he snatches my arm and walks himself up the side of the house. I grab his harness and yank him onto the roof with me.

"You didn't really think I'd let you get all the glory yourself, did you, sir!" he yells over the Hummer's revving engine.

We start to crawl across the roof, but it bends immediately under our weight, *caaht-hunking* like a soda can crushed inward when the tin folds. I get on my belly to distribute the weight and low-crawl, arms and legs spread wide. I am almost level with the barricade when the roof folds around me and pops its rivets, totally collapsed. Gunny and I go sliding down the metal and crash onto a table inside the house, shattering it. Somebody's kitchen. A man grabbing a little girl, pulling her into another room, screaming instructions, charging out with a big cutting knife, eyes wild and shouting, me raising my rifle, shouldering it, screaming back at him, don't make me pull an Indiana Jones, the man closer still with the knife held up.

I put the bullet into his shoulder and duck. He jerks and trips over me, scraping the knife across my flak vest as he goes, then rolls into the sitting position, eyes still wild and arm slashing. Gunny slams the butt of his M-16 into his head like he's cutting an oak.

As we walk out the door onto the Main Skinny Route I hear the little girl yelling. Everyone has something to say in this country. My heart is thundering, but the fear is not overwhelming this time.

The hovering helicopter is just up the road to my left. A quarter mile. One minute in this gear. Sixty seconds. Fifty-nine.

I cannot see the vehicles or the crowd; another smoky fire barricade one block away separates us from the convoy. I sprint to it and clamber up the drainpipe of another small house. This roof is sturdier. When I'm past the barricade, I hop off, a twelve-foot drop, rolling with my feet, then knees—both pairs locked together for stability—striking the dirt, onto my hip, over my shoulder and back onto my feet. Gunny, with a grunt, follows right behind.

Two smoke trails streak up past the Huey—rocket-propelled grenades or Stingers—and a third ends its run at the tail of the helicopter. The Huey shudders and begins to smoke, wobbling backward, just barely clearing a tree. Then it spins around and tips forward, flying past me on a horrible tilt, toward the airport.

I am running now but feel the heavy lethargy of a dream state in my legs. For the life of me, literally, I feel as if I am running at half speed, my legs refusing to carry me forward, Gunny leaving me behind. But the houses rushing past tell me that I have never moved faster. A Banger with an AK-47 steps out of a house in front of me and points his rifle at Gunny's back. I run him over. He manages to get out a shout, snuggling with me there on the dirt, before I cave in the side of his head with my weapon. Here, leaning over him now, sweating over my first confirmed hand-to-hand kill, I know the blood is in me, too, the irrepressible gene rising now that I need it most. No regrets. No tears.

Gunfire. Gunny kneeling next to me, firing down the street. Movement in the house to my left. I bring the rifle up to my shoulder and shoot two Bangers who are moving toward me from just inside the door. One of them just melts in place, like the Wicked Witch of the West, but the other drops his rifle and staggers forward, his bleeding mouth wide open like a Skinny version of *Jaws*. I admire the shot for a millisecond, then stand and greet his face with the butt of my rifle. He has a hard head and my hands sting the way they do when you hit with an aluminum bat when you're not wearing a glove. I am irritated that I did this to a man who was already dead.

Two holes, now three, now four open up in the side of the house next to me. Gunny jerks me flat and screams something, but the lightning cracks drown him out. I spin around in time to see the flame flash of a muzzle in a window across the street. Banger's hiding now, most likely below the window or next to it, and I'm not going to waste my own ammunition on a prayer. I grab the dead Banger's AK and fire the entire clip in a U around the window, sending ten bullets into each of the three likeliest hiding places. I hear a high-pitched wail, the screech of an animal, and the howl continues until he is out of breath, then starts again in a second. Gunny flicks a grenade from his pouch, plants his forward foot, and hurls the metal glob right through the window.

I grab my M-16 and begin to change magazines before I realize that I've used only three bullets. Gunny yanks me up and we continue our sprint forward. I hear a few rounds snap over my head but they are well high. I don't even duck. The grenade explodes behind us. I don't flinch.

Armstrong. Darren. Thayer-Ash.

At the next barricade I kick down the door to the house on my left and surprise a Skinny sitting in a chair at a table. He raises his hands and kicks something underneath. A woman walks into the kitchen. Gunny rips off the table-cloth and when he sees the rifle he tips over the entire table, more for effect than necessity, everyone screaming now, the Tower of Babel with automatic weapons.

The Somali puts his hands in front of his face and begins to babble incessantly, grabbing Gunny's harness, shaking his head. I am suddenly in a scene from *Platoon*. This is the ultimate obstacle course: fires, street fighting, Texas draws, and enemy villagers. The mother of all video games. And I'm not sure if I care about my own life.

Gunny pats him on the head gently, takes his rifle, nods at his wife, and we go racing through the house. When I get to its far end, I'm certain I'm far enough past the barricade to exit. I grab a chair and toss it through the bedroom's front window. I don't hear the breaking glass, but, then again, I don't hear anything for the ringing. I grab the thick rug from the floor and the Somali is suddenly in the door-way. His mouth is moving, opening and closing like a gold-fish and just as silent. I look down at the bare floor and see a trapdoor. Ah. I don't have to open it, my man, because I've seen the movies. I know what I'll find. No need to expose the kids to America like this, me looking like I do; they'll be clamoring for *Melrose Place* and a visa soon enough.

I wrap the camel-skin rug around my torso and dive

through the window, rolling in a half somersault on the street, particles tinkling everywhere, the glass absorbed by the thick camel skin. Gunny rolls out just behind me, without a wrap.

The crowd is fifty meters north of us, split into two separate groups on opposite sides of the street, and it is not at all what I expected. I sprint forward and pull the trigger on my M-16, barrel up, then pop the magazine free and struggle to insert another. I can faintly hear the spent clip clank on the ground and see that both groups of Somalis are looking at me. I enter the final sprint.

The CNN Range Rover is backed up against the side of a house on the left side of the street. Behind it, close to me, Darren is on his hands and knees crawling toward the second group of Somalis—mostly women—who are standing in a circle on the right side of the road, what, dancing?

"Go check out the right side!" I scream at Gunny.

He nods and barrels over toward the women. I'm twenty meters from the Range Rover when a Banger climbs to the top of it, machete held high. I'm running quickly and it will take two seconds before I can get a solid bead and shoot him. I skid in the dirt and drop to a knee but I see that I will be too late. The Banger jumps off the jeep and raises his machete over Darren, who turns at the sound and sticks out a futile leg. I put the M-16 in my shoulder and stare frantically over my sights. The machete is already coming down and Armstrong is suddenly there, unarmed. He sticks his arm out, reaching across Darren, and the machete cuts off his thumb and scrapes most of the meat of his forearm off cleanly as it works its way lower. The blade comes to rest in the bend of his arm, just below his bicep, and blood squirts all over his attacker. The hunk of meat falls into the dirt and is immediately encircled by a cloud of dust, a miniature A-bomb that was his forearm.

Before I can shoot the Banger, Armstrong grabs him around the throat with his good arm and slams his head into the trailer hitch on the back of the truck. The Banger's head bounces up just a bit, like a bowling ball dropped on concrete, and his body slumps below the bumper, lifeless. Armstrong sits on the corpse, holding what's left of his arm up in the air, yelling something at me.

Darren starts to crawl forward again. Two Bangers hop from behind the truck and I squeeze the trigger four times. One falls dead and disappears behind some grain bags. The other slumps forward and begins to wrestle with Darren. Bad call. Darren rolls him over and crushes his windpipe. A third Banger vaults over a body and I drill him. The bullet shatters his AK and the man drops it, shaking the sting from his hands, reaching for his knife. Darren rises from the earth to take him, bent in his wrestler's crouch and hopping on one leg, the Somali jutting the blade forward, keeping him at bay.

Gunny rushes out from behind a tire stack and puts a bullet in the Banger's head. The Somali collapses and Gunny grabs Darren—who's obviously severely injured—around the waist and tries to move him toward me. Darren struggles against him and points frantically at the circle of women jumping up and down on the other side of the street. They start moving that way.

I'm close to the Range Rover when a Banger steps around a burning stack of tires and shoots Armstrong in the left shoulder with a shotgun. He's blown back into the bumper of the truck and the tatters of his uniform catch fire and flop back and forth. I fire high at first to make sure I don't hit Armstrong. My third round is a tracer. I watch the red streak zip forward like a heated wasp and when it strikes the Banger it rips a large piece of his face off. Armstrong nods vigorously and he's screaming something. He grabs the dead Banger's shotgun and manages to stand. The rest of his left arm is now gone.

He stumbles back against the tailgate, sits on the bumper, glances at his left arm—pieces of it are spread across the dirt—chambers a new round with his good arm by racking the pump action violently up and down, and then tosses the shotgun just high enough so that he grabs it by the pistol grip. He turns to me quickly, yells something, and there, with one arm and a dozen holes in his upper chest, his eyebrows tipped forward and arched down to his nose, *he smiles*. It is a sinister grin, a furiously unyielding statement. A green tracer skips across the top of his helmet and he goes to his knees, dazed.

Armstrong leans around the back of the truck and fires. I can't see what he's shooting at. He tosses the shotgun up again, grabs it by the pump action with the same hand, jars it violently with a *cah-chunk!*, chambers another round, tosses it up in the air again, grabs it by the pistol grip, holds it out in front of him, and fires again, the other arm bleeding out and dead. I run up to him in time to see a Banger blown backward three meters, into a stack of grain bags.

I kneel down behind the truck, reach forward, and yank Armstrong back. The ground is muddy where we are and my knee sinks an inch into the red ground. *He needs a tourniquet.*

"Help me," he mumbles.

"I am! You need a tourniquet!"

"Noooo! I mean, help me *kill them*. Keep 'em offa the civvies."

He leans back around the corner of the truck and fires. Two bullets rip through the back of his flak vest but I know by the way he is shaking, as if he is being electrocuted, that more rounds are zinging around inside him. The chatter of the AK-47 near the bags has penetrated the tone and I am suddenly red from the waist up, the top of a blender off and wet everywhere.

A Marine is dead. Jake Armstrong. Sergeant. Twenty-eight years old. Lubbock, Texas. And for what? And for *what!*

For me. For Darren. For Thayer-Ash. That's it.

And that's enough.

My turn.

I pop up and put a bullet into the eye of the Banger on the other side of the truck, just a meter away. In the instant before the trigger breaks and the hammer falls, I see his eyebrows streak for the sky and his mouth open and I feel good about our mutual understanding of his destiny on this earth. I pull my former team leader behind the truck, but he isn't Armstrong anymore, just a faceless mess. Gunny skids on his face right next to me, bullets stitching his trail. A bullet clips my rifle and the butt shatters.

I point across the street. *"What's up?"*

"Just women over there! Shooters are over here!" Gunny screams.

I glance across the street. Darren is on his feet but he's limping badly, trying to push through the crowd of women on the right side of the street who continue to act as if nothing is happening over on this side. The Wild Side.

Thayer-Ash.

"Ready to pop up!"

Gunny nods and scoots toward the front bumper. I crawl toward the tailgate and hunch behind the wheel for cover. I back away just far enough so that my weapon has room, nod at the big man, and stand. Three targets present themselves on my side and I work the trigger and the sights in quick succession. My ears must have healed a little; in the distance I hear the metal of the recoil spring working in my M-16 every time I fire. *Claaangk. Claaangk.* And the smell. Gunpowder and . . . *blood?* Brass shell casings tinking on the ground. Next to me I hear Gunny's M-16 clapping and in my peripheral vision there are more Somalis dancing and dropping where he's killed them. I feel like I am standing side by side at a video game with the world champion. My God, do I feel a bond with Gunny right now.

I don't think any of the Bangers on my side got a round off. One of them is draped over a stack of food bags, quivering and grunting. I level my weapon, eyes scanning over my sights, and move the M-16 right past the man, the thin aiming post moving with my eyes as if one. A black mass is moving behind my front sight tip and I end it with a tracer, the third in a row.

A few rounds zing by my shoulder. The bead is so accurate that I'm forced to duck behind the truck, the 7.62-millimeter bullets missing by less than a meter. A Skinny in a house. My own tracers told me that I need a new magazine—the government only issues the unlimited clips to action stars—so I pop in a new magazine and crawl over to the wheel, next to Gunny, who's also hunched down changing magazines. I take a turkey peek across the hood. The result: at least fifteen Skinnies, including Farrah Fawcett, are sprinting toward me, firing at the truck as they approach. Two rounds snap over my head; one strikes the house next to me and the other cracks over my head toward the other side of the street, moving in the other direction. Farrah and his boys have some cover fire, to boot. Worse, it's from both sides of the street and it's highly accurate. The windows of the truck explode and the sidewalls pucker and burst in frozen blooms of jagged tin. I try to huddle next to Gunny behind the wheel but we are too big.

It's official. This is my coronation . . . king of the motherfucked.

And I've let Armstrong die.

I take four grenades from my gear harness and Gunny and I toss them over the truck and down the street, at different distances. I crouch behind the tire, in his arms, both of us fighting to protect the other. He wins. The first grenade explodes, but when I hear someone jump up onto the back of the Range Rover I know I've underestimated their speed and thrown too far. I hear the clatter of men hitting the deck just on the other side of the truck, then two more explosions that rock the vehicle and plink metal into its skin, then Somali babbling. I pull the pin on another grenade, release the fork, count to three, and toss it on the roof. It explodes immediately and a two-meter section of aluminum peels away and smashes the window just above my head.

A Skinny hand flies past me and strikes the house with a *thump!* but his arm flies much farther. A commie grenade skips under the truck and comes to rest just beyond me. I try to jump on it but Gunny smashes me in the shoulder and plops himself on top. *Not again!*

The explosion never comes. Thanks, Ivan.

There's more babbling and before I can get another grenade loose, I hear a bunch of them rushing the truck. *Better to burn out, sir.*

Feet hit all parts of the truck at once, so I flip the selector switch to Burst. It's fitting, really. I never thought I'd use it—automatic fire is highly inaccurate and not recommended—and now I finally get to blaze away like they do in the movies. My final thought: I'm going to die in some shithole country in Africa on a Wednesday morning and nobody has the faintest *idea* that we are even in any danger to begin with. No one knows. *No one cares.*

I'm going to die in *Africa?*

I coil my legs under me, take a breath, and pull the trigger as I stand up, sweeping the rifle from left to right, from the hood of the Range Rover to the back. It's immediately clear that I'll shoot the three Bangers on the hood, and possibly the fourth one on the roof, but the others are flanking us too quickly and there are too many. Gunny's M-16 closes my eardrum again. Enemy rounds are snapping in close now. I see the Cowboys jersey behind Bangers on our right flank and I am not surprised. You have to be stupid to stand on the vehicle. Or a henchman.

My eyes are ahead of my rifle now and Farrah is clear. I see every detail. I enter a zone of perfect clarity. He is wearing number eighty-eight. Who wears number eighty-eight? Oh. Michael Irvin. It'll make for a good story: Did you hear? Kelly and his platoon sergeant were killed by a guy named Farrah Fawcett wearing a Michael Irvin Cowboys jersey!

Behind Farrah's gang—*there are so many*—across the street, Darren is on the ground getting kicked to death by women and children. Thayer-Ash is already dead, probably next to him right now. Stretch Armstrong is dead, four feet away, right under Farrah Fawcett. When I go to hell, I wonder if I'll be bunking with Farrah as punishment.

The warlord's chest opens and he drops his rifle. The maelstrom of bullets is so furious that the back of the truck, and everything just beyond it, disintegrates in a tornado of red sparks and dust. It is an overwhelming force, the hand of God, and Gunny wilts and covers his head. I shrink behind the cab but I cannot shut my eyes. It keeps coming, the storm does, increasing in its intensity. Everywhere I look flesh is being nicked and scratched from jerky bodies. The road is filled with windblown chunks. The air roars past me, my breath sucked along with it, down the road with the scraps, a stampede of thunderheads that pushes me down and down. I cannot move. I cannot think.

Farrah's body is still jerking around and the red dots continue to chew into him. He's lying on what's left of his front side, staring at me with his mouth open. He could have used a dentist while he was alive.

"Recon!" someone yells. Montoya.

I try to yell but my throat catches. "Yuh," I say.

"*Recon!*" Montoya yells again.

I stare across the road at the crowd of women and they are looking back at me. Some of them are still dancing. "Recon!" I scream. "Recon!"

"Stand and be recognized!" he yells.

I pop up and someone jumps on my back, wraps an arm around me, punching me in the chest with the side of his fist. I look down and it's a knife. I'm turning around when my back is set on fire, a string of firecrackers exploding inside my flak vest. I can barely hear someone screaming behind me. "*Toma! Cabrón! Te voy a matar! Pendejo!*"

I face Montoya and he stops firing to reload. He jerks me to my knees and points at my shoulder. "Part of him still on you, sir. Got my rifle between him and you and I cut him in half."

A fist is rigored shut around my gear harness. I untangle the fingers and a sack drops off my back, scraping the heels of my boots. It's a Banger's torso, completely severed from the legs. Draining.

"Thanks," I say and reload my rifle. "Watch the snipers

in the houses over there!" Montoya waves his team forward and they surge across the road in bounds, like a coordinated pride moving under the cover of violent storm. *Craaack! Craaack! Craaack!* The Hummer comes shooting across the road and fishtails to a halt in the middle.

"Hey! Watch for snipers on the sides—"

"Got them, sir! Couple on each side," pants Montoya. "We saw them in the windows when we were sneaking up. Got my team clearing that side—that Armstrong?"

I nod—what is there to say?—and sprint across the road.

I yell my approach but the women just scoff and continue screaming and jumping around. I pull two women from the outer ring and dive forward, kicking and punching my way in. It's like entering a feeding frenzy. There are kids in here, in the innermost circle, learning their trade under their mothers' eyes. I shove one aside and suddenly I am straddling Darren. He's lying facedown, his arms wrapped around Thayer-Ash, shielding her.

I shout, "Darren!" as loudly as I can. My ears are ringing again. I see his chest rising and falling. His mouth is moving. Telling me . . . what?

I lean in close and say, "Is she okay?"

His mouth moves but I cannot hear.

A woman grabs my harness and yanks me up. She's a strong one. I kick her hard in the stomach and it's like kicking a board. "Damnit, sir. It's me," Gunny says. "We need to get out of here. *Now.* Doc'll look at him in the Hummer."

The Marines have shoved many of the women to the ground and they're just barely keeping a hole open. I tap Darren on the head and scream, "Let's go!"

He tries to stand but his leg buckles and he falls. I grab

him and he slaps my arm away and stands again. He reaches for her but struggles to move her.

"I got her," I say. "Gunny, help Darren out."

"I'm fine!" he hisses. "We need to get her to a doctor. These bitches beat her really bad."

"That's where we're going, Phillips. Now if you'll allow me, we'll be on our way." Gunny dips his head, and before Darren can back up, Gunny squats, rams him, tosses him over his shoulder, and sprints toward the Hummer. Rounds begin to snap at him when he runs, and I can hear the steady response of the friendly cover team, probably Montoya. Gunny is sprinting through a gauntlet. *Please, God, let him make it.* I understand how it works now: Armstrong dies for Darren, Gunny, and me, Gunny dies for Darren, Montoya dies for Gunny, I die for Thayer-Ash. In all this madness, dying for each other is the only thing that makes sense.

"Let's go, sir. I'll grab—"

"I got her!" I take Mary Thayer-Ash into my arms and heft her over my shoulder. The Marines are more aggressive now, throwing blows to keep the infuriated women away. I turn and begin to sprint out but something is wrong. She's too heavy. I glance back and there is Little Joe, holding on to Thayer-Ash's hand with all his strength. He's slashing at her arm with the small Swiss Army knife that Doc gave him, drawing thin red streaks from her elbow to the middle of her forearm, opening her flesh, bloody now. It is totally startling.

"*Joe!*" I scream. "Let her go, Joe! What are you doing? Get . . . off . . . her." I take my foot and put it in his chest. He doesn't let go, so I push. He tumbles onto his back.

But he's up just as quickly, growling, rushing forward. I lift Thayer-Ash out of his reach but I don't have the strength to keep her up for long. He's jumping at her, swiping with his knife, the fox and the grapes. A Somali woman rushes me with a pipe and I kick her in the gut as hard as I can. Guess that's why they call them combat boots. Little Joe has Thayer-Ash's ankle now and he's cutting again, slashing at her Achilles. I snatch his wrist with my left hand and shake him as violently as I can.

"Joe, stop! STOP, JOE! Why are you *doing* this? She . . . I said . . . STOP! JESUS, STOP!" I pull him into my thigh and grab his neck. I squeeze it for a second and fling him back again.

Tears of rage run down his cheeks. "She kilt Tamar! De lady kilt Tamar!" he screams. "She die, too!"

He rushes me again with his knife and I plant my boot in his sternum with all of my might. When his ribs crack they don't sound like mallets on crab shells. Instead I hear several snaps, like twigs. His body flies back several feet and one of the women screams bloody murder, which it isn't. Strictly superficial damage.

Perhaps peace in Somalia is just an unwelcome pause sandwiched by violence, an intermission from the continuous cycle of ripping and blood.

A horn blares.

I am shoved forward through the gauntlet and suddenly the Hummer is right in front of me. "Give her here, sir!" screams Doc. Marines are firing out the back and there's brass everywhere.

I pitch Thayer-Ash into the back and someone shoves me in from behind. I shout, "I can't go until everyone's—"

"STAY THE FUCK IN THERE!" screams Montoya. His M-16 is firing.

"Where's the boy? He's hurt. Grab Joe!"

"Got him here!" He tosses Joe into the Hummer and then dives on top of me. Someone yells. The Hummer lurches forward and, lost under the crush of bodies, I am not sure if we are moving forward or backward, or even moving at all, for that matter.

"Space. I need space. That means you, sir," says Doc. I am lying on top of him. He's on his hands and knees, protecting Thayer-Ash.

I roll away from him and back myself into the bodies on one side of the Hummer. "*Give the Doc room,*" everyone is yelling. "*Give him room!*"

"The boy—"

"He's okay, sir. She needs the help."

Ash is in her white shirt, resting on her back in the bottom of the dirty Hummer. Her eyes are closed. A bad sign, I think. Doc's hands are moving rapidly across her body. "Please, God," I am saying out loud—I think.

The Hummer crashes into something and I lose my grip on the leg behind me. I roll on top of her and try to push myself off when the vehicle straightens. Someone grabs my harness and yanks me back into some bodies.

"How is she, Doc?" I yell.

"Working here!" he says.

". . . count, sir?" Gunny yells from the cab.

"Repeat!" I scream.

"We're on Lenin Road now!" he yells. "Did you get the count?"

"No!"

"Armstrong is dead. Phillips is okay. I took a round in my shoulder. Flesh wound. Kessler took one in the ass. He's fine. All others fine. Counted at least thirty Skinny bodies. That reporter back there, how's she doing?"

"I DON'T *KNOW*, GUNNY. GET OFF MY FUCKING BACK!" screams Doc.

He's hunching over her and I am watching her face, hoping to see an exhale. Just a twitch. A sigh. *Anything.*

Doc has inspected her entire body and when he gets to her head he lifts it just enough to stuff a rolled camouflage blouse under it. "Oh," he says. "Oh, Jesus Christ have mercy."

A section of Ms. Thayer-Ash's scalp, from the top of her neck halfway up her head, flops loose, dangling in front of me on the wet floor of the Hummer.

Doc rolls her on her side and gently peels back the hair. He takes two pressure bandages and presses them into the wound. "Grab that Ace and wrap her, sir!" he says.

I kneel over her and tear at the plastic wrap in which the bandage is packaged. My nails are not long enough and my hand is too slippery to grip the corners.

"Give it here!" someone yells. I hand it to Darren and he rips it open, tosses it back, and says, "Hurry, Gavin."

I wrap her head several times and the blood penetrates right up until the final few wraps. "Where's another, Doc?"

"I, right . . . in my unit one, sir. But . . . that's not the problem, sir," he says. "She's bleeding big time from . . ." He rolls her over again and screams, "GET ME MORE PRES-SURE BANDAGES! SHE'S BEEN SHOT HERE, NEAR HER ARMPIT! OH, MAN, IT'S THE AXILLARY ARTERY. *SHE'S LOST A LOT OF BLOOD!*"

"Should we—"

"Shut up, sir! Give me a clamp!"

I grab two metal objects from his bag and hand them over.

"*Clamp,* I said!" Doc screams. "Give me the whole damn bag!" He riffles through, finds the clamp, and starts probing into her armpit. "Damn. Hold this, sir." He rummages and emerges with a scalpel.

"Can't find the vein. Gonna have to cut. Montoya, hold her *steady.* Sir, give me that clamp when I tell you." Doc makes a face that nauseates me as he cuts, slicing into her arm, and when I lean in to look he startles me by screaming, *"Clamp!"* Her side is so slick with blood that I cannot see the wound. When the Hummer accelerates around a corner, I see the blood wash forward in tiny waves separated by the corrugated metal floor of the Hummer.

I hand the clamp to him and after a few seconds he lets go and screams, "Got it! *Bandages!* Hold her still, Montoya."

"Her head might need—"

"Shut up, sir! Her head's not the problem!" He grabs the bandages and begins to stuff them into her side. "Here. Pressure *here,* sir! Hold these down till we get there. We have a chance now."

Doc is performing so wonderfully. I can't even differentiate a clamp from tweezers. I am deeply ashamed for ever having doubted his competence.

———

". . . now, Lieutenant!" Colonel Capiletti is yelling at me in the fog.

"What?"

"Get out of the way! Let's get her out of there!"

I recognize the hangar. We are inside the airport compound. I am alone in the Hummer with Thayer-Ash. Someone grabs my arm and says, "Let her go, brother. Let her go." Darren is apparently here, too, wedged behind me.

A corpsman helps Doc lift her out of the vehicle. In the sun the Ace unwinds and her scalp swings back and forth, the movement giving it new energy, a sheet on a laundry line flapping in the wind.

I turn to Darren. "What happened?"

"Those fucking animals tried to scalp her."

"They were trying to kill you."

"I know."

"They killed Armstrong."

He bows his head. "I know," he whispers.

My throat closes. I hop into the sun. They are all watching me as I enter the medical tent. Corpsmen and surgeons are swarming over Ms. Thayer-Ash, and Little Joe, and Lance Corporal Kessler is shouting orders, a coordinated and perfectly executed attack. Gunny is standing, refusing aid, pressing a bandage into his shoulder. In the back of the tent I see a corpse, alone. It is Armstrong.

It was Armstrong.

I back up next to the others and Colonel Capiletti says, "Lieutenant Kelly—"

"Please save it, sir. Please. You can court-martial me later."

In the distance I feel a hand on my shoulder. "Kelly," I hear, "you did good."

———

It is quiet when the surgeon walks over and tells us. "Boy's fine . . . just some busted ribs. Marines are fine. Thayer-Ash's stable. Head full of hair as thick as hers will cover that nasty scar. Got some O-positive flowing into her now. Your corpsman saved her life, Lieutenant. No question about it. She's taken three pints so far." She'll always have a little Marine in her now.

"Armstrong?" I nod at the corpse.

"Sorry. We'll get that covered up. It's a terrible sight." That's all he says. *We'll get that covered up.*

Behind me someone shouts, "Oh, God, Stretch. OhmyGod. Not Stretch! Not *Stretch*." It's our new Team One leader, Corporal Johnson. He pushes past me and half-sprints to Armstrong's body. He pulls back the camouflage poncho and twists his face away, reeling. His eyes are nearly bright red. He sits hard on the dirt floor and balls his fists.

"You see what they did to him, sir! We should kill those motherfuckers! Lieutenant Kelly? Sir? We gonna do something about this? I mean . . . let's get out there, sir. Right now! *Let's get out and there and kill all those motherfuckers!*"

He starts to sob and folds in half, hands shaking violently. I can feel my own cheeks going rigid and my throat closes again. But I don't give the crowd the satisfaction. I walk over to Johnson, stand him up, and put my arm around him as I lead him out of the tent.

"You should get out of those cammies, Kelly," Colonel Capiletti whispers. He pats me on the shoulder again.

Before I glance down I actually smell him; Armstrong is all over me and I have been wearing him for thirty minutes. My blouse is soaked red and smells rusty. "Well, I'm going to go write Armstrong's parents," I manage. It is the final, ironic stab of punishment for a failed lieutenant.

Darren is slumped over a set of crutches, crying. "Saved my life," he groans. "That Marine back there . . . died for me."

Johnson and I move toward him and he straightens up and extends his hand, perhaps expecting our first embrace. I walk right past and out of the tent, stone-faced. I've got a duty to perform. I think I have a pen and paper in my duffel bag.

The rest of Armstrong's team is waiting outside and I'm forced to run the gauntlet. They stare at me and I bow my head. So many times in Somalia, this sense of shame.

"Is he dead, sir?"

"Yes."

"Did he get any of them?"

"Yes."

"How many?"

"I don't know. Maybe twenty."

"Fuckin' A. We goin' out there after the rest of 'em?"

I don't have a good answer, so I just stare at my canvas boots. Johnson sniffles and pats me on the back. "I'll take over from here, sir. Thanks."

Beyond the five remaining team members, there is a crowd of other Marines pushing toward me, cordoning off my egress route, watching and whispering, crushing me down, hunting me like a lynch mob with torches burning and pistols cocked. They aren't moving, mind you—they remain at their posts, or sitting cleaning their weapons, or rehearsing patrol-reaction drills, or digging fresh foxholes—but their eyes are fixed on me as I walk across the red dirt to my lair, the only lieutenant they've ever seen who has lost a Marine. *That's him! That's the one, right there.*

I arrive at my hole breathless. Jake Armstrong saved my life twice and I plan to visit his parents to tell the stories face-to-face. Gunny said he had no parents, but I was certain he had listed a couple on his record of emergency data. I loosen my pack straps in a panic and after a struggle yank the notebook free. Armstrong's is the first file in the book.

> Next of Kin: *G. I. (Nickname: Joe) and*
> *Barb Dahl (Parents)*
> Address: *1775 Worldsbe St., Mari, NE*
>
> Seriously though, sir, if you're reading
> this for real, just give my SGLA benefits
> to the guys in the form of a keg party.

Armstrong *has* no parents to write. No sisters. No brothers. No, that's not right. Jake Armstrong is survived by his brothers. Twenty of them—and I'm the young one he looked out for the most. I sag inside my hole, put my face in my hands, and weep.

– 23 –

5 FEBRUARY 1993

Lasky: Has your father ever killed anyone before?

Rusty: Oh, just a dog. Oh! And my Aunt Edna.

Clark: You can't prove that, Rusty.

Gunny fills the door of our hooch, which is hard to do since it consists of a square of desert cammie cloth held up by four long sticks. Gunny erected the curtain when he moved in with me as a means of gaining some privacy before the hearing; I'm convinced that everyone is always watching me. Last night I asked the Gunny if, as a veteran of three combat actions, he had ever met a junior officer or NCO who had lost a Marine in a firefight. He had not. It severed our conversation and we spent the rest of the night in silence, listening to our memories chide us.

Inside our hooch is a stack of MREs, two packs readied for the movement to the ships this afternoon, two rifles, and a bunch of green-colored notebooks—my office, my home. Sometimes I stay late at the office. My classmates tell me the hours are hell on Wall Street, too. Only they have cubicles, while I have the air. Hell, on a clear day, I can see all the way to the ships that have returned to pick us up before the sun sets.

But right now my view is blocked by this man-mountain. The sun is at his back and I am engulfed in his shadow. We have rehearsed our statements and have come to believe we may yet skate on the charges. The Corps will target the senior man in the platoon—me—and hold me accountable. Problem is, my prints aren't on the card. So they'll try to get Gunny to testify against me in return for immunity. No dice.

"Big Duke's inbound to talk with you, sir. Remember what we discussed."

"No prob, Gunny."

He disappears and I notice that the entire platoon line has vanished with him. Where are my stalwart fellow dogs of war, bloodthirsty idolators, acolytes of Mars, scourge of Gangbangers, cold-eyed recon Marines? Fled, disappeared, gone without a trace and with a few yips after one growl from the Duke. My estimation for their common sense soars. I long to join them. Duke has other ideas.

"You and me need to talk, sir." It is a command. "You just go on sitting, sir. I'll just stand here and be direct with you and leave."

It isn't sweat on his face; it is steam. I've let everybody down, haven't I?

He squats down as if he's confiding in me. "The way I figure it, the chain of command was broke on the beach that night. Which means the Gunny dealt with Armstrong alone. They were pretty close and Gunny protected him. I doubt you'd be fool enough to hide those press passes.

"So you, sir, did not know about the passes, because at night you would have had to have been right up close. But you were with the cameras. And your prints aren't on the cards. So you're sitting here, planning how to protect the Gunny for something you didn't do. That's how I figure it. Sir, Marines do not lie. All the colonel's going to ask you in there is to tell the truth. So do it. That's your first duty."

"I'm confused, Big Duke. What are you worried about?"

"I'm worried you'll take on something you're not responsible for and destroy your career. You're feeling guilty about Armstrong—your men have been coming up to me concerned that you're suicidal about his loss. So now you're trying to jump on the grenade for Gunny. You got a bright future. Don't do it."

"*Bright future?*" I would laugh if I were not so close to tears again. "In two tours I've lost two men."

"And? And? Let me tell you something, sir. In my day those would have been impossibly good results."

"And in my day they are the harbingers of an incompetent who will screw up again."

Big Duke inhales. I grip the sides of my hole to keep from being sucked in. "This may come as a surprise, but you're wrong about that, sir. The colonel believes you have real promise. 'Tactically gifted,' is what he said. You have a feel for combat. You know how to kill, sir. That's what you like, isn't it?"

I am not going to answer him. But yes, I like it, not the blood, not the killing itself, but applying the fires and being *with* the men when we're winning or training to win—my *compañeros*. I have never before been part of something like the Marines, and I fear if I lose the Corps I won't find the feeling again. How does he know so much? Has he been there? Is he there now?

Big Duke nods and says, "Thought so. Let's just get this mess cleaned up and you're on your way. Keep your trap shut."

"What's next, Big Duke?"

"Formal statements, sir." He straightens up and cracks his neck. "Please present yourself in the colonel's office in thirty mikes, sir, at 0900. You'll be leaving for the *Denver* late this afternoon."

"Thank you, Sergeant Major."

"You do well in battle, sir. I would have been pleased to serve with you in combat."

Marines don't cry. So why am I misting up? Fuck. Please let me stay a Marine. Why did Colonel Capiletti, of all people, have to say something good about me? He was put in a difficult situation and I didn't help him. I'm running out of people to mock. Except when it comes to me, of course, because new material just keeps on coming.

————

I am standing with my heels touching, feet angled away like a duck, shoulders back, arms straight, head up, mouth shut. Colonel Capiletti nods to a tall Marine officer on his left. "This is Colonel Weston from the judge advocate general's office. He was kind enough to fly out from D.C. on my emergency request to make sure I don't screw something up."

Behind Colonels Capiletti and Weston, I see General Bellissimo smirk and shake his head, unimpressed by what he must take to be a Keystone Cops investigation.

This is called a "preliminary inquiry." My rights under Article 31 of the Uniform Code of Military Justice have not been read, so I know they're just sweating me, trying to form their case. If you've seen *Homicide* or *Hill Street Blues,* you know the drill. Colonel Capiletti is holding the inquiry now because if he waits until we're on the high seas the rules change for the worse; he's doing me a favor. With Armstrong dead, though, he doesn't have a case against me unless the Gunny squeals. *Not . . . bloody . . . likely.*

"Before I let Colonel Weston get down to the charges, I want to ask you one question, Lieutenant Kelly. What do you want most out of this inquiry?"

"I want to remain a Marine, sir."

"That's your goal?"

"Yes, sir, it truly is."

General Bellissimo bolts out of his chair and hisses, "Then why did you kill an innocent man?"

Colonel Capiletti steps out to block his path. "This is *my* Marine, sir, so please don't speak again. I was doing you a courtesy by allowing you to sit in."

The two men stare hard at each other before Bellissimo says, "And *you* are in *my* command now, Vincent."

"Please leave this room, sir."

"You're asking me to leave my own office?" asks Bellissimo, incredulous.

"That's what I'm telling you, sir."

"You've just thrown away my support in this case, Colonel," says Bellissimo, circling around my immobile battalion commander as he makes for the hatch.

"We never had your support, sir. You know it and I know it."

When the Italian is gone, Colonel Capiletti faces me and sighs, a faint smile still lingering on his face. "This is what you call a 'high-profile' problem, Lieutenant Kelly."

He walks over to survey the damage Bellissimo has done to his former desk, then raps his knuckles on it gently. "From what Colonel Weston here tells me, you're going to skate on this. So you're going to get your wish. Congratulations."

I nod stupidly—are we off this easy?—and Colonel Capiletti leans in close. "But let me tell *you* something . . . One of two things happened the night Armstrong killed that Somali bodyguard. Either you were involved in the conspiracy to hide the press badges or you were so out of touch with—and mistrusted by—your Marines and Gunny Ricketts that they kept you out of the loop. I'm not sure which one is worse, frankly, but from what I've seen of you, my hunch is that you lied. And Marines don't lie. It's really that simple, Lieutenant." He waits for a few seconds before he continues, "Have nothing to say to that or are you just awed again by my presence?" He smiles at me. He must be playing good cop.

"I guess I'm taking the fifth, sir. And I think Gunny will do the same."

The JAG lawyer laughs and says, "Hey, guess what, hotshot? You don't *get* to take the fifth when this goes to courtmartial. *You* aren't tasting any charges, so you, my friend, will be *compelled* to testify."

He has a looser, nearly civilian manner and he gives me a *Don't mess with me because I know my business* stare. I'm a bit put off by it.

"*I'm* the senior man, Colonel. So who am I testifying against? Because if it's the Gunny, I'd say you're off your rocker. But I wish you luck, sir."

Colonel Capiletti walks around the JAG shaking his head and addresses him as if I am not even present. "Well, what'd I tell you, Colonel Weston? Lieutenant Kelly is too *smart* and too *loyal* to his men to tell us the *truth* about that first night. And like you told me, we have no case against Kelly himself without testimony. No way in hell the

Gunny will roll over on him. So if you're planning on using him as a witness for the prosecution, well, I hope this changes your mind. Because it's clear he'll just lie. Won't you, Kelly?"

"Sir, I . . . I don't know what you're trying to say. I'm not testifying against my platoon sergeant, if that's what you mean."

Colonel Capiletti sighs and walks over to the hatch, opens it, and says to me, "You're free to go about your business, Lieutenant. Dismissed. Oh, and send Gunnery Sergeant Ricketts in here so we can read him his rights."

This is really strange. Military prosecutors always target the senior officer. *Always.* Taking full responsibility for the actions that occur on your watch is a staple in military leadership, a bedrock principle that gets admirals relieved when their ships run aground and base commanders fired when there are sexual harassment problems. Certainly they won't target the Gunny alone, considering I was a hundred meters away on that beach.

"I said you're dismissed, Lieutenant."

What the hell? "Sir, if I may, how is the Gunny being charged?"

Colonel Capiletti nods at the lawyer, who opens a folder and pulls out a sheaf of papers. "Well, for starters, Article 134, Obstruction of Justice; Article 81, Conspiracy to Obstruct Justice; and Article 107, Giving a False Official Statement. I think a military jury will find him guilty on all counts. At a minimum your Gunny is looking at some brig time, a severed career, and a bad conduct discharge. And that's the best scenario. God only knows what that International Criminal Court will do if they get hold of him."

Colonel Capiletti baits me by raising his furry eyebrows, and I take it. "What's the International Criminal Court?"

"A nightmare for Gunny Ricketts, that's what," the colonel says. He opens a folder that I see is labeled "confidential" and begins to read. "The International Criminal Court will investigate and bring to justice individuals who commit the most serious crimes of concern to the international community, including torture of civilians, murder, rape, and war crimes. The ICC is a global judicial institution with international jurisdiction, and its diverse panel of judges—balanced in terms of both gender and background—will have ultimate authority to apply international law and determine sentencing of criminals who appear before the court."

"What does that have to do with us, sir?"

"Everything, lieutenant. The president signed off on this thing and congress is now debating its ratification. The Joint Chiefs are on the Hill as we speak, lobbying against it, but if we sign on, we're hearing that Gunny Ricketts may be one of its first test cases. The commandant is absolutely determined to keep Gunny out of this hornet's nest, but even his resignation won't stop this thing once it starts rolling. Like I said, Lieutenant, this is *high profile*."

"I can't believe this. Gunny isn't a war criminal, sir. He's not guilty of any of this."

"He's not?" Colonel Capiletti holds up the plastic bag with the press cards. "This alone ensures a 107 violation. I've got a signed statement where he tells us he never saw a press badge—same one you signed, by the way—so with or without your testimony, he's a goner. No one will buy some trash theory that Armstrong somehow got his fingerprints and framed him, so I think the obstruction charges will stick, too. Even if he doesn't go before the ICC, he's finished as a Marine."

"He's got fourteen years in, sir!"

"He should have thought of that on December ninth."

"But I'm the senior officer in the platoon."

"Yes, well, not that night, it seems." He purses his lips and sits down. "My preference—*everyone's preference*—was to risk the shaky case and charge *you,* as is proper, but I was told we had no chance. Not without the Gunny's testimony. So the Gunny takes the fall. It's his fingerprint, not yours. Right? I guess you weren't there, were you, Kelly?"

I stay quiet and he slaps the desk gently and sighs again. "Now. Dismissed, I said. Send the Gunny in."

"He's got five daughters, sir. You yourself said he was the epitome—"

"*Dismissed.*"

But Colonel Capiletti doesn't rush me out. Instead, he watches me watch him, then raises his eyebrows.

I hear someone cough outside the office hatch. No way it's going down. Not like this.

"Your preference was to charge me, sir?"

"Damn right it was. As you said, you were the senior man. Well, you were *supposed* to be senior, anyway."

"I want to go on the record right now, sir. When my Article 31 rights are read I intend to testify to this fact: that I ordered Gunnery Sergeant Ricketts to destroy those press badges. I gave him no choice in the matter, although he argued against it. There was no conspiracy. It was simply a case of a Marine following bad orders. All subsequent testimony he gave was engineered and coached by me."

Colonel Capiletti raises his eyebrows even farther and says, "Seems *you're* not giving *me* a choice now. You'll take a hell of a fall, what with the media attention."

"It's my fall to take, sir. In return for my testimony and full cooperation, I want the Gunny to come through unscathed. If that isn't going to happen, there's no deal and I stay quiet. Then you'll have to risk the nasty public court-martial of a superior Marine armed only with circumstantial evidence. You don't want that. Nobody does."

Colonel Capiletti pauses for a long time and he is a weird combination of happiness and sadness. He winks at the JAG officer. Finally he breathes and says, "It's a shame, Gavin, because I think you might have made a good senior officer. You proved that to me right now. You've accepted responsibility for this messy incident, and that's the right thing to do. I had a hunch you'd step up. You'll face a general court-martial in a month, and worse if we are forced to feed you to the wolves."

"Fine, sir. What about the Gunny?"

"You used the word 'unscathed.' Well, the Gunny lied, too, so he'll sustain some collateral damage. Reputational, mostly. But, yes, we'll give him immunity and, yes, he'll remain in the Corps and, yes, he'll continue up the ranks when this skin dies and peels off. As for you, though, this time next month you will no longer be a Marine. They're going to dismiss you. You know that, right?"

My throat closes and I simply nod.

"I'm sorry, Lieutenant," Colonel Capiletti says, "but with the coverage this is getting I can't simply accept your resignation. We're going to have to kick you out. And you did wrong. *Marines don't lie.*"

I am walking out the hatch in a buzzing daze when he says, "Everything else was right though, Gavin. Especially what you did in here. And out there. Now send Gunny Ricketts in here and find Darren Phillips and send him in, too. I want to deliver some good news for a change."

"Aye . . . aye, sir."

"Oh, one more thing—we're going to have to serve you up to the press, Lieutenant, so steel yourself. They took a ton of heat for that first night and they'll be looking to give it back in spades. You were a good Marine except for this. Remember that a month from now."

"I will, sir," I manage, and walk out the hatch into the passageway.

Walk out the door into the hallway, I mean.

———

In the warm dark I am chilled. The sun has been gone three hours and my platoon has been out of Somalia for two. I've been gone for six but I'm still in this country, waiting for the aircraft that will take me to Quantico. The wind blowing in off the water is hot and I am sweating, but I am cold, shivering, listening to some Somali babble drift over the wire and dunes up the beach from where I'm standing.

I am in tune with this world. I know how to smoke people. It's official, Dad, and it gave sense to what I was doing. The only thing I did well. And now I'm out. Rejected.

Fellow rejects are out there below the shiny black, patrolling the night, never sleeping. They care only about eating. And eating, for them, is killing. I walk in up to my shins. Maybe I'm testing. Maybe I just don't care. I watched one of my men die yesterday.

I kick vigorously and jump up and down, splashing, announcing my arrival. Try me. Not a fucking *scratch* from that fight, yet a Marine who saved my life no longer has a face.

EPILOGUE

3 MARCH 1993

Forget it, Jake, it's Chinatown.

Bernard Shaw is sitting upright, his shoulders back. He's got great posture, though that is not extraordinary considering he is both a nationally recognized anchorman and a former Marine.

As am I. Former.

"Sit down, Dragomir, your blimp head is blocking the television."

The big Serb sergeant frowns at me and sits back down in one of the the jail's recreation room chairs. "You have big mouth, Kelly. Maybe I stuff it someday, yes?"

Drag Queen's serving ten to twenty for his part in a torture case. I should also mention that he was caught impersonating an officer, which is pretty much the reason I'm here.

"Now a report from Operation Restore Hope. It's been

three months since United States Marines landed on the beaches of Somalia on a mission of peace. The objective? To stop the terrible famine that had devastated the country. Once that mission was accomplished, though, the Marines found themselves in a series of violent clashes with Somali warlords. One of our own reporters was involved in several of these battles. You are about to see an *extraordinary* report by an *extraordinary* woman, but please be advised: It contains scenes of graphic violence. Viewer discretion is encouraged. Reporting now from Mogadishu, Somalia, here is Mary Thayer-Ash."

———

She is wearing a clean white cotton shirt with two buttons open. Her hair is piled up inside a CNN baseball cap, a few stray strands looped behind her ears, lighter than when I last saw it. That's not her real hair. Her right arm is in a sling, the proper badge and credential for the "war correspondent." Her neck is unblemished, thinner than before, and a shade paler than her tanned face. Even with what must have been an extended hospital stay she has managed to get a tan for this report. Her face is glowing.

She is standing in a Mogadishu intersection. It is familiar. Two boys are kicking a tin can in the background as she speaks.

"A month ago CNN recovered and turned over to Marine authorities an NBC press badge that belonged to a Somali killed by the Marines. Lieutenant Gavin Kelly, a Gulf War veteran, stands charged with concealing evidence and obstructing justice. The badge may have implicated one of his men—Sergeant Jake Armstrong—in a wrongful death.

"On that same day I was riding with a food convoy attacked by a Somali mob. The convoy came to save lives—

at this very spot—but the mob wanted to take our lives instead. Ironically, Sergeant Armstrong was killed fighting off the mob, defending me. And it was Lieutenant Kelly's reaction force that saved my life and the life of my cameraman.

"But there are no medals for Lieutenant Kelly. Instead, he faces a court-martial. The Jesuitical culture of the Marine Corps is built on strict discipline and rigid rules. But what are the rules in a country *without* any rules?"

Three men with AK-47s walk into the frame behind Thayer-Ash and I get right out of my chair and walk up close to the television. They push the kids with the can out of the way so the camera can have a clear view of them, I guess, and plop down in front of a house not fifty feet from her. They are totally relaxed, rifles across their laps, chewing khat and spitting occasionally, sharing an in-joke. Then they start to laugh wildly and all three Bangers look right at the camera—right at me—and wave.

They say I'll get two or three years of brig time for what I did. When I get out maybe I'll organize a tour group and go on a safari to unwind, bring some coolers of beer, see the sights. Big Duke will be retired by then and I'm pretty sure I'll be able to convince the Gunny to take some leave. I know Johnson and Montoya are in—they sent me a letter telling me what a great time they had in Africa and how they can't wait to get back. That makes five of us—not nearly enough to get a discounted group fare on an airline, but just one shy of the perfect size for a rubber Zodiac rental. Yeah, instead of flying into Africa I think we'll swim; my old man's pretty cheap, so I think he'll like that option better.

ACKNOWLEDGMENTS

I've never achieved anything alone and this novel is no exception. I view it as a small culmination that might have been sparked over fifteen years ago. So, thanks first to my mother who grabbed me by my scruff when I was thirteen, yanked me out of the junior high in which I was floundering, and put me on a new path by sending me . . .

To St. Paul's School, where I received an education far superior to my schooling in college, learned how to fail and make changes, and was surrounded by an incredible group of people whom I still consider my best friends (especially Stovkesschehersh productions).

To all my Harvard friends, especially Harry and his rowers, the ROTC geeks, the hooters, and the gang that formed freshman year.

To everyone at Stanford B School, with a special note to Jim King, who helped me hatch this plot in Business French class.

To D. Henry and Shandler, for buttoning their laughs when they read the first draft.

To my wife, Susanne, for not attacking me when I'm hacking on our stupid laptop. Actually, on second thought . . .

Special thanks are due to two rising stars in this strange industry. To Marysue Rucci, my extraordinary editor, whose eye for story and ability to fix a broken manuscript are just superior. How she took a confluence of disparate ideas—including a brutally boring two-hundred-page flashback—and molded a novel escapes me. If you don't like the book don't blame her; you should have seen it a year ago (though I still vow to get the college beer-bong scene into another novel). And *Sharkman* simply would not exist without überagent Dan Mandel, who fished a lonely letter out of the slush pile and gave my story a chance at life. He helped make some critical changes to the book, always has good advice, and when he's not siphoning off his fair share I consider him a friend.

I owe the greatest thanks to all the Marines with whom I served. From the LPA (Lieutenant Protection Association): Auggie, B-Man, Scooter, Jonesy (MOS notwithstanding), Manbo, Hindy, TommyO, Monty, TJ surfboard, Ben-Waugh, and Weston. All the D-dogs in Third Herd, 1/1 ("North Korea, come on down! You're the next contestant . . ."), especially Prink, Garza, Hutch, Lieuallen, Web, Peña, and the rest of the Mexican Mafia. To all my compañeros from 2nd Platoon, 1st Recon Co., especially the TLs and the HQ bitchompers: Big Duke Ricketts, Special E, PJ (Sman 4), Vance, Moore, Hoyt, "Teddy" Levan, Finny, K-Manbeast, and Doc. To three terrific (former) skippers: Killer Killion, Woody, and Blackhurst. Finally, to the otherwise happy officers who were forced to chew me out from time to time: Brick, Dunahoe, T. E., Zilmer "can't hang," and especially Easy Ezell. What great, adventurous years in the Corps. Man, do I miss it. *Semper Fi.*

SIMON & SCHUSTER
PROUDLY PRESENTS

FOUR DAYS TO VERACRUZ

OWEN WEST

Coming soon in hardcover
from Simon & Schuster

Turn the page for a preview of
Four Days to Veracruz. . . .

CHAPTER 1

Acapulco, Mexico

Darren Phillips awoke to a splitting headache and punched the air. He often dreamed of Somali warlords with machetes come to cut him again and he took a moment to orient himself. Alive. A hotel room. Mexico. Honeymoon. Tequila. He heard the slat of a blind clap open and felt a painful stab of sunlight.

In the haze, two naked women approached, both blurry and multi-colored. He blinked his eyes several times and the shapes merged. She was deeply tan with the creamy white outline of a bikini painted on her body. She stood over him now, about five-foot-seven, flat stomach, small breasts, unwanted fat long ago burned off her curvy frame. She was obviously athletic—he could now see the sheath of muscles that rippled her stomach. She had loose, straight dark hair wrapping an angular face, eyebrows that dipped toward a long nose giving her a vaguely feline look.

My wife. Oh my God, my *wife*.

"Good morning, snuggle bunny," said Kate. "Not feeling so well, are we?" She hopped on the bed and straddled him, playfully bouncing him into the hotel bed. Bounce. Bounce.

"Leave me alone," he croaked. "And you promised to stop calling me that." The term of endearment did not seem befitting for a Major of Marines, though in secret he enjoyed the moniker. Problem was, Kate liked to joust in public, often to break up a sea of testosterone. She had even dropped the S-bomb in front of the president and he used it like a humorous cattle prod on his dogmatic aide.

"Sorry, cuddle bear. I'm just trying to roust you. It's past eight. I want to be at the cliffs by ten and I still need to get my morning loving." She planned a full day of rappelling, hiking, and sea kayaking near Acapulco's famous cliffs. Kate Phillips'—well, she was still mulling Kate *North-Phillips* but was waiting for a time to broach it—idea of a vacation demanded activity and discovery and *doing*, not lazing around in a beach chair. "Plus, we still have about ten shots left on the camera. I'm not sure if I got your good side."

"I'm never drinking again," moaned Darren. Before that honeymoon night, Darren had been drunk just one time in his life, the night before he flew to Saudi Arabia for Desert Storm. The night of the Crime Against Nature. After committing the Crime, he had stumbled back to the San Clemente bachelor pad and stared at himself hard in the mirror asking, *Who am I? Who am I?* before purging himself and treating his shower like a biologic decontamination drill. He detested the fact he had lost some control of his actions, however slight. His best friend and roommate, Gavin Kelly, had laughed at him and said, *Welcome to the club, I guess you're as prone to beer goggles as the rest of us.* But Darren Phillips didn't make mistakes like that. Not mistakes of judgment. Kelly might laugh at him for being wound too tight but Kelly was too short-sighted to realize that if you have hundreds of skeletons like the CAN they'll come back to haunt you when you run for office. What if she sold the awful tale to the tabloids?

Darren peeked out from behind his pillow and a flash went off.

"That'll be a good one," Kate laughed, raising the Canon Elph again. "Rated G, but our kids will have to be allowed to see something from the honeymoon."

Out of the recesses of Darren's memory came the blurred images of the couple rolling around naked and drunk, flashes occasionally lighting the room. "Oh no. What did you make me do, Kate?"

"I got you drunk and took advantage of you, that's what I did. The self-timer is a wonderful invention. You'll see the details later. Now let's finish this roll."

Darren suspected that her voracious sex drive had something to do with her athleticism, maybe boosting her estrogen level or feeding some female hormones or something. Whatever. Lately it had been off the charts. He pulled the covers up right against his chin even as she tried to snake her way under them, marveling at the role reversal. The death of sex some of his friends talked about was simply inconceivable in his marriage, he thought happily. "If you want access you leave the camera behind. I'm too sober now. Let's expose the film. Could ruin my political career."

"Or make it. Look at Pamela Anderson." She tossed the camera on the sofa and peeled back the covers. He sat up to kiss her but she shoved him back down on the bed and leaned over him, her hair falling down and capturing his face, soft and warm.

An hour later they had parked their rental car by the kayak shop at Estero Beach and were carrying their K-2 down to the surf zone. Darren was irritated with his wife; the rental shop had been specific about using the ramp in the protected cove as a launching point and now Kate had convinced him to sprint across the busy street to make a surf passage from the main beach. Darren believed in rules and law. He was a man who understood the need for conformity and excelled in bureaucracies: at Harvard, in the Marines, at CNN, and then as a Marine again where he currently served in the plum role carrying the nuclear suitcase alongside the president. The true test of a man was how well he performed within guidelines, playing by the rules and beating others with determination and merit, competing on the same field under the same set of laws. If everyone made exceptions or bent those rules, he reasoned, there would be chaos.

"We're supposed to stay in the lagoon," he said.

"We'll be fine," she said as they negotiated the rookery of tourists, mostly college kids on Spring Break who were already digging into Pacificos. Scorched bodies littered the beach like a battlefield waged among alcohol, the sun, and common sense. Everyone seemed to have a tattoo. To her right, a young woman with a glittering jewel embedded in her belly button removed her string bikini top and raised her arms above her head, gyrating. Her breasts must be three times as big as mine, Kate thought as she watched them sway. She twisted her own torso for fun, chuckling when her breasts showed scant residual motion under her tight tank top. Too many laps in the pool. Too many paddle strokes.

Kate glanced back at her husband. Typically, he was just staring at the kayak, still grumbling. Sometimes he reminded her of one of those Wall Street types with whom she used to ride the subway, immersed in his own thoughts even as the micro-world around him erupted. Still, he didn't have a wandering eye like her father and most of the time his focus was just wonderful. It was a magnet.

"I'm not talking about our well being. I'm talking about rules," Darren said, stepping between a comatose boy's legs.

"They told us where we should go. They didn't tell us where we *shouldn't* go. Don't worry so much about dumb rules. They weren't made with us in mind."

This from a woman who often ignored laws that she considered ridiculous, thought Darren. She sneaked food into movie theaters—*whole meals!*—took their dog running on the beach without a leash, rappelled off the side of their apartment building. It was a spot that had been long ago rubbed raw. And a spot that was often sweet for some maddening reason. She is so right for me, he thought. His was a rigid personality that needed to be dragged kicking and screaming toward the boundaries in life that she regularly exploded. Besides, he secretly loved to be prodded, unsure if it was self-righteous attention or genuine therapy that he craved.

Kate's plan would take them on a leisurely kayak near the cliff divers, then an extended paddle south to a deserted beach surrounded by cliffs where the couple could drink beer, picnic, and get the blood up with a few rappels. And, she hoped, the fulfillment of a beach fantasy to boot. She had stuffed the camera, suntan lotion, six Coronas, and foil-wrapped tortillas filled with guacamole, lettuce, chicken and onions into the waterproof pack alongside the harnesses and the climbing rope they called the Hell Bitch. The rope was slightly frayed but she could not part with it and buy a replacement, much to Darren's chagrin. Too much history lugging it around Eco Challenge courses, she said.

When the kayak was at the edge of the wet sand, Kate slipped into the rear compartment and picked up her paddle, struggling to seal her spray skirt when her belt buckle caught on the lip.

"You should take that damn buckle off," said Darren when he leaned over to help. "It's so big, it could get caught and prevent you from getting out if we roll. I don't know why you wear it with shorts in the first place. Looks . . . weird. Like you're a rodeo chick or something."

"Yee-hah." She smiled. Kate had been wearing the heavy silver prize whenever she could in the nine months since they finished the Eco Challenge, style be damned. The buckle was just a finishers prize so Darren refused to wear it, but of the seventy-five teams that had started in New Zealand, fewer than fifteen had finished. She was proud of eighth.

"Really. I'm worried," he said.

"I'm fine, babe. Besides, if we capsize, we'll just Eskimo Roll back up."

Darren slid into his hole and tested the rudder steering pedals with his Teva sandals. He waited for a lull in the surf to scoot forward but Kate, behind him, wanted to taste bigger waves like those in the set just rolling in. He could feel her scooting the craft forward.

A big blue plunging wave crested white and slammed shut in a foamy froth not twenty yards from them, hissing as the bubbles burst up across the sand, turning it from white to brown. "Isn't it beautiful? Let's go!" she shouted over the roar.

A small crowd had gathered so that when Darren turned to refuse, he was staring at some college kid in a Brittney Spears T-shirt who said, "You two aren't going out through those waves, are you dude?"

"Hell yes, we are," Darren said.

"Right on."

Darren pried the kayak forward until it was floating and started to churn the water, catching hold of it and powering it past, charged by the sound of the surf zone. The undertow snatched the kayak and it gathered speed. Kate joined him on the paddle and the speed the boat shot forward, spray flying past like BBs, then the waves themselves crashing over the bow and knocking Darren back against his seat every few seconds even though he was bent forward and pinning his paddle flat and parallel to the gunwale so it would not be stripped away be each greedy wave. The couple paddled hard when they were clear of each wave to build momentum for the next plunger. The boat pitched wildly and the final breaker in the set sucked up its face and spit it out on the ocean side.

"WAAhoo!" screamed Kate when they were clear.

The Pacific was a deep, cobalt blue and they paddled easily for several hours, taking time to admire the kindred spirits that leapt from the hundred-foot cliffs at La Quebrada before they turned north and skimmed toward the secret beach—deserted, she reasoned, because of the severe terrain that protected it. It lay in a long stretch of private property carefully delineated on her map. She didn't tell Darren about the red lines and the warnings, of course.

Their beach was more beautiful than she had hoped: a tiny crescent of sun-bleached sand, not more than fifty yards long, surrounded by towering cliffs that announced their presence by kicking the surf with their coral feet. She could see a crew of sandpipers working the edge of the high water line, scurrying up and down the beach like giant ants. Above them, a precarious set of steep wooden stairs led from the cove up over the cliffs.

"Wow. Isn't it perfect?" she asked, leaning back against the plastic seat rest and resting the paddle across the raised oval lip of her compartment. "Wouldn't it be great to own a place on property like this? Build a house somewhere up on top of that cliff? Just work out, have sex, and listen to the ocean?"

"Yeah, but I get the feeling that a Marine and a full-time adventure athlete might not be able to afford it." Darren had retired from endurance racing after Eco Challenge New Zealand to concentrate on his military career. His new assignment to the White House didn't allow for a life, let alone hobbies that demanded three-hour daily work-outs to compete and lead others. If he was going to transition into a high government office, his spare minutes would have to be spent networking, not riding some mountain bike into the ground the way Kate seemed to do every other month.

Kate had never stopped racing and had been anointed the ambassador for the fledgling sport of adventure racing. She used her notoriety to found an adventure academy for girls called You Go Girl!, where she taught them—beyond all the outdoor skills—what self-esteem really tasted like. She had been featured in most of the fitness magazines by then, and had even appeared in *Sports Illustrated* naked. Well, not *really* naked, she had laughed with Darren, pointing out the gray clay that covered her as she ran with a full pack, chased by a camel.

"Well, we own the beach today, babe. And I've got plans for it that I think you'll like."

Darren had heard the fantasy several times and he paddled a little harder toward the beach.

The couple pulled the kayak past the high water mark and stretched their towels for a picnic. Kate stuck her feet into the soft sand and happily kneaded it with her toes. The sun broke free of the cliff and the sand sparkled and winked at them like glitter painted by the swiftly retreating shadow. The water turned a light aqua and dazzled them.

"What'd I tell you, baby?" she said.

"You were right. It's unbelievable."

"I'm just getting warmed up." She positioned a Corona against a log, popped her hand down hard against the cap, and extended the foaming beer to her husband.

"Where'd you learn that?" he asked.

"College."

"And the salient difference between Princeton and Harvard is revealed. No wonder I pinned every Tiger I ever wrestled." Kate tossed him the Corona and he continued, "No mas. My head is killing me, babe."

"You want to cure that hangover? Drink it and see what happens."

The beer was still cold and his hand would not release it. He tipped it back. He didn't think he liked the taste of beer but in a few seconds that had changed. It was really goddamn good. Careful, he thought, this is how the weak are taken prisoner.

Kate pulled off her tank top and stepped out of her shorts, then reached back and untied her silver bikini top. Darren smiled dumbly.

She smiled at him and pursed her lips, swaying her hips in a hula motion, pushing her bikini bottom slowly down past her strong thighs and stepping out of it. She flicked it with her right foot—still missing its big toenail she lost during the last race—and Darren caught it before it smacked his face. She tossed the sun tan lotion at her husband and lay down on her stomach. "Back rub," she said.

Darren glanced up around the cliffs and then back at his new wife. I am truly a lucky man, he thought. He knelt beside her and squeezed the tube, lathering her shoulders and knotted back, kneading her neck and grinding his fingers into the dense muscles of her lats. Her build did not ruin but accentuated her curves. "Ummmm," she hummed happily. "That's a good boy."

He was not used to alcohol and on an empty stomach his stomach he felt a buzzing warmth. When he cupped his hands and stroked her hamstrings and calves he had the urge to drink a second beer. And a much, much stronger urge, as well. She started a slow hum and the vibration in his hands felt like a purring cat. When he reached her ankles, Kate spun around and stretched her arms behind her head, sighing slowly, almost a coo, and arching her back. Her breasts and pelvis were vanilla except for her nipples and the slick black rectangle of hair. "Front," she said simply. Then she brought her hand up to her temple to block the peeping sun and said, "And get those clothes off."

"You better fix that salute when I get back, Marine."

Darren walked over to the pack and grabbed another Corona, then glanced up at the cliffs—only blinding sun, though—and took off his clothes. He rubbed the bottle across his neck and then did the same to her, drinking some more now, pouring some in the belly button well of her flat stomach, licking it off, pouring it across her breasts and watching her nipples grow and tighten, finishing the beer and tossing the bottle up the beach, happy and buzzed and excited, straddling her chest and dripping the lotion down on her, massaging her breasts even as she massaged him with those soft, wet hands and pulled him in tight, surrounded.

"You're so beautiful," he said.

"I want to do this in the water," she whispered. Her voice was husky and he carried her into the Pacific as quickly as he could. The water was cool and he was standing waist-deep when she wrapped her arms and legs around him and pressed herself down.

"*¡Hola! ¿Qué hace usted? Usted sabe que esto es la propiedad privada!*" the shore shouted at them.

Kate pushed down on Darren's shoulders and hopped off him with a startled squeal. She hid behind her husband and peeked at the shore.

Three men were standing next to the kayak. Two of them wore white slacks and jackets like *Miami Vice* holdouts, and the third—an enormous fat man with a pony tail and square sunglasses like her grandmother wore—was dressed in an ugly purple Hawaiian shirt and long khaki shorts that were stretched wide by his tree trunk legs.

"*Usted rompe la ley, mis amigos. Usted ensució. La natación desnuda no se permite. Entrar ilegalmente tampoco!*"

"What'd they say?" asked Darren, once again fuming at the fact his mother had pushed him into French at prep school instead of Spanish.

"They say we're trespassing on private property. And that skinny dipping is illegal. And that you littered on the beach with the bottle." Kate backed up until the ocean was deep enough to cover her breasts, then stepped aside of Darren and shouted, "*Arrepentido, nosotros no supimos. Nosotros no saldremos las botellas. Hacemos nunca sucio este lugar hermoso.*"

The fat man said something and the two men in jackets laughed. "*Bien entonces, sale del agua y me lo explica a mí!*" the fat man shouted. Kate could see the tattered triangle of sweat that darkened his shirt and matted his chest hair. His tongue was hanging out the same way her Black Labrador, Neptune's, did after their long runs.

Kate pressed into Darren's back and whispered, "They want us up there, babe. You're probably going to have to pay them off."

"Wait one."

She pushed him forward. "Go."

He looked at her and nodded toward his waist. "I *can't* right now, baby, I've still got to calm down a little. He's still a tad excited."

She laughed, looked down at the water and said in a baby voice, "Don't worry, little guy. Mommy will take care of you real soon." She laughed again and shouted to the men.

Darren began to wade forward and he said over his shoulder, "How much do you think this will cost us?"

"I'm sure you'll figure out a way to pay the minimum."

She watched her husband emerge from the Pacific and felt comfortable and unafraid; the ocean revealed him as he walked, his muscled form tapering sharply from his wide shoulders to his waist, eventually unveiling the big scar on his knee from the bullet that shattered his kneecap in Kuwait. He kept himself is superb shape, well-muscled but not bulky. "Lean enough to keep my jab speedy," she once heard him tell Kelly during one of their ridiculous Macho Marine Talks, "but strong enough to cave in a man's face." At six feet, Darren wasn't bigger than the men on the beach but you couldn't see that in his confident approach, naked-ness notwithstanding. She was sure the men would just give her husband a warning and send them on their way.

To lighten the mood, she shouted, "¡Usted es agradable a mi esposo o él lo quizás golpee con su herramienta masiva!"

The men in front of Darren broke into wild laughter. When he neared, they pointed at him and shouted back to Kate in Spanish, enjoying an in-joke. The chuckling fat man was even holding his great sweaty belly as if worried that it might burst. Darren was sure the joke was made at his expense. His stiff nature made him an easy target for people with keen senses of humor like Kate and his buddy Kelly so he was used to it. In fact, some part of him enjoyed the ribbing.

He smiled and turned back to face his wife. "What'd you tell them?"

The water was shoulder high on his wife and her long hair was flopped back flat behind her head. She looked so beautiful. It made him slightly nervous.

"Just that you'd do whatever they told you," she said.

Yeah, right, Darren thought.

Gil Saiz looked at the black man walking toward him and laughed again. The man's penis was shriveled and small, certainly not the "massive tool" that might flog them if they weren't nice to him as the lady said. But it was a funny warning and Gil immediately warmed to the woman in the water. She was good-looking and had some American Indian traits, he thought, what with her severe eyebrows and jet black hair. But even her deep tan couldn't hide her European roots. Tall and fair. Maybe Irish or Scandinavian years back but American now, a mixed breed like most of the mutts up there.

And the impurity was going to get worse. Here she was, *naked,* with a negro. A hot white woman like that with a black! It was the same unholy rap fantasy that these fucking college kids shoved in his face every spring when they took over the clubs, all the white kids dancing to spoken nonsense and acting black, baseball caps backward and pants pulled down. Confused gringos! Bad influences, too, beaming their fucking rap crap into his house by satellite television when his son was home alone.

Still, Gil hoped the Jackrabbit might just let the girl in the ocean go. He glanced at her and she was smiling. He could see her teeth. A feeling of dread flooded him—he had been in similar positions too often. This woman was too striking to be ignored by Jackrabbit. Her smile would be gone soon. Gil had worked as the Jackrabbit's bodyguard for seven years and though the soldiering never bothered him—that was business—he felt a weighty guilt when it came to all of the women who had come in contact with his equally weighty boss.

The black man came up to the three of them gesturing with his hands apologetically, speaking English like all of the spoiled tourists. It's Spanish down here you arrogant fuck, thought Gil. At least the girl speaks it.

The black shouted to the woman and she relayed the stupid message: they were sorry and could the man pay the fine, take their clothing, and leave the private beach? The black nodded stupidly. Then he put on his shorts, pulled out a wallet and raised his eyebrows, extending a ten dollar bill. *Dollars.*

"This son-of-a-bitch is trying to bribe me?" said the Jackrabbit. *"With ten dollars? I could buy his woman from him right now. Get her out of there . . . I want to see her."*

Gil could tell by the look on the black man's face that he did not speak Spanish so he slapped the wallet from the man's hand and shoved him back roughly. The black stumbled back and came up in a crouch. He has good balance, thought Gil. And no panic yet.

At close to 150 kilograms, Gil was a big man whose job demanded he be comfortable in a fight, relaxed enough to think even while absorbing a lucky blow. He saw in the American's face some of the same, looking back at him like some little fighting dog, black eyes moving across the Jackrabbit and his *companero* Juan, then back to Gil. The black was shifty. He's not afraid for himself, thought Gil, but he's afraid for his woman.

"Come out of the water now, girl," shouted Gil in Spanish. *"Come out and get your clothes. My boss wants to speak to you."*

"What'd he say, Kate?" Darren asked calmly. Unlike most of his generation, Darren Phillips understood real violence, both its consequences and its requirements.

"He wants me to come out of the water, too."

"You stay put."

Darren glared at the men and shook his head. He recognized that the fattest man wearing the shorts was in charge and turned to him, gesturing apologetically and shaking his head. He tried to explain. "Sir. I am sorry . . ."

The Jackrabbit recoiled and said, *"Get this nigger out of my face and get her out."*

Gil reached for the black man, missed his elbow but snared his wrist and yanked him backwards, tripping him onto the sand. He moved in for a kick—to get the girl's attention—but the black swiveled around and was on his feet too quickly, fists balled. *Fast!*

"Tell them we don't want trouble!" Darren screamed.

He heard Kate yelling in Spanish. The men babbled, then the biggest man in the jacket moved in again. "No—

no—no," said Darren, but the man's hand was moving so he flung the sand he was clenching into the man's eyes and blocked the punch, returning a sharp jab that he pulled. *Could have been much worse, amigo.* His left fist returned to its defensive position.

Gil went to his knees holding his head and thinking that the man must have used a blackjack. He swore loudly and rubbed his fingers across his bumpy eyelids. The pain was a hot one and his neck tingled.

When Darren turned to face the other two he saw the pistols, both automatics and large caliber, one of them silver and reflecting the sun.

The second jacketed bodyguard in his white suit moved forward shouting and put his pistol in Darren's face. *Nine mm Baretta. Thumb safety. Won't fire if the barrel's depressed.* Darren considered a grab, but when he heard Kate scream he raised his hands. *Too late now.*

Miami Vice punched him in the stomach and seemed to be trying to drill the barrel of the gun into his ear. "*¡Si usted mueve otra vez y yo fucking lo mata cabron!*" he screamed. Darren allowed the man to pull his hands behind him and felt the sharp squeeze as flex-cuffs bound his hands tightly. Darren tried to engorge his wrists by clenching but the man continued to yank even as the plastic handcuffs broke the skin. Darren felt blood trickle south past his thumbs.

Juan pulled Darren to his feet by yanking his hands up past his shoulder blades. Darren screamed and twisted around in time to catch Gil's fist with his face. He crumpled down onto the sharp volcanic coral. A black spike drilled into his pectoral but there was plenty of meat to keep it from penetrating more than a centimeter. His cheek was submerged in a tiny tide pool and he could taste brine with the blood.

"*Yo no hecho con usted,*" Gil said. He stepped on the

black's lower back, careful to avoid scuffing his polish on the coral.

Darren didn't speak the language but he understood nevertheless—understood the dark underbelly of power and domination, the evil that men do. He twisted his head when he heard Kate babbling and saw her run out of the water, naked and wet. Vulnerable. He didn't want Kate to be within miles when men reverted to their truculent natures, let alone having her as their sole focus ten meters away on a deserted beach. He kicked Gil lightly, just to get his attention, and said, "Hey! You touch her and I'll fucking *kill you*."

Gil slid his shoe up until it rested on Darren's neck then twisted his shoe back and forth leisurely before turning his attention back to the naked woman. He didn't like to ogle but she was worth the twinge of shame. Her thighs were big for a trim girl and they hardened beneath her tanned skin each time she placed weight on a leg.

"*Stop!*" Kate shouted in Spanish when she ran up. "*Here I am. You are happy now?*"

"*He's making it bad for you,*" said the Jackrabbit.

Jackrabbit looked her over and decided that he had never seen a woman with so many muscles, a mash of wicked curves. And still somehow she is feminine, he thought. And long! Her hips were wide and full but not fat. Nice dark skin that yielded to a pure cocaine white bikini line. He stared at the black rectangle of pubic hair like it was a hundred dollar bill or a pile of freshly cut product or a newly oiled pistol—impossible to take his eyes away.

Jackrabbit's extremities flooded with anticipation. He considered sending Gil and Juan to finish off the *mulatto* so he could take her right there on the beach. *This will be a good one!*

"*We don't want a problem,*" she told him.

He barely heard; he was watching the muscles between her hips. "*Tell him to calm down so we can have a discus-*

sion. *This fighting with police makes it worse. You have enough trouble.*"

"*Okay. Relax. Relax.*"

Kate walked over to the pack and grabbed her shorts and bikini. "*You boys get a good look or do you want another second or two?*" She pulled the bikini bottom up over her hips, followed by her shorts, and flipped the tank top over her head. She reached into her bag for her squeegee and tied her hair in a ponytail.

Darren was struggling to get his footing under Gil's shiny white leather shoe. His bride stroked his face. "Darren, just let me handle them. Calm down. They're police. People have seen me naked before, you know."

She smiled weakly but Darren was in no mood for levity. "Kate, I want you to get in the kayak and *get out of here.* Are you listening? Get the hell out of here. I'll take care of myself. Please. They are *not* police."

"*You two talk too much,*" Jackrabbit interrupted. "*Did he say he was going to be a good listener now?*"

Kate stood defiant with her hands on her hips. "*Please, sir. This is my honeymoon and we wanted . . . we just stopped on the beach. I'm sorry. Okay? Let us get back in the boat and we'll go.*"

Jackrabbit laughed and his henchmen joined in a second later out of habit, though Gil felt increasingly guilty, especially when he heard it was the woman's honeymoon. He had never participated in the games with the women and the Jackrabbit accepted this. He would stay in the guest house while he and Juan delved.

"*No, it's not that simple, girl,*" said the Jackrabbit. "*We have to take you back for some questions. Then we let you go.*"

Visit the
Simon & Schuster Web site:
www.SimonSays.com

and sign up for our
mystery e-mail updates!

Keep up on the latest
new releases, author appearances,
news, chats, special offers, and more!
We'll deliver the information
right to your inbox — if it's new,
you'll know about it.

2350-01